THE GREAT LAND

The Great Land

Derek Lambert

CORGI BOOKS
A DIVISION OF TRANSWORLD PUBLISHERS LTD

For Barrie and Christina Mullins

THE GREAT LAND

A CORGI BOOK 0 552 10795 6
Originally published in Great Britain by
Arlington Books

PRINTING HISTORY
Arlington edition published 1977
Corgi edition published 1978

This book is set in Intertype Plantin

Corgi Books are published by
Transworld Publishers Ltd.,
Century House, 61–63 Uxbridge Road,
Ealing, London W5 5SA

Made and printed in Great Britain by
Cox & Wyman Ltd., London, Reading and Fakenham

There's a land where the mountains are nameless,
And the rivers all run God knows where;
There are lives that are erring and aimless,
And deaths that just hang by the hair;
There are hardships that nobody reckons;
There's a land – oh, it beckons and beckons,
And I want to go back and I will.

Robert W. Service,
The Spell of the Yukon

Part One

CHAPTER ONE

THE Japanese dropped from the ceiling of fog. He was dead by the time he hit the ground a few feet from the foxhole where Richard Larsen was crouching.

Larsen, who had been watching a sea-otter playing with its pup while shells from the *Nevada* monotonously pounded the mountainside above the fog, stared with fascination at the body.

It was the first body he had seen and he couldn't comprehend that a few seconds ago it had been breathing, thinking, living. Blood and saliva dribbled from the mouth of the Japanese onto the sponge-like tundra.

Still Larsen stared. Until the arrival of the body, tossed like a puppet from the fog, he hadn't totally accepted that the enemy were on the island. Only kittiwakes and ravens and foxes and sea-otters swimming in the shallows.

And, watching the sea-otters, he had been thinking how vulnerable they were because they were a protected species and they didn't care about man and his guns, not even the 14mm shells from the battleship *Nevada*.

The shells continued to punish the mountains. The otter with the pup dived for sea urchins. Blood seeped from a wound in the back of the dead Japanese.

Richard Larsen forced himself to look away from the body. He stared at the rock where the pup was waiting for the return of its mother and he thought: they belong here, we are the intruders. And he wondered if this island, this hump of pumice washed by the Pacific and the Bering Sea, was as important as they had been told. He doubted whether any animal, for all its ferocious territorial instinct, would be foolish enough to fight for this place.

9

Larsen looked again at the dead Japanese. Plump face, uneven teeth, eyes already glazing. He began to tremble.

Above the thunder of the bombardment he heard the sharper rattle of gunfire. He stared up into the fog and was surprised when the sergeant grabbed his legs, pulling him into the mud at the bottom of the foxhole, shouting: 'You could lose your head that way.'

Sitting in the mud with the sergeant – an Irishman with a creased face who claimed he had once sparred with Joe Louis – and Gold, a small-time crook from Detroit, Larsen said: 'I didn't think they could see us.'

The sergeant shook his head in disbelief. 'They can hear guys like you thinking.'

Gold laughed. He claimed to have worked for the Mob and, Larsen decided, he must have looked tough enough in Detroit. Dark suit, black shirt, white tie, three gold teeth to match his name: here in the foxhole he looked foxy-faced and puny in combat gear a size too big for him.

Larsen asked the sergeant: 'When do you think we'll go over the top again?'

'Over the top? Where do you think you are? The Somme?' The sergeant stuck a wad of chewing gum in his mouth. 'We go when the colonel says we go like we did last night.'

They had attacked twice the previous night, moving up the valley towards Jasmin Pass, getting cut down each time by mortars and machine-guns firing from ridges on the flanks of the mountains above.

Larsen said hopefully: 'There can't be many of them left, not with a bombardment like that,' jerking his head towards the flaming guns of the battleship.

'Want to bet?' The Sergeant shifted the gum to the other side of his mouth, tilted his helmet onto the back of his head.

Richard Larsen thought how different it all was from what he had expected. Ever since he had enlisted he had geared himself to fighting in monsoons, in booby-trapped jungles, in thick brown mud hearing the Japs calling from the under-growth. Landing on silver sand with big guns picking off diving

Zeros. Instead here he was in a foxhole on an island named Attu at the tip of the 1,100-mile-long tail of Alaska, the Aleutian Islands. The mud was dark and cold; so was the sea and the beaches of volcanic sand.

And the men around him. Different from anyone he had known on Long Island. Cowboys and clerks, Indians, negroes from the ghetto, the youth from Chicago in the bunk next to him at Cold Bay who had carried a razor in his sock – all with a knowledge in their eyes of which he was ignorant.

At first one or two of them had tried to get tough with him. But there was a composure, an insularity, maybe even a serenity, about him that made them falter and veer away to find more recognizable targets.

He said to the sergeant: 'Maybe the Japs will attack us.'

'If they're crazy they will,' the sergeant said. 'If they're out of their little yellow heads.' He spat out his gum, covered it with mud with the toe of his boot. He looked at Larsen with resignation. 'Christ, would you attack if you were sitting in a fortress watching a lot of toy soldiers floundering around in the mud, knowing they can't see you? If you knew the toy soldiers had their toy howitzers stuck in the goddam mud? If you knew they hadn't eaten any food since they landed and that the wounded toy soldiers were still sitting in the cold waiting for a field hospital to arrive? Would you attack?' He paused and then said: 'I guess *you* would,' and smiled faintly.

Above them a patch of sky, a blue rent in the fog. It was a starting signal for the snipers; bullets plugged into the tundra; the three soldiers crouched, heads down, like tortoises beneath their helmets. Then the shooting stopped. The guns of the *Nevada* continued to flame.

'They must have known there would be mud and the guns would get stuck,' Larsen said.

'Sure, someone knew. But someone else knew better.'

'I heard that we'd take the island in three days,' said Gold, his face small beneath his helmet.

'They underestimated,' the sergeant said. 'They underestimated the strength of Japs here and the weapons they got.'

'And the mud,' Larsen said.

'Sure. And the fog and the wind and the rain and the cold and the mountains.'

'But they must have aerial pictures of the island,' Larsen said.

'Yeah, pictures of mountain peaks and fog. I heard that the only map they had went inland for one thousand yards.'

'Jesus!' Gold exclaimed. 'And they sent us in not knowing a goddam thing about the island. Oh the bastards! The goddam bastards!'

Larsen said: 'I heard they tried to sink a whale.'

They looked at him. 'Who tried to sink a whale?' the sergeant asked.

'One of our destroyers. They thought it was a sub.'

Gold said: 'Beats me why the hell anyone wants this fucking island – the Japs or us.'

'Because,' the sergeant told him, selecting another wad of gum and sticking it into his mouth, 'the Aleutians are the stepping stones to Tokyo.'

'Yeah. I heard that lecture, too.'

'Can you think of a better reason?'

Gold nodded. 'Sure I can. Because the generals thought we'd wipe up the Japs in a couple of days and they'd all get gongs. Maybe college boys would get gongs, too,' looking at Larsen from under his helmet.

The fog pressed down. Richard Larsen who had learned about Alaska and its glacial beauty tried to find comfort in the grey rocks and khaki tundra around him. But there was none.

Instead he thought about white frame houses in a village overlooking the Sound on Long Island. And about a girl he had kissed at Jones Beach. It was then that the lieutenant arrived in the foxhole. Feet hitting the mud with a thick splash, squatting in one movement like a gymnast, hand on the butt of the pistol at his hip.

Larsen wondered: What the hell do we do? Salute?

The lieutenant said: 'We'll be attacking soon. I'll stay here with you.' He glanced at the sergeant. 'You know me, sergeant?'

'Lieutenant Browning, sir.'

'Right. I lost all my men in the second attack last night,' answering their unspoken questions. 'Two dead, the rest wounded.'

'It certainly isn't Errol Flynn's sort of war,' the sergeant remarked.

The lieutenant regarded him doubtfully. He was young, medium height, fit-looking, black-haired with an educated voice, not too sure of himself giving orders to a man of thirty who claimed to have sparred with Joe Louis.

The lieutenant shifted his attention to Larsen and Gold and said to Larsen: 'How's it going, soldier?'

'Okay, sir.'

'I see you had a visitor,' pointing in the direction of the dead Japanese. 'Dropped in, did he?' The lieutenant smiled showing white, even teeth.

'One of the *Nevada*'s shells got him, sir.'

'What's your name, soldier?'

'Larsen, sir.'

'Scandinavian?'

'Way back,' Larsen told him.

'We'll be landing reinforcements soon,' Browning told them.

'And supplies?' the sergeant asked. 'We could do with some chow. The coolies' – the infantrymen manhandling supplies up from the beach – 'don't seem to be reaching us.'

'Food? Sure, you'll get food. These things take time. Any of you hurt?' Browning asked.

No, they told him, they weren't hurt.

Ignoring Gold, Browning said to Larsen, 'You look as if you're in pain, soldier.'

Larsen told the lieutenant about his feet, about the cold aching in them.

'But it won't affect you?'

'Affect me?'

'Stop you going over the top.'

Like they did at the Somme. Larsen grinned.

'What are you grinning about, Larsen?'

'Nothing sir.' And then: 'No, it won't stop me . . . going over the top.'

Suddenly the *Nevada*'s guns stopped, leaving a cold, tangible silence. A few stones came rattling down from the fog. Fear returned.

Browning whispered: 'This is it.'

'Either that or they've run out of ammunition,' the sergeant murmured, breaking up the fear.

They waited.

The silence thickened.

A voice shouting into a bullhorn. Browning peering over the lip of the foxhole. 'Come on,' he said, 'let's go.'

They stood up but Larsen couldn't move. He didn't know why he couldn't move. Was it fear or was it the ice in his feet? Oh Christ, he whimpered to himself without speaking.

The lieutenant was out of the foxhole followed by the sergeant and Gold.

Browning peered into the foxhole, took his pistol from its holster. 'Move,' he shouted, waving the pistol.

Larsen's feet belonged to someone else. He was trying to pick them up; they felt like chunks of concrete. Dear God, help me. To be brave you have to know fear . . .

'For the last time – move!'

And he was over the lip of the foxhole, standing on the tundra beside the body of the Japanese, and some of the fog had shredded so that they could see the valley ahead of them, and they were moving forward.

Behind them the otter reappeared nuzzling its pup. Then the Japanese guns opened up.

CHAPTER TWO

RICHARD LARSEN sometimes suspected that he wouldn't have enlisted in the Army if it hadn't been for his mother and an Indian named Ott.

Somehow his mother brought out the worst in him. Her calm sorrow, her inner grief, her sacrifices, her quiet fortitude were making him act perversely, even cruelly and this, he knew, was unfathomly sad.

He was an only child. His parents weren't rich, neither were they poor; they lived in a split-level white frame house at the Suffolk end of Long Island.

By the time he was seventeen he knew he would have to leave this house and the village of his youth and he was puzzled by the pain of the self-inflicted wound.

His mother was a tall woman, blonde hair greying, with a noble face and an arrogant nose; yet she rarely attacked. Instead, she implied deep inner grief, internal wounds inflicted by those nearest to her.

'If that's what you want to do,' she said, knitting needles clicking, 'then we mustn't stop you. But it will be hard for your father.'

His father said: 'Don't worry about the business, son. I'll make out somehow.'

'But you must know I've got to go,' Richard Larsen said. 'You must realize that.'

'Yes we know,' his father said. 'It's just that with your mother going into hospital' – needles clicking faster – 'it's come as a bit of a shock.' He lit his pipe, a greying, plumpish man, wearing a cheap suit crumpled by daily journeys to Manhattan on the Long Island Railroad.

His son said: 'I'm sorry but, you know, it's only a minor operation.'

'Of course it is, dear,' his mother said, smiling at him as though she were concealing the truth.

'You wouldn't like it if I was the only kid in the village who didn't join the Army.'

'Some of them haven't,' his mother said. 'Josh Woolfolk and Ronald Saunders—'

'They're semi-cripples,' Richard Larsen interrupted.

'And you mustn't forget your heart—'

'For God's sake,' Richard Larsen exclaimed, 'that was thirteen years ago and the doctor said it was a systolic murmur and nothing to worry about and I haven't had a systolic murmur since.'

'But you should tell the Medical Board about it.'

'Why don't I just shoot my big toe off?'

His mother pulled at the wool making the blue ball spin in her lap.

His father pulled on his pipe breathing out grey smoke that billowed across the window-frame. It irritated Richard Larsen and he didn't know why. He wished he were out collecting clams.

He patrolled the room touching familiar objects. No, they were more than familiar, they were the trappings of his youth. He lit a cigarette and his mother coughed.

His father regarded the smoke-dribbling stem of his pipe. 'Of course I suppose you could still get into Princeton and then maybe you wouldn't have to serve Uncle Sam for a while.'

'I guess I could.' *But why the hell should I when, not so long ago, before Pearl Harbour, you were just as upset that I wanted to go to college to study zoology because it would postpone my entry into The Family Business. For Chrissake, a tiny store on 2nd Avenue, up in the 80s, that sold newspapers and cigarettes and novelty postcards and chocolate bars and lent out old novels at a nickel a time.* 'But, don't you understand, it would seem as though I was just going there to get out of the draft.'

16

'You said you might get a scholarship.'

'Yeah. But that was months ago. Things have changed since then.' He stopped under the ship's clock, looking at his parents, knowing they were divided between conventional patriotism and Family, understanding and yet wondering if there wasn't some hypocrisy involved. Parents were like teachers and the family doctor; suddenly you realize they are fallible and from then on there is always doubt.

His mother put down her knitting and said she was going to make some tea.

His father said: 'I suppose you'll be applying for a commission.'

Here we go again, Richard Larsen thought, and said: 'No,' still trying to be kind.

'Why not? The Lubitsch boy . . .'

'I know about Sammy Lubitsch.'

'Then why . . .'

Richard Larsen smiled. 'I guess I'm not officer material,' knowing that his mother who was making a lot of noise in the kitchen could hear every word. 'I am not a leader of men.'

'How the hell would you know, only just eighteen?'

'I don't want to lead men. I know the leaders at high school and I know I'm not like them and I don't want to be.'

'You're so different, huh? A loner?' Richard Larsen could tell that his father was getting angry and said: 'Not different' – although he wasn't sure about this – 'but, you know, I'm not a jock and I'm not a scholar—'

His mother came back carrying the silver tray bearing the silver teapot and the best china.

She poured the tea – lemon and sugar – and said: 'I couldn't help over-hearing. You know, Richard, it would be wonderful for your father if he could tell customers that you were an officer.'

Oh hell, Richard Larsen thought. Why would it be wonderful? Would he sell any more White Owls that way? Wasn't she really telling his father that he hadn't made it and the only way he could get back at the well-heeled customers who dropped by for their *New York Times* was by telling them that his son was

17

a lieutenant leading his men up the beaches of some island in the Pacific? And wouldn't she enjoy telling members of the Literary Circle likewise? And he asked himself: Do they really care? and was immediately ashamed.

'I don't have to be an officer to become a hero,' he said.

'But you should think of your family,' she said. 'I know your country comes first. But you should think of your family because they're the units that make up the country.' She handed him his tea.

'Oh, let him be a buck private,' his father said. 'Then maybe he'll learn what life's all about. Come up the hard way like I did,' said his father who had fought in France in the last war. 'You don't remember the depression. You didn't know what it was like trying to hustle a few bucks to keep you and your mother clothed and fed. Maybe if I had come back Stateside as an officer things would have been different.'

'You haven't done so bad,' his son said.

'Yeah? You think I like getting out of bed in the dark and riding the train every day and bussing it to the shop and picking up the papers and selling gum to kids and breaking off for a hamburger and a beer and getting a pain down here' – pressing his stomach with his free hand – 'and getting back too tired to do anything except falling asleep listening to the radio?'

His mother said: 'Your father had plans for you.'

'It doesn't matter,' his father said.

'He was going to buy a place in midtown Manhattan,' his mother said. 'Down in the fifties. An antique shop. And he thought you might go in with him. You know, as a buyer, something like that.'

Richard Larsen realized then that his mother had always believed that she had married beneath her – *My husband's in antiques* – and he was depressed by the knowledge. 'Maybe he can still buy it,' he said. 'I guess I'll travel in the Army and I'll come across antiques. Maybe some real good ones. You know, not the usual stuff from the Civil War.'

'I can't run it myself,' his father said.

'Then get some help?'

'And pay them with what, potato chips?'

His son fished in his pocket for his packet of Camel, thought better of it and left them there. 'There's nothing I can do. We're at war and like everyone else I've got to go. I'm sorry.' And he was because it seemed to him then that there was nothing left for them; that everything had been done for nothing; that they had surfaced from the Depression for nothing; that the train rides every day had been for nothing.

Outside a seagull swooped past the window. A squirrel ran along a branch of a birch tree, balancing itself with its tail, smelling spring. A dog barked. In the village they would be gathering at the soda fountain and lining up outside the movie house to see Bob Hope and Bing Crosby and Dorothy Lamour.

'I'm sorry,' he said again.

But his ingratitude, his treachery, hung between them. His mother began knitting again.

'I've got to go,' Richard Larsen said. 'You must see that.'

His father nodded and in a dull voice agreed: 'I see it. Your country needs you.'

His mother, head bowed over the darting needles, said: 'We'll make do.'

And it was then that he knew that it was partly his mother who was making him go. In the world of animals the mother teaches the cub to feed, to walk, prepares it for departure; but the human mother cossets the child, chains it with reproach. And then he thought: But I am an only child, a son; and he knew that he loved her, loved them both. But I have to leave the nest, I have to.

But, looking back, he realized that it was Ott the Indian who had exerted the greatest power: Ott would have guided him outside the boundaries of his upbringing even if there hadn't been a war.

He met Ott one drizzling summer day in Central Park Zoo. There were a few children around, waving balloons and trailing popcorn behind them. The odour of the animals was strong in the rain so that you could smell their misery.

Richard Larsen was watching a lioness padding up and down its cramped cell when a man stopped beside him. He had a strong, brown, lined face with half a cigar stuck in the middle of it and a bottle of whisky protruding from the pocket of his jacket. His shirt was open at the neck and he didn't seem to mind the rain.

'Well,' said the brown-faced man, 'what do you think?'

Richard Larsen said he wasn't thinking anything at all. He was intrigued by the man, and a little apprehensive.

'Not a good day for them,' the man said, pointing the chewed cigar at the animals. 'There aren't too many humans around for them to look at.'

'I don't quite understand,' Richard Larsen said politely.

'You don't imagine they built this dump for humans to look at animals, do you?'

'What did they build it for?'

'The idea was to create a sanctuary where animals can observe the curious habits of humans. You know, so that they can learn a thing or two. How not to eat and drink and gawp and giggle. That's why animals are what they are – because they've observed us.' He took a swig from the bottle of whisky. 'But today's not a good day for them. No, sir, there aren't too many exhibits around for them to observe today. You see humans don't like rain, it makes them clean.'

The lioness stopped for a moment, gazed at them with expressionless yellow eyes; but it seemed to Richard Larsen as though it had made some sort of contact with the man beside him.

'You know what I'm doing here?'

'Showing them how not to behave?' Richard Larsen ventured.

The man with the brown face laughed, too loudly. He stuck the cigar back into his mouth, biting with his teeth so that a little juice ran down his chin. 'No, sir, I'm here planning my campaign.'

Richard Larsen waited.

The lioness began to pad up and down again.

The man said: 'One day soon I aim to set all these critters

free. All I need is a little explosive delicately applied and maybe a hacksaw or two. But the timing's the thing,' he said. 'They all got to go free at the same time. Say midnight. Can you imagine an elephant in Tiffany's, a polar bear in the Plaza?' He laughed and a woman in a white macintosh hurried two children past them.

'That wouldn't be any good,' Richard Larsen said seriously. 'They'd be killed.'

'Better dead than imprisoned in this dump. Better the electric chair than jail for life.' He took another pull at the bottle and put his arm round Richard Larsen's shoulders. 'Are you in, boy? Will you join the campaign?'

'Sure, why not?' The apprehension was dissolving.

'Great. We'll set up a command headquarters. Now come and see another animal. Imprisoned in bronze,' he added, turning and heading out of the shabby zoo towards a rise in the ground in the park.

'Ott's my name,' he told Richard Larsen as they walked across the stringy grass. 'I'm an Indian.'

'My name's Larsen. Richard Larsen.'

'Where you from, Richard Larsen?'

'Long Island,' Richard Larsen said.

'Know it well,' Ott said, pausing to take a pull from the bottle. 'Lot of good species there. Especially up the east end. They wear mink up there, Richard, and leopard. Do you know how they kill a leopard so that some broad can have a nice unblemished fur?'

Richard Larsen said he had no idea.

'They stick a red hot poker up its ass. Fact,' he said, observing the disbelief on Richard Larsen's face. 'And sealskin. You've seen those cute little hats the well-heeled New Yorkers wear, haven't you Richard? Well, I'll tell you how they kill seals. They talk to them nicely and the seals blink at them and wait for some candy or something and then they crack them over the head with a baseball bat. And do you know something else?' he asked, not waiting for Richard Larsen to reply, 'they tell you it's the kindest way to kill them. How about that? As if it was a necessity' – Ott had a little difficulty with necessity – 'a necessity of life to kill them in the first place.' He spat out the ragged butt of the cigar onto the grass.

'It's terrible,' Richard Larsen said.

'Damn right it's terrible.'

He spoke with a slight accent and Richard Larsen wasn't sure whether it was because he was drunk or an Indian or both. He asked Ott if he was from a reservation.

Ott grinned, new creases arriving on his face. 'Yeah, you could say that. I'm a Tinglit, ever heard of them?'

No, Richard Larsen said, he hadn't. He was sorry.

'Don't let it worry you, kid. They come from Alaska. Many a good red-blooded American doesn't even know where Alaska is and what's more he doesn't give a shit.' Raindrops fizzed on the glowing end of his cigar. 'Yeah, you could say I'm from a reservation. A territory, they call it ... a reservation ... twice the size of Texas, bigger than Europe. Some reservation, huh?'

Richard Larsen decided it was time to make a stand. He liked Ott but that didn't mean you could be put on. And so he told Ott: 'I know where Alaska is, for Chrissake, and I know how big it is.'

'Good on you, kid. What's its capital?'

'Anchorage,' Richard Larsen said.

'Anchorage my ass,' Ott remarked. 'Ever hear tell of Juneau?'

'I guess so. That's the capital, huh?'

'Yes,' the Indian said. 'That's the capital, or so I'm told. That's where they govern the Indians and the Aleuts and the Eskimos from. Juneau and Washington.'

'Why are you so bitter?' Richard Larsen asked. 'I mean, you seem to be bitter about everything.'

'Do you want a drink?'

'Okay.' *Why not?* He took the bottle, wiped the neck, swigged and retched. 'Strong stuff,' he said, wiping the neck of the bottle.

'Yeah. And, as you know, us Indians can't take the stuff.'

'Have you drunk much?' Richard Larsen asked.

'About two bottles,' Ott told him. 'Maybe that's why I'm

bitter. Or maybe I drank two bottles because I was bitter in the first place.'

'But why?'

'This and that,' the Tinglit Indian said. He waved the bottle. 'This park used to be Indian country. Did you know that Richard Larsen?'

'I guess so. It was all Indian once, wasn't it. But you didn't tell me why you're so bitter.'

'I guess old Balto sums it up,' Ott said, stopping beside the bronze statue of a dog staring out across the park which was a lonely place now, with the drizzle thickening, with only lovers and cranks and men with dogs walking the paths beside the fine battlements of Fifth Avenue. 'Do you know about Old Balto?'

Richard Larsen hesitated. Taking another snort from his bottle, Ott told him: 'Balto, now there was a mutt for you. He had his day back in 1925 in the forgotten territory of Alaska. They had an epidemic of diphtheria at Nome on the west coast. They flew the serum into Anchorage and then had to take it from Nenana to Nome six hundred and seventy-four miles away by dog teams.' Ott patted the bronze head of the dog. 'They made it in six days in temperatures of fifty and sixty below. Can you imagine cold like that, Richard Larsen?' taking another swig as though an Arctic wind had knifed through the park. 'Can you imagine a temperature that freezes the flesh in thirty seconds? One guy, Leonard Seppala, made three hundred miles in seventy-eight hours and forty-four minutes. You know, they did it in relays and it was old Balto here that made the final burst, leading Gunnar Kassen's team into Nome. He even got a mention in Congress, did this old mutt,' patting the bronze head again.

'I don't understand . . .' Richard Larsen began.

'Sure you don't. Do you know how they rewarded him? Put him and six other mutts on a vaudeville tour. In 1927 they were found tied to a sled in a dime museum in Los Angeles. Bet he wished he'd never made that final burst, huh, Richard, old buddy?'

'And that's why you're bitter?'

'Kind of sums it up, doesn't it.'

23

'I guess so,' not sure what it summed up, but feeling it some-how did. 'But why did you come here if it makes you bitter?'

'Maybe the bitterness does me good. Maybe it purges me. Or maybe,' Ott said, 'it's just an excuse to get drunk. Hey,' he said, punching Richard Larsen in the chest, 'let's go and get our-selves a beer.'

They walked towards Fifth, smelling wet dust and earth, dodged through the cabs, clean in the rain, and walked down 65th to Third where they found a dark bar with a wise-cracking barman, bottles paraded in front of ornate glass and a drunk with his head hung low over his glass.

Ott drank thirstily, wiping the foam from his lips with the back of his hand. 'White men don't like to see Indians drink-ing,' he said.

'How old are you?' Richard Larsen asked curiously, sipping at his beer, seeing the two of them in the mirror and thinking that his face looked very white and downy beside Ott's brown face.

'Ninety-eight,' Ott said.

'No, seriously.'

'Why be serious?' He found another cigar and lit it clumsily. Then, with the furtive, confidential air of the drunk: 'Do you really want to know why I'm bitter?'

Larsen felt very young and sober and a little superior. 'Sure I want to know. I asked you, didn't I?'

'Then I'll tell you.' He belched. 'Because at last they've dis-covered Alaska, the Great Land.' He pulled a black notebook from his inside pocket and extracted a newspaper clipping. 'Here, take a look at this,' and to the barman: 'Me big chief want another beer.'

Richard Larsen read the clipping. It described the discovery of Alaska since Pearl Harbour. It recalled how American Civil War Secretary William H. Seward had bought Alaska for 2 cents an acre; how Alaska had then been called Seward's Folly and Seward's Ice Box and how it had been forgotten except by the gold prospectors and canning companies and fur traders. Then Japan had attacked and Washington had realized that Alaska was the shortest route from the U.S. to Japan. Alaska had been rediscovered and now they were building the Alaskan Highway from Canada, building airfields with mile-long concrete strips, hustling troops and firepower into the territory whose garrison in 1939 numbered two hundred and ninety-seven. *Let us hope,* the article concluded, *that after the Japs have been whipped we never again forget Seward's Folly.*

'See what I mean?' Ott addressed himself into the mirror behind the bar.

'You mean they're spoiling your country.'

'My territory,' Ott corrected him. 'My goddam territory. Your territory, America's goddam territory.'

He got up off his stool and made for the men's room. While he was gone the barman who had slick hair parted down the middle put down the glass he had been polishing and said: 'Your coloured buddy has had a few belts too many, why don't you get his ass out of here.'

Richard Larsen, digging his fingernails into the palm of his hand, said: 'He isn't coloured, he's Indian.'

'Same thing,' the barman said, but picked up the glass and went on polishing it as Ott returned.

Richard Larsen glanced at his wrist-watch. He had a date and he wanted to get to Penn Station to get back to the Island, but he didn't want to leave this drunk, this Indian, this man who smelled of the outdoors, this man who was cramped in Central Park, this man who beckoned him to come out from behind the drawing-room curtains of his village.

'You got to go?' Ott dropped his cigar on the floor crushing it with his heel as though it were a snake. 'I got to go, too.' He was struggling now to articulate. 'Say, maybe you'd like to hear more about your territory. Maybe we should meet again.'

Richard Larsen stood up. 'I'd like that. Can we make a date?'

'Same place,' Ott said, staggering slightly as he stood up. 'Day after tomorrow, same place.'

'Here?'

'Here? To hell with here.'

'Where then?'

'Outside the lion's cage, of course. Where else, Richard Larsen?'

'What time?'

'Any time. I got plenty of time.'

'Midday?'

Ott stuck out his hand in the general direction of Richard Larsen's hand. 'Don't forget.'

'I won't forget. But will you?'

'I won't forget. Do you know what the national flower of Alaska is?'

Richard Larsen shook his head.

'The forget-me-not. Now, ain't that something?'

But it was a different Indian who turned up outside the lion's cage at midday. He was sober. And so he was most of the times when they met and drove in Ott's Oldsmobile up beside the Hudson or into New Jersey or to the eastern shores of Fire Island, to drink beer and eat cold chicken in the sand dunes and watch the gulls finding the currents in the sky.

From Ott, young Richard Larsen learned more about animals and birds than any book had ever taught him. Mostly he learned about animals and birds that live in wild places, in particular he learned about the creatures who live in the great bulge to the north west of North America that is Alaska.

With a bottle of Schlitz in one hand and a leg of chicken in the other he listened and saw and smelled black bears growing from hairless, helpless cubs to five hundred pound killers; grizzly bears asleep in the sun or taking salmon from waterfalls; herds of caribou moving unpredictably across tundra and forest. Moose with great foolish noses, dewlaps and ridiculous tails; dall sheep, coyote, fox, lynx, beaver, otter, flying squirrel ... and, of course, wolves.

Ott put Larsen right on wolves one day as they sat among the dunes on Fire Island with the gulls wheeling like pieces of paper caught in a gale and the Atlantic, grey now in the fall, pushing and pulling at the cold sand.

'I suppose you think they're mean bastards,' he said. 'Mean, cowardly and treacherous.'

Larsen said cautiously: 'I don't know too much about wolves.'

'One of the most fascinating animals in the world. And the pack is the most complex society in the animal kingdom. Grandparents, parents, kids, uncles and aunts – they all live together and they could teach us a thing or two about getting on. You know something? They even have babysitters when the old lady's away. And you should see the hunters when they come home. They get kissed and hugged which is more than most breadwinners get when they return home in Philadelphia.'

'But a wolf is a killer, isn't he.'

Ott was disgusted. 'Of course he's a killer, how else would he eat? And you should see 'em bring back food to their pups. The pups give 'em a bite or two around their muzzles and they regurgitate the meat. Clever, huh?' Ott didn't wait for a reply. 'And as for organizing their lives – American Society could learn a thing or two there. The leader's the leader and that's it, boy, no arguing, no fighting, not till he quits by submitting to a younger wolf.' He paused. 'I suppose you think a wolf's howl is blood-curdling?'

Larsen said he hadn't thought about it one way or the other.

'You would if you'd heard it. One of the most exciting sounds in the world – the real call of the wild. And as for being vicious, why they make the most gentle pets in the world. Better than any pooch or pussy ... Not of course, that you should tame 'em. They belong to the wild ...'

It was one day when they had driven north and were sitting overlooking a fat curve of the Hudson near Bear Mountain – Indian country, according to Ott – where stems of smoke arose from the red and gold banks of the river, that Richard Larsen discovered that Ott was an Indian with a difference.

He had been telling him that, with a few pounds of polar meat in your belly, you could walk on ice for five hours or more without pain, and Richard Larsen had asked: 'What sort of gun do you shoot them with?'

Ott was silent for a moment, yellowish eyes staring across the river and beyond. Carefully he lit a cigar, blew smoke into the thin air and said: 'I don't shoot them.'

'What do you mean about the meat then?'

'I don't shoot them,' Ott repeated. 'Others do.'

'But I thought—'

'You thought wrongly.' Ott picked up a smooth stone and flung it towards the river, but it fell short. 'I'm a freak,' he said. 'I'm an Indian who doesn't shoot, doesn't hunt. That's one of the reasons why I left Alaska,' he told Richard Larsen who had been wondering. 'Not only was I an Indian which is bad enough up there but I was a non-hunting Indian, a weirdo.'

Richard Larsen, seeing smoke signals and the Apache moving down from Bear Mountain, asked Ott if he was a thoroughbred Indian.

Ott said no, not thoroughbred, maybe threequarters and maybe it was the mongrel quarter that made him feel the way he did about hunting.

'You've never carried a gun?'

'Oh sure, I've carried a gun. If there's a polar coming at you – the hardest bastard in the animal world who will kill you for the hell of it – then you've got to shoot him and you've got to know where to shoot him. But I don't go looking for him. I leave that to the Eskimos and the big white chiefs from Seattle and Vancouver who go hunting in light aeroplanes.'

They walked down the hillside where the birch trees stood out like bones among the autumnal oak and maple.

Finally Richard Larsen asked the questions that had been bothering him. If Ott felt like that about Alaska why did he leave it (because Richard Larsen didn't accept the outcast theory)? And why (hesitantly) wasn't Ott in the Army?

'Good questions,' Ott said, following a trail through a patch of briars and making no effort to answer them.

'I mean, how do you live?'

'A good question,' said Ott, stopping and picking up a stick, taking a knife from a sheath on his belt and starting to whittle it.

They reached a mouldering wharf beside the river. There was a rowing-boat moored alongside it; there was water in the bottom of the boat and the varnish had long since peeled from its hull. Ott contemplated it for some time, whittling away at his stick. 'Fancy some fishing?'

'You don't mind fishing?'

'If the fish are for eating. I don't like killing for sport, that's all.'

He knocked at the door of a wooden shack leaning towards the river and asked the stubble-jawed old man, if he could hire tackle and buy some bait. He got the tackle and some worms and the hire of the rowing-boat for two dollars.

He rowed across the river where they found a stretch of calm water protected by a headland. He baited the hooks and let the line, weighted with lead, slide into the water.

He lit a cigar and said to Richard Larsen: 'So you want to know why I left Alaska?'

'It puzzled me,' Richard Larsen said.

'Well, I'll tell you. You see, being a mongrel, I don't know what the hell I want. But I figure Alaska deserves more than she's getting. I figure that the States has used Alaska for so long that it's about time that they at least did her the honour of making her a State. So I came south to do some lobbying in Washington.' Ott peered over the side of the boat and stared down the length of cat-gut until it disappeared into mud-grey depths. 'As a matter of fact,' he said self-consciously, 'I was the Indian representative. I wanted statehood so that the natives – me,' he grinned, 'could have decent education and food and housing because we've been exploited ever since the Russians found us. And I wanted the wild life preserved,' Ott said, testing the line.

'And then the war came?'

'Sure, the war came and Alaska suddenly became strategic.' He tasted the word. 'Yeah, that's what it became – strategic. And so now the spoilers have arrived and I tell you this, Richard Larsen, they'll never leave because once a man's found Alaska he doesn't want to leave. And one day they'll do to Alaska what they did to an island known as Manhattan.'

The line jerked and he began to pull it in; then it straightened out again as a fish tore free from the hook. 'And you want to know how I earn a living? Why I'm not serving old Uncle Sam?'

Richard Larsen had the decency to look ashamed.

'I teach,' Ott said, folding a grin at him. 'Now how about that? I teach kids like you about animals, about evolution, so that you can all grow up and take your baseball bats to seals and trap lions and put them in Central Park zoo. As a matter of fact,' Ott said, searching Richard Larsen's face, 'I'm a professor. Now how about that? And do you know where I teach?'

'Here in New York?'

'To hell with that,' Ott said, testing the line again. 'I'm an Ivy Leaguer. I teach at Princeton.' He paused for effect. 'You want to know why I'm not serving Uncle Sam?'

'It doesn't matter,' Richard Larsen said.

Ott flicked his cigar butt into the water, watched it drift downstream towards New York. 'I'll show you.' He took off one shoe and sock and Richard Larsen counted four toes. 'Frostbite,' Ott told him. 'Lost the big one mushing in a race. Seems they don't want toeless soldiers in the United States Army. But hell, who wants to fight anyway? And what would I be fighting for? The Indians, Alaska, America . . .?'

'You shouldn't be so bitter,' Richard Larsen said.

'Bitter? I reckon the frost did me a good turn. Did I ever tell you what happened to old Balto in the end?' he asked.

Richard Larsen watched a kingfisher skim over the water. 'You said he went into vaudeville.'

'That wasn't the end of it. The good people of Cleveland got up a subscription. Raised more than two thousand bucks. They put him out to grass in a zoo, then they stuffed him and put him in Cleveland Museum.'

Richard Larsen who couldn't see much wrong with that said so.

'I guess not,' Ott said. 'I suppose it's better being stuffed than being in vaudeville with the clowns.'

The line jerked violently and Ott began to haul it up. As the tackle neared the surface they could see the fish wriggling, silver and bright. As the tackle reached the surface it broke free, leaped and dived and disappeared.

'That's the sort of Indian I am,' Ott said. 'I can't even hook a fish.' But, as they rowed back towards the far shore, it seemed to Richard Larsen that Ott was relieved that they had lost the fish.

Larsen had gone shooting once on Long Island. With three other boys and two Daisy air-rifles between them.

They had climbed a hill covered with birch. There was a dusting of snow on the deep pile of the leaves and the twigs of the trees were sheathed in ice so that, when a breeze came in from the Sound, they clattered together like the fingers of skeletons.

Larsen was thirteen years old and he hoped they wouldn't see anything to shoot. He didn't want to be there; but he wasn't yet brave enough to say so.

He didn't carry a rifle. He walked in front of the other three boys making as much noise as possible to scare away the quarry.

'Hey,' shouted one of the boys, 'stop making that racket. How the hell can we get a bead on anything with you sounding like the cavalry?'

'Maybe he doesn't want us to shoot anything,' said another boy.

'Yeah, maybe he's chicken,' said the other.

One of them fired his gun into the slippery, polished branches. Two birds took off into the cold sky.

'You couldn't hit a teddy bear at five yards,' one of the boys said.

'Yeah?'

'Yeah.'

They reached the brow of the hill, crossed a pond concealed by leaves; their boots broke through the crust of ice and one of them went thigh deep into the water. He laughed it off, holding his Daisy air-rifle high-port, like a Marine landing at a beach-head.

Now they were looking down on woodland where stems of smoke rose from houses stripped of their summer camouflage of leaves.

Larsen said: 'Maybe we should go back. Harry will get his legs froze.'

31

'You go back,' Harry said. 'I ain't chicken.' He broke the barrel of the air-rifle, slammed it together again. 'How would it be if the Lone Ranger went back every time he got his legs froze?'

Larsen saw it first. A squirrel looking at them from a branch where it joined the trunk of a birch. He coughed, clapped his hands loudly and said: 'Hot damn but it's cold.'

The squirrel scuttled along the branch and looked down at them. Larsen swung his arms round his chest and gave an Indian war-cry.

'For Pete's sake shut up,' one of the boys said, as the squirrel moved nearer and the branch bowed towards them under its weight.

The boy who had fired the first shot spotted it. He held up one hand, put his fingers to his lips, brought the barrel of the air-rifle to his shoulders.

The squirrel gazed at them, chip-toothed, paws up to its throat.

The boy squeezed the trigger and the rifle fired with a thick, compressed sound.

The squirrel fell from the branch. Then it began to move slowly towards them, its movements growing slower, until when it was a few feet from them Larsen saw that the slug had blinded it in one eye and that blood was oozing down its sleek winter fur.

The boys stared at it. The boy who had fired the shot said to the other boy with a rifle: 'For God's sake finish it off,' and the other boy fired at the slowly moving squirrel and the slug seemed to hit it in the side but it still came at them, pausing once to brush at the blood on its face.

Larsen picked up a large stone and brought it down on the squirrel's head. And only then did the squirrel die.

It wasn't until they were nearly back at the village with the cold getting inside them that they spoke.

One of them said to Larsen: 'Gee thanks, I guess you weren't chicken after all.'

Larsen said: 'I was chicken. I shouldn't have been there.' He stopped outside his house; the dusk was cold and cruel. 'And I won't be again,' he said as he walked towards the house, past the trees where the squirrels played.

Ott was very drunk the last time Richard Larsen saw him in New York.

He was in the zoo and he was addressing the polar bears. It was cold, with a little snow on the ground, and the polar bears seemed happy. Ott, whisky bottle in his jacket pocket, cigar in his mouth, had attracted a small crowd.

'Some good specimens today,' he told the big bear whose fur was yellow against the snow. 'We shipped 'em in specially for you to look at.' Ott scanned the crowd. 'I reckon that specimen over there' – pointing at a six-footer wearing a Stetson – 'is from Texas. You'd like it down there, everything's big.'

A keeper hovered uncertainly in the background. A few flakes of snow were peeling off the grey sky and the cold air smelled of smoke from a hot-chestnut stall. Pigeons flapped overhead.

Ott pointed at a fat man eating a hot-dog. 'Interesting specimen there, Bruin. He doesn't eat like you because he's hungry. He eats all the time except when he's sleeping and he makes a point of eating all the wrong kind of food – fats and starch and sugar – and he wonders why he's fat. Yes, sir, a very interesting specimen and we're sure grateful to him for coming to the zoo today.'

'Hey,' said the fat man, 'I don't have to take that crap from you. I reckon it's you who should be behind bars, not the bears.'

A few people laughed but not too loudly because there was menace about Ott and everyone knew what Indians were like when they got on the juice.

Ott drank from the bottle. 'You got it wrong fella. We're all behind bars. It's the critters who are watching *us* and *we're* behind bars.'

'He's nuts,' said the fat man. 'Someone should call the cops.' He looked round for the keeper.

'He ain't doing any harm,' said a middle-aged woman, hair in rollers beneath a headscarf. 'You don't have to stay and listen.'

'He's nuts,' the fat man said.

That was the situation when Richard Larsen approached from Fifth Avenue. He wondered whether he should intervene, then decided not to because this was The Ott Show. So he stood at the back of the crowd thinking: Why the hell does he drink like this? A couple of days ago we were sheltering from the wind in the dunes at Fire Island watching Oyster Catchers and he was sober and vitally alive. Now he's plastered, hamming it up like some Hollywood Indian playing a drunk in a Randolph Scott movie. It was stupid and it was ugly. So he stood and waited for a couple of Hollywood cops to end the show.

Ott was shouting: 'You imagine you've come here to see the animals? You're crazy. They've been brought from the four corners of the world to observe the habits of the civilized American.'

'Turn the record over,' the fat man said. 'Play us another tune, for Chrissake.'

A little girl in a fur-lined parka said to her nurse: 'He's a funny man. I like him.'

Her nurse said: 'He's a silly man. Now come on, let's go and buy an ice-cream soda,' leading her towards Loeb's boating house.

'But,' said Ott, taking a pull from the whisky bottle, 'the animals don't just want to watch you while you're all behind bars, they want to come and meet you. So, folks, I'm going to do something about that. I'm going to get rid of some of these bars.'

He picked up a parcel. With the knife he cut the string; he tore off the paper and there was a new hacksaw, teeth strong and shiny.

He climbed over the outer bars and began to saw at the bars of the cage.

The bears watched him with minimal interest.

The fat man dropped his hot-dog. 'Hey, stop him someone. That guy's crazy.' He looked over his shoulder. 'Where's the keeper? Where are the cops?'

The woman in the headscarf said: 'He could lose an arm that way.'

No one moved.

Richard Larsen decided that it was time he made a move. He pushed his way through the crowd and shouted to Ott: 'For Chrissake knock it off. They'll lock you up in a minute.'

Ott looked up, 'Hi, Richard Larsen. Come to help?'

'I've come to stop you making a fool of yourself.'

'Too late for that,' Ott said. 'But I wish I had some dynamite.'

'Let's get the hell out of here,' Richard Larsen said. 'Before it's too late . . .'

'It's too late now. It's always too late.' He began to saw at the bar again.

And it is too late, Richard Larsen thought, as two cops pushed their way through the crowd, one with his hand on his night-stick, the other with his hand on the butt of his pistol.

They grabbed Ott, bent one of his arms behind his back, twisted the other until the hack-saw fell from his hand. Richard Larsen was surprised that he didn't make a fight of it; but you could never tell with an Indian who didn't like hunting.

The two cops were broad and dark, and they tackled the job at hand with muscular efficiency. 'Better come with us, fella,' one of them said, frisking him and taking away the knife.

'Sure, why not,' Ott said; and Richard Larsen realized for the first time that he didn't know Ott's first name and that it didn't matter.

Richard Larsen followed them to the car parked on an access road and said: 'Is there anything I can do?'

One of the cops looked at him. 'And who are you?'

'He's my buddy,' Ott said.

'What is it with your buddy?' one of the cops asked Richard Larsen.

'He's an Indian,' Richard Larsen said. 'He doesn't like to see animals locked up in cages.'

'He's the one who's going to be locked up,' the other cop said.

'Does he have to be?'

'Sure he has to be. One he's plastered, two he's probably crazy.' He took the bottle of whisky from Ott's pocket and put it in the back of the car.

'He teaches at Princeton,' Richard Larsen told the cops.

'Jesus,' they both said.

Ott leaned against the car. 'No more,' he said. 'No more teaching. Now I'm going to fight.'

The older of the cops frowned. 'How's that?'

'Uncle Sam wants me. I signed on this morning.'

'God help the Japs,' said the younger cop.

'I was celebrating,' Ott told them.

'Yeah?' The younger cop was thoughtful. 'As a matter of fact I'm going, too. Military police. What unit you joining?'

'The Alaska Territorial Guard,' Ott told him.

'Come again?'

Richard Larsen who was suddenly very sad told them about Ott's background.

The younger cop turned to his colleague. 'You know something? When I turn in my badge I might have a few belts. I mean, it's natural ain't it?'

'But you won't go trying to free polar bears, huh?'

'I guess,' said the older cop, 'that you're entitled to hang one on when Uncle Sam's called you.' He put his hands on his hips and addressed Ott. 'You going to behave yourself? I mean if we let you go we're strictly out of line and if the lieutenant hears about it then he'll have our balls.'

As they climbed into the car Ott said: 'And I've only got nine toes, how about that?'

They walked down Fifth Avenue without speaking, the Indian, an alien imprisoned by high-rise, breathing gasoline fumes instead of air scented with pines.

So Ott is going and I shall return to the village, Richard Larsen thought. The adventure is over but nothing will ever be quite the same again.

He said to Ott: 'Why do you have to go?'

'Seems I'm needed. Seems I know Alaska better than most and now, because they've suddenly realized Alaska is part of America and it's in danger and therefore the United States is in danger, they want me to go and help save it from the Yellow

Peril.' Ott patted his inside pocket. 'I got a letter from Washington the other day.'

'But I thought—'

'So did I,' Ott said. 'But have you tried getting a broad these days if you're not in uniform?'

'What about Princeton, what about your work?'

'It can wait,' Ott said. 'Like they say, everything's got to wait till this war is finished.'

Richard Larsen was silent.

Ott said: 'It's their look-out. They know I've only got nine toes but it seems they don't know I'm crazy.'

'You were certainly crazy this morning.'

'Sure, why not? It's good to be crazy. You know, it helps. A little Scotch and a little craziness.'

'Who are you fighting for?' Richard Larsen asked. 'Alaska or America?'

'Both, I guess. And when the war's over I'll be fighting the Americans so that Alaska can have a piece of the pie. And I tell you this, they'll be as tough as the goddam Japs because one day the United States is going to need Alaska more than any other piece of land in the world and they won't want to make us a state, they'll want to keep us as a territory, a goddam colony. And do you know why, kid?'

Richard Larsen shook his head.

'Because there's oil up there, that's why.'

So Ott departed and he didn't write and Richard Larsen told himself: That's all you can expect from a crazy, nine-toed Indian. At first he was hurt, then he decided that they had established a permanence that didn't need letters. Ott had picked him up and pointed him in a new direction.

And by the spring of 1942 Richard Larsen was a buck private in the United States Army.

By the early spring of 1943 he was at Cold Bay in the Aleutians, part of Alaska, but bearing no resemblance to the Alaska

Ott had described. The island had been scoured by rip-tides and storms, shaped by glaciers, ruptured by volcanoes. More often than not they were covered by fog and from an aircraft the mountains looked like rocks, protruding from the ocean. Very few of the military personnel at Cold Bay could understand why the Japanese or the Americans gave a goddam about the Aleutians; but the Japanese had captured two islands at the tip of the chain, Attu and Kiska, and the enemy had to be driven off.

If Larsen's will to escape permanently from his upbringing ever faltered then it would falter in this place.

He lived in a Quonset hut and he ate tinned Vienna sausages, bread without butter and powdered eggs. It was wet and cold and, while the generals drew up their plans, he yearned for his home, for his parents and sometimes at night for the feel of a girl's breasts in his hands.

He observed with awe the reactions of some servicemen who had been too long at Cold Bay. Most of them were stoic – after seeing *The Fighting Seebees* for the fifth time at the improvised movie house – but some caught Cabin Fever, one or two committed suicide, some indulged in homosexuality.

It was at this time that Larsen decided that he wanted to fly. He made a point of talking to the fliers, listening to their accounts of bombing runs and reconnaissance flights over the islands to which the Japs clung like limpets. They told him about Aleutian static that blacked out communications, about the Williwaw that tossed them around the sky, about targets reduced to a few crags, about flying with ice-sheathed wings, about the damp that sabotaged carburettors, about ditching in dark waters and feeling your blood freeze while you waited for a Catalina to come to your rescue.

And he heard about a pilot they loved and hated: Major William Eareckson, a lanky, crop-haired buccaneer who sent them on interminable missions – and flew them himself.

Once Larsen borrowed a flying jacket and sat in on a briefing:

'We're going up to about ten thousand. Head north then turn in towards the island at Pillar Rock. Make a ninety degree

38

diving run. The first wave will use a 7,000 base, the next 6,000. The first wave goes for the hangars' – stabbing at a green, brown and blue relief map of the island with his finger – 'the second the sub base.'

Larsen wanted to go with them. Not to pulverize a rock in the Pacific but just to be high and free above the clouds.

One day, Larsen thought, I'll fly.

Then, on May 4th, 1943, Larsen set sail from Cold Bay with the 7th Infantry Division bound for Attu.

CHAPTER THREE

LIEUTENANT CHARLES BROWNING, who had left Harvard to enlist, was one of the first to reach the shore when the Southern Force landed at Massacre Bay.

By 5 p.m. on the first day all three beaches – Holtz Bay, Beach Scarlet and Massacre – were in American hands without a shot being fired and Browning felt cheated. He had come prepared to die, to see a line of splashes in the sea and feel a bullet hit him in the stomach, to die with his pistol in his hand. Instead he was alive, cold and hungry, amid fog and khaki colours, and he was scared that fear would take advantage of the anti-climax and return.

With his men behind him, Lieutenant Browning slogged inland, his calculations, and the calculations of the generals, based on a Coast and Geodetic Survey chart that penetrated one thousand yards inland, and a few blurred aerial photographs. The tundra sucked at his combat boots, the silence thickened, and for a while he forgot about the Japs perched up there somewhere in the fog.

What opportunities have been missed here, Browning thought as he led his men along Massacre Valley. These humps of rocks, inhabited by a few Aleuts, have been ignored because they are ugly and inaccessible; but there are harbours and fish and God knows what minerals beneath the tundra – gold, silver, uranium, nickel, lead, tin, maybe coal, maybe even oil. One day, he decided, I'll return to reap the harvest.

Behind him on the beach, blocked by vehicles and guns stuck in the mud, a 105mm howitzer of the 48th Field Artillery Battalion fired the first round of the Battle of Attu at a Japanese mortar position spotted by an observer through a hole in the fog. The mortar position was destroyed with the third shot. Perhaps, Browning thought, the Japs will give up without a fight and he hoped so and at the same time, hand on his pistol, he hoped they wouldn't.

Ahead of the Southern Force, on the heights above Massacre Valley, two companies of the Japanese 303rd Infantry Battalion, waited for the enemy to come within range. They were hidden by the fog but they could see the Americans below; it was like looking down from an observation balloon.

The message from Northern Imperial Army HQ had been simple. DESTROY THE ENEMY. Colonel Yasuyo Yamasaki wasn't too sure about that. He had only two thousand, six hundred and fifty men and he had deployed them to strategic points above Holtz and Massacre Valleys. But he would fight until the last man was killed and that would take time because, despite their limited fire power, the Japanese had other allies – fog, snow, tundra and Williwaw.

As the Southern Force moved up Massacre Valley the *samurai* fingered rifles, machine-guns and mortars.

On one side of Browning was a Negro corporal, on the other a private, a country boy from Nebraska.

The fog above them was a roof and the light was beginning to fade. The cold closed in from the sea and the sky and the ground. Above the fog they heard aircraft engines. The noise grew louder, then faded as the aircraft returned to base at Umnak.

Then the snipers opened up. Bullets coming from the grey ceiling, whining from boulders, burying themselves in the tundra and snow.

The advancing troops faltered, took stock of themselves and began to move forward again. Browning felt fear move inside him but only briefly because it became an exultation like the feeling on the football field when, with a broken rib and the taste of blood in his mouth, he had burst through the defenders to touch down. He took the heavy pistol from its holster, raised it aloft and shouted: 'Forward.'

To his left the boy from Nebraska groaned, dropped his rifle, clutched his stomach and died. And all that Browning saw on his face was: *Why me?*

The sniping increased in intensity. A bullet struck a boulder in front of Browning, a chip of stone striking his helmet. Now he wanted to take cover, to drop behind the nearest clump of boulders to escape from the whining, zipping, killing bullets. But he was officer material, so he stayed there on the football field, knowing that the Japs could pick them off at their leisure from the fog that was their fortress. 'Keep moving,' he shouted. 'Keep your heads down and keep moving.'

Another man fell, blood staining the snow. And another. 'The bastards,' Browning shouted, 'we'll show 'em.'

But just then a voice from a bullhorn shouted to them to take cover, and they did so thankfully, dragging the dead and wounded with them.

Later that evening, with night crowding the fog, the order to attack came again. As the artillery marooned on the beach opened up the troops broke cover and charged the hillside.

But the earlier sniping had been play, toy muskets. Now machine guns and mortars opened up, ripping the tundra apart. Men fell ingloriously, heads lying in olive-green sponge.

Facing death, Browning was heroic. On the baseball diamond, on the football field, leading his men. He pointed his pistol at the fog above and fired it, imagined a Japanese clutching his throat. 'Come on, follow me.'

The Negro corporal jogged along beside him, face impassive.

A mortar exploded to Browning's right throwing two men in the air like marionettes, jerked by strings. One of them lay screaming, holding the pulp that had been his belly.

The bombardment from the ridges guarding Jarmin Pass increased in ferocity and now the troops were scattering.

Browning was confused because it had never been like this in the lecture rooms when the only direction was forward and you could see the enemy and your guns weren't bogged down on the beach and there were good maps of the terrain with great curving arrows showing how the enemy was going to be encircled.

The attack faltered, stopped. Became a retreat.

They attacked once more that evening; then, as darkness fell, they dug in for the night.

Browning took cover behind a crop of boulders. He had lost all his men, killed or wounded. The Negro corporal was among the dead.

Browning waited until dawn before setting out in the direction of the command post. He was cold and he was hungry and he was angry that the Army was making a balls-up of what should have been a simple operation.

He found a major and a sergeant lying behind a patch of scrub.

Browning knelt down beside them and asked where the commanding officer, Colonel Edward Earle, was.

The major, a middle-aged Southerner with brown liver spots on his hands, said: 'He's touring the forward positions wherever the hell they are.'

Browning told him that he had lost all his men.

The major leaned on one arm and stared at him. 'Survival of the fittest, huh, lieutenant.'

'I was lucky,' Browning said.

'How's the battle going?' Browning asked.

'How does it look as if it's going, lieutenant?'

'How are the other units getting on?' Browning asked.

The major stared at him for a moment, then pointed at the field radio. 'Dead as a dodo, lieutenant. We also are in one helluva mess,' said the major.

'But they can't hold out for ever,' Browning said.

'Who can't?' the major asked. 'Them or us? The air force has dropped enough bombs to sink the island.'

'We'll be okay when we get reinforcements and supplies,'

said Browning, thinking: This is the sort of creep who gets us into a shitty position like this.

'Oh sure,' the major said. '*When* we get them. *If* we get them. When the *Nevada*'s finished loosing off its shells we'll be attacking again. I suggest, lieutenant, that you go and round some men up.'

Browning made his way back to the crop of boulders where he had spent the night. How in the hell have we made such a God-awful mess of it? he wondered. And he decided that bullshit was one of the reasons – someone had bullshitted about the enemy strength, about the terrain, about the weather.

He crawled across the tundra, stopping at three foxholes and telling the men sheltering there to follow him when the next attack came. Then he dropped into the foxhole where Larsen, Gold and the sergeant were squatting.

The sergeant, he decided, was a pro, the backbone of the Army. Gold was cannon fodder and Larsen ... Instinctively Browning disliked the tall soldier with the ice-blue eyes and blond hair. Why? Browning wasn't sure; but there was a self-sufficiency about the man, an assumption of superiority, a latent defiance that implied that Army rank didn't matter a goddam.

When the time for the attack came and he pointed his pistol at Larsen's head to get him moving he wanted to pull the trigger. His excitement at the thought surprised him, but it didn't shock him.

It was the worst barrage yet. Men fell wounded, men died, men fled as the metal poured down from the fog.

It's crazy, Browning thought as clods of mud fell around him, as a mortar exploded thirty yards away. We should have waited till the fog lifts because, surely to God, it has to lift sometime; we should have waited until reinforcements and supplies reached us.

Instead they were committing mass suicide, just like the Japanese except that the Japs died with purpose and this was futility. But at least there was bravery here; no one could ever deny that there had been bravery at the Battle of Attu; if, that is, anyone ever remembered the Battle of Attu.

He held his pistol tightly, feeling fear take a sudden bite at him, but refusing to acknowledge it. That was surely what it was all about: experiencing fear but fighting it.

Suddenly a machine-gun opened up from another angle, bullets sang around them. One bullet hit Gold in the chest as he stood up, a snarl frozen on his face, the snarl of a fox in a glasscase; he fell sideways, hitting his head on the butt of his rifle.

The sergeant got to him first, put his ear to his chest, then shook his head and said: 'Poor little bastard.'

Browning intended to go forward, but no one else was – the Southern Force was in full retreat again. It was farcical, humiliating, tragic; it was like nothing they had ever been taught to expect.

The third day was a little better. They got to within two hundred yards of the Japanese positions before crossfire forced them back.

The fourth day was the worst. It was a débâcle, a rout.

Despite the decision to withdraw the Southern Force it was decided to test the enemy strength with the 3rd Battalion because, as someone reasoned, the Japanese might have withdrawn during the night.

At 11.00 hours the 3rd Battalion made its move, advancing into a mesh of gunfire which cut men down, chopped them up, shredded flesh and dignity and morale.

Gripping his pistol Browning moved forward, ducking behind cover, but always forward, knowing that this was what he had to do even if he thought it was crazy, wondering what the impact of a bullet was like and how long it was before you felt the pain.

As a mortar exploded near him, erupting snow and black mud, he thought he would have liked to have achieved something, at least to have sampled a little more of the world. I would like to have made money and I would like to have had lots of girls. This is injustice, this is suicide, this is a crime but I have to go forward.

He fired his pistol, feeling the recoil.

He looked round for Larsen.

But there was no one there.

I am alone.

Then he was moving back. Running without crouching, just running back towards the first line of trenches.

And then he was in a trench beside the Irish sergeant. And he saw that now the sergeant had only one foot. He turned to vomit but he fought it back and he didn't vomit.

CHAPTER FOUR

No one objected to Charles Browning enlisting even though he was in his sophomore year at Harvard. Least of all his mother and father.

At the time of the War of Independence his ancestors had been Loyalists; and his parents still were in a way: they were all-American but London was the centre of their world. When Britain and Germany went to war they waited impatiently for the United States to join in; shortly after Pearl Harbour their son enlisted and became an officer in the shortest possible time.

Not that there was anything brilliant about Charles Browning: it was his awesome single-mindedness that always won the day. This was abetted by a zealous regard for doing the right thing, or, more precisely, not doing the wrong thing.

The Browning forebears had been smugglers (merchants, in the family chronicles). After the War of Independence they had sailed for the Bahamas where the family fortune had been founded on rum.

There was some speculation that the Browning energies had reverted to liquor during Prohibition but Charles's parents were vague about this period and, in any case, it was surely unimaginable that any family whose lineage went back to Henry VII would have associated with Al Capone and the likes. Certainly they built railroads and a mansion on the shores of Lake Michigan with stables, ballroom and liveried servants.

In the 30s, Charles's father, with the unerring family instinct for world supply and demand, sold up the railroad interests and went into oil. Eight years later, with black gold gushing from his wells in Texas, he allowed himself to be bought up for a phenomenal sum by one of the oil giants with its headquarters in Manhattan. He accepted a vice-presidency and the corporation was grateful for his mannered presence.

Charles Browning continued to live in Chicago with his mother and the servants until he went to Harvard which Mr. Browning considered the next best thing to Oxford and Cambridge. He was soon an All-Ivy tackle, not because he particularly liked football but because it was the thing to be and he applied himself to its rigours.

Despite all this Charles Browning wasn't entirely happy. Because he was, in his way, honest – at least with himself.

He knew he was typecast by circumstance and he resented this. He resented the trappings of his heritage, not because he despised their benefits – and was too sensible ever to reject them – but because he wanted to create his own opportunities. It seemed to Charles Browning that his whole personality had been stamped upon him.

'All I can do,' he told Grace Meredith, a girl from Radcliffe, as they walked along State Street, Chicago, looking for a ring for her birthday, 'is to accept what's been handed to me on a plate and use it.'

'Very sensible,' she said, hand tucked in his arm.

Grace Meredith was a beautiful girl from Los Angeles. She was also intelligent and yet to Charles Browning she represented everything that he resented. She was the sort of girl that a boy of his birthright was bound to marry. We are well-matched, he thought; maybe we will marry and reproduce ourselves. Like sausages.

They stopped outside a jeweller's where trays of rings glittered in the sunlight behind thin bars.

'Anything take your fancy?'

'All of them,' Grace Meredith said.

'You're my kind of girl,' he said.

They stood close together and he could smell her perfume (expensive) and the warm smell of her hair. We're too young to become engaged, he thought, and yet I know it's written. Like everything in my life's written if I don't watch it.

'So, which one?'

She pointed at a brilliant-cut three carat stone and he said:

48

'Jesus, Grace. I haven't made it yet,' admiring her for it.

She tossed her long, honey-coloured hair. 'At least I'm ambitious. That's what you admire, isn't it, ambition?'

We understand each other, he thought, saying: 'What about something a little more modest until I make my first million?'

She settled for a small rosecut Silver Cape and they walked back to his open green MG which he had left at Grant Park.

He drove back too fast, glancing at the girl beside him, hair flailing behind her, seeing himself in ten, fifteen years, with Grace, his wife, beside him in their Cadillac and two Browning sausages in the back.

The dinner was very English.

Before the meal they drank Amontillado sherry in the drawing-room before adjourning to the baronial hall where they drank tomato soup followed by cold and bloody roast beef and for dessert apple pie and cream.

Mr. Browning, silver-haired with pink polished cheeks and a white moustache that was a little too rakish, spoke about the Chicago weather comparing it with the fragile beauty of English summers. Mrs. Browning spoke about the difficulty of getting reliable servants before – over the apple pie and cream – questioning Grace about her background and aspirations.

Charles Browning listened, despising the interrogation and yet approving of it, guessing that Grace understood because it was ritualistic.

Grace answered the questions adroitly.

Her parents owned vineyards in California. They were of Irish extraction – ah well, you can't have everything – but there was a peer mixed up in her ancestry somewhere and one of her relations in Co. Cork was a Master of the Hunt which was something.

They moved back to the drawing-room for coffee and liqueurs. Mr. Browning drank brandy in a large glass which he warmed with his hands, then selected a Havana cigar which he crackled at his ear, smelled, snipped with a gold cutter and finally lit.

They talked for a while, Grace gaining points by telling them that she played tennis and Mrs. Browning asked if she had ever been to Wimbledon.

The conversation faltered.

Mrs. Browning looked at her husband. 'Well, dear, I think I'll turn in. There's a new cook coming tomorrow and I've got to have my wits about me.' She turned to Grace. 'You stay on with the men if you want to, dear,' precluding any such possibility.

Charles Browning was left with his father.

Mr. Browning, glass in hand, began to patrol the room.

'A pleasant girl,' he said after a while.

'Very pleasant,' Charles Browning agreed.

'But you're both very young, of course.'

'We're not engaged or anything.'

'No, no, of course not. But I have a feeling that you think this might be *the* girl.'

'It's possible,' his son said. 'She's very attractive and she'd make a good wife. Keep the family line going, huh, dad?'

'I don't know about that,' his father said, pouring himself more brandy from the crystal decanter.

Charles Browning frowned. 'What do you mean by that?'

'Do you know much about her?'

'Enough I guess, now that mother has cross-examined her.'

'She was a very good witness,' his father said.

'You mean she handled herself well? Okay. I know she's not related to Royalty—'

'She certainly isn't.' He unlocked a desk, took out a sheet of typewritten paper and glanced at it. 'She comes from Los Angeles all right. But that's about the only accurate statement in her account of herself.'

Charles Browning looked at his father in astonishment. 'You mean you had someone check up on her?'

'In your interest,' his father said. 'Her father is a clerk with a firm of accountants and her mother once played walk-on parts in the movies some years back. Grace is one of three children and she was going out with a lifeguard before she won her scholarship.'

'So what?' asked Charles Browning.

His father sat down in the leather chair; it sighed as he sat down. 'I just thought I'd help you out. No harm in dating the girl. But . . .' He brushed ash from the watered silk lapel of his tuxedo.

'But she hasn't got class?'

'A vulgar expression,' his father said.

'For Chrissake we've only been out half a dozen times. There's been no talk about marriage, we're both too young . . .'

Mr. Browning stared at his son without speaking. Charles Browning caught a glimpse of total impersonality, this was the man who won boardroom battles, not the dinner-jacketed host who talked trivia over the claret.

His father said: 'I was taking a precaution. You learn to take precautions, in business.'

'But . . .' Charles Browning protested.

'She lied,' his father said flatly.

'Haven't you ever lied in business?'

'Many times – but I never got caught.'

'But it doesn't matter a goddam what she was, it's what she is.'

'They're one and the same thing,' his father said. 'And now, if you'll excuse me, I'll turn in, I've got a busy day tomorrow.' He put the typewritten sheet away in the desk and locked it. 'Think it over, son. Think it over.'

An hour later Charles Browning made his way quietly up the curving staircase to the landing where another Browning in oils stared across the hallway above a Ming vase. He turned in the direction of the guest bedroom, unsure of his motives but sure about what he was going to do as he always was.

He opened her door gently and she said: 'Is that you, Charlie?' She didn't speak again while he undressed, and climbed into bed beside her.

At first he had meant to confront her with his father's findings but, he reasoned, that would only thwart his intentions. 'Charlie,' she said, 'oh, Charlie,' and he could feel the warmth of her skin, as though it still held the warmth of the sun, and he could smell her perfume, somehow part of the warmth. He kissed her mouth, her breasts, and stroked her between her legs where the hair was soft as he had known it would be.

Then they were together. It was quick, perhaps too quick, but he didn't care. They came together. And only afterwards as she lay with her head on his arm did he question his motives.

He kissed her gently. Then he thought: The future Mrs. Browning wouldn't have allowed me to do that without resistance. What's more the future Mrs. Browning is expected to be a virgin.

Charles Browning didn't question her about her background. Instead he kissed her again, dressed and made his way quietly to his own bedroom.

And only then did the door of his father's room close with an oiled click of the lock.

Charles Browning never told Grace Meredith that he knew her background. It no longer seemed to matter. She stayed in Chicago for a few more days before returning to Los Angeles and he slept with her a couple more times. There were other girls that vacation and he took them to see the White Sox and to the restaurants and bars and movies in Rush Street. Sometimes he drove them into the country in his MG where they excited each other on blankets spread on the ground. Sometimes, on the third date, they went the whole way, as they put it, but if they resisted, he didn't pursue it because he had no wish to be compared with other clammy-handed boys. He had an abundance of partners and was almost indolent in matters of sex, declining to fumble because that wasn't the Browning way. He wasn't sure why he attracted the girls but he knew that it would prove to be a great asset in the future.

And he didn't waste his time. He was no genius and he knew it. So he spent a lot of his vacation studying and working out theoretical ways of making a fortune from the war that he believed would soon be waged.

Munitions, he decided, would be the answer. But would they? Everyone would be into munitions and you didn't want to waste your energy scrapping for Government contracts. No, he wouldn't go directly into munitions; he would buy out a small factory and adapt it to manufacture some small component vital for the production of shells and bombs.

He made the most of his plans knowing that they were fanciful because he would be in the Army.

He went to the oil company's offices in New York where he was treated with wary respect by junior executives and avuncular interest by the senior members of the board. He assessed them all, despising the servility of the Dale Carnegie graduates, admiring the older executives with their growling voices and boiled faces, telling himself that he would make his money younger, while he had time to enjoy what he had won.

He enjoyed going with them to a restaurant off Madison where lights, furniture and staff were subdued and decorous. He drank beer while they drank highballs. And he listened while they became slurred and childish. It made him feel mature and he was grateful to them, but he noted their vulnerability under the influence of alcohol, how it peeled off their masks, eroded their power; and he filed away his knowledge asking himself why the hell they allowed it to happen.

During the first two highballs he listened attentively while they talked oil. About new discoveries in the Middle East and Texas, about the potential of Siberia, about the requirements of the armed forces in the event of war.

One thing struck Charles Browning forcibly: these men, drawling Texans and Madison Avenue types with quick tongues, were as much concerned with suppressing news of oil strikes as they were with striking it.

Once, on the fourth highball, he heard a middle-aged Texan with a seamed face and a shoestring tie, refer to the Alaskan agreement.

What agreement? Charles Browning took a Yankees programme from his pocket and studied it and listened.

'It looks like the others are going to play along,' said the Texan.

'I hope to Christ you're right,' said one of the Madison Avenues. 'There's a helluva lot of oil up there. If it ever starts to flow the prices will hit rock bottom and we might as well go into the candy business.'

'Don't worry,' said the Texan, ice from his highball clinking against his teeth. 'The other guys see it our way. They don't want a glut, no one wants a glut.'

'Let's hope it stays that way,' Madison Avenue remarked. 'Let's hope the Eskimos use it all up lighting their lamps. And let's hope the Navy doesn't realize what it's got,' he added thoughtfully.

The Madison Avenue man glanced at Charles Browning. His face became wary. 'Hey, let's knock off the business talk.' He summoned the barman, clapped Charles Browning on the shoulders. 'Have you heard the one about the Army major telling his girlfriend about his unit in Georgia? He said they had white officers with black privates and his girlfriend said: "How exotic?" '

Mr. Browning senior who didn't get drunk said: 'I think it's time we ate.'

Once Charles Browning dated the company president's daughter, borrowed a company Packard and took her to a country club in New Jersey.

She was nineteen with page-boy-styled auburn hair and green eyes in a heart-shaped face. She was studying at Vassar, she was a snotty bitch and he admired her for it.

After they had swum in the pool where you took calls on telephones floating on trays, they put on terry-towel robes and walked across the lawn towards the trees.

And my little rich bitch is wondering when I'm going to make a pass, Charles Browning thought.

Judy Thackeray's robe had fallen open. Underneath she wore a fashionable flesh-coloured bathing costume and she looked naked and knew it.

Charles Browning put his hand on her back, feeling her warmth, beginning to want her but knowing this wasn't the way to play this one, saying, 'We'd better be getting back,' and feeling pleased with himself.

They walked back across the grass and he knew that she was analysing the situation just as the daughter of the president of an oil company should.

Half-way back to the clubhouse she said: 'You know you spoiled it for me then. I had a little speech rehearsed.'

'But you adapted to the unexpected. You'll go far, Miss Thackeray.'

'I don't have to try, do I?'

'No,' he said, 'I guess you don't.'

'Nor do you for that matter.'

He stopped and took her arm and stared into her green, knowing eyes. 'No, I don't have to, that's for sure. I could have my own office with a leather-topped desk and an ice-water dispenser and a secretary with good legs as soon as I quit Harvard if I wanted to. But I don't want it handed to me on a platter. No ma'am.'

'Very admirable. But you've got to admit you're starting off with a few advantages denied to a kid from the Bronx. Whatever way you look at it, whatever you achieve in life, the foundation stone is what your father's given you.'

They sat down at a white, wrought-iron table beside the pool and he ordered two beers from a black waiter wearing gloves. 'You're quite a bitch, aren't you,' he said wiping foam from his lips. 'You know where it hurts.'

'You should write B-movie scripts.'

'Only if they'd make a lot of dough.' He watched the tanned bodies of the young and privileged thrashing through the water.

'What I mean is I've come to terms with what I've inherited. You know I'll use everything that was dished out to me on that platter but I'll make my own way.'

'You're very sure of yourself, aren't you, Charlie?'

A small aircraft, a blue Lockheed Vega, flew overhead. 'I don't know if I'm very sure of myself. I know what I want and I've looked around and I don't see much competition. But no, I'm not sure of myself. I mean there are too many imponderables to be sure of oneself. Like any day now we're going to get involved in a war. How the hell can you be sure of yourself then?'

'And you'll enlist?'

'Natch.'

'I should have thought the war would have been the time to start making your fortune.'

'Maybe, but I wouldn't want to make it that way.'

'Quite the little patriot, aren't we?'

'Quite,' Charles Browning said.

'My father doesn't reckon we'll get involved in the war.'

'Maybe Hirohito doesn't think the same way as your father.' He stood up, a little bored with her. He took off his robe, stretched, executed a racing dive and swam a couple of lengths under water.

When he surfaced in front of Judy Thackeray he had decided that, when the time was opportune, he would ask her to find out about this Alaska agreement between oil companies that the executives had been discussing over their highballs.

When he got back to the apartment block a woman in a fur coat was walking down the carpeted corridor from the direction of his father's apartment towards the elevators. She was wearing a mink wrap; she was fortyish, attractive and yet her features were blurred, the face of dissipation or disillusion or both or neither . . .

His father was standing at the french windows leading out to a balcony where geraniums and cacti grew in wooden tubs. He was wearing a brocade dressing-gown and his silver hair which grew in neat wings over his ears was ruffled.

The room smelled of expensive perfume.

His father turned and smiled, hand wandering to the wings of hair. 'Had a good time?'

'So, so.'

His father looked disappointed. 'Care for a beer?' Charles Browning nodded and his father fetched two bottles from the fridge in the clinical kitchen.

'You don't seem very enthusiastic,' his father said, 'she's a fine looking girl.'

'I guess so. Another rich bitch.'

'That's no way to talk about the opposite sex.'

'Who was that woman?' his son asked. 'The one I saw walking down the corridor?'

His father tugged at his moustache. 'Just an old friend. I've known her for years.'

'A friend of the family?'

'You could say that,' his father answered carefully.

His son let it go. The fact that his father shacked up with women in New York didn't bother him; he doubted whether it would bother his mother as long as there was no scandal. What lodged in his mind was another insight into vulnerability.

His father said: 'You shouldn't judge girls like that too hastily,' feeling for his words. 'She's a very attractive girl—'

'And the president's daughter?'

'Precisely. Don't ridicule it, son.'

The trend of the conversation irritated Charles Browning. He was aware of the potential of a relationship with Judy Thackeray. But, hell, I don't want him guiding me towards the obvious, stamping the die once again.

His father said: 'You're the only child I've got. I intend to see that you make good.'

'I aim to do that, too,' his son said.

'Good boy.' His father stared into the cold, imitation log fire, the dressing-gown slipping open revealing blue silk pyjamas with navy piping and a glimpse of a scrawny chest. 'I'm returning to Chicago tomorrow. I want you to come with me. You know I still have a small interest in the railroad company. Well, they're giving their annual picnic the day after tomorrow. You know the sort of thing?'

Charles Browning knew very well. A big spread with cheap champagne in the grounds of some executive's house to give the lower echelons of the staff the impression that they were wanted, appreciated and loved and that a pay rise wasn't everything.

'Do you really want me there?' Charles Browning asked,

failing to see how he could enhance the prospects of the railroad company.

'Not just you,' his father said, staring at a picture of his wife on the mantelpiece above the fireplace.

'You want me to invite Judy Thackeray?'

His father shook his head. 'She's already invited.'

Charles Browning sighed. 'You know, I don't think it would break her heart if I wasn't there.'

'I suggest you come.' His father's voice hardened; it was his hiring and firing voice, a little cruel.

His son thought: Not much longer, and telling himself that, in any case, he preferred Chicago to New York, said: 'Okay I'll be there.'

The picnic was held in the grounds of the Browning mansion at Evanston, Chicago. The Mayor and a couple of Congressmen dropped in for a while before moving on to other picnics; there was a small band playing decorous music, a cold buffet and waiters in gold-braided jackets serving the good champagne to the important guests and the other stuff to the company's loyal servants. The grounds contained arbours and a couple of summer houses for champagne-inspired courtship. One or two executives would spoil their chances of promotion, which was partly the reason for these affairs. But the atmosphere was, generally speaking, well-bred.

There was also a blue, kidney-shaped swimming pool with a bar at one end adorned with lifebelts from a famous cruise ship.

One man seemed unimpressed by the gentility of the occasion. He was about fifty, balding and sweating with a long sour face and mud-coloured patches under his eyes. He wore lightweight grey trousers spilling over thick-welted shoes and his jacket was slung over his arm. He was talking to Browning senior and his voice was raised.

Charles Browning, talking to a boring young man about business management, eavesdropped.

The man was referring to some incident many years ago when his father had been boss of the railroad company. As far as Charles Browning could make out the man thought he had been swindled, 'screwed into the ground'.

His father, wearing a hacking jacket and silk Paisley scarf knotted at the neck of his white silk shirt, nodded sagely, beckoned a waiter who gave the man a glass of the good stuff. Then he put his arm round the man's shoulders and led him away, behind the arched walls of a rose arbour. Charles noticed the outline of a hip-flask in the man's trouser pocket; he also noticed his father beckon to two swarthy waiters with muscles straining the fabric of their gold-braided jackets.

Charles Browning wandered into the rose arbour where he could hear the voices of the two men on the other side of the wall. He picked a rose from a bush and listened.

The man was saying: 'You've got to do something, Mister Browning, you've got to. They reckon she's got TB and I haven't got the dough to get her the right treatment.' Charles Browning assumed that his father had already refused to help because the man went on: 'If you don't, Mr. Browning, then I'll spill it. You know what I know. I don't want to threaten you but I've got to have the cash. You know, I've kept quiet all these years. I've never given you any trouble. But I've got to have some help. Otherwise—'

His father cut the man short. 'I don't like blackmail, Bob.'

'This isn't blackmail.'

'It sounds very much like it to me.'

'It was a wrong thing you did, Mr. Browning.'

'Normal business practice, Bob.'

A pause. Perhaps the man named Bob was having a slug from the hip flask. Then: 'I've got friends on the papers, Mr. Browning.'

'Have you,' Mr. Browning murmured. 'Have you indeed.'

Charles Browning smelled the rose and stuck it in the buttonhole of his cream suit. Dear old decent old upper-crust dad, more chilling than any conventional all-American tycoon because it was all such a surprise.

'I don't want to—'

'You won't have to.'

There was a sound of a scuffle, a muffled cry, a crackling of undergrowth. Thoughtfully, Charles Browning made his way back to the guests, took a glass of champagne and joined Judy Thackeray who was wearing a green silk dress and a jade necklace. She was talking to some wives, although why she should bother Charles Browning couldn't imagine; except, perhaps, that her father, and his father, were part of a greater free-masonry than just railroads, linking American business above the boardrooms, ruling America, gazing down on its restless suburbs and slums from summits of high-rise.

He took her arm and they walked over to the swimming pool.

'Why did you come all this way? Because your father suggested it?' he asked.

'I'm not my father's vassal.' She paused. 'Do you think we're being manipulated?'

'Damn right.'

'Do you want to be manipulated?' she asked.

He grinned at her. 'Do you?'

'Like I want scarlet fever.'

'Then let's not be manipulated,' he said, steering her back towards the lawn. 'Looks like the party's over.'

The champagne had run out on time. The hosts were glancing at their watches, the band were packing away their instruments, guests were being escorted to their cars walking on champagne bubbles.

When they were all gone the Brownings and Judy Thackeray and a few other guests retired to the baronial hall for dinner. Charles Browning wanted to ask about the man named Bob but instinct told him: leave it alone. You had to be tough in business: you couldn't have ex-employees blackmailing you.

When they had reached the coffee and cognac Charles Browning and Judy Thackeray went for a stroll in the grounds.

They headed for the pool illuminated with under-water lighting. There were spare costumes in the changing rooms and they decided to swim.

Charles Browning emerged first. He walked to the end of the spring-board and gazed down into the bright blue water.

The shape was directly below his feet. Like a sack, drifting slightly with the current from the circulating pump.

He shivered. Because he already knew what the shape was. And when he dived and swam round the shape he gazed into the dead face of the man named Bob.

Back at Harvard he studied hard but he reckoned he had learned more of value during the vacation than he would learn during the term. He continued to date Grace Meredith for a while, wondering why he had ever considered it to be anything more than a casual relationship. She never asked why his attitude had changed and he never asked her about her Los Angeles background; but she knew, ah yes she knew; and she understood, he decided.

At first he wondered about the dead man in the pool, dreamed about the staring, dead-fish eyes and the thinning strands of hair waving like seaweed. To Charles Browning it looked like murder, not that it was any of his business. But the official verdict was a heart attack. The man named Bob had suffered a heart attack at the edge of the pool and fallen in. And if there had indeed been a coronary then it wasn't murder, Charles Browning concluded. After a while the dreams stopped and he stopped thinking about it. Although he was pleased that the railroad company had given the widow five thousand dollars.

Charles Browning continued to be on-the-way-up until, in May 1941, the Japanese bombers fell on Pearl Harbour and savaged the United States Fleet. Two weeks later he was in the army.

CHAPTER FIVE

THEY were winning. Or so it seemed.

Browning and Larsen and half a dozen men who had been relieved were sitting in a tent behind the forward positions drinking soup.

Browning said: 'Looks like we've got them licked.'

No one answered and Larsen thought: Yes, we're winning but at what cost? The generals had estimated that it would take three days to capture the island. The battle was now into its second week. We came here as greenhorns and now we're veterans.

He had seen men with trenchfeet and frostbite; he had seen the mess when the medics cut away blucher boots and the medics shook their heads because the feet would have to be amputated; he had seen starving men who had been cut down by Japanese crossfire vomiting their own juices; he had seen LTs sink in the shoals; he had seen men trying to haul the big guns fall exhausted beside them; he had seen men disobey commands because their minds were stunned.

And I have seen bravery. Christ, what bravery. I have seen what men are capable of and this I will always remember when I am cheated or betrayed.

He dipped the scoop into the can of steaming brown soup, making sure that he fished out some meat and lentils.

Larsen drank his soup from the scoop and looked at the other soldiers sitting listlessly on their sleeping bags. Only Browning looked alert, self-composed, deliberating.

Soon they would have to go out, up into the ice-sheathed mountains where snow was beginning to fall and men looked like shadows and you could shoot an American in mistake for a Jap.

Larsen knew that the men drinking soup and smoking and thinking about their wives and children, as he was thinking about the white-frame house and his mother cooking breakfast on the other side of the world, all hoped that the battle would be over before they were ordered out to fight again.

The Northern Force had taken Holtz Bay and the Japanese, with their position at Jarmin Press now unprotected from the rear, had withdrawn. A Southern Force patrol had finally walked into the deserted Japanese positions and met up with Captain Willoughby and one of his Scout Battalion patrols. The Japanese were then encircled at their main base at Chichagof Harbour by sea, mountains and American troops.

Sure, they were winning but there was no victory until the last Jap was killed. It sounded like a newsreel commentary but here it was true.

After that there had been three days of fighting for the heights around Chichagof against Japs entrenched on a mountain named Point Able. Drifting snow and fog and drizzle and bayonet combat.

Oh God the bayonets. Larsen felt the weakness in his legs again. He put down the scoop and sat down on his sleeping bag and lit a cigarette, remembering how he had tried to pretend that the man in front of him was one of the straw-filled sacks which he had bayoneted during training.

The Japanese had appeared suddenly in front of him on the third day of the assault on Point Able. At first he had thought it was an American because sleet was falling and the figures of all the soldiers were blurred shapes.

The Japanese came at him with his bayonet. Larsen's bowels moved and he heard himself scream. He had known that he might have to kill, with the impersonality of a bullet or even a grenade, but not facing a man, not having to stick the knife at the end of his rifle into his flesh.

But he did not wish to die that way either.

The Japanese, wearing a hood, small and squat and hissing, lunged at him. Larsen parried the strike, side-stepping at the same time. One of us has to die. He lunged and missed, then the Jap was coming at him again. It was unreal.

63

The Jap slipped on the ground where the drizzle had turned to ice. Larsen stood over him, bayonet poised. No, he couldn't do it. Not steel into flesh. The Japanese tried to kick his legs from under him. Larsen stared down at the straw-filled sack, thrust the bayonet down, down; put his foot on the sack and withdrew the blade, not seeing the blood on it, leaving the sack on the ice, following the other blurred shapes up the hillside into the mist.

They had taken Able Point. Reinforcements had arrived in the shape of the 4th Infantry Regiment. The village of Chichagof had been destroyed by attacks by B-25s and P-38s. An air attack by Japanese Betty's had been beaten off. After the battle for Able Point came the battle for Sarana Nose. They took Sarana Nose; then the Battle for Fish Hook Ride that was still raging.

Larsen picked up his rifle and ran his hand over its cold metal. The sack that he had left on the ice became human, eyes staring at him without fear, without hatred, sacrificial. Larsen put down the rifle, lit another cigarette with shaking hands and lay down on the sleeping bag, staring at the roof of the tent.

Browning drank the hot soup carefully, spacing out the gulps, chewing the meat thoroughly so that his starved stomach would accept it. As he drank he tried to work out exactly what had gone wrong with the operation; certainly it had become loused up, probably by a combination of factors, and heads had rolled; well one had at least – that of General Albert Brown, commander of the landing forces.

It was this in-fighting in high places that intrigued Browning because of its likeness to boardroom battles. He didn't believe that General Brown was the culprit, but there always had to be a scapegoat no matter how many people had fouled it up.

If my plans ever go wrong, Charles Browning thought, then I'll make sure there's always a sucker to take the can. 'Yes,' he said aloud, 'I guess we've got them on the run now.'

Later that day the battalion was ordered to join the attack on Fish Hook Ridge.

One soldier stood up, saluted and told Browning that the pain in his feet was so bad that he couldn't move.

Browning nodded understandingly. 'Okay, soldier,' he said, 'I'll see you at your court martial.'

May 26th.

A miracle.

The sun shone from a sky of eggshell blue and there were jewels in the snow and it was Christmas in the land.

There was even birdsong and seabirds floated high in the air-currents. Boulders and tundra had a brightness about them and even the cold smelled good.

They folded their sleeping bags, drank their coffee, which tasted sharp and sweet. There should have been carols and church bells; instead there was silence – and for the moment that was enough.

The silence lasted until the bombers came. At first there was a beautiful innocence about them as they flew in the sunshine. Then they were dark and dreadful and loud with the sunlight splintering in the fuzzy circles of their propellers. There were more than fifty of them and the sky was black with them.

They flew over the mountains and laid their eggs. The weather was suddenly their ally, the enemy of the Japanese. The weather was a turncoat.

And as the bombs tumbled from the bellies of the aircraft, straightening as the air caught their fins, tearing up the Japanese base at Chichagof Harbour, covering it with smoke and dust, Colonel Zimmerman's infantry began to move up towards the Japanese.

Browning was in front of his men when the machine gun opened up. One of the bullets hit him in the stomach and he fell on the snow feeling as if he was pinned there. Behind him his men took cover.

He didn't think he was going to die because he had overcome that fear. At first there was no pain, just a wonder that it was he lying there with the snow cold against his cheek and the blood spreading on the whiteness. He rolled over and felt the hole in

65

his combat jacket; it was just a hole, warm and wet. *But I am not going to die.* There is too much ahead. Bullets churned up the snow. All he could feel was the cold, the knife of cold in his belly, and then a little pain. And then he cried out with the pain. He tried to get up but he still felt as if he was pinned there, as if he had been bayoneted to the ground.

He gazed without interest at the grenade that came rolling down the hillside.

He watched without interest as Richard Larsen reached the grenade, picked it up and threw it back in the direction of the Japanese.

He saw it explode in the air.

Then he closed his eyes and didn't see Larsen fall as a chunk of the grenade hit him in the thigh, throwing him onto the snow. Nor did he feel arms round his chest as Larsen, taking the weight on his uninjured leg, tried to drag him back to cover, only giving up as a corporal and three soldiers reached them and pulled them both out of the line of fire.

Later, lying on a stretcher carried by two orderlies, Richard Larsen thought how strange it was that he had been wounded on the first clean bright day since the landing when he had seen the gulls in the sky and the sun on the snow.

CHAPTER SIX

THE Eskimo named Taluk had left it too late.

He had left Shishmaref on the north-west coast of Alaska before break-up hoping to get as far south as possible before the thaw when there would be black mud and water beneath new green leaves and small bright flowers as the sun grew warmer.

Taluk preferred to travel on ice with the runners of his sled hissing and the breath of the dogs smoking in the air. He liked the prickle of cold in his nostrils; he liked to see the flying wings of snow that guided him; he liked to see ice around him, flat ice or the broken ice of the ocean or the blue ice of glaciers.

He had no thought for the kind of beauty that only finds expression in these white, wide places: it was merely that the cold was a comfort to him behind his dogs, knowing that it was waiting outside while he crouched inside a snowhouse, the frost on his eyebrows melted by the heat from his body and the heat from his Primus stove.

Before leaving his village Taluk had loaded his sled with muk-tuk, pickled and sweet, cut from a bowhead whale harpooned in the Fall, dried seal meat, dried tom-cod, blueberries preserved in seal oil, ice-cream made from reindeer fat, seal oil, water and berries. He had also loaded the stove, with fuel, coffee, a caribou tent and rotten seal meat for the dogs.

And, because he was an enlightened Eskimo, four bottles of Vat 69 whisky and two rifles, a ·22 and a ·243 Winchester.

But enlightenment had brought no joy to Taluk, merely a restless ambition that had confused him until, lying in the wood and sod hut where his family lived, he had reached a decision. I am living in two worlds, the Eskimo's and the white man's, and I must make my choice. He chose the white man's world.

He would leave the poverty and tuberculosis of the village

and go south and find the riches of which white men spoke. He was twenty-four years old and the white man had educated him so that he could speak English and was equipped for whatever awaited him in the cities to which the small red, blue and yellow planes flew.

He grieved for a while because of what he was leaving. He grieved for the whaling expedition, the feasts that followed when the meat was stripped and cooked and the dancing and blanket tossing. And he would grieve for the long hours trapping white foxes when they came inland off the ice, hooking shea fish from the sea and listening to the beat of drums made from walrus stomach.

And he would grieve for the hot, oily smell inside the huts, the naked baby on a mother's back in the summer, the old women darning with sharp broken teeth; he would grieve for the sharing of possessions and happiness and sadness.

This is what Taluk believed he grieved for, but much of it was pictures in his mind, as old men see green fields where cities have been built. There were still some such pictures in his village but in Nome, to the south, there were gas-heaters and Singer sewing machines in the houses and furniture ordered from Sears-Roebuck. There was even a jukebox in the community centre.

It was Nome that had brought Taluk's ambition out of hibernation. The white man had arrived there many years ago in search of gold; had plundered the land – as the Russians had once plundered it of furs – and departed, leaving behind disease, a taste for liquor and big mining dredges stranded in the snow.

But the white man had also brought education and his own religion and these had stayed even when Nome's population had shrunk to a couple of thousand. White man still came to hunt and to search for new wealth in the Norton Sound and to watch the Eskimos dance; to Taluk they had transmitted this curiosity, this restlessness, this ambition that slavered inside him.

Why was he leaving? He couldn't really say. He told himself that it was the poverty around him – and the coughs deep in the

68

chests of the young men; but he knew he was making excus[e]
he had to leave as a swallow migrates through instincts as yet
undivined by Man.

And yet, although he wanted to see their cities and their
automobiles and their great houses, the white men puzzled him
because in many ways they were stupid. According to the old
Eskimos, the prospectors who had come looking for gold,
camped on the beaches, extracting it from the black sand with
rockers that looked like butter machines, had never wanted to
share what they found. And if they didn't share what they won
what pleasure was there in it?

They were also obsessed by time and ageing when all that
mattered was night and day, the long dark of winter and the
light-filled days of summer; you were born and you lived and
you died and there was nothing to fear from that so why, with
all their cleverness, were they so bothered?

Taluk, who was something of an engineer, had further evidence of their stupidity. Some Eskimos had wandered down
from the north, from Barrow, taking two years over the journey.
They had brought with them a barrel of thick black fluid and
they had explained to Taluk how it proved the curious foolishness of the white men. Taluk had listened to the explana-
tion, then he had filled a Coca-Cola bottle with the liquid; this
he had corked and carefully packed on his sled before heading
south.

At first the journey went according to plan. He reached
Nome, then struck east along the coast of Norton Sound and
then south to Unalakleet and then north east to pick up the
Yukon River which bisects Alaska, roughly following the trail
in reverse that the relays of dogs had once taken transporting
the diphtheria serum to Nome.

The huskies, their feet shod with sealskin boots, ran well
along the Yukon. At dusk each day Taluk built himself a snowhouse, treading the snow until he heard the deep noise, like a
door opening on rusty hinges, which meant that the snow was
deep enough to cut the blocks; he dug a pit then laid the blocks

around it, tilting and tapering them until the house was the shape of a cone. Inside the house he fitted the last block into the hole in the roof, cut a small doorway, brewed coffee on his Primus, ate dried fish or muk-tuk, smoked a pipe and slept on caribou furs hearing the whine of the cold outside.

The first three nights Taluk was happy. Chewing his meat and smoking his pipe, he was proud of what he had done and, lying beneath caribou skins, scorning his sleeping bag, with the dogs curled up in the deep snow outside, he slowly allowed the pride and excitement to be overcome by fatigue; and in his sleep, secure with the cold outside, dreaming that he was a small boy eating ice-cream while the elders butchered a beluga whale on the ice and stacked the meat beneath the flat of the whaling captain and the Stars and Stripes. He smelled the cooking meat and in his sleep he smacked his lips.

On the fourth night he felt uneasy. There was cruelty in the air outside and the dogs whimpered.

On the fifth night he hardly slept. He was in alien territory now and there were subtle differences abroad; the tracks in the snow were different, the texture of the snow was different, and so was the smell of the cold.

Later, when he struck south from the frozen avenue of the Yukon at Ruby, the land began to change, a few trees and shrubs, soft with snow and yet without comfort.

One night he didn't sleep at all. These weren't the changes he had anticipated: they were more frightening than cities and broad highways. He was *inland*, the messages of wind and snow and the tracks of the animal herds were foreign to him. Perils seemed to press around him, especially at dusk, arising from the past, from superstitions which the white men had taught them to laugh at without noticing the uneasiness of the laughter. He wanted to reach back to the time before the white men had come with their Bibles to consult the shamin, to ask him to clear the trail and frighten away the spirits. Taluk was ashamed because of these thoughts.

He slept briefly in the morning and he dreamed of the tundra of the north melting over granite-hard ground that never thawed; of yellow arctic poppies and mauve campion and bright red lingonberries cramped close to the ground. He had never noticed their beauty before but in his dream he did. There was a trail leading to his home, paved with bright blue stones; only when he stepped on them they were pools in the summer tundra reflecting the sky.

But later with the runners of the sleds singing and the dogs barking he thought how stupid I am, how cowardly, how superstitious. What sort of spirit is this to enter the white man's world with? And it wasn't until the afternoon that the uneasiness returned.

First the dogs quarrelled, snapping at each other, lips curled, taking no notice of his commands so that he had to dismount from the sled and strike the lead dog, a fine animal with fur the colour of a polar bear's. The dogs came to order but thereafter they were hostile; they didn't pull as strongly as before and often he had to push the sled.

Next morning one of the dogs was dead. There was no wound but the body was already frozen, its legs as stiff as tent-pegs.

Taluk continued on his way wondering if there was any curse on Eskimos who left their own, immediately banishing the thought. But during the day he heard the distant cracking of ice parting for the summer and, when he crossed a stream, he noticed that there was water above the ice.

By nightfall the cold had returned, whipped many degrees below zero, the combination of cold and wind being what the white man called the chill factor. Inside his two suits of caribou, one with the fur worn against his flesh, the other with the fur on the outside, and his parka with his hood lined with wolverine, Taluk didn't feel the cold; but he hadn't expected such weather this far south.

During the night there was a blizzard. He had to dig himself out of the snowhouse and when he did he found the snow had been thrown into a drift on one side of the sled. The dogs snarled and were reluctant to leave. Perhaps, Taluk thought, they could feel a curse as they stood in front of him, the fur standing up on their backs.

But soon the snow was wet under his feet as the wind

dropped; if the thaw came quickly he would have to abandon the sled and make his way by foot. However, Taluk comforted himself, that was no great worry because he was on a trail. Or was he? There was a clear way through the spruce trees ahead but now, under the new snow, there were no signs that anyone had been there before him.

And no one will come looking for me. I will die from exposure just as my grandfather did when he went hunting alone on the Serpentine River because meat was short in the village.

After dawn the greyness lifted and the sun rose in pink shoals of light and by midday the snow was melting fast, fingers of it plopping from the branches of spruce trees. Ahead Taluk could see the white crests of the Alaskan Range. He had studied the maps in Nome and he knew that when he saw these mountains he was three-quarters of the way along the route south. And he was so happy with this knowledge, that he failed to notice the danger that was worse than blizzards or rebellious dogs or the premature crack-up of ice.

It wasn't until he was inside his skin tent – the snow was too soft to cut into blocks – that he realized that he must have crossed a stream with water flowing above the ice and that his mukluks, his fur boots, were encased in ice. And it wasn't until he sat down in front of the Primus stove after feeding the dogs that he noticed the tear in one of the boots and felt the ice inside. He could feel the ice but he couldn't feel his foot.

Then Taluk was scared because he had seen men lose a foot this way.

He tried to take off the boot but it was stuck to his foot by the ice inside. He warmed it before the Primus stove; at first he felt nothing but, after a while, the boot came free and he poured the water from it. Then he moved away from the Primus and began to massage his foot. The pain came slowly, working its way out from the bones. He went on massaging; the ache became a throb of pain so that he felt faint and paused, thrusting his head between his knees to bring the blood back to his brain, before continuing to knead back the foot to life, coaxing the blood back to the toes.

He examined the foot which was now burning. There were

patches of white on it, the beginning of frostbite, and he massaged these again telling himself what a fool he was, how the elders of the village would have mocked him for his stupidity, how he yet had to tackle his ultimate stupidity: he had brought only one pair of mukluks.

He sat on his pile of caribou skins and began to stitch the rent in the mukluk. What sort of Eskimo am I? he thought, and seeking a culprit, blamed the white man who had dissipated so many of the old skills, so much of the instinctive knowledge, with their zeal to improve the natives.

Or was it a desire to bring the natives down to their own standards? They talked so much about progress. But is progress improvement? Taluk wondered as he opened a bottle of whisky and rubbed the spirit into his foot. Were they not perhaps jealous of the natives?

He took a swig from the bottle feeling the whisky burn his stomach. After the burn a sort of glow expanded inside him. He took another swig and, after a while, the fear was dispelled and the pain in his foot subsided once more to an ache which wasn't all that unpleasant. He ate some muk-tuk and some blueberries and drank some more whisky. When he climbed into the sleeping bag the bottle of whisky was half empty. Or was it half full? he thought, smiling and closing his eyes, opening them once more to see the roof of the tent reeling, then sleeping until the barking of the dogs awakened him and he raised himself on one elbow and vomited.

The back of his head ached as he harnessed the dogs, packed up the tent and loaded it onto the sled. He was late this morning; the sun had risen, daggers of golden light finding the peaks of the mountains where Mount McKinley reigned.

By midday the snow was melting again and Taluk could feel the water seeping in through the darned rent in his mukluk. He stopped and massaged his foot again, let the sun get to it; but he had to get on so he put on his mukluk and mustered the dogs. The markings of the dogs gave them smiling masks but they weren't smiling these dogs, not since he had struck the lead dog, not since one of them had died in the night.

That night Taluk again massaged his foot noticing that his

toes were swelling; after long exposure to cold, not necessarily sub-zero temperatures, the flesh died; he had known men with feet like this whose legs had been amputated. He climbed into his sleeping bag and finished the whisky; then the pain faded, the fear was calmed.

He was woken in the night by the barking of the dogs. He didn't bother to find out what was making them bark because of the warmth in the sleeping bag which protected him like his mother's womb. If there was a curse upon him there was nothing he could do except curl deeper in the warm and try to sleep to forget his shame.

In the morning he found that what was left of his muk-tuk and dried fish had been taken from the sled. He should have taken the food into the tent, or at least bound it so that neither the dogs nor marauding animals could get at it. A wolf must have crept up in the dark while the exhausted dogs slept; he cursed the dogs, hitting the new lead dog across the snout, until he remembered that they had barked and he had done nothing but burrow deeper into his sleeping bag.

What kind of Eskimo am I?

The swelling in his foot was worse, making it difficult to pull his mukluk on, and he walked with a limp. He mounted the sled but the dogs were so lethargic that he had to dismount and walk, occasionally push, until there was a slope when the dogs ran away with the sled chasing them, swerving away as the sled buried itself in a drift.

Now the warmth of the sun was stronger and he longed for the chilling winds of the north because this steady thaw was treacherous: in the north you knew there was tundra beneath, sedge and moss and lichen, and beneath it the permafrost that was the foundation of the earth; here there might be a ravine or a drift of snow that would take the sled and the dogs down and it would take hours to dig them out. Normally the dogs scented such dangers but now they were tired and hungry and hostile, so perverse that when he ordered them to make a left turn they went to the right. He had always known dogs, talked to them so that they responded, but the feeling between them was gone.

They were hungry and so was he. He unstrapped the Winchester hoping for caribou or moose, or perhaps a bear. A caribou was his best bet, one from the McKinley or Delta or Nelchina herds.

That afternoon the ice began to crack up around him.

At dusk, with the sun blood-red in the west, he pitched camp in a clearing in a spruce wood. He had just laid the traps to snare small animals when the dogs took off. He shouted to them but they took no notice and he went after them in a limping run.

Outlined against the skyline, now a cold mauve, he saw the silhouette of the caribou the dogs were chasing, the sled bouncing behind them. Taluk returned for his Winchester, then went after them again. The caribou was running into Taluk's line of fire.

He knelt with the butt of the Winchester rammed against his shoulder, finger light on the trigger, and he stopped breathing but listened to the beat of his heart, and told himself that this was the moment he had waited for, this was his test, this was red, bloody meat to eat.

The light was fading fast. The caribou with its great antlers sharp against the mauve of the sky was swerving away from him. Or was it a trick of the light? Without knowing why, involuntarily without reasoning, he pulled the trigger, jerking back with the recoil, knowing that he had fired too soon, before the caribou was near enough for a certain kill.

The caribou swerved again and was gone. The dogs returned.

That night Taluk heard wolves howling.

His foot was swollen like a bladder.

Taluk prepared to die.

He journeyed once more, after retrieving the empty traps, through mountainous country, pitched camp in mid-afternoon, fed the last of the rotted seal meat to the dogs and cut them loose.

He decided to go no further. He could, perhaps, have gone further, but he no longer saw any point because the spirits that had ruled his people long before the God of the Bible had been brought to them had followed him.

He pitched tent at the end of a valley at the foot of the mountains. Then he prepared a fire, a good fire because it would be the last thing he would do and he would do one good thing before he died.

He took his axe and collected wood from the trees at the end of the valley. He built a platform with the bigger branches, stripping off the bark and laying this across them. On top of this he placed the driest wood. He lit a shaving and applied it to the bark tinder, blowing gently on the glowing bark when the flame went out. When the flames returned he continued blowing so that they dried the wood above. When the heart of the fire was red with butterflies of flame leaping at the logs above he placed green wood on the top.

The dogs gathered round the fire. But they sensed that there was something wrong. It was too early to pitch camp, it was too early for a fire; the routine had been broken, so they lay, noses between their paws, staring at him while he lit his pipe and opened his last bottle of whisky.

There he would stay until the fire died away and darkness fell and the cold took him. He had no particular feeling about dying: it was merely that he believed his time had come: the signs were too strong to be ignored. He didn't think that he lacked courage for not trying to continue because courage wasn't a quality that he understood.

No, this is the way it has to end. This is the end of my span and the end of my foolishness.

He stirred the red heart of the fire and sparks spiralled in the afternoon air which already had the chill of night upon it and he tilted the bottle and drank two great gulps of whisky that dropped straight into his stomach where they soon passed into his blood stream so that he smiled at death.

He put the last of the green branches on the fire watching the thick white smoke rise into the sky.

The dogs licked their lips, wagged their tails.

He drank more whisky. The pain in his foot was gone. He took his Winchester and fired a couple of shots into the spruce trees.

Then he lay down.

The pilot of the old, one-engined Fairfield 51 equipped with skis saw the smoke. He circled the valley, then he made a low-level run through the flanks of the mountains, skimming the tops of the spruce trees as he climbed steeply.

He saw the tent and the fire and the dogs and the figure of a man lying in the snow. He calculated that he could just about land in the valley if the snow was hard enough; it was melting fast on the low ground but up here it was probably firm enough.

He put the Fairfield down at the far end of the valley and stopped twenty yards from the tent. He pushed his goggles up to his forehead, climbed out of the small aeroplane and walked over to the figure of the man.

An Eskimo.

He knelt and turned the man over. He smelled his breath and saw the empty whisky bottle. A drunk Eskimo.

He saw that the Eskimo was wearing only one mukluk; he saw the bloated flesh that was the Eskimo's foot.

He tied the dogs to a spruce, fetched them meat from the plane, kicked out the fire, picked up the Eskimo and threw him over his shoulder.

He piled the Eskimo into the Fairfield, then his gear; then he revved the engine, took off and headed south.

There were only four beds in the small ward of the military hospital near Anchorage.

Larsen was the only serviceman from Attu, therefore he had prestige. The other occupants were a young Air Force man who had broken both legs rock-climbing, a young man employed by the United States Bureau of Mines to prospect for antimony near Mount McKinley who had been charged by a cow moose with calf, and an Eskimo with an acute case of trench foot, so acute that at first the surgeons had feared they would have to amputate.

Larsen had observed the Eskimo with interest because it was the first he had seen. Once he would have imagined them squatting in an igloo, greased with blubber, rubbing noses; but Ott, the Indian, had taught him better.

At first there were screens round the Eskimo's bed and all they knew about him were the strange sounds he uttered in his fevered sleep and the smell from his foot.

Then the screens were removed and they saw him sitting up against his pillows, black hair cut in a fringe, flat nose, watchful brown eyes slitted in pouchy flesh, broad shoulders, strong, podgy-fingered hands.

He smiled a lot but hardly spoke.

When they asked him what had happened he said: 'My feet froze in water,' and smiled.

After the first couple of days they stopped asking him questions. The airman read paper-back books and Guthrie, from the Bureau of Mines, talked excitedly about the discovery of antimony in a deserted gold mine twenty miles from Mount McKinley.

But Larsen held sway. He expounded on the Battle of Attu without dwelling on the errors: it was the courage not the carnage that mattered. And he told his fellow patients what he had learned since being wounded.

'Instead of defending Chichagof the Japs attacked, would you believe. And they actually stormed Engineer Hill and fought hand-to-hand with the engineers up there before they were beaten back.'

'Jesus H. Christ,' Guthrie said.

'And even then they weren't beaten. They attacked again and when they were thrown back they killed themselves by holding grenades to their chests. Their commander, Colonel Yamasaki, was shot dead with his sword in his hand. His sword!'

'How many did they lose?'

'About two thousand. We only took twenty-eight prisoners.'

'And the Yanks?'

'About one thousand dead. But I reckon the total casualties will be nearer four thousand what with exposure, frostbite, trenchfoot ...'

Larsen remembered the sergeant saying that it wasn't Errol Flynn's sort of war and he surmised that the campaign with all its miscalculations would be unsung in the history books and that only legless men would tell the story and that no one would be greatly interested.

Now, he thought, I am in Ott's territory, Alaska from an Aleut word meaning The Great Land, so Ott had told him. And I must see what I can of it before they ship me out because they had dug the shrapnel out of his thigh and the wound was healing fast.

When the windows were open, summer breathed into the ward. As the wound healed he was allowed onto the balcony and he could see the mountains in the distance, green with streaks of snow still clinging to their peaks.

While he sat on the balcony, wanting to journey beyond the white-streaked peaks, he was joined by Guthrie, his broken ribs mending well. It was Guthrie who continued the work on Larsen that Ott the Indian had started.

He talked of the great seamed face of the Mendenhall Glacier near Juneau; of the Valley of 10,000 Smokes, a valley of salmon-coloured pumice, still smoking in places, after the eruption of Mount Katmai; of the fizzing Northern Lights and the green Matanuska Valley; of the North Slope in the Arctic where sea and sky and land were one and on blue and white mornings you could see mirages of mountain ranges.

With a map Guthrie indignantly explained to Larsen that Alaska was not the great white wilderness that people on the Outside believed it to be. 'I consider myself to be an Alaskan,' said Guthrie who was born in North Carolina, 'and Outside they talk a lot of crap about this place.'

Guthrie who had been in Alaska two years longer than Larsen was belligerently defensive about the territory. 'I suppose,' he said, pulling at his beard, 'that you think there's a hell of a lot of snow up on the North Slope.'

No, Larsen said, he didn't particularly think that.

'Well there's snow, of course. But not as much as you might think. It's pretty dry and Barrow only gets 4·3 inches of precipitation a year. But it's what lies beneath the surface that interests me,' Guthrie went on. 'Did you know that thirty-one of the thirty-three strategic minerals can be found in Alaska?'

Guthrie reminded Larsen of Ott and he wondered if Alaska affected everyone like this. He said: 'With your knowledge of this place you should have known better than to fool around with a moose cow with a calf.'

'Huh?'

'Even the experienced hunters steer clear of them.'

'Yeah? And what the hell do you know about moose?'

'Quite a bit,' Larsen said.

'And how the hell was I to know it was a female?'

Larsen grinned at him. 'Because it's only the bulls that have antlers.'

'Yeah? Well I didn't know that, smart-ass. And I wasn't fooling around with the great stupid bastard, I was just minding my own business looking for antimony when it came at me.'

'Then its calf must have been near.'

'Well I didn't know that.' Guthrie felt his ribs and winced. 'Stupid looking animals, aren't they?'

'No more stupid than us,' Larsen said.

'Okay, okay.' Guthrie followed him back into the ward. 'Maybe if we get some sick leave I could show you a bit of the country.'

Larsen sat in the wicker chair beside his bed. 'I'd like that,' he said.

The airman was lying on his bed reading *The Thin Man*; he read more than he talked and Larsen, war-scarred veteran, guessed he was homesick. The Eskimo lay on his pillows staring at the wall.

Guthrie nodded towards the Eskimo and said: 'I guess he could show both of us a thing or two, couldn't you, Pete?'

The Eskimo smiled and said nothing.

Larsen asked: 'Why Pete?'

'I call all Eskimos Pete.'

'I wonder what they call you.'

'I don't know. *Cheechako*, I guess, like all Alaskans call Outsiders.'

The next day the Eskimo spoke, not answering questions but of his own volition, as though he were coming out of a spell. He said: 'I must have a Bible.'

They looked at him. The airman put down his book and Guthrie stopped talking about minerals.

After a pause Guthrie said: 'Have a look in your bedside table, there might be one there.'

But there wasn't. The Eskimo flung aside his bedclothes and put his good foot on the floor and tried to lift the metal framework that protected his foot from the bedclothes.

Guthrie shouted at him. 'Hey, for Chrissake don't do that.' He swung his legs out of bed, one hand pressed against ribs. 'I'll get you a Bible.'

The Eskimo hesitated, then swung his good leg back onto the bed. Guthrie pressed the bell behind the bed and an orderly arrived and Guthrie told him the Eskimo wanted a Bible.

The Eskimo sat for half an hour reading the worn, black-leather Bible. It stopped Guthrie talking; the airman finished *The Thin Man* and started on Edgar Wallace; Larsen stared out of the window at the mountains which advanced and retreated according to the clarity of the air and wondered what lay beyond.

The Eskimo laid down the Bible on the white coverlet and said: 'Ah, the good word.'

They didn't know what to say and now it was they who were smiling and he was talking. And then they couldn't stop him talking.

He said: 'I doubted. Back there I doubted what the Reverend Franklin had taught us.'

Guthrie asked: 'What the ... what was that, Pete?'

'My name is Taluk.'

'Oh, sure, well, what did the Reverend Franklin teach you, Taluk?'

'That God is looking after me, that is all.'

Larsen propped himself on one elbow. He glanced at his watch but he didn't bother to calculate the time difference. Some time today his father would ride to Manhattan on the Long Island Railroad and the kids would whack a baseball around the field at the end of his road and someone would climb the water tower and here he was in Alaska with a hole in his thigh listening to an Eskimo named Taluk talking about God. 'Well of course he's looking after you, Taluk. He's looking after all of us.'

'But I doubted,' said Taluk, shame on his face.

'Why?'

'Because I thought he had deserted me.' And then he told them about the journey omitting the part about his belief that a curse had travelled with him, too ashamed to admit his fear.

When he had finished Larsen said: 'I don't think there's anything bad about doubting in circumstances like that. Maybe you were just questioning, Taluk, not doubting.'

'Thomas doubted,' Taluk said.

'Yeah, but that was different,' said Larsen.

'But although I doubted God came to my help. He sent a plane and he had me delivered to this hospital.'

The young Air Force man, Polish-American, blond and crew-cut, said: 'Why did you come south, Taluk?'

'I have asked myself that many times. It is strange but I don't know the answer except that I wanted to live as the white man lives.'

'That wasn't so smart,' Guthrie said, but Larsen frowned at him and said: 'We're two of a kind, I want to see how people live here.'

Taluk stared at him without comprehension. 'But you know, you *are* a white man.'

'But I don't live here. I live in New York.'

'New York.' Taluk pursed his lips. 'That is many, many miles away.'

'It's a helluva long way,' Larsen agreed.

'I have come a long way but not as long as that.'

'How far?' the Air Force man asked.

'Two weeks.'

'Yeah, but how far? I mean, how many miles?'

Taluk spread his hands. 'I don't know, two weeks.'

The Air Force man said: 'Jesus, I didn't know they were that primitive.' Guthrie turned to him: 'How would you like a punch in the mouth?'

'Don't get sore,' the Air Force man said. 'But, you know, you'd think anyone would know how far a place was . . .'

'Yeah? Where do you live, soldier?'

'I'm in the Air Force.'

'Yeah? Well where do you live, airman?'

'Nevada.'

'How far is that from here?'

'Nuts,' said the Pole picking up Edgar Wallace again.

Larsen said to the Eskimo: 'Where did you say you came from?'

'I come from a village near Nome.'

'I'm sorry,' Larsen said, 'but I don't know where that is.'

'That,' Guthrie said, 'is because you're ignorant. Nome,' he said, 'is on the west coast. Years ago whoever discovered the place wrote on a map NAME with a query mark after it. The query got lost and when they came to make another map they thought it was NOME.'

'That's cute,' Larsen said.

'Nome was the gold rush. They found gold on the beaches would you believe.' He turned to the Eskimo. 'That's right, isn't it, Pete?'

'They find much gold in Nome.'

'Sure they did. But not enough. Most of the prospectors died penniless. But a few made it . . .'

'Maybe you'll strike gold,' Larsen said.

'Maybe I have. Do you think I'd tell you?'

'I thought we were buddies,' Larsen said.

'Not that much buddy, old buddy.'

'There's still gold there,' Taluk said.

The airman put down his book. 'How much?' he asked.

'I don't know how much. But I find gold there.'

'Jesus, you must be some sort of millionaire,' the airman said.

The orderly brought them lunch, hamburgers and mashed potatoes and pallid beans, rice pudding and weak coffee.

While they ate Guthrie told them that, sure, there was still

83

gold in the Nome area but not enough to make it worth anyone's while to go prospecting. He waved his knife at the Eskimo. 'What did you do with your gold, Pete?'

Taluk ate his hamburger without enthusiasm. 'I left it there. Gold is bad. It brought much unhappiness to my people.'

'Could you find it again?' the airman asked.

'Maybe if I went back.'

'Was it a lot of gold?'

'No, not a lot.'

The airman lost interest, pushed aside the trolley with the empty plates on it and began to read again.

When the orderly came to take away the trays Taluk touched his arm. 'Please, can I ask you something?'

'Sure, what is it?'

'My possessions, where are they, please?'

The orderly shrugged. 'Stored away, I guess.'

'Can I have them?'

'I don't see why not. What are they?'

Taluk listed his worldly possessions. 'Two rifles, sleeping bag, caribou skins, Primus stove . . .'

The orderly put his hands on his hips. 'This is a hospital ward, buddy, not an igloo.'

Taluk appealed to Guthrie and Larsen. Larsen was kind and so, beneath his jokes, was the man with the beard. 'I don't want the guns,' he said.

'Then what do you want, Pete?' Guthrie asked.

'I want a bottle.'

They waited until tea-time. At 3 p.m. the doctor came on his rounds. He was in his middle twenties, pale-faced with a red mark on his nose where his spectacles rested. He scanned the charts hung on the ends of their beds, peered under their dressings, placed his long-fingered hands on Guthrie's chest, smiled reassuringly at the four of them and to each of them murmured: 'Fine, fine, that's coming along just fine.'

'They reckon he was a pox doctor back in San Francisco,' Guthrie observed when he had left.

The airman finished Edgar Wallace and picked up a paperback Agatha Christie with the jacket missing and a purple stamp on the title page informing the reader that it was the property of the hospital library. 'Speaking of pox . . .' he began.

Guthrie who was looking into a hand mirror trimming his beard with a pair of nail-scissors said: 'Who was?'

'I read somewhere that the Eskimos have all got the clap.'

Guthrie put down the scissors. 'You surprise me,' he said, stroking his beard. 'You surprise me a lot, old buddy. In the first place you surprise me reading these books. You know, they haven't got pictures and I can't make out what the hell you keep turning the pages for. Then you surprise me that you don't know how far Nevada is. Now you surprise me with your knowledge of the Eskimo race. Hot damn, pretty soon you've got to stop surprising me. Oh sure, I know what you're getting at. The Russians gave them syph, am I right?'

'That's what I read,' said the airman doggedly.

Taluk asked: 'What is this pox? Maybe I have it?'

Guthrie sighed, flicking needles of hair off his coverlet. 'No, Pete, you haven't got it. It was eradicated – you know, cured – a helluva long time ago.'

At 4 p.m. the orderly arrived with bread and margarine and plum jam and mugs of syrup-sweet tea and, on Taluk's tray, the Coca-Cola bottle full of thick black liquid.

Taluk smiled his beautiful smile, the toothy smile of a child, and held up the bottle aloft because in addition to liking jokes he had a touch of theatre about him. 'Oil,' he said.

Guthrie held the bottle to the light, uncorked it and smelled it, poured a little into the palm of his hand, rubbed it between his fingers. 'Black gold,' he murmured, with the awe of a man who believes that the essences of the world are beneath its crust. 'Where did you get this?' he asked the Eskimo who was still smiling from his pillows.

'It is good oil?'

'Sure looks good. Did you get it on the North Slope?'

Taluk went on smiling because the oil was proof of the curious stupidity of white men: they travelled the world in their quest for oil and yet there it was on the surface of the

85

Arctic. He told them that it had been brought to him by an Eskimo who had travelled from the North.

'A lake, huh?'

Taluk looked disappointed. 'He said lake, yes.'

Guthrie nodded. 'Probably somewhere on the Colville River or near Prudhoe Bay. There's oil there, all right. Oceans of it waiting to be tapped.'

'Then why hasn't it been tapped?' the airman asked.

'As a matter of fact I hear that the Navy's going to start drilling there. Why haven't they done so before? Search me, I'm not an oilman. But the day they make a big strike watch out for your precious birds and animals, old buddy,' he said to Larsen. 'If they start fooling with that permafrost they could turn this place into one big bomb site. Scratch the tundra, expose the permafrost to the sun and you've got yourself a lake, an ocean.'

Larsen stared through the open window at the crests of the mountains as remote as the stars. 'But there would be controls, wouldn't there? I mean the Government wouldn't allow them to ruin the countryside . . .'

'Want to bet?'

'I'm sure they wouldn't.'

Guthrie handed the bottle back to the Eskimo. He stood in front of the window, arms folded. He said to Richard Larsen: 'Get this straight, the Government doesn't give a fuck about Alaska.'

'I can't believe that.'

'Don't believe it then. But ever since the Russians sold out America has regarded Alaska as a place to plunder. You ask any full-blown Alaskan, they'll tell you. Gold, timber, canning, furs — all owned by tycoons on the Outside and some of them have never set a foot inside Alaska. And, boy, if they struck oil don't kid yourself that anyone would give a monkey's toss whether they spoil the Last Frontier or not. Where there's oil there's dough and any Texan oilman would bulldoze Central Park if he thought there was oil underneath it.'

The Eskimo was smiling again because, although he wanted to inhabit the white man's world, they often amused him. He shook the Coca-Cola bottle watching the soft, sluggish movement of the oil. 'Don't worry,' he said, 'they won't find it.'

'You've got to be kidding,' Guthrie remarked.

The Eskimo laughed. He was the centre of the conversation and this pleased him. 'My friends have seen them looking for oil,' he said. 'But they are blind.'

The airman shook his head and returned to his book.

Larsen lit a cigarette. 'They can't be that blind, Taluk. I mean your Eskimo buddy found it okay.'

Taluk shrugged eloquently. 'Maybe he knew where to look. But I tell you, the white man looks with unseeing eyes.'

Guthrie said: 'I hope you're right, Pete, but I doubt it.' He sat down in the wicker chair beside his bed and, staring out of the window, occasionally glancing at Larsen and the Eskimo, talked about what lay under the North Slope.

Eskimos, he said, had known about the oil for centuries. They had seen lakes of it, sometimes burning, and they had burned it in their lamps with wicks made from tundra moss and, when it was frozen, they had cut it into bricks and burned it. White men found it at the beginning of the last century; a man named Thomas Simpson, who worked for the Hudson's Bay Company, found deposits on the Canadian side of the Slope.

The airman said: 'So what. For Chrissake, can't you talk about broads or something?'

Guthrie ignored him.

He related how in 1914, a teacher named William Vanvalin also found oil on the Slope, two springs spouting what he described as looking like 'engine oil'. And in 1923 President Warren Harding set aside a huge parcel of land for the Navy.

'It was called Naval Petroleum Reserve Number Four,' Guthrie said. 'Better known as Pet Four.'

Larsen's thigh was beginning to hurt; he shifted his position in the bed. 'Then why haven't they exploited it?'

'Search me. Old Pete here reckons they've had a look around. I figure the main reason is that there's a glut of gasoline in the world. Now there's a war on and all that's going to change.'

'I don't understand,' Larsen said.

'Nor do I, old buddy.'

'Why didn't the oil companies stake claims at the same time the Navy got its reserve?'

'They did,' Guthrie said. 'And they took a beating. It was maybe the only time Alaska won out against outside interests. The oilmen charged up to the Slope all right, but you've got to improve land to establish a claim and they sure as hell hadn't improved a damn thing.'

He was saying: 'Who knows, maybe they would have just sat on it even if they had staked their claims,' when the doors swung open and Charles Browning came into the ward in a wheelchair, pushing the wheels with his hands.

The bullet wound had been clean, straight through and out the other side; and it was healing well enough, although when Browning asked the doctors if he would be completely fit when it had healed their faces tightened and they were enigmatic in the way of doctors who resent letting you in on the secret of what's wrong with you. The bullet had done a certain amount of damage, they said, and he would just have to wait and see.

He had written to his parents in Chicago and they had taken the news well although Browning suspected that they would have welcomed a modest medal. But in the boardroom, in the restaurants and the dark bar off Madison Avenue and at garden parties on Lake Shore Drive the news that he had been wounded in action would be well received.

But did he want to return to that life? Lying in bed behind screens, during the first fever after the wound, this had bothered him. In his dreams and periods of consciousness which jolted together like an old movie badly patched together he had kept shouting at the principal of his school at Evanston, a sardonic man with dry hair and a scaly skin, and the words were always the same: 'It's my life, it's my life' and the principal always replied: 'You are a Browning,' and smiled distantly, picking at the skin on his face.

Later when he lay quietly in bed with the sun warm on his

body he tried to work it out rationally. There was a fair chance that he would be discharged as medically unfit; this he guessed from the tight, wary faces of the doctors. And I will have to adapt to this. This is what I will always have to do: adapt. But I would be a fool to reject the Browning legacy. I will accept it and use it but I will make my own way.

Then he learned that Larsen was in the same hospital and he knew that he had to thank him although he resented being rescued by the Viking. He wasn't sure why he resented it and it puzzled him. Larsen had dodged bullets to get to him and had thrown away the grenade that would have torn his body apart and yet I resent it. Why? There was between them an instinctive hostility complicated by the difference in rank.

But I have to thank him. He is a brave man. I knew I wouldn't die and he was the instrument of my knowledge. But why did it have to be him?

And so he wheeled himself to Larsen's bedside. 'I came to thank you.' He felt self-conscious.

Larsen nodded, smiled. 'That's all right, sir,' he said and they were both aware of inadequacies of speech. You saved a man's life and he thanked you and all you could say was, 'That's all right, sir.'

'If it wasn't for you I would be dead.'

A long, embarrassing pause.

Then Guthrie came to their aid. 'Hey, what's all this, I didn't know we had a hero with us.'

Browning stared at him. 'He didn't tell you?' And when Guthrie shook his head Browning told them what Larsen had done.

'Jesus,' Guthrie said, 'when does he get his medal?'

'I shall be recommending him for one,' Browning said stiffly.

'I don't want a medal,' Larsen said.

'You don't have any say in the matter, soldier,' Browning said trying to make a joke of it.

Larsen tried another smile. 'How are you feeling, sir?'

'Okay I guess. But I think the bullet rearranged my guts a little.' And then: 'How's your leg? They tell me you got a piece of shrapnel in it.'

89

'It's healing fine,' Larsen said.

Browning remembered how he had pulled a gun on Larsen. 'Well,' he said carefully, 'when this is all over if I can be of any help to you . . .'

'Thank you, sir.'

'You know, if you're looking for a job.'

The words were patronizing; they hung in the ward. Browning turned to the airman and asked him what was wrong with him. The airman told him about the climbing accident and Browning lost interest. He questioned Taluk and commiserated with him, then turned to Guthrie who had resumed clipping his beard. 'And what happened to you?' uncertain who he was and how to treat him.

'I was run over by a moose,' Guthrie told him.

'Are you kidding?'

'The moose wasn't.'

'You're a civilian?'

'I don't have a uniform,' Guthrie said.

'But you work for Uncle Sam?'

'I guess you could say that. I go hunting – for metals to make your guns and your explosives.'

Browning was interested now. 'There must be fantastic mineral wealth here.'

'It's the treasure house of the world,' Guthrie said. 'Just like Siberia. You name it I could find it.'

Excitement stirred inside Browning; hidden antennae quivered; saliva flowed. *It's my life.* 'Gold?' he asked. 'Is there still gold here?'

'Bet your ass there's gold. But not enough for another gold rush. And in any case, what is it with gold? There's better stuff deep down in Alaska than gold. Maybe there are minerals you and I have never heard of. What line of business were you in, lieutenant, before the Army got you?'

'The Army didn't get me,' Browning said. 'I enlisted.' He refused the cigarette offered by Larsen; now he was sounding pompous. He wanted to leave but he wanted to know more about what lay beneath Alaska's crust. He told Guthrie: 'I was at college.'

'What about these jobs for the boys after the war?'

Browning didn't like him; he sensed an alliance between Guthrie and Larsen. He said: 'My father has connections. He was in the railroad business. Now he's in oil.'

Taluk spoke for the first time. 'I have oil,' he said. He held his bottle aloft; he was in command again.

Browning wheeled himself over to the Eskimo's bed and picked up the bottle. 'Where did you get this?' he asked.

And half an hour later Browning knew about the oil on the North Slope.

Guthrie was wary now, and hostile. 'Don't get any ideas, lieutenant. The Navy owns that oil. But I doubt whether it's a commercial proposition,' he lied.

'Why not?'

Guthrie lied wildly. 'It's too scattered and it's probably too deep.'

Browning picked up the Coca-Cola bottle again. 'That wasn't too deep.'

'Just a pool, lieutenant. Maybe a couple of feet deep at most. Not enough to take your Cadillac from here to Seattle.'

Browning nodded thoughtfully. Why was the man with the beard lying? He examined the oil in the bottle. Thick and soft and black. He swallowed the saliva running in his mouth. He would find out about this oil. If you were successful in business the unsuccessful always talked about your luck and this was true; but it was a question of recognizing your luck and using it. My luck is in this Coca-Cola bottle, he thought, giving the bottle back to the Eskimo.

'Well,' Browning said, 'I guess I'd better be getting back.' He wheeled himself over to Larsen. 'Thanks again. You know, I don't know what the hell to say,' knowing that Larsen was also remembering the time he had drawn the pistol. 'But if it wasn't for you I'd be dead.' He began to back away towards the swing doors. 'And don't forget what I said about helping you when the war's over. Just give me a call in Chicago or New York and you've got a job for life.'

'Thank you sir,' Larsen said.

'Well, take care.' Browning smiled at all four of them. He

pushed open the swing doors with his wheelchair and was gone.

'Jesus,' Guthrie said. 'Why did you bother to save him?'

'I haven't the faintest idea,' Larsen said, smiling.

'Oily,' Guthrie said. 'That's what he is – oily.'

Within three weeks they had all been discharged.

Taluk was given the address of a native welfare association in Anchorage; he was driven into town by jeep and deposited on the dusty sidewalk with his belongings.

The airman was given a week's sick leave and headed for the library.

Browning was given a couple of weeks' leave and told to report for a medical at the end of it. He took the railroad to Fairbanks, Alaska's second largest city in the heartland, where there were men who knew about the hidden wealth to the north.

Larsen was given a week's leave and, with Guthrie, headed for Mount McKinley.

CHAPTER SEVEN

THE brown bear, *ursus arctos*, was old and irritable. He was seven foot tall when standing, he weighed eleven hundred pounds; his claws were straight, the colour of ivory, but becoming discoloured; his fur was dark brown touched with blond patches although he had shed much of it since the spring, perhaps in preparation for the thick new growth in the fall, perhaps in preparation for death. He had been born a hairless cub, and this is what he had become after eighteen years of good feeding, rutting, and sleeping.

Until now he had always followed the trails, ambling or shuffling or galloping at a great speed. But now the speed was gone and, since the fight with the young bear two weeks earlier, he had felt tired. He had left the trails and settled beside the log cabin on the foothills of Mount McKinley.

The fight had been brief but it had exhausted him. The young bear had moved onto the old bear's feeding grounds where the berries were bright and sweet, the grass and sedge were sappy with juice and the roots which he dug out with his claws were soft and moist.

He had warned the young bear but it had taken no notice. The anger of the old bear who had killed moose and men in his time was wild and terrible, the anger of a bear in its prime in the frame of an ageing bear with bad teeth.

When the young bear ignored him he knew he had to fight because this was the way it had always been: the young had to respect their elders, they could not poach. The young bear knew all this and the young bear had to die. Once upon a time a cuff round the head might have been enough; no longer – the young bear would turn and fight and the old bear was too weak for prolonged battle.

The old bear approached diffidently, scenting the young bear rather than seeing him with his short-sighted eyes; then seeing him clearly, berry juice running from his jaws, the anger expanded inside him and he lunged with one paw and the young bear fell and the old bear lunged again and the fight was over.

Then he tore the stomach and intestines from the young bear and hauled the carcass half a mile to the gravel beach of a river where he had always buried his kills. Digging with his claws, he felt a burning pain in his limbs, a tightness in his great chest. He pushed the carcass into its grave, shovelled the gravel on top of it.

He rested for a while, curled up with his head resting on his paws, then he left the burial ground and the feeding ground and the trails and made his way up the green slope where yellow Arctic poppies grew, past a copse of moose-chewed willow, to the log cabin in a clearing in a belt of spruce.

Carefully he smelled the cabin. Men had lived here but they hadn't been there for a long time. He had no great fear of men, he had no great fear of any living creature. The sun was hot and the bark-stripped logs of the walls were warm. He lay down beside one of the walls and slept, this time on his back with his feet in the air.

During the next week he left the clearing in the spruce several times to feed on berries and grass, but he always returned to the cabin where the sun was warm by day and he was sheltered from the winds that sometimes sprang up in the twilight of the night.

Then on the seventh day when he was returning he stopped at the edge of the clearing in the dark shade of the spruce. There were fresh, harsh scents on the air, the smell of man, unmistakeable because there was no purity about it.

He stayed hidden by the spruce until the light weakened a little just before midnight. Then he approached, the anger once again swelling inside him, anger at the intrusion of men into the peace he had found beside the sun-warmed logs.

There were slits of light between the logs and smoke rising from the chimney, but he only saw all this as a vague silhouette, relying as always on his sense of smell which was still keen. He smelled the wood-smoke and he smelled food and, as he got nearer, the smell of man was strong in his nostrils.

They had no right to this cabin just as the young bear had no right to poach on his feeding ground.

The old bear stopped outside the cabin and waited.

Inside the log cabin Richard Larsen was telling Guthrie about bears.

'You know, bears are pretty harmless. It's just that they're so goddam big that people are scared of them just as they're scared of Alsatian dogs and say they're savage. They don't say some bitty little mongrel snapping at their heels is savage because they can tread on it like a centipede.'

Guthrie handed him a mug of Russian tea which is made with tea and lemonade and any other available liquid and whisky. He swallowed; the first swallow tasted terrible but the second wasn't bad at all.

'In fact,' lectured Larsen as Guthrie barbecued steaks on the blazing, resin-smelling fire, 'bears are more scared of us than we are of them. I mean they're so short-sighted they can hardly see us. Once they smell us they take to the hills.'

'Yeah?' Guthrie turned the steaks and the fat hissed in the heart of the fire where he had pushed aside the logs that were fizzing with sap. 'Well, I wouldn't like to meet bruin on a dark night. That's why I wear this.' He shook the bell that he wore round his neck. 'They say it scares them off and I like to think they're right. But if not—' he pointed at the Winchester leaning in the corner of the cabin '—then I'd let them have it.'

'You disappoint me,' Larsen said.

'But I'm alive to disappoint you.'

'Maybe the bear's got more right to be here than you.'

'Maybe you don't want to eat this steak,' Guthrie said. 'It was once alive.'

'That's different,' Larsen said.

'Oh sure.'

'It's different because it's killed humanely and we've got to eat.'

'Nothing to say you shouldn't be a vegetarian.'

'You don't understand. I'm against the senseless killing of animals – killing them for sport and pretending that you're doing the world a service by controlling pests.'

'Okay, okay,' Guthrie said. 'Maybe I even agree with you. But don't become some sort of nut about it.'

Guthrie tested one of the steaks with the point of a knife. It was tender with a little blood in the pink meat. He laid the steak on two wooden plates and ladled string beans and boiled potatoes from the saucepans bubbling on the portable gas cooker.

After they had eaten Guthrie brewed coffee and they drank it, occasionally belching contentedly, their feet stretched out in front of the fire. It was past midnight and yet it was light outside and the knowledge gave them an odd satisfaction, a Sunday afternoon satisfaction instead of the log-cabin snugness when a wind is driving the snow against the door in the darkness of the night.

After a while Larsen, whose thigh ached, said he would take a stroll. Guthrie allowed himself a last, weak belch; he stretched and yawned and said he was turning in and that if Larsen was going to go wandering about in the twilight then he'd better take the Winchester and when Larsen shook his head he said: 'Well, at least take my bell,' and handed him the bell, a small, alpine cow-bell. 'Anyway,' he said, 'I should have thought you'd had enough walking. It's been quite a day, huh?'

Larsen massaged his thigh; there was still a dressing on it stuck down with plaster but there was no longer any blood seeping through the gauze. He pushed a log with his foot and watched the sparks spiral up the chimney. He decided to stay another five minutes.

Outside the cabin the stomach of the old bear who had smelled the food rumbled loudly. Berries and roots and grass no longer seemed to satisfy him: he should be taking more substantial food to build up fat for the winter. His hunger made him more angry; he moved round the cabin a couple of times sniffing at the slits in the timber; then he lay down, nose between his paws, and continued to wait with the patience that endures like the snows of winter

They had landed the previous day in a single-engined Cessna on a mountain airstrip. It was dawn – sometime after 2 a.m. – and McKinley, the highest mountain in North America, was there waiting for them, a scarf of cloud round its peak.

They had brought packed meals and, after leaving their gear in the cabin which Guthrie and two other Bureau men had built last year, headed up the slope of the hill facing The Mountain across a plain of spruce and streams fed by glaciers, until they were above the timberline where the slope was clean and bare and the trees were only shoulder high and the pressure of their boots on the dried sponge of the tundra released the scent of herbs.

Larsen was excited because this was the Alaska for which he had been prepared by Ott. Here he was in the folds of the Alaskan Range, the great knuckles of granite that separate the south from the interior. And he was here in that brief time, between melting and freezing, when the land had to refurbish itself, when flowers had to bud and blossom and die and birds and animals had to mate, give birth and kill with breathless speed.

This was the time of survival, Larsen thought, as they breathed the cold, filtered air from the north, warming up now in the sunlight that had dispersed the cloud from The Mountain; not the long, boxed-in winter of sleep; no, this is the time of struggle when the roots of yellow bush buttercups and the pink pin-cushions of campion have to search for life in the thawed soil above the permafrost. When the eagle has to find its prey. This is the time of survival and this is the time of death.

It frightened him a little.

They were on higher ground now with patches of crusty

snow in the hollows. They stopped on a plateau where already the petals of pink rhododendrons, cramped close to the ground, were dying. They drank coffee laced with brandy and ate hunks of brown bread and cream cheese.

With a pair of field-glasses Larsen scanned the mat of vegetation. A couple of hundred yards away a stone moved. Larsen frowned, adjusted the focus, saw a small animal chewing at the stone. He handed the field glasses to Guthrie. 'What do you make of that?'

'An animal eating a stone,' Guthrie said. 'He must be desperate.'

'He's getting the salts out of it,' Larsen told him.

He glanced up and saw a black and white jaeger swooping, long tail as straight as a javelin. Larsen stood up, shouted and waved his arms. The bird faltered in its dive, levelled out and flew away up the valley.

'So you saved a small critter,' Guthrie observed. 'Your good deed for the day.'

Larsen didn't reply. He sat down and drank some coffee. He felt a little foolish.

Guthrie cleared up the utensils and packed them into the haversack he carried on his back. 'You also deprived a bird and its family of a square meal. In my book you shouldn't interfere.'

'I guess you're right,' Larsen said.

'Damn right I'm right.'

They saw a few moose and a couple of wolves from one of the packs that roam the area around McKinley, then they headed back towards the cabin. They were both silent, Guthrie alone with his thoughts which he rarely divulged, Larsen, overwhelmed at what he had seen, his wonder balanced on a razor of fear sharpened by the scent of death that hovered in the mountains, the patterns of survival and extermination which humans had imitated and improved upon so that, as the evening air chilled, although the sky was still cobalt bright, it seemed to him that there was no hope for anything.

But when the fire was lit inside the cabin, and the Russian tea was warm in his belly, and the steaks were spitting on the fire, and there was a togetherness with this man Guthrie with the smile in his beard, the mood passed and there was hope for everyone.

Larsen stirred lazily in this sort of Sunday-afternoon sloth; it reminded him of the times after lunch, before supper, with church music on the radio, his father asleep and his mother embroidering a tablecloth with yellow silk marigolds and blue cornflowers; he saw it all from a distance, when he had been a boy.

He had written and told them about his wound, making light of it, but he hadn't gone into details because he didn't want to disturb their lives because if nothing else, they at least had the right to remain undisturbed in their cocoon hanging from the Long Island Railroad.

He stood up, stretched, walked round the cabin. He touched the objects in the cabin, the moose antlers in one corner, the hurricane lamps, the pieces of rough-hewn furniture; he avoided the gun leaning in one corner and felt the log walls with their beads of viscous sap that might one day become amber.

Then he heard the singing.

Guthrie who was cleaning his boots looked up. 'What the hell's that?'

Larsen was silent for a moment, listening. Then he said: 'The call of the wild.'

'Coyotes?'

'No, wolves.' Larsen stayed very still and tried to visualize the pack as they followed the leader who had started to howl, as they stood with their heads tilted to the sky and cried and listened to their voices chasing one another through the folds in the mountains, perhaps warning another pack to keep clear, perhaps hollering for the hell of it. He thought of Ott, what he had told him about wolves. 'Beautiful, isn't it?'

'Everyone to his own taste.'

'I'm going for a stroll.'

'Well, watch yourself, old buddy, and don't try and make friends with the wolves.'

Larsen opened the door. He would just take a short stroll because he had to walk in this lambent light beneath the green-ish sky at one in the morning. Guthrie walked with him to the door. They could smell the woodsmoke from their own fire. Abruptly the wolves stopped howling. It was very quiet.

Larsen walked into the centre of the clearing just as the old bear came from behind the cabin. Guthrie shouted a warning and Larsen turned, stared at the great animal moving towards him with the rolling gait of a sailor.

'Don't move,' Guthrie shouted.

Larsen stayed perfectly still. Don't startle it. Let it get used to you. It can hardly see you, only smell you. Oh Christ! Rich-ard Larsen shouted within himself. He knew that the injuries from one swipe of a bear's paw were as bloodily terrible as a shark-bite. But bears don't want to savage humans, they don't gobble up babies . . .

He stayed still, hardly breathing, hearing the thump of his heart. The bear continued to come towards him and he could see its rotten teeth and the shabbiness of its fur. Then he re-membered reading that you could talk to bears in a gentle but authoritative way.

He started to talk nursery nonsense. His voice broke and he tried again. The bear stopped and peered at him. Its ears were flattened and it was growling softly. Larsen continued to talk until the bear cocked its ears and stopped. 'I'm a friend,' said Larsen, then saw Guthrie loading the rifle and kneeling down at the doorway, and shouted: 'Don't shoot.'

But the shout frightened the old bear who may have been merely puzzled by the man who talked and didn't move and would have attacked anyway, or may have been thrown out of his stride by the enigma and may have wandered away into the spruce.

But it was the shout that did it. The ears of the bear flattened again and as he came forward he raised one paw.

The bear was eight feet from Larsen when Guthrie squeezed the trigger and the shell hit the bear just below the ear and flung him onto his back. Guthrie ran across the clearing, stood behind the bear and shot it again in the head.

The eighteen years of the bear ended then. Without dignity. Larsen turned on Guthrie. 'You didn't have to do that.'

'Are you crazy?'

'I could have handled him.'

'Like crazy you could.'

'He had stopped. He wasn't going to attack.'

'So, what were you going to do, stand staring at each other for the rest of the night?'

'I could have handled it,' Larsen said stubbornly.

'Well, don't thank me for saving your goddam life.'

'Thanks,' said Larsen.

They left the old bear there and they went back to the cabin and closed the door and climbed into their sleeping bags while the light strengthened over the wild pastures around The Mountain.

Larsen lay awake for a while; he wondered how much longer the bear would have lived if they, the intruders, hadn't camped in the clearing in the spruce.

He found that his eyes were moist so that, when he closed them, they stang.

Later in the morning they told a ranger about the bear. Then they walked to the airstrip where they were picked up by a blue Fairfield.

When they landed at Anchorage's Merrill field they had hardly spoken to one another. They booked into a wooden hotel just off Fourth Avenue and that night Larsen got drunk.

CHAPTER EIGHT

CHARLES BROWNING went straight to Fairbanks on business. He had seen sepia photographs of the town in the old pioneering days with bearded men in punished hats standing outside shacks staring shyly at the camera; apart from the beards, it didn't look much different now, he thought. True there were concrete buildings and establishments like the four-storey Empress Theatre but the wooden shacks, where steam was forced through the rafters in the fall to make a roof of ice, were still there. And the dust of summer.

He booked into the Nordale Hotel and later, very sharp in his olive, tailored uniform, pale-faced after his convalescence, walked the streets beside the Chena River where old Model A Fords and a few sleek sedans and jeeps whipped up the dust and blared at drunken Indians and servicemen.

Joe E. Brown had once stared down Anchorage's Fourth Avenue and remarked: 'My what a large liquor store.' Fairbanks was also a large liquor store – bars, clubs, beers and liquor stores and a few general stores.

The biggest change was in the inhabitants – servicemen based at Fairbanks and the Army engineers who had laid the Alaska Highway fifteen hundred miles through forest, tundra and muskeg, linking for the first time the United States with Alaska via Canada.

Browning decided that the Alaskan Highway, the Alcan, might be very useful to him one day. But he had little interest in the town itself choking in the heat. He thought it was cheap and scruffy, a place to lay foundations and control their growth from an office in a sturdy high-rise in Chicago.

But to know how to lay those foundations Browning had to find the man who had done it before him. His name was Ben Harper and he was said to be the richest man in Alaska.

Ben Harper was seventy-seven and he *was* very rich and he looked miserable, as though his whole money-making experience had been a painful necessity. His face was seamed with dollar signs and his clothes were cheap, the seat of his trousers sagging with the bagginess typical of old men whose shanks have withered, old men who haven't the interest to buy a new pair of pants. Ben Harper looked as if the moths had been at him. Unless you took in his hair and his shoes.

His hair was white, a great cloud of it, and it wasn't the smoke-cured whiteness of some old men; it was a pristine, bleached, shining whiteness and it looked as if it had been brushed all night. When he bowed his head you expected the shine of his hair to be reflected in his black shoes which had been polished until he walked on black mirrors.

Ben Harper had made his dough indirectly through gold. He had provided prospectors with transport and provisions, with sleds and dogs, lamps and spades and caribou-skin tents, candles and loans to anyone with nuggets in his pocket. Then he warmed Fairbanks by mining coal; educated them by publishing a newspaper and opening up a radio station; then he took care of their money by opening a bank; now he owned a cinema where he showed patriotic movies.

Browning nailed him in his office.

The office surprised Browning who judged people by their trappings. In his books the trappings of those-who-had-made it included wall-to-wall carpets, mahogany desks with gold leaf on leather-covered surfaces, dictaphonees, an obedient secretary and an iced-water fountain with cardboard cups.

One of the legs of Ben Harper's desk was supported by an old Baedecker. Where the ice water should have been there were piles of old newspapers which had been gnawed by mice.

Ben Harper was reading the proof of the front page of his newspaper. The proof was wet and Browning could smell the ink.

Ben Harper handed Browning the paper. 'It ain't the *New York Times*,' he said, 'but the folks here like it.'

Browning glanced at the page and handed it back. 'Do you write it?'

Ben Harper lit a White Owl cigar. 'What makes you think I can write?'

'Can't you?'

'As a matter of fact I can. But most of you youngsters reckon us old sourdoughs can't read or write.'

Browning grinned; his grin had been described as boyish and he used it. 'I reckon most of you old sourdoughs are pretty belligerent.'

'You're right, son. We have to be or the folk from Outside would run us into the ground. I guess you could call us defensive. We ain't got much but what we got we're proud of.' The smoke from his cigar made patterns in the dusty light.

'I think you've got a hell of a lot,' Browning said.

The old man looked at him suspiciously. 'Yeah? Such as what?'

Browning gestured towards the grimy window. 'Everything. The sky, the mountains, beauty . . .'

Ben Harper prodded the wet end of his cigar at Browning. 'Don't come that old fancy talk with me, son, I'm a pretty good judge of character and I know that sort of talk doesn't come natural to you. I know that and I know it because I reckon you're a pretty cute sort of young fella. Beauty? I say horseshit. There's beauty all right but it ain't just pretty mountains and forget-me-nots and salmon leaping waterfalls. No, sir, that kind of beauty is skin-deep. That's *cheechako* talk.'

Browning's smile was fixed. '*Cheechako?*'

'Yeah. Greenhorn. You know, the sort of talk from Outside people who think we're all hill-billies and panhandlers and when we're starving we eat our boots and we've all got icicles hanging from our balls.'

This time Browning's laugh was genuine. 'I reckon yours thawed a few years back.'

Ben Harper didn't smile.

'Now perhaps you'll tell me why you came to see me.'

'I was told you owned Fairbanks.'

'A fair chunk of it. But youngsters don't seek the company of old men just for the hell of it. Bob out there' – he nodded towards the door – 'said you wanted to say you had shook the hand of Ben Harper. Now, what sort of horseshit is that?'

'Sure I wanted to shake your hand. I hoped some of the gold-dust would rub off.'

'Coal-dust,' Ben Harper said. 'What do you want, son? I'm a busy man.'

'Okay, I'll tell you. I want to know how you made your money and I want to know how I can do the same.'

Ben Harper eyed him. The whites of his eyes beneath the frosty eyebrows were yellowing and there was a cataract in one of the pupils. He said: 'You look kind of rich to me.'

'How can you tell that?'

'I can tell,' Ben Harper told him. 'Like I said, I can tell people and I figure that's one of the things *you* have got to learn first. I figure you take people at face value and that's a mistake, son, because that way you'll get screwed. First of all you've got to judge a man right and then you've got to assess his ambition. And don't misunderstand ambition neither. Ambition ain't just lusting after a lot of loot. No, sir, ambition can be just wanting to spend your days in the forest with the stars as your ceiling. Ambition can be a full bottle of whisky.'

'I don't know about the bottle of whisky,' Browning said.

'There you go. You accept too much of what you've been taught, boy. That's the second lesson. Black ain't black and white ain't white – there's many shades. You've read someplace that a man drinks to forget. That he's lonely, that he's bitter. Has it ever occurred to you that a man drinks because he likes it? That his *ambition* is to prop up a bar and chew the fat and drink. Maybe he'll die from it but that's his choice and maybe he'd rather die from that than overwork.' Ben Harper squashed the wet cigar butt. He stood up, very straight. 'Now, tell me why you've really come to see me, son. I'll show you the print-works and you can tell me then because this office sure ain't the place for an interrogation.'

The print-works was beneath the office, down a wooden

staircase that moved when you trod on it. 'Want coffee?' Harper fetched two tin mugs, the insides stained the colour of old teeth, poured in the coffee and topped it up with condensed milk. He drank, smacking his lips. 'Well?' he said.

'I told you why I wanted to see you.'

'I figure you want me to tell you how to rob Alaska.'

'I wouldn't have put it quite like that.'

'Exploit then. What's your angle, son, gold?' He considered this, then shook his head. 'No, you're too slick to be after the yellow stuff. What are you after, boy?'

'Anything I can lay my hands on.'

Ben Harper poured himself more coffee. 'Want to see the paper go to bed?'

Browning watched as the old flat-bed began to thump up and down.

'Alaska wants business,' Ben Harper said. 'But it wants business put into the place, it wants investment and it doesn't want any more Outsiders creaming the profits.'

'It's part of the States, isn't it?'

'It's a territory,' the old man said, sucking at his coffee. 'Down south they reckon it's a place to be sucked dry of its riches.' He paused. 'What line of business are you in? Or what line of business is your old man in?'

Browning said quickly: 'Railroads.'

'Railroads, huh? I heard different.'

Browning looked at him in astonishment. 'What did you hear?'

'I heard your old man was in oil.'

'Okay, so he's in oil, but who in God's name told you?'

'Lesson number three,' the old man said, 'Know your adversary before you meet him.'

'But I only arrived a couple of hours ago.'

'Sure, but you came up by train. And young Charlie Gaynor was on that train.'

Browning remembered talking to a man who hadn't seemed all that young to him. 'Son of a gun,' he said.

'You've got a big mouth,' the old man said. 'Lesson number four, keep it shut.'

'You don't have to—'

'If you want to learn, son, you've got to take a few knocks. I'm short-circuiting them for you.' He put down his mug. 'Now let's take some air.'

It was hot outside. Browning's shirt was damp with sweat. He wished he hadn't decided to impress the old bastard with his uniform. He put on Air Force-issue shades to keep out the flying dust.

Ben Harper said: 'So you want me to tell you how to get the oil out of *them thar hills*?'

'I guess that's about it. After all, you got the coal out.'

'Yeah. And it keeps Alaskans warm, it doesn't fuel the central heating of the Empire State Building.'

'Oil would keep your automobiles going.'

'Looks like they're going pretty good now,' remarked Ben Harper as an open jeep filled with soldiers overtook a Model A, two wheels mounting the sidewalk.

'You'd get your gas cheap.'

Ben Harper stopped outside his picture house where Danny Kaye in *Up in Arms* was showing. 'Are you kidding?' he asked.

'Don't you want cheap oil?'

'Does your old man want to sell it cheap?'

'I guess not. But I—'

'Horseshit,' said Ben Harper. He took out a key and opened up the cinema. 'Sometimes,' he explained, 'I like a private showing.'

They went into the auditorium with its rows of red-plush, cigarette-scarred seats and heavy maroon curtains pulled across the screen. It smelled of celluloid and disinfectant.

Ben Harper shouted up the stairs to the projection room. 'You up there, Charlie?'

Charlie said he was.

'Start it rolling in five minutes.'

They sat half-way down the stalls.

The old man took out a White Owl and lit it. 'So, what makes you think there's oil here?'

'Everyone knows it.'

'Not everyone, son. Don't generalize, it can lead you into trouble.'

'Lesson Five,' Browning said. 'Well, a hell of a lot of people know.'

'Yeah, and most of them are keeping their mouths shut about it.'

'The Navy's up there.'

'Yeah, and they're going to start drilling soon. But I'll wager you a silver dollar that they don't find nothing.'

'But if it's there—'

'Ain't got nothing to do with it,' Ben Harper said, enjoying himself.

'I don't understand,' said Browning. But he was beginning to; he remembered the talk in the dark bar off Madison.

'You will. Maybe you already do because you're slick.'

'Okay,' Browning said, 'I'll play. Why won't they find the oil that we agree is up there?'

'Because,' Ben Harper said, 'your old man don't want it found.'

'What the hell's that supposed to mean?'

'Put it this way,' Ben Harper said. 'The oil companies have learned their lesson – they caught a cold with that big strike in East Texas in the 30s and they sure as hell don't want to catch another one. If America was flooded with oil from Alaska the whole price structure would collapse. There would be a glut and it would be a buyers' market.'

'But the Navy doesn't give a damn about that.'

'Maybe not. But do you know who's going to do the exploring for the Navy?'

Browning shook his head.

'There ain't no prizes for the answer – the oilmen. Who else? They're in uniform now but they know which side their bread's buttered. They'll be thinking ahead, son, and they won't be finding any oil even if they're standing up to their necks in it. They've got enough in California and Texas and Louisiana and the Middle East without wanting any more. They want us to have cheap gas like you want leprosy.'

Browning was silent for a moment. Then he asked Ben

Harper if he would be prepared to help 'if I decided to go looking for oil.'

'No, son, I wouldn't. You see I might be filthy rich but I kind of like it here. If you strike oil Alaska will be scarred for life. The oilmen will rip it apart. You might say Alaska's a virgin: stick a pipeline through it and it ain't a virgin no more.'

'Does there have to be a pipeline?' Browning asked.

'Sure there does. They've got to move the stuff to the States somehow and they'd have to get it to an ice-free port and there ain't any of those up north.'

The lights dimmed, a shaft of light shone from the projection room.

'In fact,' the old man said, 'it's not just a question of not helping you: I'd fight you.'

'You'd lose,' said Browning abruptly.

'You ain't the first to say that.'

'You'd lose,' Browning said again.

The curtains parted noisily. No hushed expectancy, no usherettes. The credits came up on the screen.

'Well,' Browning said, 'I'll be leaving you.' He paused. 'But you have been helpful to me, Mr. Harper. Oh yes, you've been very helpful.'

The old man shrugged. He was lost in the movie now and, as he walked up the aisle, Browning heard a strange sound. Like water gurgling in a rusty pipe. Ben Harper was laughing.

Browning took the railroad back to Anchorage and travelled in a De Soto automobile, the scooter on which the railroad general manager, Colonel Otto Ohlson, rode his five hundred miles of single track. The wheels of the black automobile were adapted to fit the tracks; it had an air brake for a footbrake and there was no steering wheel.

Ohlson was a neat man of seventy with a clipped moustache; he wore a fedora and carried a rifle in the back seat of the car.

They were travelling at seventy miles per hour when Ohlson told Browning: 'Once the wheels came off and the scooter took to the fields.'

Browning asked why the railroad which started at Seward went no farther than Fairbanks.

Ohlson pointed at a porcupine staring from the brush, at a couple of ptarmigan in their summer feathers that rose slowly from the track in front of them, at the fields of red, spiky fireweed. 'That's why,' he said.

'I don't get you.'

'We don't want to disturb any more of the land. Fairbanks is far enough. Beyond that there's nothing – a vast, beautiful, nothing – and that's the way we aim to keep it. We don't need a Santa Fe.'

Browning shrugged. One of these days, he thought, I'll have a fight on my hands with these people. Suddenly he remembered the dead face of the man named Bob at the bottom of the swimming pool.

A couple of Indians squatting beside the track waved and Ohlson waved back. 'It's their country as well,' he said.

'Maybe they'd like more railroad. Maybe it would give them work.'

An old Stinson passed overhead. Ohlson said: 'That's the way Alaskans travel – by the seat of their pants. They don't need railroads.'

Browning said nothing. He was thinking that one day he would bring progress to The Great Land. And he saw the banners of flame above the oil wells in the north and high-rise among the clapboard houses of the towns and he heard the sound of oil flowing through great pipes.

They stopped at a junction while a freight-train came past loaded with merchandise from Anchorage; probably with supplies from Stateside which, because of the transportation costs, sold at prices which made the territory the most expensive in America. (Everything, they said, cost a dollar – unless it cost more.) Yes, Browning thought, there was money in freight. And railroads. And pipelines.

He failed to notice McKinley, its peak hidden by cloud in the distance. When the De Soto arrived at Anchorage he thanked Ohlson for the ride, refused a dinner invitation, called at a bookshop and bought a book on the mineral wealth of

Alaska. As an afterthought he bought a yellow booklet about the Gold Rush and took them both back to his hotel to study.

Ten days later Browning went for his medical.

The doctors were understanding. They realized that he wanted to go on fighting for his country but he just wasn't fit enough and he would have to be discharged.

'Nothing to worry about,' they said, toying with the stethoscopes round their necks. And a major with a fierce face and a woman's hands said: 'You'll find you'll get stronger but not strong enough for Uncle Sam. Not for a couple of years anyway. But there's nothing to say you won't live to be a hundred.'

Browning wasn't surprised; nor was he disappointed. You must adapt just as you must know how to handle luck when it's presented to you on a salver – or in a Coke bottle.

He packed and was flown back to a base in New York State for the formalities of discharge. Then he flew to Chicago. He had learned a lot, he was grateful to the Army. He was a modest hero at the dinners in the Browning mansion and it was several months before he remembered that he hadn't recommended Richard Larsen for a medal.

CHAPTER NINE

RICHARD LARSEN wanted a girl.

The need came to him stiffly in the early morning as he lay in bed in the Forces hostel in Anchorage. He took a shower and went down to the cafeteria where he ate ham and eggs and drank a lot of coffee and thought about girls with warm bellies and strong thighs.

He tried to think about Alaska, but everything was vanquished by these big healthy girls. He drank more coffee. It was ridiculous that a battle-scarred veteran was still a virgin. Ridiculous and humiliating, so he confessed his virginity to no one and when the conversation got around to girls he smiled leerily and hoped his companions inferred a series of casual conquests on the degenerate shores of Long Island.

He walked out into the hot, dust-choked town. There were lots of girls about but they were outnumbered ten to one by men so they were haughty, able to choose.

A tall, blonde girl with long legs walked along the sidewalk and a GI in uniform winked and said: 'Hubba, hubba' and, without turning her head, the girl said: 'Get lost, soldier' and swept on and Larsen imagined he could hear the swish of one silk-stockinged thigh against the other.

He stopped at a drugstore where he drank more coffee in the company of old sourdoughs who asked him where he came from and told him their names – Moose Charlie, Esky Bill who had once had a taste for Eskimo girls, and two-fisted Harry who had taken on all-comers at the Olympia Theatre in Nome in 1900.

They told him about the Gold Rush. About the gold on the beaches of Nome, about the safe stolen from Wintermantle Store with twelve hundred dollars in it, about Hoagy Car-michael on piano and his father on violin in the Northern Saloon in 1906, about the Wild Goose Railroad with its open wagons, about the gold strike in Anvil Creek in 1898, about the Great Fire at Fairbanks in 1906 and the Great Storm in Nome when cabins and tents were swept away.

They asked for the price of a cup of coffee and, while Richard Larsen thought about girls, told him about great dog-sled racers such as a Cheechako Scot named Charles Fox Maule Ramsay who at the first stop on a race had asked for a bath and some toast and marmalade. They told him about suicides, prizefighters, and wild girls and it was then that Larsen paid for his coffee and left.

He turned into Fourth Avenue. In the background the aloof Chugach Mountains emphasized the tawdriness of the main street where Pabst, Budweiser, Schlitz and Olympia reigned between the Western Auto Supply, Sears-Roebuck, the Northern Commercial Company, the Bank of Alaska and Hewitt's soda fountain. Behind this Larsen glimpsed the broad flat waters of Cook Inlet where Captain Cook had sought the North West Passage.

He went into a bar and ordered a Rainier beer. The walls of the bar were decorated with Varga girls from *Esquire*, varnished and stuck on wooden plaques; the girls had lovely tilted breasts and superb legs and pubic hairs added by the bar's patrons. The bar smelled of disinfectant and it was infested with mosquitoes which didn't seem to bother the barman who stood in the gloom staring into the street as if waiting for a ship.

Larsen drank his beer slowly. He was beginning to feel depressed but the lust still raged within him. He had fifty dollars in his money-belt; it was easy to get a girl in Anchorage if you had money but he was determined not to pay. Perish the thought, Larsen said to himself, gazing at the black-pencilled crotch of a Varga girl.

Half-way through the beer he made a decision. He didn't know whether it showed weakness or strength. He decided to forgive Guthrie for shooting the bear. He went to the telephone at the end of the bar and called him at the Anchorage Hotel.

When Guthrie came to the phone Larsen said: 'What about some lunch?' and when Guthrie said: 'Sure, why not,' he experienced a warmth of pleasure not unconnected with the notion that Guthrie might be proficient at finding girls.

They went to a restaurant overlooking the Cook Inlet with a view of a mountain known as the Sleeping Lady and, while they watched the ravens floating in the currents over the water, they ate King Crab claws, hot rolls with firweed honey and mounds of green ice-cream.

It cost Larsen a lot of money, but everything cost a lot of money in Alaska. A bottle of beer could cost forty cents, a shoeshine was twenty-five cents.

'So how are you making out?' Guthrie asked. There were tiny wrinkles at the corner of Guthrie's eyes and lines from nose to mouth so that he always looked amused.

'Fine,' Larsen said. 'Just fine.'

'Doing anything tonight?'

'Nothing in particular.'

'Feel like taking the town by storm?'

'Sure, why not.'

'Maybe we could find a couple of broads.'

'Sure, why not,' Larsen said with terrible nonchalance.

That afternoon they went to a movie house that charged Broadway prices and sat through a double-feature, Roy Rogers in a Western, and a film starring a young singer named Frank Sinatra who was making the girls swoon in the aisles in the States but not here in Alaska.

Afterwards they bought a newspaper with headlines about an inquiry by Governor Gruening into allegations that booze was being shipped into Alaska from Seattle in preference to food and machinery.

'That's a bit of luck,' Guthrie said.

The bars were beginning to fill up as servicemen came into town, freshly-shaven and barbered, uniforms and civilian clothes pressed with soap behind the creases to keep them sharp. The doors of the bars opened and swallowed them. An hour or so later the girls arrived in their splendour with filmstar hair styles and liquid-cosmetic stockings which streaked when they spilled liquor on them and cupid lips and ankle-straps and red shiny claws.

'Boy oh boy,' Guthrie said, wiping foam from his beard. 'You guys' – prodding Larsen in the chest – 'think you've got it made because you're GIs. Me, I've got it made, too. Because,' he said, 'I've got the dough.'

Larsen was thinking that he had never seen a girl totally naked. He was wondering if he would have the nerve to ask a girl to go to bed with him. And he was wondering if it would be all right when he got a girl into bed and suddenly he thought: Christ, supposing I can't.

'Let's move on,' Guthrie said.

Out into the Fourth Avenue, into another bar with a picture of Capri painted on the wall and a juke-box playing in one corner. In the other two soldiers squaring up.

The beer dropped ice-cold into their stomachs. I mustn't drink too much, Larsen thought. He was excited and it seemed to him as if he had been wanting a girl for years; and today his desire, harnessed for so long, had broken loose. Tonight's the night. Tonight's the night for battle-scarred virgins to strike.

But not here. I want a beautiful girl who will love me for myself and lead me to her bed, not one of these bags soaked with scent that smells like gin. Each woman was surrounded by clusters of competing males and they smiled as flirtatiously as college beauty queens as they tapped their cigarettes with tobacco-stained fingers.

Larsen and Guthrie went into another bar where, in a dark corner, some Alaskans were playing 4-5-6, money jingling in their swollen pockets.

A couple of military police came in. One with a red, bad-tempered face who kept slapping his pistol while he asked Larsen for his papers. Larsen, wearing a leather windcheater and grey trousers, didn't realize that he looked so much a serviceman. The discovery pleased him.

The MP scanned the papers and told him to keep out of the bars in the red light area.

Guthrie said: 'We don't have to go that far.'

The MP looked at him, slapping his gun. He didn't like this

man with a beard but there wasn't much he could do about it. 'Put a uniform on,' he said, 'and then I'll tell you where you can go. What was your trouble, flat feet?'

Larsen began to speak but Guthrie put his hand on his shoulder and said: 'Don't worry, I get it all the time.'

'Are you two in love?' the MP asked.

'No,' Guthrie said, 'we're just good friends.'

'You make me want to spew,' the MP said. He went into the street with the other MP who hadn't spoken since they came in.

'Why didn't you tell them what you do?' Larsen asked Guthrie.

'Because I don't have to tell punks like that any goddam thing. I don't have to tell them that the Government thinks I'm doing valuable work for the Bureau and I don't have to tell them that I get into more shitty positions in a white-out with the temperature fifty below than they could ever dream of sitting on their fat butts in the guardhouse.'

They went to another bar where Guthrie took out his wallet flush with dollar bills and a woman with long back hair, dye fading at the roots, asked him for a light and then asked if he would buy her a drink.

Guthrie bought her a drink. Later, when Larsen asked why, Guthrie said because she reminded him of his mother.

Then they went to the Seven Seas where Guthrie said there would be girls and Larsen took the news with the same terrible nonchalance. Above the entrance were the words NO NATIVE TRADE SOLICITED.

'So you won't meet Taluk here,' Guthrie said as they sat down at a table amid bamboo and coconuts. On the wall Polynesian girls took the place of the Varga girls.

'Is it the same in all these places?'

'Yeah, anywhere where you can get liquor. They reckon that the natives can't take their booze and they may be right but there's a helluva lot of whites who can't take it either.'

'*Whites.*' Larsen savoured the word. 'That seems kind of funny up here. You know, I thought they only talked that way in the south.'

'They're as colour-conscious here as any town in Alabama.

But,' Guthrie said thoughtfully, 'the girls get whiter every day. If you feel like an Eskimo girl or an Indian then you've got to go somewhere outside the city limits where you can find yourself a nice plump *klootch*. Indian girl,' he explained.

Guthrie ordered two rounds of Johnny O'Farrells which the waiter said he hadn't got until Guthrie slipped him another bill and he brought two shots of corn whisky and two glasses of beer.

'Good hunting,' Guthrie said, swallowing the whisky and pouring the beer down his throat after it.

Larsen did the same. The whisky burned and he felt sick.

Where was *his* girl?

There were girls all right, dancing and jiving with servicemen in uniform and shirtsleeves or snappy suits with bright, fat-knotted ties loose at their necks. They whirled and they spun and they knocked over chair and drinks. But none of them was Larsen's girl.

Guthrie spotted a girl coming in the doorway. He asked her to dance and then brought her back to the table where she ordered Old Grandad bourbon and called him Beaver.

Guthrie asked her if she had a friend for his buddy and she shook her head and Larsen was glad.

Sometimes the girls left the Seven Seas with their partners and returned ten minutes later peering into small mirrors and repairing their lipstick. Larsen wondered where the hell they went to. He ordered a Johnny O'Farrell for Guthrie and a beer for himself.

Then *she* came in.

She was slight with shadows under her eyes and her legs seemed unsteady in her ankle-straps. She wore pink lipstick and her hair was brown and straight and long, like Veronica Lake's except for the colour. Her eyes were greenish and she looked lost and Richard Larsen was in love with her.

He was beside her, inviting her for a drink, hearing it all coming out wrong, feeling his cheeks flush. She put her head on one side with a bird-like gesture. Yes, she said, she would love a drink.

They sat down. Guthrie who was a little drunk now slapped

his thigh and said: 'Attaboy.' Larsen wished him in hell.

She sat there, shabby black purse on the table, while he ordered her a Coke. He offered her his cigarette case and she took a cigarette which he lit with his lighter, his hand trembling.

So, what the hell did he say? She was making no effort to talk; she seemed content to sit there smiling, head a little to one side. He judged her to be about eighteen. *What's a pretty girl like you doing in a joint like this?* My God, battle-scarred veteran, what is it with you? Haven't you an angle, a line? Don't you know how to make a pass, for Chrissake? Don't you know a single sentence in the English language?

'Where do you come from?' he asked.

'Me?' She seemed surprised at the question. 'Oh, I come from Boston.'

'Ah,' he said, 'Boston.'

She puffed at her cigarette, letting out tiny smoke-signals from her mouth.

Perhaps I should show her my wound!

'I've never been there,' he said.

'Oh.'

She was wearing a dark green skirt and a silk, apple-green blouse under which he could see the shape of her small breasts. Inspiration came to him. 'What's your name?' he asked.

'Mary,' she said.

Quite contrary, he thought wildly, asking: 'And your second name?'

'Just Mary,' she said. 'The rest doesn't matter, does it?'

'It doesn't?'

'Not on meetings like this.'

Larsen took a swallow of his beer, spilled some on his shirt. 'How do you mean?'

'I mean that we won't know each other for very long so what is the point of second names?'

'Mine's Larsen,' he said. 'Richard Larsen.'

'You didn't *have* to tell me.'

'I wanted to.'

'Oh.' She stubbed out her half-finished cigarette.

A well-built blonde was punishing a piano in the corner. Larsen asked the girl if she wanted to dance.

She said. 'Are you a good dancer?'

'No,' Larsen said.

'Then what's the point?'

'I thought—'

'Let's just sit here quietly and watch.'

A soldier in shirtsleeves with sweat dripping from his face came up to the table, put his hand on the girl's shoulder and said to Larsen: 'Do you mind if I cut in?'

'Yes,' he said, 'I do.'

'Oh you do, huh?'

'Yes,' said Larsen, 'I do.'

'Well I want to hoof it with your girl so what the hell are you going to do about it?'

'If you don't beat it I'm going to punch you in the throat,' Larsen said.

'Yeah?'

'Yeah.' Larsen stood up. He was surprised with himself but quite sure of himself. He felt the power and the confidence just as he had felt it when he threw the grenade away from Browning and he knew that now he would stop behaving like a tongue-tied hick with the girl.

The girl watched them without much interest. Guthrie was on his feet asking if Larsen needed help and Larsen turned and said abruptly: 'No, this is mine.'

In the background he could see two bouncers moving towards them. Larsen felt calm; if the sweating soldier took a swing at him then he would be the quicker so that he would parry the blow with his left hand and hit him on the jaw with his right, a blow which would knock him onto the dance floor, although Larsen believed that this soldier wouldn't throw a punch: if you knew animals you could sense things like this in men.

The soldier asked: 'Are you in the Army?'

'Does it matter?'

'I asked you a question.'

Larsen said: 'Just get your ass away from here, buddy.'

The soldier hesitated, glanced around.

'Beat it,' Larsen said.

'If I thought you weren't in the Army—'

Larsen sat down because he knew it was all over and, when the soldier had gone, the girl said: 'That was all very childish.'

Larsen grinned at her, relaxed. 'Did you want to dance with him?'

'I didn't have much chance, did I?'

'Do you like it here?' he asked.

'No.'

'Would you like to take a walk?'

'Yes,' she said, 'I'd like that. Down by the water. I like to be by the water,' she said in her small, feathery voice.

Larsen said good-bye to Guthrie who had his arm round the blonde and Guthrie winked lewdly and said: 'See you in church.'

They turned their backs on the mountains and headed for the shore of the Inlet. It was late and the sky was twilight green and the water had a dawn calm about it.

She tucked her arm into his. He felt proud and proprietorial. He asked her: 'How long have you been here?'

'Oh, not long. Does it matter?'

'Not really. It's small talk, I guess.'

'We don't have to talk all that much, do we?'

'Not if you don't want to.'

'I mean there's so much.' Her voice was a little breathless. 'So much all around us without having to talk.'

'Perhaps we should talk every five minutes.' He glanced at his watch. 'Just so that we know we're still together.'

She laughed for the first time. 'All right, time us.'

Five minutes later they were on an expanse of wasteland by the water. But in the half-light it was no longer wasteland, a place where trucks dumped garbage and stray dogs died: it had magic at this time between the nightless summer days. Ripples on the water came to them slowly, dying at the shore; they could smell the water. They sat on a charred log. They lit cigarettes and Larsen glanced at his watch. 'Time for a few words,' he said, taking her hand and holding it.

'You limp a little,' she said. 'Why's that?'

He was glad she had asked. He told her about THE WAR WOUND.

'What sort of man was he, the one you rescued?'

'He was all right, I guess.'

'You don't sound too sure.'

'He was a materialist, I'm not.'

'What are you?' she asked.

'All of a sudden you're asking lots of questions.'

'All of a sudden I'm curious. About everything,' she said, staring across the water at the Sleeping Lady. 'What are you?' she asked again.

'I'm too young to know,' he told her.

'What do you think you are?'

He picked up a stone and tossed it into the water; it plopped and pushed out a circle of ripples that made a noise like silver when they reached the shore.

'Perhaps,' he said carefully, 'I'm an idealist. But more than that. I don't want to preach and I don't want to patronize. I don't know what I want to do and I wish I did.' He threw away his cigarette and put his arm round her waist so that her warmth reached him. With his free hand he pointed to the north. 'I suppose I would just like to understand.'

'I wonder,' she said, 'if we are both seeing the same things.'

He thought about it. 'They say we all see a different world but I think maybe we're both seeing the same one.'

'I think so.' She touched his hand round her waist. 'I think that if we stared into the sky we'd see the same star.'

'Why won't you tell me your second name?'

'Because it doesn't matter.'

'You sound very mysterious.'

'I am very mysterious. I'm an enigma.'

'What were you doing in that place?' he asked.

'What were you?'

'Waiting for you,' he said smugly.

'And I was looking for you.'

'Smart, aren't you?'

'Yes,' she said. She shivered. 'Shall we go?'

'Okay,' he said and thought: But where?

'I've got a one-room apartment on the other side of town,' she said. 'Would you like to come?'

He nodded but fear stirred. Was it possible that she wanted money? He was ashamed of the thought but it persisted.

'What are you thinking?' she asked as they climbed up the scrub in the strengthening light.

'I didn't realize you had an apartment.'

'Where did you think I lived, in a Cribb? That's what they call these black-tarred huts they're putting up for the construction workers,' she explained.

'No,' Larsen lied, 'for some reason I thought you lived in a hotel. You know, you haven't given me much of a clue as to what you're doing here.'

They turned into Fourth Avenue where they picked up a cab. They sat in the back holding hands. The girl said: 'I know what you were thinking just now.'

He sighed. 'What was I thinking?'

'You were wondering if I was a good-time girl, a Lou.'

He had to laugh. 'And are you?'

'Yes,' she said.

He kissed her very gently, with tenderness but without passion, until her lips parted slightly which made him shiver inside but it was more than passion, oh much more.

The driver said: 'Don't mind me.' The cab had stopped outside a small apartment block on the outskirts of town.

The apartment was a studio; one room, a bathroom and a kitchenette behind a yellow curtain.

'I'll make coffee,' she said, drawing the yellow curtain.

Larsen moved around the room looking for clues, feeling furtive. There was a photograph on a table of a middle-aged man and woman, both of whom resembled the girl in different ways; they both looked scholarly but there was a touch of arrogance about the man with his white moustache and the woman had the patient Victorian smile of a woman who knows her place. He turned to the bookshelves which, he had once read, is a good indication of character. But she said from the kitchenette: 'Those were here when I took the apartment so they won't help you.' There was a vase of fireweed on the table, a photograph of Mount McKinley and a water-colour of arctic flowers on the walls; there really weren't any clues and, in fact, the apartment was oddly impersonal.

She handed him a cup of coffee and sat on the edge of the divan which he assumed turned into a bed and said: 'You really do think I'm in it for the money, don't you?'

He sat opposite her on an easy chair, taking his time before replying. He took so long that she said: 'You needn't worry, I understand perfectly. After all I was in that night club alone.'

'It's just that I can't understand what you're doing here alone.'

'Minding my own business,' she said, sipping her coffee.

'Well, I'm sorry.'

'I told you, there's no need to be.'

He stood up and sat down beside her and took her hand again. 'I wouldn't want you to think—'

'I don't. What are you going to do, Richard? In the future, I mean.'

'Come back here,' he said. It was the first time he had fully realized this and he was grateful to her for making him say it. 'I'd like to show you what I've seen. I'd like to share it with you.'

'We've already shared a lot. You can share a lot in a few minutes seeing the same things. Maybe as much as a lot of people share in a lifetime.'

'I guess so,' he said, disappointed. 'But I'd like to take you north. I'd like you to see the mountains and the animals and feel the freedom.'

He paused and told her about the bear.

She traced the outline of his mouth with her finger. 'You mustn't be too much of an idealist, Richard. Who needs a dead idealist?'

'I still figure I could have stopped him attacking.'

'And I think I must thank Mr. Guthrie for saving you for me.'

'I suppose you're right. He's a nice guy,' Larsen said.

She stood up, brushed her green skirt, disappeared in the

bathroom. Larsen heard the splash of water. He walked round the room a couple more times. He stared at the middle-aged couple who stared back. He sat down again and waited. She seemed to be taking a hell of a long time in there. He glanced at his watch: it was 3 a.m. Outside it was bright now so he pulled the drapes. He sat down and continued to wait, hearing again the splash of water.

When she came back she was wearing a white terrycloth bath robe. She had washed her face and she looked very young and Richard Larsen, scared, asked her how old she was.

'Eighteen,' she said.

She pulled the back of the divan so that it turned down into a bed.

Larsen went to the window, peered through the drapes, and when he turned again she was under the blanket and her bath-robe was lying on the floor. She didn't smile, she didn't beckon: she merely looked at him.

He went to the bathroom. He undressed and washed. The thought of what was to follow frightened him. He reasoned that if she was the sort of girl he hoped she was then she wouldn't be behaving like this. Perhaps she thought it was expected of her; yes, perhaps that was it because, after all, he had patently been hunting in the Seven Seas. And yet they had surely progressed beyond that, on the wasteland with the ripples pushing at the shore; surely she understood that it was more than that now; that, as she had said, it was the sharing that mattered, the knowledge of the sharing that transcended talk, and that she didn't have to go to bed with him the first evening.

He stared at himself in the mirror and said to himself: 'Christ, you hypocrite.' And then anticipated his disap-pointment if he found that she was . . . experienced – 'Christ, you goddam prude.' But the first night! That was for the good-time-girls, the phantom girls who paraded themselves beside his bed in the stiff, pulsing dawn. You smug bastard, Larsen; you with your double standards, one for men and another for women. *When she discovers my inexperience will she laugh?*

Then he thought: How the hell am I going to get from here to the divan naked? He opened the door cautiously; she was

124

lying with her back to him and he made it in three strides; then he was lying beside her, his arms around her softness and her warmth, his hands reaching for her small breasts.

She turned to him. In the fragile light that reached them through the drapes he could see the greenness of her eyes; the pupils were large but he didn't know what was in them, unless it was wonder. He kissed her breasts, the nipples that were larger than he had expected, and felt the power in his own loins. He stroked the curling hair between her legs while, hesitantly, she searched for him, found him, stroked him.

'I love you,' he said.

She smiled at him. 'This is sharing,' she said.

She turned on her back, guided him into her, moaned as he entered her. Then he knew that she was a virgin and he was ashamed, not because she was but because it shouldn't have mattered.

Then they climbed together, to the peaks, to the skies, to the final freedom. This is as it should be, this is as it will always be, this is what I sought and I'm glad it happened this way, the first time, so that I will always remember this is how it should be, this is the seeding of life, the sharing, the love.

Afterwards he said: 'It was the first time with me,' and she said: 'I know,' which pleased him which was ironic because he had feared her reaction to this knowledge.

She touched the dressing on his wound. 'Does it hurt?'

'Nothing hurts any more.'

'I always knew it should be like that.'

And then she told him that he must go. He left without question, telling her that he would return when they had both slept.

'Yes,' she said. And, when he had dressed, she stood naked in front of him, put her arms round his neck, kissed him, and said: 'You know, we will always share the same things. Whatever happens the sharing will be there. Don't ever forget that.'

The caretaker was in his sixties, stomach flowing over his leather belt, smelling of whisky.

He met Larsen at the entrance to the apartment block. 'Name of Larsen?' he asked.

Larsen nodded.

'I got a message for you.' He handed Larsen a pale blue envelope. Inside was a single sheet of blue notepaper.

Larsen read it slowly, hardly comprehending and yet knowing before he read it what it said.

I'm sorry, my love. You were my first love, my only love. Nothing will change that.

But there had to be more. He searched inside the envelope. He felt cold as though he might faint.

'Anything wrong?'

'Where is she?'

'Search me, buddy. She only took the apartment a couple of days ago. She was packed and gone by ten o'clock this morning.'

'Where did she go?'

'She told the cab driver to take her to the airport. She didn't look in too good shape to me. But that was only to be expected . . .'

'What the hell do you mean?'

'Don't get sore with me, buddy.'

'What do you mean, "That was only to be expected . . ."'

The caretaker scratched himself under one armpit. 'She was a very sick girl. That I did know. She came here from the hospital. She said she wanted the apartment for a week to recover but' – the caretaker yawned – 'she didn't look like she was going to recover to me. Not this morning anyhow.'

'What was her name?'

'She didn't give it.'

Larsen stepped towards the caretaker. 'She must have.'

'Are you calling me a liar?'

Larsen stepped back. 'I'm sorry, but she must have when she took the apartment.'

'Well, I'm telling you she didn't. She paid all right and said she would give me her particulars later. And that was okay by me because, as a matter of fact, she paid over the odds.'

'You mean she bribed you?'

'Now look,' said the caretaker, thumbs in his belt, 'I don't have to take any shit from you, mister.'

'You've no idea who she was?'

'As far as I'm concerned she could have been Hedy Lamarr.'

'Can I go up to the apartment?'

'Ain't much point unless you want to take it.'

Larsen gave him a five dollar bill. 'I just want to see it.'

The caretaker took the bill.

But the apartment looked as if it had never been lived in. The blankets were neatly piled beside the divan; the caretaker standing at the door told him that the sheets had been taken away to be laundered. The bathroom had been cleaned out; the photograph on the table had disappeared. The room was like a stage-set, waiting to be dismantled at the end of a run.

'You know something,' the caretaker said, 'I reckon that girl was going away to die.'

He took a cab out to the airport. There was no sign of her. There had been several flights out that morning to Stateside and, yes, a passenger could have got a connection to Boston on any one of them.

It took him three days to find the doctor who had treated her. He told him that she had a rare bone disease, that she had about three weeks to live. That she had left instructions that her real name and address should be given to no one.

'I guess you've got to respect that,' said the doctor.

'But didn't she have any family?'

'Sure she had a family. She said she wanted a couple of days by herself before flying back to the States with them. A nice old couple they were but, you know, broken up by it. They'd only been out here a couple of months. They were going to settle but when she fell sick and when they knew the truth they wanted out.'

The doctor, middle-aged and compassionate, added: 'I know one thing – she wouldn't want you to find her.'

'She was so young,' Richard Larsen said.

'You know what she wanted?'
Larsen shook his head.
'She wanted a couple of days of life.'
'And love,' Richard Larsen said.

CHAPTER TEN

HE had intended to try and locate Ott, but now he didn't think he could face him.

In the *Anchorage Daily Times* he read about an Indian named Ott who was dividing his time between the Alaskan Territorial Guard (Gruening's Guerrillas) and the Bureau of Indian Affairs at Fairbanks.

Larsen called Ott from the hostel which he hadn't left for two days. Ott was enthusiastic. 'Son-of-a-gun, so you made it to the promised land. Better than a zoo, huh? When you coming up?'

Larsen said he didn't think he could make it.

'You got to make it. We've got quite an outfit. At least we think so but the Eskimos don't because some idiot called it Indian Affairs instead of Native Affairs. Did you know we were slightly higher on the social scale?'

Larsen knew his lack of enthusiasm sounded in his voice and he regretted it, but there was nothing he could do; nothing interested him. He told Ott about his wound, but he wasn't proud of it any more. 'They're flying me out to Seattle today,' he said. It was a lie but it was the best he could do.

'Goddam, that's a shame.' Ott hesitated. 'Will you be coming back?'

'Maybe,' said Richard Larsen who didn't care where he went.

'Is anything wrong?'

Larsen said: 'I'll tell you about it some time.'

'You sound like you're suffering from battle fatigue.'

'Look,' Larsen said into the receiver, 'I've got to go now. But I'll write. And maybe when the war's over we can get together.'

'Is there anything—'

'There's nothing anyone can do,' Larsen said thinking of a girl who was dying somewhere.

'Well, it's great to hear your voice, old buddy.'

'I'll write,' Larsen said and hung up.

Next day he went for a medical. They examined the wound now covered with tight pink skin. A couple more weeks convalescence, they said, and he would be fit. He told them he didn't want any more convalescence and they looked at him in surprise because he was the first casualty they had encountered who wanted to get back to active service.

While Larsen waited in the corridor outside listlessly flipping through copies of two of the Service newspapers, *The Kodiak Bear* and *The Williwaw*, the medical officer made a couple of calls, then called Larsen back into his office.

He said: 'How would a couple of weeks in Seattle suit you?'

'Can't I rejoin my unit?'

The doctor shook his head. 'It's Seattle or staying here. Take your pick.'

So Richard Larsen who had found Alaska and had now rejected it because here he had found a girl and lost her forever elected to go to Seattle.

Fourteen days later he was posted to London, England.

CHAPTER ELEVEN

THE tables stretched the length of the gap-toothed London street. Everyone had cooked and there were pyramids of cakes studded with hoarded currants and glacé cherries, towers of corned-beef and Spam sandwiches and jugs of lemonade and dusty-sweet Tizer.

There were three pianos with yellow keys, one of which had seen service at a silent movie house, and a set of drums with a cymbal missing. Bunting looped from the budding plane trees and there were two Union Jacks bought for the Coronation standing at either end of the street.

It was a coming-out party.

Throughout the war, after they returned from work, from school, from battle, the people of Denmark Street had retired indoors. To cupboards under the stairs, to Morrison shelters, with gas-masks and first-aid kits and Thermos flasks of tea handy, listening on the wireless to Tommy Handley and Winston Churchill, playing cards and knitting while the blades of searchlights switched the skies and the planes droned overhead and the bloody great gun one street away loosed off shells and the bombs whistled down and shrapnel tinkled on the roof-tops.

The war had taken five people from this street of terrace houses near Clapham Junction station. From the grubby trains nosing their way into London, the terrace looked identical to the ranks of streets shouldering each other to the horizon; but, of course, it wasn't, each house possessing its own touches of affection. Three houses had been flattened by bombs, and old Mrs. Higgins had died in the bed she refused to leave, crushed by a falling beam, and a young mother whose husband was on the Russian convoys, had been buried with her baby in rubble. Jack Davenport, who had spent much of his time in prison, had been killed at Dunkirk and Maurice Hart had caught his at El Alamein.

All in all Denmark Street had been luckier than many streets. Now Hitler had been beaten and on this balmy May day in 1945, Mrs. Logan was in charge of the victory celebrations. As she had been in charge of most functions during the war – First Aid, Knitted Comforts for Sailors, Dig for Victory, Saucepan Day when everyone gave a saucepan to build a Spitfire, Austerity Cooking (the manufacture of carrot marmalade and suchlike) and the collection of greenstuff from the flowerless parks to feed rabbits in the yards behind the houses.

During the war Mrs. Logan, a shapeless woman in her fifties, had worn a siren suit and a turban; now she emerged in a cotton frock that still smelled of the lavender she had picked in the country before the Battle of Britain and stored in the drawer with her clothes.

Mrs. Logan had also been in charge of Morals, trying to make sure that none of the wives and fiancées of Men at the Front entertained servicemen from foreign countries in their homes. She did not laugh at the joke about Americans and austerity knickers – One Yank and they're down. And it was a great sorrow to her when her daughter, Ruth, became a Windmill girl, posing naked in patriotic tableaux, and confessed that she had slept with a British paratrooper.

Today Mrs. Logan in her print dress, barmaid arms as white as flour, arranged the children at the tables, separating those who tended to fight, replenished cakes and sandwiches, tried to regulate the supply of Guinness and brown ale because, all right, the men could get drunk this evening but not now beneath the plane trees with the children.

Occasionally she popped into her house, No. 15, for a nip out of the bottle of Gordon's gin that had been kept unopened in the sideboard since 1939. Mrs. Logan, a widow, was taking a nip when her daughter who had been late the previous evening came downstairs dressed in slacks and white blouse.

She was a pretty girl, like Mrs. Logan had been in the wedding photograph on the mantelpiece, but she had the serene expression of her father, and his eyes and mouth. With her father's serenity and her mother's determination she had in her time scared off several young men. She had dark curly hair and a voluptuous figure and a mole on her cheek like a courtesan's beauty spot.

She was also ambitious, determined from the age of fifteen to make something of herself. By listening to the voices of the BBC announcers she had taught herself to speak well, she had studied shorthand and typing and had worked in a munitions factory before a slick-haired young man in a draped jacket had introduced her to the Windmill management; when he had suggested a private showing at his apartment in Frith Street she had laughed at him with such derision that he had slunk away.

She came down yawning.

Her mother said: 'Out late, weren't you?'

'I was working.'

'Showing off your body again. Disgusting.'

Ruth yawned again and bit into an apple. 'Not today, mother, it's VE Day.'

'I don't know what your father would have said.'

'He saw your body didn't he?'

'And he was the only one,' said Mrs. Logan. 'I didn't parade it in front of thousands of men.'

Ruth shrugged. 'It gives them pleasure so what's wrong with it? In any case they only see my breasts' – she touched her breasts – 'and the rest of it's in their minds and we're not allowed to move anyway.'

'I should hope not,' Mrs. Logan said. She put the gin bottle away. 'Now come out and help.'

They went out into the sunlight. Mickey Kelly was playing *Roll Out the Barrel* on one of the pianos, dogs were taking scraps from the children, a cat with one blue eye and one green was curled on the seat behind the drums.

Ruth moved along the tables filling up the jugs. The children liked her, so did most of the inhabitants of the street which had become a sort of club during the war, although one or two of the women disliked her because she was stuck-up and shameless. 'Probably on the game,' they said with satisfaction over

133

their tea. 'Sitting on a fortune,' they said as their husband's eyes followed Ruth Logan walking down the street to the station.

When all the jugs were filled Ruth sat on a low wall – its railings removed for the War Effort – lit a Sweet Caporal cigarette from a packet a Canadian sergeant had given her and watched this wonderful, guzzling, belching occasion in this branch-line of houses.

Bill would have enjoyed it today, she thought. But Bill would never come here again because he had died at Arnhem, suspended by a parachute from a tree, six machine-gun bullets in his body. She took out his photograph from her wallet; these days she had to look at the photograph to remember clearly what he had looked like and she was ashamed of this, although she knew that the present drowns the past in deep water. A fierce, blond man with a moustache, grinned at her from under his Red Beret, thumbs stuck in his webbing belt. She had known him only for three weeks and they had made love once in a hotel at King's Cross and, contrary to the legend of the first night, it had been wonderful. Hard and lustful and tender, waking to see him dressing to go away to die. Remembering the movements of his muscles as he pulled on his vest.

He had been a North Countryman with vowels like broken slates. She wondered if she would have married him; they had been engaged but war-time engagements weren't pledges, more acts of faith in a holocaust, a gesture of affection before love-making. If they came back then you sorted things out, that was tacitly understood. You might marry or you might agree that the engagement had been a token.

And she hadn't slept with anyone since.

When she looked at the photograph and remembered the night in the wretched hotel room she experienced a warmth in her loins. She put the photograph away in her wallet, away in the past.

Mickey Kelly was playing *Underneath the Spreading Chestnut Tree* and on the pavement they were miming it; a small boy had got at the drums and, watched reproachfully by the cat, was making a lot of noise which made the old people who had lived through the Blitz jump in their chairs.

It was 2 p.m. A few of the men sitting on the walls were mildly drunk. The sun shone. Mrs. Logan was organizing games.

Ruth poured herself a Guinness. Later she and a friend were going up to the West End. She paused to talk to one of the old men sitting on the wall, as old men sit watching bowls or cricket content with their moth-balled memories.

The old man's name was Harry Sharp. He wasn't as old as he looked but he had been gassed in France in the First World War. He wore four brightly-polished medals on the jacket of his worn, pressed brown suit. He leaned with both hands on a walking stick, smoking Three Nuns in a blackened pipe.

'Well, Harry,' she said, 'so it's all over.'

'For a while,' he said.

'Don't be so pessimistic.'

'Difficult to be anything else while there's politicians around. We beat the Hun once and this war should never have happened.' He pointed the chewed stem of his pipe at the tables. 'This should be a wake for what the politicians allowed to happen. They talk about war criminals, there's peace criminals too. Lloyd George, Bonar Law, Baldwin, Chamberlain, the whole damn crew of them. They threw away what we'd won.'

'They won't let it happen again,' she said.

'Oh yes they will.' He coughed his mustard-gas cough. 'A politician will never take an unpopular decision unless he's forced into a corner. Loses his votes, you see. Mark my words, in a few years time the Boche will be rich and powerful and we'll be going down the drain.'

The children were singing now

> *Just whistle while you work,*
> *Mussolini is a twerp.*
> *Hitler's barmy, so's his army,*
> *Rub 'em in the dirt.*

And if he was right Bill had died for nothing and so had everyone else. She couldn't accept this. 'We fought evil,' she said, 'and we won.'

'Aye,' he said, 'but they should never have let it happen, should they?'

'I suppose you're right,' she said, but she refused to let his pessimism spoil the day.

> *Just whistle while you work,*
> *Mussolini bought a shirt.*
> *Hitler wore it, Churchill tore it,*
> *Rub 'em in the dirt.*

She heard a clock chime. 'Ah well,' she said, 'cheer up Mr. Sharp, I've got to be off now.'

'Going up West are you?'

'I think I should, it only happens once in a lifetime.'

'You hope.' His pipe gurgled. 'Don't forget the Japs haven't been beaten yet.'

Ruth had.

She patted his shoulder and left him with his mustard cough.

In her bedroom she put on her grey costume nipped in at the waist that had cost all those clothing coupons and one of the pairs of nylons that the Americans brought to the stage-door as bribes. She put on a filmy, high-necked blouse and a pair of court shoes; she combed her curls, painted her nails and was ready.

In the street her mother looked at her with reproach. 'I thought you might have stayed in tonight.'

'But tonight's going to be fun.'

'All tarted up, I see. No wonder they talk in the street.'

'I'm glad I give them pleasure as well as all those thousands of men,' Ruth Logan said. 'Have a good time.' She kissed her mother on the cheek and was gone in the direction of Clapham Junction Station, heel-taps crisp on the pavement as the men watched her go.

At the Junction she caught a train that had arrived from outer suburbs where the playing-fields were green and the houses detached. She gazed through a hole in the anti-blast netting at the grey terraced inner suburbs moving past. There were parties in many of the streets; here and there she saw a terrace with its walls ripped off, bathroom, bedroom, lounge, bared for everyone to see. Shops with blind, boarded windows, the pub at the corner rebuilt with hard-board, a school punched flat; all stitched with flags this victorious day.

But what had they won? Ruth Logan wondered as the train crossed the Thames and swayed over the mesh of rails outside Victoria. A return to those bricked-in days between the two wars with the only escape at the penny library, the cinema and the pub? She thought about Harry Sharp's words and she saw the politicians as the people who lived at the railheads of these suburban tracks, in country mansions and Mayfair apartments. The people who had lived in the terraces had fought for them, but what would they gain?

No, it has to be different this time, she decided as she heel-tapped her way along the platform. THEY couldn't pull the same shabby tricks this time.

And she thought: Of one thing I *am* sure: I shan't return to that life.

She met her friend, Eileen Fielding, outside the station and they walked along Victoria Street in the direction of the celebrations. They had a couple of drinks in a pub in Whitehall and, with arms round the waists of two sailors, sang: '*There'll always be an England*'.

But it will never be the same, she thought. Never.

They headed for Piccadilly, the hub of the party. But the party had spread itself, sprawled through Leicester Square to Trafalgar Square; darted up Regent Street and the Haymarket and Shaftesbury Avenue, overwhelmed Soho, charged the Strand and St. Martin's Lane and collapsed, exhausted, in Green Park and St. James's Park with giggles and sighs, with pretty heads pillowed on military jackets.

It was dusk when Ruth Logan and Eileen Fielding arrived in Piccadilly having been kissed by all the world except the Axis powers. By then, in scattered pockets, even the Allied Powers were falling out, fist-fighting with exuberance.

Ruth wore an American sailor's hat; Eileen Fielding wore a fairground hat bearing the legend KISS ME WHILE MY LIPS ARE STICKY.

Overhead rockets smeared the skies with soft, slowly-fading

stars. Londoners who had come up from the suburbs or emerged from their burrows on the Underground, remembered the shells that had wounded those skies and the bright, white moonlight of magnesium flares.

In Shaftesbury Avenue, near Rainbow Corner, the HQ of the GIs, a member of the United States Air Force made one kiss with a girl with one ear-ring last for fourteen minutes. Applause.

In Regent Street a duchess lifted her skirts and danced *Knees Up Mother Brown.*

In a pub in Trafalgar Square someone from the city drank a pint of beer from his bowler hat.

In the sweating, jostling streets they danced the *Hokey Cokey* and the *Palais Glide.*

Somewhere up Shaftesbury Avenue, Eileen Fielding who was blonde and pouting-pretty, disappeared with a member of the Free French. She had never been reliable.

Ruth retraced her footsteps down Shaftesbury Avenue, pushing through the throng at Rainbow Corner, dodging the clutching hands of servicemen – British, Americans, Canadians, Australians, New Zealanders, South Africans, Belgians, Poles, Czech, French, Dutch and a Russian or two – and made her way back to Trafalgar Square where there was a knees-up in progress around Nelson's Column.

But she had lost the spirit of the occasion: you couldn't celebrate by yourself, not if you were a girl. She turned into the Mall intending to bear left at Buckingham Palace in the direction of Victoria. In St. James's Park to her left she could see couples moving on the grass beneath the trees. She hastened her step. She was half-way to Buckingham Palace when two American sailors came out from behind the trees. They were amiably drunk.

They were very young, crew-cut, walking on waves. One of them tried to put his arm round her. She dodged him and he said: 'Hey, what's the matter? It's VE Day, didn't anyone tell you?'

She smiled at them: she had become adept at dealing with drunks. 'I'm exhausted,' she said. 'I'm going home.'

'No hurry,' the other sailor said. 'Come on, let's have some fun.' He nodded towards the park. 'They're having a lot of fun in there.'

'I'll come back when it's VJ Day,' she said.

'Huh?'

'When the Japs have been beaten.'

'Aw come on,' they said and they both made a grab at her.

She was angry now. 'Please leave me alone.'

'Come on,' they said and began to pull her into the park.

'I mean it.'

'Aw, come on.'

She kicked one of them on the shin. He yelped. 'Hey, she's got spirit, that's what I like.' Neither of them let go.

She was frightened now. She tried to break loose and get back to the pavement but one of her shoes came off. She screamed. One of the sailors put his hand over her mouth. 'Knock it off, sister.' The mood had changed: there was a throatiness in their voices.

She bit a finger clamped round her mouth. The sailor raised one hand to hit her when a third figure came up from behind. The newcomer caught the raised arm, spun the sailor round and hit him in the throat, the sailor fell choking.

The other sailor let her go. Ruth saw that the newcomer was an American Army corporal.

'Well, well,' said the sailor, 'a fucking soldier boy. Now ain't that something?' He swung at the corporal but the corporal ducked and the momentum of the blow sent the sailor staggering across the grass. He came back, fists raised. The corporal waited.

The sailor stopped in front of the corporal and said: 'Put your fists up you jerk.'

The corporal didn't move. He said quietly: 'I could kill you with one hand behind my back.' Above them a rocket exploded dripping stars. 'And I don't have to remind you what the penalty for rape is?'

The sailor stared at him uncertainly. 'Rape? We were just going to have some fun.'

'Beat it,' said the corporal, 'and take your buddy with you,' pointing at the other sailor who was getting to his feet, one hand at his throat.

The corporal handed Ruth her shoe. 'Come on,' he said. 'Now,' he whispered, 'while we're winning.'

They walked away; the sailors didn't follow. They reached Buckingham Palace. There they stopped. There were still crowds around; a couple of lights burned in the great oblong building.

She turned and faced him. 'Thank you. I know it sounds inadequate but, anyway, thank you.' She tried to make a joke out of it. 'Thank you for saving me from a fate worse than death.'

'That's all right.' He smiled at her. 'Where are you heading for?'

'Victoria Station,' she said.

'I'll walk you there. You must feel shaken up. Here, take my arm,' he said, and took her hand and tucked it beneath his arm.

'Perhaps,' he said, as they neared Victoria, 'you'd better have a coffee or something.'

'All right,' she said.

They went into a café with steamy windows where black coffee and sweet, stewed tea were being dispensed to white-faced revellers. They sat at a table covered with oilcloth beneath a notice CARELESS TALK COSTS LIVES.

'What's your name?' he asked as he sipped his coffee.

'Ruth,' she said. 'Ruth Logan.'

'I'm Richard Larsen,' he told her. 'And I doubt if I could have killed that guy with two hands let alone one.'

'I'm very grateful to you, Richard Larsen. Are you on leave?'

He nodded. 'I've just come back from France.'

'You don't look as if you've been celebrating.'

'Oh sure I've been celebrating. I celebrated all day, then I thought I'd take it easy. You know, consider this day. Everything that led up to it, everything that's going to come after it.'

'When are you going back to America?'

'Soon, I guess. It's all over now, isn't it. I mean the Americans will stay in Europe but I've been over here long enough.'

'Don't you like it here?'

'Oh sure I like it. But I have another place to go.'

'Where's that?'

He told her it was Alaska and smiled when she frowned. 'The Frozen North? That's about all most people know about it. In fact it's as big as Europe.' He gave her a cigarette and they both smoked. 'What do you do?' he asked.

For the first time she found that she was reluctant to tell someone. It was ridiculous because she wasn't ashamed of it. It was the connotation that was the trouble. She told him: 'I'm in the theatre,' and was ashamed of the half-truth.

'An actress, huh? I don't know much about the theatre. Are you famous?'

'Not exactly.'

'A straight actress?'

'Not really.' She glanced at her watch. 'I think I'd better be getting along or I'll miss the last train.'

'Of course.'

They walked to Victoria.

On the platform beside the grimy train, she said again: 'Well, thank you Richard Larsen.'

'Scandinavian,' he said. 'It's a Scandinavian name.' He opened the carriage door for her. She leaned out of the window and it wasn't until the train began to vibrate that he asked her if she would like to come out next day.

'I thought you'd never ask,' she said.

She telephoned the theatre from the call-box at the end of Denmark Street and said that she had 'flu. The manager said that a lot of girls had 'flu today and it was an odd coincidence that 'flu had struck in epidemic proportions the morning after VE Day.

They went to Hampton Court and took a rowing boat on the river. It was a filmy day with the sun dull and golden through the mist, swans gliding over the brown, gold-touched water and green-headed mallards paddling slowly beneath the over-hanging branches. When Larsen dipped the oars into the water they left behind swirls ~~that~~ flattened out so slowly that the water might have been mud. Other rowing boats slipped silently past. The day was a Japanese print.

He wore civilian clothes, jacket and open-necked white shirt and slacks. She wore a pink dress and a pink cardigan with a string of imitation pearls at her neck. As he rowed Larsen admired her legs.

After a while he stopped rowing and let the boat drift. He could sense the latent heat above the mist.

She said: 'I've got a sort of confession to make.'

'You're married,' he said.

'Nothing like that. I don't know why I didn't tell you last night because I'm not ashamed of it or anything.'

'My God, what is it? Are you out on parole or something?'

'No,' she said, watching his face for reaction, 'I strip.'

'Strip?'

'Yes, I take my clothes off on the stage.' His face registered nothing. 'Well, I don't exactly strip. You know, not your idea of stripping.' She was becoming confused. 'I'm at the Windmill. You've heard of it?' she asked.

'We never closed?'

'Some of the girls there are debutantes,' she said.

'Really?' He was smiling.

'I mean it's quite artistic, it really is. We pose in tableaux on the stage. I can't see anything wrong in it. I mean it's only wrong surely if you're ashamed of your body or if it's vulgar. You know, we're not even allowed to move.'

'We never moved,' he said.

'This is all coming out wrong. Perhaps,' she said desperately, 'you'd better come and see the show.'

'Perhaps you can get me a ticket.'

'You don't book,' she said, thinking of the scramble before each show to get the seats nearest the stage. 'It's continuous performances and you just go to the box office. It's best to get there early because there's usually a queue.'

'I'll be at the head of the queue,' he told her.

For some reason it mattered to her whether this young American with the bright blue eyes and the Army-cropped hair cared about the way she earned her living. She trailed her fingers in the water as they drifted downstream. 'Does it bother you?'

'Does what bother me?'

'That I appear nude – or semi-nude – on the stage.'

'Why should it?'

'I don't know, I just thought it might.'

'It might have once, I don't know. I guess I was a little prudish when I was younger. But war changes a lot. War changes everything,' he said.

'How old are you?' she asked.

'Twenty-two. An old man.'

'That's silly.'

'No, you can grow old in a day. Or you can die innocent at eighty.'

'Did you see much fighting?'

'Enough,' he said. 'I was in the D-Day landings.' He began to row again as the sun grew stronger above the mist; a swan glided past without bothering to look at them. 'But I reckon you had it as badly as anyone. You know, just sitting there waiting for the bombs to drop.'

'The Flying Bombs were the worst,' she said. 'You heard them cut out and then you waited for them to hit the ground. The V-2s – the rockets – weren't so bad because there was just the explosion, no warning.'

'I think a lot of us were thinking of London when we were fighting. Not just London, I guess, all the other cities that were bombed. And yet we're not all that popular with the British, not with the men anyway.'

'Well,' she said, 'you do have a lot more. Money, clothes, cigarettes.'

'Maybe, but there's more to it than that. No one loves a benefactor.'

'I suppose you're right. You're very wise, aren't you. Old and wise.'

'Like I told you, you grow up quickly in war.'

'Do you mind me asking questions? I've always been in-quisitive.'

143

'Ask away,' he said.

'Well . . .' She hesitated. 'Do you have anyone back home?'

'Sure, I have a mother and father on Long Island.'

'That's New York, isn't it?'

'Sort of.'

'But I didn't really mean that. This is terrible, isn't it.' She crossed her fine, nylon-sheathed legs. 'I mean do you have a fiancée or anything like that?'

He was rowing hard as though he were in a race. 'I had a girl once.'

'Oh,' she said.

'It was a very short romance. It lasted six hours.'

She didn't ask him any more.

He stopped rowing; the sweat was trickling down his chest, the muscles in his arms burned. The sun beat down and the shreds of mist scattered and were lost and in places the water was now deep and green, with silver fish suspended in the depths. 'Let's go back and eat,' he said. He held one oar steady in the water and rowed with the other so that they turned; then they were heading back to Hampton Court at a steady pace with the water unfurling before the prow.

They went to a pub with horseshoes on the wall, its ceiling pickled brown by tobacco smoke. It smelled of stale beer and you had three choices of sandwiches – Spam, corned beef or peanut butter.

They took their sandwiches and half pints of bitter into the garden with oak tables and unsteady park benches. They sat under an ornamental cherry tree while the last petals of blossom fell around them.

'What will you do when you go back?' she asked.

'Have you ever thought of becoming a reporter?'

'Well, you ask some questions then. Haven't you got any curiosity?'

'About certain things.'

'But not about me?'

'You wouldn't like the questions.'

'Try me.'

'Okay. What does it feel like when you're on stage naked in front of a few hundred men?'

'It doesn't feel like anything,' she said. She threw the crumbs from her plate to the waiting sparrows. 'I mean why should it?'

'I don't think you're telling the whole truth.'

'Well,' – she sipped her beer – 'I sometimes feel cold and would like to be wearing woolly underwear. But I suppose you're right, I do feel something.' She had sometimes wondered if there was anything sexual about her reactions. She tried to speak honestly. 'I feel quite proud. I mean I've got quite a good body. I like the feeling that it's giving pleasure. But I don't *think* I get any sort of kick out of it.'

'Don't you ever consider what all those sex-starved guys out there are thinking?'

'Yes, I suppose I do.'

'And you're quite sure it isn't that knowledge that gives you pleasure?'

'I suppose it might,' she admitted. 'But there's nothing wrong in being desired, is there?'

'Not a thing,' he said. 'I just wanted you to be honest.'

As they left the pub a small boy in a green blazer came up to them and said: 'Got any gum, chum?'

Larsen fished a pack out of his pocket and explained to Ruth Logan: 'I don't chew gum myself but I like to give it to the kids. I wonder how he knew I was American.'

'You're not serious?'

'I am.'

'Because you couldn't be mistaken for anything else. You're in uniform even when you're out of it. Those trousers, that shirt – American, American.'

They went into Hampton Court maze and got lost and didn't bother too much about finding their way out. They found the benches at the middle of the maze and smoked cigarettes there. When they got up to go he took her hand. The sun was strong on them as they wandered around the tattered hedges, into dead-ends, past familiar stretches of hedge, back to the benches at the heart of the maze. She had a theory that if you kept turning right you would come to the exit but it didn't work. It took them half an hour to get out.

Then they had tea and cakes that tasted of sawdust in a teashop run by two old ladies in pinafores. They walked beside the river in the evening which smelled of grass and blossom, and boats and Larsen thought: This is what I was fighting for.

They went to the movies – all newly-met couples went to the movies – and they saw Abbot and Costello and they laughed a lot and he took her hand and she squeezed it staring steadily at the screen.

They had a final half pint of beer before catching the train back to London. They were alone briefly between two stations so that was when he kissed her. Softly with one hand touching her cheek. When he drew back she gazed at him for a moment; her eyes were green and there was a quality about her expression that reminded him of another girl a long time ago.

The following afternoon Larsen went to see Ruth Logan in the nude.

He lined up for half an hour with Servicemen and civilians – the civilians were more self-conscious about their presence and hid behind newspapers – before entering the theatre during an interval and finding a seat six rows back from the stage between an Australian soldier and a youth of seventeen or so.

The curtain arose; the audience sighed. The opening number was patriotic with lots of red-white-and-blue, the girls in short skirts dancing in a line, with beautiful legs, shoes tapping metallically on the stage, breasts apparent beneath filmy tops to the long-sighted and the imaginative. Larsen searched for Ruth but spotted her only as the curtain came down because, from six rows back, the girls all looked much the same which was perhaps intentional to prevent a concerted rush from the stalls.

It wasn't until the third act that the audience saw what appeared to be four girls totally nude. None of them was Ruth. They were grouped around a maypole, hanging onto green and yellow ropes, motionless – flesh statues. Their breasts were beautiful, marbled and cherry-tipped, but their other charms were invisible, like the nudes in a nature magazine where an artist has erased the crotch.

They were followed by a Cockney comedian who made jokes about GIs, spivs, rationing and nylons. He was politely applauded by men who had come to see women; he seemed grateful.

Larsen finally saw Ruth stripped in a tableau depicting the French Resistance. She was kneeling on a pedestal in an attitude of defiance and he had a clear view of the profile of her face and body.

The Australian beside him said: 'Fantastic tits.'

Larsen ignored him. He wasn't certain of his feelings. Certainly not disgust; jealousy, perhaps, that all these randy men were staring at the unclothed body of the girl who had been with him in a Japanese print only yesterday. He hated what they were thinking. I'm goddam jealous, that's what it is, jealous of every man in this theatre. And yet up there on the stage she was enjoying it. Hadn't she told him so? So what right have I to cast judgement?

The curtain fell and the Australian said: 'Jesus, those tits.' He turned to Larsen. 'They say they cover their fannies with sticky tape. Painful, huh?'

Larsen said: 'Just as painful as it would be round your mouth.'

'Hey, what's eating you? Did you come here just to hear the comedian?'

'I didn't come here to hear you,' Larsen said.

The Australian shook his head, a big, shaggy, wounded animal. 'You bloody Yanks, you don't know your ass from your elbow. What's eating you?'

Three rows ahead a young man in a striped blue suit who looked like a British officer stood up to leave. There were movements in the auditorium but they subsided as the Australian climbed over the backs of the chairs and slid into the empty seat.

Larsen waited for the next tableau.

What, he asked himself, do I think of this girl? Since the girl in Alaska there had been other girls in England and France and one in Germany but he had been honest with them, they were the fortunes of war, and in his wallet he still carried the message from the girl in Alaska, but you can't carry on a courtship with the dead; you don't forget them – ever. But there is only the present, so you must love as best you can, or hope to find someone to love, even if it's only a compensation and, even if it's only a compensation, find a girl who loves you, because when you're a battle-scarred veteran you've seen too many loves stemming from infatuation and pity, and you know that there has to be more, there has to be more.

But it's peace now, he thought.

And I've known her, what, two days?

A soldier pushed his way past the row of knees to reach the vacant seat; he joked and apologized as he made his way there. Larsen couldn't place the accent and the soldier who was used to this sat down, sighed happily, turned to Larsen and said: 'I suppose you think I'm a South African.'

The curtain was down and the audience was fidgeting.

'I couldn't place you,' Larsen said. 'Is that a South African accent?'

'You wouldn't be far out,' the soldier said, beaming.

'I'm afraid—'

'I'm a Rhodesian, man, and proud of it.' He offered a pack of Rhodesian cigarettes. 'You a Yank?'

Without thinking Larsen said: 'No, I'm an Alaskan.'

The curtain went up and they both forgot all about it.

It was another symbolic setting; Larsen didn't know what. On an impulse he got up, the show only half-way through, and said to the Rhodesian: 'Enjoy yourself.'

'Don't worry, Yank, I will.'

He took in a movie at the London Pavilion. Then he made his way to the stage door of the Windmill. With a pair of nylons in his pocket.

They had been going out for ten days and, in their respective ways, they both dreaded visiting Denmark Street.

As they walked in the rain in Hyde Park he said: 'What is it with you? Are you ashamed of me or something?'

'It's not that, it's just, oh well, you don't know my street.'

'I haven't got leprosy,' Larsen said.

'You mean you *really* want to go there?'

'Well,' Larsen said carefully, 'I think I should, don't you?'

'Yes,' she said, 'you should.'

'Well, when? I promise I won't break wind or stick gum on the piano.'

'We haven't got a piano.'

'On your mother then,' he said. He took her arm. 'I know how you feel. I know how I'd feel. But it's got to be done if—'

'If what?'

They walked on in silence along the wet paths of the park, hearing the hiss of tyres along the Bayswater Road.

When they reached Marble Arch they agreed that he should make the pilgrimage to Denmark Street on Sunday when Ruth didn't work. It was very important to Richard Larsen that he should be accepted and for three days he worried about it.

Americans were greeted with reservation in Denmark Street: it was up to them to prove their calibre with something more than nylons, candy and cartons of Camel and Lucky Strike. Girls who went out with Americans changed stature in the eyes of the vigilantes behind the lace curtains: Americans were fast, they came from the fast cities of the movies, and by implication the girls who went out with them were fast. In a nearby street an American Marine who had got a girl into trouble had been savagely beaten up by two British soldiers. But the Americans had helped to win the war, they were smart, personable, clean-cut and loaded, and if their intentions were honourable, then the elders of the street accepted them. An engagement ring helped.

Mrs. Logan prepared the lunch with care. She had not yet conceded defeat and, while a bony leg of Australian lamb roasted in the oven, she planned her tactics.

Ruth was nervous. She dressed in slacks and blouse and sat in front of the mirror in her bedroom as the slothful, lunch-smelling Sunday morning developed; she could measure her life by these Sunday mornings – newspapers, tea-in-bed, the men off to the allotments – and it seemed significant that Richard Larsen should be intruding into this summer Sunday morning, a spectre of change.

She picked up the photograph of Bill on the dressing-table; he smiled at her and loved her from the past. If she had married him then the future would have been comfortable, assured, predictable. Nothing was predictable any more. The fortunes of war had brought her an alien from a celluloid world.

She thought she was in love with Richard Larsen but she wasn't sure of his feelings. He was attracted to her but war, or its aftermath, distorted emotions: you invested attraction with false depths, seeking permanence amid the impermanence.

Since Bill had died hanging from the tree at Arnhem she had wondered who would take his place; she had never doubted that someone would because she knew that in the young, grief, however genuine, doesn't endure. But she had never anticipated that he would be supplanted by an American, a race more foreign than any European. If he asked her to go to America could she do it? It would seem, she thought, applying lipstick, like an act of betrayal.

And what would he think of this street, lazing in dusty Sunday torpor, and this cramped little house? In a way she hoped that he would be condescending because then there would be no decisions to make: stop patronizing us and be off back to your Hollywood home on Long Island.

Ruth went downstairs. It was eleven-fifty and Larsen was due in ten minutes.

Mrs. Logan was in the kitchen in a housecoat and turban. The tiny joint crackled and hissed and the Yorkshire pudding blew bubbles. It smelled cosy; oddly enough it smelled of peacetime.

Ruth said: 'I hope you're going to change before he arrives.'

'He'll have to take us as he finds us,' Mrs. Logan said. 'This isn't Long Island.'

'Long Island doesn't mean anything in particular,' Ruth said.

'And I haven't got any ice for the drinks,' Mrs. Logan said, opening the glass door of the oven and peering in, 'so he'll have to sing for that.'

'He won't mind,' Ruth told her mother. 'He isn't fussy. You'll like him,' she said without conviction. 'He's very English in a way.'

'Does he want to stay in England?'

'I don't know about that.'

'I doubt it. They come and get what they can' – looking at Ruth meaningfully – 'and then they go back to their grand homes and forget all about us.'

'They haven't all got grand homes,' Ruth said. She smiled. 'Haven't you seen the Dead End Kids?'

Ruth went into the dining-room. The gate-legged table had been brought in from the drawing-room and it was set with lace mats that her father had once bought in Cyprus and wedding-present cutlery. There was a bottle of Algerian wine on the table and, on the sideboard, a quarter bottle of Haig. She looked around the small room with its tiled fireplace, its red-plush three-corner settee in the corner, the fawn wall-paper with the gold border that they had chosen years ago from a catalogue, the prints of The Changing of the Guard and Sunset over the Yorkshire Moors and felt immensely proud.

She hardly remembered her father. Only his patience and his rectitude and the Friday-night smell of beer on his breath and the expression on his face that night when he had been fired from his job at the sweet factory. He had loved sweets, had her father; not in the great vats of bubbling chocolate or vanilla-smelling toffee, but in the shops, on trays in the expensive shops up West; the toffees in twists of cellophane with silver paper underneath, the chocolates with little crusts of violet and rose-petal and crystallized fruit on top. She remembered him more clearly now. He had talked of owning his own sweet shop one day when, he said, she could eat herself sick; but, so her mother had subsequently claimed, he had been sacked because he was too artistic. One evening, after collecting the dole, after drinking two brown ales at the Royal Standard, he had been run down by a bus – outside a sweet shop.

Mrs. Logan passed Ruth on the way upstairs. 'I think he's coming,' she said. 'I heard the gate click.'

He was in civilian clothes and he had bought a bunch of red roses for her mother and a box of chocolates for her.

She felt very self-conscious, very conscious of her home. 'Would you like a drink?' she said.

He sat down on the edge of the three-cornered settee. 'Please,' he said. 'A beer will do.'

Oh God! 'We haven't got any beer. Will a Scotch do?'

'Sure – on the rocks.'

She began to resent his attitude. 'We haven't got any ice, we don't live in the tropics.'

'That's fine, I'm not a great Scotch drinker anyway.'

'Well, it's all we've got,' Ruth said.

'Scotch and water will be fine.'

He sat as though he were awaiting an interview while she poured them both a Scotch.

'Here's to us,' he said. He took a drink and dropped the glass just as Mrs. Logan came down the stairs.

He stood up, bunch of roses in one hand. 'I'm pleased to meet you, Mrs. Logan. I'm sorry about the—'

'Don't worry,' Mrs. Logan said. 'I'm glad to see it go. We had six. An anniversary present. That was the last.' She took the roses and smelled them. 'They're beautiful. Do you like flowers, Mr. Larsen?' And to Ruth: 'Get a cloth, dear, and clear up the broken glass.'

'I really am sorry.'

'Think nothing of it. Get him another drink, Ruth.'

Mrs. Logan sat in the easy chair beside the empty fireplace opposite Larsen. 'Well,' she said, 'I've heard a lot about you young man.'

'All of it good, I hope.'

'Most of it,' Mrs. Logan said.

A long, ticking pause. The Westminster clock on the mantelpiece chimed and an aeroplane droned across the sky. 'One of ours,' joked Mrs. Logan.

'I beg your pardon?'

'We used to try and decide whether they were one of ours or one of *theirs.*'

'Ah.'

Ruth came back with the fresh drink and took the roses from Mrs. Logan and put them in a jam jar in the kitchen.

When she came back her mother was saying: 'Everything must seem very cramped to you, Mr. Larsen.'

'Richard, please.'

'Doesn't anyone call you Dick?'

'No, as a matter of fact they don't. I don't know why.'

'Can't be helped,' said Mrs. Logan. 'And a drink for me, please,' she said to her daughter.

Larson, holding his glass very tight, said: 'I don't find it cramped. You know, there isn't too much space in the Bronx.'

'I suppose not,' Mrs. Logan said. 'Do you have a . . . a big home, Richard?'

'Just a frame house,' Larsen said. 'Nothing very special. My father's got a store,' he said, holding the glass with two hands.

'My late husband always wanted his own premises.'

'Ah.'

Ruth joined them, sitting next to Larsen on the three-cornered settee. 'Richard was wounded in the war,' she told her mother.

'Just a flesh wound,' Larsen said. 'In the thigh.' He patted his thigh.

Mrs. Logan looked interested, Red Cross instincts alerted. 'The Germans?'

'No, the Japs.'

Mrs. Logan relaxed; that was another war. 'Where was that,' she asked, 'in Burma?'

'No, Attu.'

The clocked chimed again. 'I don't think—'

'Don't worry.' Larsen took a sip of his Scotch. 'I doubt if many people in the States know where it is. It's in the Aleutians,' he told her and, to save her further embarrassment, 'in Alaska.'

'I didn't know there'd been any fighting there,' she said, and Larsen said: 'No, nor does anyone else.'

'Well,' said Mrs. Logan, 'lunch won't be long. Nothing special, mind. Just an ordinary, honest English Sunday lunch.'

'I've been looking forward to it,' Larsen told her.

'I'll go and see how it's getting on,' said Mrs. Logan, finishing her whisky.

When she had gone Larsen put his hand on her knee and said: 'Well, so far it's been a disaster.'

'That's because of your attitude,' she said.

'*My* attitude?'

'At least I'm being honest with you. Letting you see my background. Not like some girls who've gone out with Yanks. One girl I know said she lived at Castleford Estate and he thought it was some sort of ancestral estate and she never told him it was an estate of pre-fabs.'

He laughed. 'Stop apologizing. I think this is great, these streets, the people, it's all so compact. Hell, you should see some of our slums.'

She said: 'Mr. Larsen, this is not a slum.'

He held up his hands. 'I didn't mean that. You know I didn't mean that. I'm just trying to tell you that America isn't all honey and roses. I know of one guy who's dating an English girl. She thinks he owns a ranch when in fact he lived in a shack in the Appalachians. You see, it works both ways.'

Mrs. Logan brought in the lamb in its nest of roast potatoes. Then she brought in the Yorkshire pudding, its bubbles deflating, the first peas from the neighbour's allotment and a dish of mint sauce.

Mrs. Logan carved thin slices of meat. 'Cold meat tomorrow,' she said, 'and cottage pie on Tuesday. Corned beef on Wednesday, heaven knows what on Thursday and fish on Friday. That's the way it's been for years.'

Ruth uncorked the Algerian wine and poured it and grimaced as she sipped it. Larsen ate his lunch with enjoyment.

'Well,' said Mrs. Logan, as she cut open a floury potato, 'you two have been going out with each other for some time now, haven't you?'

154

'Two weeks,' Larsen said.

'And I suppose you'll be going back to America soon.'

'I don't know, Mrs. Logan. I'm waiting for a posting.'

'Have you ever thought about settling down here?'

Larsen chewed a piece of meat. He spoke guardedly. 'It's difficult to think of anything like that when things are so uncertain. You know, we're still fighting the Japs.'

Mrs. Logan was undeterred. 'What will you do when the war's over?'

'I don't know yet. I don't reckon anyone really knows.'

Ruth poured more Algerian wine, missing her own glass. 'Richard's thinking of settling in Alaska.'

'And live in an igloo?' Mrs. Logan asked.

'Alaska's not quite like that, ma'am.' Larsen told her about Alaska; it sounded as remote as the moon in the little lunch-smelling room.

'We've never travelled much,' Mrs. Logan said. 'We've always been very happy here. In many ways the war years have been the happiest.'

'I can understand that,' Larsen said. 'The cameraderie.'

'We were like one family in this road,' said Mrs. Logan. 'I don't think it will ever be quite the same again.'

Ruth cleared the plates. From the kitchen she brought a rhubarb pie, steam escaping from its crust, and a bowl of custard made from dried-eggs.

Mrs. Logan said: 'I shouldn't think Alaska's any place for a woman,' and Ruth thought: Oh God, here we go.

'Lots of women live there quite happily.'

'But they've grown up there. I mean an English girl wouldn't be able to settle there, would she?'

Ruth said abruptly: 'Who said any English girls were going to try?'

Larsen said: 'The English are probably the toughest race on God's earth. They'd colonize the place as soon as they got there.'

Mrs. Logan helped herself to a second helping of pie. 'What on earth would you do there?'

'I'm kind of interested in wild life, Mrs. Logan. I guess I'd become a bush pilot. You know, over there everyone travels by plane. They have planes like you and me have automobiles.'

'We haven't got a car,' Mrs. Logan told him.

'I didn't mean—'

'Our standards of living are very different to yours, young man.'

Ruth said: 'For heaven's sake, mother, stop jumping down his throat.' She tried to make her voice sound amused. 'He's only trying to explain about Alaska. I'd like to see it,' she said, surprising herself.

Larsen looked up from his pie. 'You would?'

'In a travelogue,' she said hastily. '*As the sun sinks low in the west* ...'

'In the summer it doesn't set at all,' Larsen said.

'Don't split hairs.'

They returned to the three-cornered settee and easy chair while Ruth made a pot of tea in the kitchen. Larsen offered cigarettes and Mrs. Logan took one, examining it as though it had a coded message inside. Larsen lit it for her. Mrs. Logan inhaled experimentally and, expelling smoke with every word, said: 'It was a great disappointment to me when Ruth took up with this life.'

'You mean the theatre?'

'I mean posing.'

'Have you seen the show?'

Mrs. Logan shook her head vehemently.

'It's tastefully done. Some of it's quite beautiful.'

'So you've already seen my daughter in ... in the flesh as it were.'

'From a distance,' Larsen said. 'And I am short-sighted,' he lied. He waited.

'And you still respect her?'

He looked at her in astonishment. 'Of course I respect her.'

'Well that's something,' Mrs. Logan said as Ruth came in with the tea on a tin tray.

Through the open window they could hear the rattle of the electric trains. A thrush sang in the laburnum tree at the end of the yard. Sunday afternoon settled somnolently.

They were beginning their second cup of tea when they heard a knock on the front door. Ruth went into the hall and opened the door.

Bill's mother stood in front of her.

'Hallo Ruth, dear,' she said, 'I've just come down from Leeds. I thought I'd pop down and see how you're getting on.'

Ruth stared at her.

From the dining-room Mrs. Logan shouted: 'Who is it?'

'Well,' said Bill's mother, 'shall I come in or shall we bring the chairs out here?'

Mrs. Logan shouted again: 'Who is it?'

'It's me, Edith.' She didn't exactly push past Ruth, but she was in the hall now, heading for the dining-room, a thin, blonde woman with Bill's eyes and the same North Country accent. Bill had been dead a long time but she still wore black.

Mrs. Logan stood up. She seemed at a loss. She waved her hand. 'This is Mr. Larsen.'

'Pleased to meet you,' Bill's mother said taking his hand.

'And you, ma'am.'

'You're American?'

Larsen nodded.

Understanding began to dawn on Bill's mother. 'You and Ruth?'

Mrs. Larsen tried to intervene but Larsen beat her to it. 'We've been going out for a couple of weeks.'

'I see.'

Outside the thrush sang with happiness.

Bill's mother said again: 'I see.' And then: 'All very cosy.'

Mrs. Logan said: 'Now, Edith—' and Ruth said: 'It was a long time ago—' and Larsen looked from one to the other and Bill's mother said: 'And to think that my Bill wanted to marry you.'

'He would have been a very lucky man,' Mrs. Logan said. 'Poor Bill.'

Bill's mother backed into the hall. 'I've no doubt you were carrying on while he was hanging from that tree at Arnhem.'

Ruth said: 'That's a despicable thing to say.'

'Is it? Not content with flaunting yourself naked on the stage

157

while he was still fresh in his grave you've taken to going out with Yanks.'

Mrs. Logan, the organizer, took over. 'Now that will be enough, Edith,' she said, standing in front of her. 'Life has to go on, you know that. Ruth loved your Bill but it was a long time ago. A long time when you're young. Now she's met Richard and he's a very nice young man. You should be ashamed of yourself behaving like this in front of him. We all know how you feel, we grieved for Bill when he died. But Ruth has her life to lead.'

'Aye,' said Bill's mother, 'on her back.'

The front door slammed behind her, like a gunshot, ripples of sound filling the house. The thrush stopped singing. They stood in the dining-room as in a tableau. Mrs. Logan sighed. Then she turned to Larsen. 'Sit yourself down. I'm sorry that had to happen. But you mustn't feel too badly about her, Bill was her only son.'

Larsen said: 'I'm sorry, too.' He glanced at his watch. 'But I think I'd better be going.'

Mrs. Logan pushed him gently into the chair. 'You'll do no such thing. You'll sit down and have another cup of tea. We've got a lot to talk about.'

Ruth excused herself. She went up to her bedroom and, when the anger had faded, wept. Downstairs she could hear Larsen and her mother talking.

They were sitting on a bench in a park that had been dug up for allotments. Even before the war it had on the surface been a drab spot, dust and string-like grass in the summer, cold mud in the winter, bounded on all sides by terraces of houses. But, despite the cracked boating pool, the deserted bandstand and the shifty lavatories it had provided pleasure for mothers and children on the balding grass, for footloose dogs, for girls on Sunday evenings awaiting overtures from loud, shy boys; for courting couples behind the laurel bushes where many of the children who later crawled on the grass had been sired.

There were no railings now, just sawn-off stumps, and lettuce and peas and beans and new potatoes grew in salad-green rows where the lawns had been.

She crossed her legs that were finely-shaped and, behind the knees, somehow vulnerable. She said: 'Well, that was a disaster, wasn't it?'

He put his arm round her waist. 'I don't think so.'

'Come off it, Richard, it was a nightmare.'

'Look,' he said, 'your previous fiancée's mother turned up. That was bad luck. But there was no secret about Bill, was there?'

She shook her head.

'I guess I can understand the way she behaved. But she did me a favour. Your mother and me were like a couple of old buddies after she'd gone.'

'And that is an achievement,' Ruth said.

'The salt of the earth your mother. She and the others like her won the war.'

'It's incredible that you got on,' she said. 'It's more than that: it's a bloody miracle.'

A mongrel dog, brown and undistinguished with a beard and begging eyes, sat in front of them and laughed as it begged.

Larsen stroked it. 'Sorry, old buddy,' he said, 'I've only got gum.' As he stroked it he went on talking. 'I don't know how to put this. No one ever does, I guess.'

She guessed what was coming: she knew the preliminaries but – Bill apart – they had never mattered before.

'You know what I'm going to say?'

She was confused. 'Perhaps . . . I don't know.'

'I'm asking you to marry me.' He went on stroking the dog which was wagging its tail. 'I haven't got much to offer but I love you and I reckon that's enough.'

'It's more than enough,' she said.

She leaned down and stroked the dog. The dog, amazed at the attention, stood up and begged.

'Well?'

'I don't know what to say. I don't know if I could ever leave all this,' gesturing at the park and the slow-moving buses and the terraces with their Blitzed, boarded-up windows. She thought it was the most ridiculous remark she had ever made.

'I understand that.' He straightened up and the dog looked at him with reproach. 'I think I know what it's like to be a Londoner. But you're a girl with spirit. You can't stay here forever.' He took out his cigarettes, lit two in his mouth and handed her one. 'You probably think I'm crazy talking about Alaska. But it's the one place I know of that's unspoiled. I know I sound like a travel brochure but it's true. You know, the Last Frontier. But it's going to need help. There are a lot of guys like me who got hooked on Alaska and most of us are going back. Alaska needs its Statehood – you wouldn't understand about that – but it's got to come. Then we've got to fight another battle.'

'Against what?'

'Against civilization. Against the spoilers. Alaska's a rich place, there are fortunes to be made and we've got to stop it being exploited. When I left Alaska I wasn't sure whether I'd go back. But I've seen a lot since then, a lot of war. It's the only place I know of where there's something worthwhile to do. And I know it sounds corny,' he finished.

'No it doesn't. It doesn't sound corny at all. But I don't know. I don't know if I would match up to it.'

Then he spoke to her as Ott the Indian had once spoken to him. He told her what he had seen; he told her about Mount McKinley and the fields of fireweed and the squeaking of the lemmings and the smell of clean snow and the green twilight of summer nights.

'First we'd go to New York,' he said. 'When the Army's all through with me. Then we'd take off for Alaska. I guess I'd get some sort of grant from Uncle Sam and learn to fly.'

He felt in his jacket pocket. 'Here, I brought this.' He brought out a purple-satin box; inside was an engagement ring, a single, brilliant-cut diamond. He slipped it on her finger. 'So what do you say?' He kissed her.

'I don't know.'

'Do you love me?'

She nodded. 'Yes, I love you.'

'Then you'll come?'

She stroked his cheek. 'I need a little time.'

It was then that he told her that they didn't have any time: he was being flown back to the States in two days time.

She worried about it in bed that night. And she knew that she had to make up her mind before he left, because when he left it would be too late; that's the way it had been during the war and it hadn't changed, not yet.

When she got home her mother had made them a cup of cocoa and said: 'He seems a nice boy.'

'He is,' Ruth said.

'He's your steady, isn't he?'

'The first since Bill,' Ruth said.

'Don't worry about Edith. She didn't really mean what she was saying. You can't stay in mourning all your life. Life is different to when I was a girl. I only went out with one boy and that was your dad. But the war's changed everything.'

They were in the kitchen facing each other across the table. Ruth was surprised at her mother's understanding and it occurred to her that perhaps she had never given her mother a chance to understand. Supping the scalding, bitter, watery cocoa she realized that the necessity of making a decision was making her into a woman; that until now she had been a spoilt girl.

Her mother said: 'He wants you to go to America, doesn't he?'

'He asked me this evening.' She took the ring which she had slipped off her finger out of her pocket and showed it to her mother. 'He wants to marry me.'

Mrs. Logan examined the ring and said: 'It's a beauty,' and asked, 'Why aren't you wearing it?'

'Because it wouldn't be honest. Not if I'm not going to go.'

'Only you can decide,' Mrs. Logan said. She lit one of the cigarettes that Larsen had left behind. 'But let's get one thing straight – don't let me influence you. Don't stay here because of me. And I mean that, Ruth. It would have been just the same if you'd married Bill and gone to Yorkshire. You're twenty now, time for a girl to leave home.'

'It sounds as if you want me to go.'

Mrs. Logan finished her cocoa. 'I want you to have a chance to go into the world and breathe. All the young men in the street have gone away and learned to breathe. You should go and breathe as well, that's what the war's done for us, taught us that we should go out and breathe. Those of us who are still young enough.' She stood up and kissed Ruth on the cheek. 'Now you go up to bed and think it over. I've got to be up early in the morning, I'm organizing a reception headquarters for the lads who were in POW camps.'

But she still worried as she lay in bed and heard the Westminster clock downstairs chime two. Many of the girls she knew wanted to marry a Yank, preferably an officer, and to go and live in a big white house in a tree-lined avenue with a couple of sharp-finned cars in the driveway and a black nanny and a cook. She knew that when their lovers were posted, many of the girls would never hear from them again; some would go to America and some might have a big white house but others would move to another boxed-in life where only the packaging was different. The Americans were different: that was their attraction, not just the nylons and the candy: they were easy and sure of themselves and they were the means of escape. Just as the girls that the British soldiers brought back from France, Greece, Belgium, Holland and, soon, Germany, were different and therefore desirable. Am I merely attracted by the glamour of a different way of life? Did I mean it when I said I loved him in the park or were those war-time words, genuine but inspired by circumstance, by impermanence, by the haste of war?

She worried about it while she slept that night and when she woke and while she posed on the stage. She worried about it while she drank tea with the other girls in the dressing-room and while she dressed before meeting him at the stage-door when he would ask her to tell him her decision.

Can I leave England for ever?

To Alaska!

The stage-door keeper handed her an envelope. 'Message for you, Miss Logan.'

She opened it. *Can't make it tonight. Had to report to base. Luv (British spelling) you.*

But he could have phoned.

And this was the brush-off. She had seen it happen many times.

And he was leaving the day after tomorrow.

She stared at the ring on her finger.

She pushed past the stage-door crowds and walked down Shaftesbury Avenue to Piccadilly.

There was a hollowness inside her. It had taken this to make her realize that she did love him.

She got up late next morning with the worthless day ahead and when she got downstairs he was there sitting on the three-corner settee and he smiled at her and, after he had drunk his tea, they went to the park where he kissed her and she clung to him crying while he said: 'Well, will you come?' and she said: 'Of course I'll come, whatever made you think I wouldn't?'

CHAPTER TWELVE

CHARLES BROWNING adapted. He wanted to stay in the Army but he couldn't so he used the remaining war years as a bounty. He applied himself to laying the three foundations of success as he saw them: graduating from Harvard, penetrating the sanctums of the oil industry and marrying the daughter of the president of the oil company that employed his father.

He had planned to leave marriage as late as possible. But his father's influence was waning in the company – his mannered charm no longer cut much ice – and Browning knew he had to get Judy Thackeray to the altar before it was too late. It was one of the top twenty weddings of the year in New York and would have been one of the top ten if Browning had still been in uniform.

For their honeymoon they went to Miami where, after they had made love in the penthouse suite of a beachside hotel, while they were drinking champagne, she said to him: 'So, you made the first round.'

'Come again?'

'You made it, you married the boss's daughter. It's a sort of classic, isn't it.' She was lying naked, the corner of a pink sheet just covering the top of her thighs.

He poured champagne, watched the bubbles rising in the glasses in thin lines. 'I guess it is.'

'At least you're honest about it.'

'Well, it's true, isn't it. The only difference is that I wasn't necessarily on the make. You know, it wasn't the chauffeur who knocked you up and put the squeeze on your old man. I mean, I'm not exactly on Skid Row.'

'Now you're being dishonest,' she said. 'You were on the

make. It was Ivy League stuff but you were definitely on the make.'

He sipped his champagne. He felt lazy after the love-making. He grinned at her. 'Okay, I was on the make. Nothing wrong with mixing business with pleasure is there?'

She moved the coverlet from his body and touched the scar with the white-flesh stitches on his belly. 'You're quite a bastard, aren't you?'

He considered this. 'I'm not sure. Does ambition make me a bastard? If it does then I'm a really mean bastard. And what's so wrong with marrying the boss's daughter anyway? We go well together.'

'Oh yes,' she said, 'we go well together. I've never believed that garbage that opposite poles attract and we're two of a kind. But it would be nice,' she said, 'to think you loved me.'

'And it would be nice,' he said, 'to think you really meant that. Let's face it, Judy, we're good for each other. Maybe that's our version of love, I wouldn't know. I know you're the most attractive woman I've ever met and I think you're attracted to me. What more could a couple want? I mean, maybe we've got more than most couples have on their honeymoon night only they're not smart enough to know it.' He drank some champagne. 'Don't worry, I'll be a good husband – and I guess you'll be a good wife.'

She propped herself on her elbow, breasts small and firm. 'And if I hadn't been the boss's daughter, would you have married me?'

'No,' he said.

'Thanks a million,' she said.

'Don't knock it. I'm telling the truth. You *are* the boss's daughter and honesty is one of my qualities that you admire. How would it have been if I'd given you a firm, dry little kiss and said, "I'd have loved you if you'd been the milkman's daughter"?'

'I would have said you were a goddam phoney.'

'And that I'm not.'

'No,' she said, 'you're not. On the make yes, a phoney no.' She touched the scar again as though feeling his pain. 'I might even accept that you're honest with me. But are you honest in business?'

'Hell no.'

'Thank God for that,' she said and laughed.

'But I'm not a crook. What's the difference between dishonesty and smart practice? What's the difference between smart practice and normal business practice?'

'You tell me,' she said.

'Okay, there ain't no difference. Only in the interpretation and outcome. One means you're a success, the other means you're a loser.'

She took the champagne glass from him and drank from it. She handed it back and told him: 'you won't be a loser, that's why I married you. But I want us to make our own way, not through my old man, not through yours . . .' She hesitated.

'You make it sound as if he's on the way out.'

'He is,' she said. 'That was another reason you married me. Now, was that smart practice or business practice?'

'Very smart,' he said. 'I'm one big smart-ass.'

'Do you ever apologize?'

'Not often. I did once – when a guy nearly lost his leg to save my life.'

'He sounds like a loser,' Charles Browning's wife said.

'Maybe.' Browning got up and walked naked to the shell-pink bathroom because he didn't want Richard Larsen in the conversation.

When he came back, drying his hands on a pink towel she said: 'I'm serious, we've got to make out by ourselves.'

He put on a yellow beach robe and stood at the window. Sometimes he wished he smoked: it gave you time, composure. Below he could see the bodies grilling beside the blue pool, paunchy men, women in curlers, beautiful girls, playboys with nose-shields perfecting their tans before moving in on the blue-rinses at the bar. Beyond he could see the beach and the waves pushing in from the Atlantic which was almost as blue as the pool.

Still staring at the sea, beyond to the horizon, he said: 'Sure, we'll make out on our own. But everyone uses what they've got, their birthright if you like, to build on. I would be crazy not to use what my father's got – his knowledge, his influence, his friends – to make the start.' He turned and faced her. 'We'd both be crazy if we didn't use what we've been given. It's our legacy.'

He half expected contempt; but, no, she was too smart. She had made her point: Independence, but qualified independence. She saw it his way: Make your own way but use the success of others to get there. It was, he decided, going to be a very happy marriage.

She said: 'Astor started from nothing. Vanderbilt started from nothing.' She caught hold of the belt of his robe and pulled him towards her. 'But I guess you're right. They'd have made it quicker if their fathers had been president of an oil company.'

'And maybe they wouldn't,' Browning told her. 'Maybe they wouldn't have had the impetus.'

'But you have, haven't you, my darling.'

'Oh yes,' he said. 'I have. Because gutters are only relative and I want to drag myself out of my particular one.'

'And you will,' she said and pulled the belt of his robe so that it fell open and put her arms round his waist and said: 'But that's not the only reason I married you.'

As his father's influence diminished so did the sycophancy towards his son; Charles Browning sensed it and rejoiced at their ineptitude: if you're going to be a sycophant for God's sake be an efficient one – go foraging and find out that I'm going to marry the boss's daughter. He noted the identities of the bullshit brigade because this knowledge would be useful when he formed his own company. He would take with him the brains and leave behind the bullshit.

After his marriage the sycophants once again invited him to their homes but, with his boyish smile, now revealing sharp teeth, he declined. And when he went for a drink at the dark bar off Madison he went in the company of sharp young men on their way up, turning his back on the worried men with alcohol flushing their cheeks and loosening their tongues.

He visited the company's wells and refineries; he studied the evolution of hydrocarbon. He studied the politics of oil and found that it didn't merely influence Washington: it was part of Washington. If you were a VIP in oil then you were a voice in the land.

When Browning senior retired with a golden handshake his son employed a Madison Avenue company to prepare a report on the commitment of oil-state governors, senators and congressmen to the oil companies. He was astonished by the report: graft, corruption and kick-backs were the rule rather than the exception. Politicians and oilmen fed off each other. Browning locked away the report in a wall-safe in the apartment he had bought on Michigan Avenue in Chicago; it would, he decided, be one of his greatest assets.

When he was promoted within the company he began to make precise plans for his future. As he saw it, it wasn't where oil had already been struck that mattered: it was where it still lay trapped and untapped that counted. But these details were as closely guarded as a miser's hoard and not even the president's son-in-law could unlock them because they were the secrets of oil giants who wanted to prevent a glut of petroleum that would cut their profits and give the American motorist cheap gasoline.

Remembering what Ben Harper had told him, Browning followed the progress of the Navy's exploration of Alaska's North Slope at Petroleum Reserve Number Four, Pet Four. They were already hinting that the amount of oil there didn't justify development. But Browning wasn't surprised when a subsequent Geological Survey indicated vast stores of gas and petroleum below the frozen crust. Even an Eskimo named Taluk had guessed it was there.

What Browning needed to find first was a nice, unprepossessing piece of land with oil beneath it, not in Alaska because old man Thackeray had confirmed that there was a gentleman's agreement not to drill for oil up there and, at the moment, the *gentlemen* were too powerful for Browning. So Browning employed a scout.

His name was Trusz and he was a second-generation Pole

from Los Angeles. During the war he had worked for Allied Intelligence and had been dropped behind the German lines at the time when the Germans were razing the Warsaw ghetto. He had enjoyed his spying and had returned to the States with his medals to take up industrial espionage.

He was a smallish man with a shiny face and pink cheeks; he was plump and he wore old-fashioned suits and stiff white collars except when he was buzzing oil installations in a Piper PA-14. The contours of his belly tended to deceive people about the strength of his shoulders, and the deception was compounded by his small hands with their manicured nails and shiny fingertips.

They were a card-player's hands and this was the weakness of Ernie Trusz – gambling. He would bet a year's wages on the depth at which they struck oil, on the outcome of a snake fight in Florida or the number of letters captioning the first cartoon in the *New Yorker*.

Browning examined the files of each of the company's scouts and settled on Trusz as his own personal spy. He decided to meet him in a conducive atmosphere and, when Trusz was on vacation in Los Angeles, Browning had him shadowed so that he was able to meet Trusz by chance in Las Vegas.

Browning found Trusz sitting at a roulette table in a house on Fremont Street with a brandy and soda on a little tray on one side of him and two stacks of chips on the other. Browning stood behind him, took a Scotch from a plump-breasted girl in a jump suit, and saw that Trusz was not merely a compulsive gambler: he was a very bad one.

Trusz, who looked highly professional with the stiff white collar sawing into his neck and his clean neat fingers drumming on the table, was playing a straight martingale system which Browning, who had studied gambling on the journey to Vegas, recognized as a guaranteed short-cut to bankruptcy.

The system was simply doubling up on even-chance bets: it had helped to make the casino proprietors of Monte Carlo and Nice rich and happy men.

Trusz was laying out $256 on the ninth bet on black when Browning took up his position behind him. The croupier, swarthy, slick and impersonal with a DA hairstyle and a tuxedo with watered-silk lapels, spun the wheel, and the group that had collected behind Trusz waited tensely. Trusz took a gulp of his brandy and soda; the pink-shelled fingers of his other hand drummed the table. The ball bounced coquettishly before dropping finally into a red slot.

Trusz's fingers stopped drumming.

Browning's only reaction was contempt. Yet he knew it was weaknesses such as this, obsessions, greeds and conceits, that would provide his footholds.

Trusz, now committed to recouping his losses, doubled up for the tenth bet, $512. He took another drink, the ball tumbled, his fingers beat their restless tattoo. Red.

The final bet. $1,024. Surely it was inconceivable that the ball could drop into eleven red slots in succession. Surely the Law of Averages couldn't fail, after all, it was a law.

Red.

The croupier scooped up the chips. The crowd sighed and broke up. Trusz stood up and walked past the one-armed bandits to the bar.

Browning sat two stools away while Trusz ordered another brandy and soda. Trusz didn't appear distressed: it had happened before, it would happen again and there would be the times when he won, the ultimate time when he would win a fortune.

Browning ordered himself a beer. He said to Trusz: 'That was bad luck.'

Trusz didn't look up. 'That's the way it goes,' he said.

'But that's a hell of a way to go about it, doubling up.'

'Yeah? You know of a better way to lose your dough?'

'Well, there are better martingales than that, I guess. But progressions are the only way to win.'

'I know about progressions,' Trusz said.

'Then why not use them?'

Trusz sipped his drink, gazing at the rows of bottles behind the bar with its brass foot-rail and cushions of red-imitation leather. Behind them a woman in a silver-fox stole, wearing a gardening glove on her lever-pulling hand, was feeding silver dollars into a machine and humming nursery rhymes.

Trusz said: 'You like 'em, you use 'em.' He fingered his neck where the collar had sawed a pink line.

Browning shrugged. 'It was just a suggestion.'

Trusz turned and stared at Browning. 'Don't I know you?'

'Yes,' Browning said, 'we work for the same company. I recognized you at the table.'

'You're Browning's son?'

'That's right,' Browning said. 'Let me get you another drink.' He ordered another beer and another brandy and soda.

Trusz looked at him contemplatively. 'What brings you to Vegas?'

'The same as you, I guess.'

'You a gambling man?'

'No, I'm on my way to L.A. I just thought I'd drop by and see the action.'

'Well,' Trusz said, 'you saw some.'

'Are you going to play the tables again?'

'You kidding?'

'Why should I be kidding?'

'I'm cleaned out,' Trusz said as Browning moved up one stool, 'broke, busted. I got the fare home and that's it. And you know something?'

Browning shook his head.

'My luck was going to change. You know, Madame Roulette was sulking back there. But she's sure as hell due to come out of her sulks. So there was a streak of reds while she was sulking. So why not a streak of blacks now? All I got to do,' he confided, 'is go back there and wait till the next run is over. Red or black, I don't give a shit. When one or the other's finished then Ernie Trusz gets in there with his chips.'

'Why not try a progression?' Browning asked.

'Because that ain't gambling. That's mathematics, mister.'

'Gambling's a mug's game,' Browning told him.

'Sure it's a mug's game. But you can be a lucky mug. Did you ever hear of the Neopolitan martingale? No? Well, I knew a guy who used to clean up $2,000 a day with it. Now he owns a couple of motels in San Diego and lets out rooms to the Marine officers from the base and their broads.'

'Anything based on luck is strictly for losers,' Browning said.

Trusz said: 'Yeah? Well maybe you're right. Maybe we all got rocks in the head. So, what the hell, we have fun. Much more fun,' he said slowly, 'than smart guys. Guys who are always on the make. Guys who can't relax to scratch their balls. You know, smart guys who have to marry some dumb broad just because she's the boss's daughter. In my book,' Trusz said, drumming his fingers on the bar, 'any guy who gives up his liberty to make his pile is a mug.'

Browning pointed at the pay telephone at the end of the bar. 'I've only got to pick that up to get you busted.'

'Pick it up then,' Trusz said. 'Then I go and work for the opposition. See how your daddy-in-law would like that. I reckon he'd be tickled pink that his smart-ass son-in-law has dispatched Ernie Trusz over to Standard Oil with all his secrets.'

Browning grinned at him: 'Maybe we're both mugs.'

'Yeah, but I'm a fun-loving mug.'

'A different concept,' Browning said. 'There are different ways of having fun. Each to his own.'

Behind them they heard the sound of money. The machine that the woman in the silver fox stole was playing was having hysterics; money gushed from its innards, spilled over the floor, dropped on the worn red carpet. The woman produced a small sack with the brand name of a fertilizer stamped on it and ladled in the money. She was still humming to herself and she looked, Browning thought, as if she were kneeling on the carpet weeding her garden.

Trusz licked his lips. 'A lucky mug,' he said.

'You really think you've got it going for you now?'

'I feel it,' Trusz said.

'How would you like an advance?'

'An advance on what, charity?'

'An advance on your salary. I have the authority.'

'And why the hell would you do that?'

'Because I think you're a mug. Because I don't think there's any such law as the Law of Averages and I don't believe in lucky streaks.'

'I'll say this,' Trusz remarked, 'you're no mug. *You* don't stand to lose a nickel.'

'And, according to you, you could be on your way to a fortune.'

'Okay,' Trusz said, 'give me the advance.'

Browning took out a notebook and made out a debit slip for $1,000 in lieu of salary. Trusz signed the slip of paper and Browning handed him $1,000 in twenties.

'You want to see the old Neopolitan martingale in action?'

'I'll count the winnings,' Browning said. He walked out of the casino, past the woman in the silver fox stole who was feeding her winnings back into another machine.

Two days later Ernie Trusz owed the company $3,000.

Browning drove out to the motel where Trusz was staying on the edge of the town rooting itself in the desert. The motel looked as if it had been half-finished for a long time, as if the owner had lost the balance of the bricks and mortar on the tables.

He asked for Trusz's room and the girl at the desk said: 'Eighteen, first floor, second door,' without looking up from her movie magazine.

Trusz was lying on one of two single beds rolling dice. He had taken his shoes and jacket off but it was the absence of the stiff shiny collar that made him look bare, but not vulnerable because you could see the thick neck and shoulder muscles. He didn't look up. He said: 'I thought you were on your way to L.A.'

'I am,' Browning said, 'when we've cleared up the matter of these debit slips.' He took them out of the inside pocket of his light-weight suit and held them up like playing cards.

Trusz rolled the dice on the soiled sheet. Two fours. 'What the fuck do you want?' he asked. 'It was a set-up, wasn't it. Now I ask you, what the fuck do you want mister?'

Browning put away the debit slips and sat on the other bed. There was no air-conditioning and the air was hot and wet and smelled of mould. There was a damp patch on one of the white-painted walls and a panel of ceiling board was hanging down; a tap dripped in the bathroom cubicle, there was a row of cigarette burns on the edge of the dressing table.

'Just a talk,' Browning said. 'Shoot the breeze a little.'

'It's got to be something to do with the company, hasn't it.'

'I think,' Browning told him, 'that you and I can do a little deal.'

'I don't like deals,' Trusz said, tumbling the dice from the leather cup. 'I work for Ernie Trusz and that's enough headaches.'

'I'm looking for a partner,' Browning said.

'You got yourself a partner, you got the boss's daughter. I can't compete with bosses' daughters. What do you want anyway?' He rolled the dice; one fell off the bed and he rolled it again. A three and a one.

'You're a spy, huh?'

'A scout is what I am.'

Browning let it ride. 'And you have information which even the boss's son-in-law isn't supposed to know about.'

He put his hands behind his head and addressed the plasterboard ceiling. 'How would you like to work for me?'

'I already got a job. Why the hell should I want to work for some junior executive?'

'Because,' Browning said, 'I'll have lots of dough soon and I'll pay you more. And as I go up you'll go up with me.'

'Bullcrap,' Trusz said, cradling the dice lovingly in one hand.

'What do they pay you?'

'None of your business, mister.'

'I know what they pay you,' Browning said. 'And I'll increase it by fifty per cent.'

'You got the dough?'

'I will have,' Browning said.

'Sure. And I'll break the bank at Monte Carlo some day.'

Browning hoisted himself on one arm. Through the finger-smeared window he could see the desert with the heat bouncing off it.

'Got a cigarette?' Trusz asked.

'I don't smoke.'

'A healthy smart ass, huh?' He straightened a butt in the ashtray beside the bed and lit it with a match from a book provided by the casino on Fremont Street. 'Why aren't you in the Army, mister, if you're so goddam healthy?'

Browning told him about Attu and his wound.

'Attu? Where the fuck's that?'

Browning told him.

'I caught a bullet too.'

'Where?'

'In the leg.'

A little cameraderie, Browning decided, had been established. 'So,' he said, 'do you want to be a partner?'

'No dice. Why the hell should I? I do all right. I make enough to lose on the tables, on the tracks, at craps.'

'Okay,' Browning said, 'then I'll make that phone call.'

'Like I said, feel free.'

'And then I'll phone Standard and every other goddam oil company in the States. These three slips of paper' – Browning patted his inside pocket – 'say that you're in debt. They also say that you're a gambler and therefore unreliable because each one says the dough was borrowed at Vegas and you don't borrow money in Vegas to buy furniture.'

'You're a nice sonofabitch, aren't you.' There was a hint of respect in Ernie Trusz's voice. 'And fresh out of your cradle too,' he said, coughing as he drew on the cigarette butt. 'What the hell are you going to be like when you go onto solids?'

'Rich,' Browning said.

'I wouldn't bet against it and I'm a betting man.' Trusz popped the dice into the leather cup and rattled it. 'What do you want anyway?'

'I want all the dope you get about our explorations and rival explorations channelled to me before they reach the top brass.' He held up his hand. 'It won't be any skin off your nose because no one will know. In return you can have these three debit slips back and another three grand on top of that. When I make the break you will come with me with fifty per cent on top of what you're getting now. How about it, Trusz?'

'Spoken like an officer and a gentleman,' Trusz said.

'How about it?'

'You got the three grand there?'

Browning showed him three rolls of $20 dollar bills.

Trusz peered into the leather. 'Let's see what the dice say.' He murmured into the cup, held it high over his head, rattled the dice, whopped it down onto the sheet.

Two sixes.

'Hallo, partner,' Trusz said.

Two years later, long after the Japanese had surrendered in August 1945 after the atomizing of Hiroshima and Nagasaki, after the birth of his first son Robert, after the death of his father, after he had sold the baronial mansion on Lakeshore Drive and rented an apartment for his mother in downtown Chicago, Charles Browning bought a vast ranch at knock-down prices in Arizona.

The vegetation was sparse and even the scrub on the low hills looked sick. The rancher who sold out was delighted with the price and the neighbouring ranchers were almost as happy that a dude had been suckered.

As the cattle died off and the scrub died of thirst Browning looked suitably stricken. But it was difficult. How can you look suitably stricken when, according to Trusz, the arid wasteland on which you're standing covers a deep dark lake of oil?

CHAPTER THIRTEEN

Judy browning understood her husband. *The trouble with my wife is that she understands me*. That's what he would have to say if he ever had an affair.

Not that she thought he would, she decided, as she walked through the streets of the Loop ordering food and drink and flowers for their wedding anniversary party that evening.

No, he wouldn't try that, she told herself again as she breathed spring for the first time that year and stopped outside a florist's window blooming with daffodils and tulips, because this marriage was the most important chapter in *Business Practice* and it was bad practice to jeopardize such a marriage.

She went into a florists. She touched the blossoms of jonquils, purple and yellow irises, maiden-hair fern; she breathed hothouse scents – summer caged inside spring. 'What beautiful flowers,' she said, bending to smell a cluster of violets. 'I'll have them all,' she said, gesturing with her hand.

'All of them, ma'am?'

'All of them,' she told him, seeing the penthouse as a spring garden, and when he had added up the total on the cash register she wrote out a cheque and told him to deliver them not later than four so that she could arrange them before her husband flew in from New York.

All I ask, she thought, as she walked down the street past girls in yellows and greens and pinks, like first butterflies, past jobless young men from the war looking for work and hopeful today in their summer suits, all I ask is that he's honest with me.

But he is, she decided, drunk with the day and the after-shower smell of the breeze coming in from the lake. Why should he be otherwise? Why should he, at twenty-six the youngest member of the board, spoil anything by cheating?

He had phoned her two days ago from New York and he had promised to be back for the party when she would tell him that they were going to have another baby. As she went into the shops she imagined she felt the baby stir but that was ridiculous because Dr. Steiner wasn't even sure that she was pregnant. But anything was possible this day, the premature stirring of a tiny, half-formed hand, a pulse in the heart that was feeding from her.

He was a good father, she reminded herself, as she crossed the street to the liquor store. In his business way. And she didn't mind that either, the partings and the late hours because it was part of her role. And in a way it was better that he spent so much time in New York because of the homecomings that were almost ceremonial. If you were an executive's wife you expected this; she had seen it with her own parents.

There would be ten of them for the party, including her parents, so she ordered ten bottles of Don Perignon. After the guests had gone they would drink a bottle together and then, when Robert was settled, and the nanny had retired to her quarters, she would tell him that she thought she might be pregnant and then they would make love. As she headed for the hairdressers, high heels tapping, yellow spring coat flapping, she wondered what snotty, Vassar-educated rich-bitch Judy Thackeray would have thought about all this *schmaltz*.

Judy Thackeray would never have admitted it, she decided as she stared at herself in the hairdresser's mirror, but she would have envied me.

She told the hairdresser to style her a pageboy because that was the way it was styled when she met Charles Browning.

He was due at seven and it was only six forty-five but she was restless in the hot-house, flower-filled penthouse while the waiter in the blue jacket circulated with a tray of champagne glasses.

'Don't be hard on him if he's late,' her father said. 'I know what it's like.'

'And that goes for me,' said her mother. 'You're married to oil, darling, you're married to a gusher.'

Her father was in his sixties. Unlike Charles Browning he had come up from nothing; he was proud of it – and told you so – but he didn't envy Browning his short-cut. 'Wish I'd been smart enough to marry the boss's daughter,' he was fond of saying before squeezing his wife's arm to indicate that he was joking. Judy's mother was younger than her husband but looked older; riches had come to her late in life and she found it difficult to become accustomed to them and used them without grace, as her servants confided to the servants of other rich families. Her frail hands were weighted with rings and she used too much perfume. But they had been good for each other, Judy thought, and they were both as hard as diamonds.

She drifted around the other guests, mostly oil men and their wives with a couple of rail-road executives from the Browning side. Browning's mother had been invited but she had been indisposed: her husband had been voted off the board and, so she believed, had died as a result. She blamed Thackeray who, she managed to imply, wasn't out of the upper drawer.

A champagne cork popped. Six fifty-five. Outside, the spring day was fading and Judy Browning began to wonder if this flower-bed of a room wasn't perhaps a little ridiculous.

By five minutes past seven he hadn't arrived and she told herself: don't be stupid, it doesn't matter. The plane's late, the traffic's heavy on the airport road.

By ten past seven she began to worry. Supposing the plane had crashed. She called the airport. No, said the girl's bored voice, the New York flight had been on time.

At seven thirty she said: 'Well hell, you guys, let's cut the cake,' but her father said: 'No, give him another ten minutes, I know what it's like,' squeezing his wife's arm.

At seven forty-five they cut the cake, demolishing the lowest tier so that there were two tiers left with HAPPY ANNIVER-SARY still intact in pink iced sugar on the top.

By eight o'clock the flowers had begun to wilt; the guests were looking at their watches. Judy Browning had drunk too much champagne.

'Don't fret,' said her mother. 'Charles will get here. Don't give him a hard time when he does. I've had a lifetime of it.'

At eight-fifteen the first guests left.

When Mrs. Browning senior, indisposed, called to see if her son had arrived from New York Judy was short with her on the phone.

She drank another glass of Don Perignon. She wondered if Dr. Steiner had been right; she didn't sense life inside her any more.

When the last guests were leaving she apologized on behalf of her husband and they all assured her they understood, business was business, but the faces of the wives were knowing and complacent because, for the moment, they were secure.

She was left with her parents.

'Don't fret,' said her mother.

'Charles knows what he's doing,' said her father.

At nine the telephone rang.

She picked it up. His voice was tinny and distorted. 'Hi, honey,' he said, 'happy anniversary.'

'Happy anniversary shit,' she said. 'Where are you?'

'Where am I?' A pause. 'Didn't my secretary call you?'

'No one called me.'

'But I—'

'Where are you, Charlie?'

'I thought you knew.'

'Where, Charlie?'

'I'm in Alaska,' he said.

They were playing golf on the tailings of a derelict gold mine. Charles Browning and a Japanese American named Nagata who had summoned him from New York.

Browning drove the ball powerfully, watched it soar into the pale evening sky, hover and drop a hundred yards short of the green. Nagata, squat and strong with slightly protuberant teeth and blue-black, razor-cut hair, dropped his ball onto the edge of the green.

They shouldered their clubs and made for the green.

The air felt wet and a great barrel of cloud hung over the small city of Juneau.

Nagata, wearing gaberdine slacks, brown and white shoes and a fawn windcheater, said: 'Did you know we're walking on a fortune?' He asked questions even when he was answering them. 'Is it possible that there's a million dollars worth of gold beneath us?'

'Why don't they get it out?' Browning asked waiting patiently for the Japanese to come to the point of the meeting, and knowing that it would be a circuitous process.

'Why should they start mining when it would be uneconomic? After all, aren't there far greater riches in Alaska than gold?'

'Such as what?'

When Nagata did make a statement it had added emphasis. 'Such as salmon, copper, a hundred different minerals.'

Were they nearing the point? Browning made the green with his second shot. The Japanese dropped his ball to within twenty yards of the hole.

As he lined up his putt he asked the Japanese which was the greatest of Alaska's riches and when Nagata said salmon he was disappointed because he knew it wasn't true. 'Anyway,' he asked as his impatience ran out, 'what's the deal? Why did you send for me?' He made his shot and the ball stopped ten yards short of the hole.

Nagata squatted by the hole and gazed at his ball. 'Did I say there was a deal?'

'You sure as hell implied there was one.'

The Japanese addressed the ball; there was fifty dollars on the game and Browning reckoned that the frustrating conversation was part gamesmanship. 'Isn't it true that you would like an interest in Alaska's future?'

'Who told you that?'

'Didn't you once meet a man named Ben Harper?'

The Japanese putted and the ball rolled smoothly into the hole. 'Before he died he told me that you were interested.'

'Ben Harper's dead?'

Nagata picked the ball out of the hole. 'He was found dead in his cinema two weeks ago.'

'Well I'll be damned,' Browning exclaimed.

'Let us hope that he is not?'

Browning was thinking of Ben Harper's rusty laugh in the Fairbanks cinema as he made his putt – and missed. He swore softly. 'So what's the deal, Nagata?'

'Would you like a share in a canning factory? You would, perhaps, like to become the major shareholder?'

As Browning drove off again he said: 'Perhaps you'd better explain and stop being so goddam oriental and enigmatic,' as he pulled the drive and watched the ball drop a hopeless distance from the green.

With a series of questions and a few statements Nagata explained his proposition as they made their way round the course.

Nagata was in the importing business, in particular importing canned salmon from Alaska to Japan. He also owned a cold-storage plant in Juneau and a couple of canning factories in Ketchikan. He knew of another factory that had been run down, the owners from Outside had made their bundle and had let it fall apart.

The factory hadn't yet been put on the open market but it was available at a knock-down price – 'a crazy price', Nagata said. So why should a smart young businessman like Browning be interested? 'I will tell you why,' Nagata said.

His company was prepared to rejuvenate the factory, to put new machinery in. If Browning bought the major share in the factory then he couldn't avoid making a fortune.

'But why me?'

'Because we need you.'

'Why, for God's sake?'

Nagata made a gentle putt into the last hole. It circled the lip of the hole, hesitated and dropped in. 'Wasn't it fifty dollars?' the Japanese said, thrusting out his hand. Sticking the bills in the pocket of his windcheater he said: 'Can we discuss it back at the hotel because it's going to rain, isn't it?'

In the lounge of the Baranof Hotel, decorated with paintings of Alaskan scenes, they drank highballs served with glacier ice.

'Okay,' Browning said, sucking the ice, 'why pick on me?'

Nagata leaned across the table. No questions now: this part of the conversation was vital to Nagata. 'Because you are in oil,' he said and held up his hand to forestall questions. 'You, Charles – if I may call you that – are a rising star, like the rising sun' – his plump lips quivered – 'in the oil industry. And the oil lobby is one of the most powerful in the United States. Am I right?'

Browning nodded.

'Well, as you may know, there is a strong movement in Alaska for statehood. They complain about taxation without representation.' He tinkled the ice in his glass, a fragile, oriental sound. 'No one Outside with business interests in Alaska wants it to become a state. You are, I am sure, aware of that.'

'Because a State government would slap whopping great taxes on your profits?'

Nagata placed his hands together as if praying, rubbed them slowly together. 'Precisely. That is the principal consideration. We fear that a State government would introduce conservation and that would be very bad for the industry.'

'But very good for Alaska,' Browning said.

Nagata spread his hands. 'Alaska is a big place. It can stand many incursions . . . Is that the right word?' He hurried on. 'But I am sure that you see my point.'

Browning ordered two more highballs reflecting that two drinks was his limit during business hours. 'I see your point.'

'You are an intelligent man, Charles.' The slightly protuberant teeth tapping on the inside of his glass. 'We in the canning industry have a strong influence in the territorial legislature. You may have heard of W. C. Arnold?'

No, Browning said, he hadn't.

183

'Well, Bill Arnold is a very smart guy. He is general manager of the Alaska Canned Salmon Industry and he has a lot of influence in the territorial legislature. He also has many friends in Washington – in the Senate and the House of Representatives. But the power of the Statehood crusade is growing. You know, there is a lot of patriotic sentiment for Alaska since the war.'

Browning grinned at him. 'Yeah, I know about Alaska during the war. Your mob nearly killed me.'

Nagata bowed his head. 'Not my mob, Charles, I fought the Germans at Monte Cassino with a sub-machine gun and a samurai sword.' He raised his head. 'But we are digressing. Is that the word?' He held up one hand again. 'As I say the movement is gaining momentum. The Governor, Ernest Gruening, is behind it and he is a man of great influence. There has been a referendum and Alaskans have voted three to two in favour of Statehood. And then there is the Alaska Statehood Association.'

Outside rain was falling steadily, the smell of rain on dust reached them in the lounge. The rain increased Browning's impatience: he had little interest in the historic development of Alaska. He glanced at his watch. 'So in return for a canning factory you want me to get the oil lobby to oppose Statehood?'

Nagata nodded twice, slowly. 'If you would be so kind.'

'I'll see what I can do. How much is my share in the factory going to cost me?'

'Well, the profits from red caviar alone will run into millions.' He took a black, gold-embossed notebook from his pocket and wrote down some figures with a gold pen. Then he looked up, lips quivering. 'You have already paid me fifty dollars for the golf. Let's say another fifty to make it a round figure, shall we?'

Standing on the brink of the deep milky melt lake, staring into the timeless blue ice, Browning was overcome by a sense of peace, of contented helplessness. Perhaps it would take a hundred years, a thousand, before oil flowed from the punctured skin of Alaska; but that didn't matter, not at this moment.

He walked back to his rented car as the glacier inexorably moved a fraction of the width of a moth's wing.

As he drove the sense of peace faded but the helplessness remained and he wasn't sure whether it was born of this view of impassive creation or knowledge of his own destiny.

CHAPTER FOURTEEN

HE sat on a tree stump in a clearing beside the rotting fishing boats watching the villagers carving a totem pole. Six of them worked on the twenty-five foot long tree and, with chisel, knife and axe, they were fashioning the top of the pole into the head of a raven, the sacred bird of the Tinglits.

Ott watched with shame and fascination as the sneering beak of the bird began to take shape under the blades of the carpenters.

The totem pole would serve no sacred purpose. The Indians were civilized – they had bad teeth to prove it – and it would be admired by tourists when it was transferred to a village on the domestic airline routes. The tourists would take coloured slides of it, grinning families gathered at its base, and would be projected onto screens all over the North American continent.

The embryonic totem pole, mysticism and commercialism combined, symbolized Ott's dilemma. Ever since he could remember his loyalties had been divided and with them his instincts.

His parents in this village where he had been born had been converted by a Presbyterian missionary who had persuaded the villagers to burn and bury their totem poles and Ott had been brought up to speak English instead of Tinglit.

He had studied hard, obtained a grant for the University of Alaska, had graduated as a fully fledged white man. But his blood was Indian and not even a transfusion could change that.

A white Indian.

A raven flew down from the swift-moving clouds and perched on the roof of a brightly-painted wood shack to look with wicked eyes at the Indians carving its effigy in wood. Goddam ravens, Ott said to himself, as he lit a cigar and narrowed his eyes as the breeze blew the smoke into them.

At college he had studied zoology and learned to respect the heart-beat of life in creatures other than humans, but even then he felt that his motives were suspect, that his subsequent crusade was a tactic to divert attention from the Indian–white man complex, that he had latched onto a white man's obsession to identify himself with the alien race, because the Indian instinct was to kill in order to eat and be warm and Ott knew that at heart he was a hunter.

When he left University he worked for equality for his territory and for its natives, he sought an end to the slaughter of animals but, when he realized that he was only playing a game, a futile exercise against the overwhelming power of the rapists of the land, he took himself to the East Coast of the United States to preach his doctrines to eager students who didn't really give a damn.

It was then that he began to drink.

And drank like an Indian, badly.

The war gave him a cause. Helping to organize Gruening's Guerrillas, he half-hoped that the Japanese would invade so that he could fight, exercise the predatory impulses inside him. He stopped drinking.

When the war was won he found that there were now worthwhile causes to fight and he rejoiced. The movement towards Statehood inspired by his war-time leader, Dr. Ernest Gruening, was gathering momentum and a few white men were beginning to accept the idea that the natives had a place in Alaskan society.

For the most part Ott kept his complexes bandaged but the bandages sometimes wore loose, resentment frequently exposed like a raw wound to the wind as when he left his office of the Bureau of Indian Affairs in Fairbanks and walked down Fourth Avenue, looking at the notices in bars and the restaurants banning minors and natives.

It was then, when he entered one of these establishments, perhaps with a white man, perhaps with his wife, a white woman, that he felt his betrayal. I should walk into these places

187

in full tribal dress with a scalp in each hand and put an arrow through the heart of the first white man who objects.

But he continued to live as a white man because was he not, after all, civilized and entitled to enjoy their benefits? Was he not living as a white man to get a better deal for the Indian? Hypocrite, he cursed himself, as he took his place at a table with his blonde wife – *they always go for the blondes, those natives* – and tasted the wine and ordered his steak medium rare from waiters who bowed and called him sir, a waiter who *knew*, as Alaskans knew, and showed that he knew with heavy-handed servility, bowing too low when Ott over-tipped, over-reacted.

But it had not always been so because the Tinglits were the bravest Indians in Alaska, they had never been suppressed by the Russians, their code was revenge, forgiveness was weakness, and it followed that Ott had to revert when he reached the bad end of Fourth Avenue where natives and roughnecks and rummies gathered one summer day before the law banning racial discrimination was passed.

The sign outside the bar stated NO MINORS, NO DOGS, NO NATIVES. In bold black letters. Now or never Big Chief Ott in your fancy grey mohair suit and your plum-coloured bow tie and the cigar screwed into your face.

He walked into the bar, shading his eyes to get accustomed to the dark until he saw the hunched shapes at the bar, liquor glasses held in two hands in case they flew away.

The bouncer was good at his job. He claimed he used his nose. 'I can smell 'em, even when they come in wearing fancy threads. The day an Indian or an Esky gets past me I quit and go back to the Outside.'

The bouncer, who was also the owner, wore baggy-assed pants and a cheap blue shirt with the sleeves rolled as tight as rubber bands round his biceps. He weighed two hundred and twenty pounds and his great belly was his bouncer, the belly of a cop who has spent too long behind a desk, a massive belly but a formidable one.

He glanced at Ott. For a moment the clothes and the haircut confused him. Then those old olefactory senses took over. He gave his gum a final chew and spat it out. Thumbs in his belt he winked theatrically at the nearest rummy who took no notice. He smiled amiably at Ott. He said: 'Sorry, buster, didn't you read the notice?'

The Tinglit blood tingled. So they were banning Indians from slop-chute bars now ... Revenge, oh how they had revenged themselves on the Russian hordes. To hell with the white man, to hell with hypocrisy. He glanced outside and saw a raven circling the sky.

He said to the bouncer in his best Bostonian: 'I beg your pardon.'

'Don't come that crap with me. You might be an Indian but you can still read.'

'Sure, I read the notice.'

'Then get your ass out of here.'

If you deny your heritage now, Ott, then you are indeed a low-caste shithead.

'I don't have a dog,' Ott said.

'Come again?'

'I said I don't have a dog.'

The bouncer felt he was losing face in front of the rummies who might be transfixed over their glasses but were listening all the same.

'Listen craphead,' the bouncer said. 'For your information no one's talking about dogs. The words say NO NATIVES.' He jerked his thumb. 'Now git.'

Ott sat down on a stool at the bar. 'I think a whisky and soda would be nice,' he said.

'A whisky and soda, huh?'

'Yes,' Ott said. 'Chevas Regal if you have it.'

'Well I'll be a sad bastard,' the bouncer said; and to the rummies: 'You guys, we have a funny man in our midst.'

'With a little ice,' Ott said. 'But not too much. You know, it's a good old Scotch and the proportion of water and ice must be just right.'

'For the last time, craphead, move.'

'But I'm over twenty-one and I haven't got a dog.'

'We don't serve niggers,' the bouncer said.

'Do you mean Indians?'

'You heard what I said.'

'Ah.'

Ott got off the stool and faced the bouncer. His voice was still Bostonian, perfect. His tone was silky. He said: 'Get me a Scotch, pig.'

The eyes of the rummies moved towards them, hands tightening on their glasses. A car roared past leaving dust in its wake. An old dog peered into the bar.

The bouncer swung. Ott moved back so that the swing lost its power and parried the blow with his left arm. He then kicked with the side of his foot, bringing the edge of his shoe down the fat man's shin so that he could feel the skin coming away from the bone and, as the fat man instinctively bent towards the pain, he brought his knee up into his face, and then chopped at the back of the neck with the back of his left hand making sure that he didn't break any bones and kill him. As the bouncer hit the floor Ott kicked away the knife he had drawn from the sheath at the back of his belt.

Ott said: 'Now get up, craphead.'

The bouncer stood up and removed a broken tooth from his mouth. This time Ott hit him on the jaw with his left elbow, followed by his left fist, then his right fist and right elbow as he fell.

The bouncer tried to get up and Ott kicked him on the side of the head. 'Us Indians fight heap dirty,' he said. He went to the door of the bar and came back with the old dog. 'I'm under twenty-one,' he said, 'I'm a native and I've got a dog. Now get me a Scotch.'

The bouncer stood up. He made his way round the bar holding on to the edge. The rummies got out of his way before resuming their positions. The bouncer poured him a Scotch.

Ott poured it on the floor.

'A Chevas Regal, pig.'

'I ain't got Chevas Regal.' His voice was thick and phlegmy.

'Then the best you've got.' Ott pointed behind the bar. 'Johnny Walker Black Label will do. Not too much soda and a little ice.'

The rummies licked their lips. He tasted the Scotch and smacked his lips appreciatively. 'Just what the doctor ordered,' he said. 'And now some water for my dog.'

'You can go and get—'

Ott broke the glass on the bar and held it in front of the bouncer. He gave the bowl of water to the old dog. Then he threw some coins onto the bar. Then he walked out of the bar.

Outside the dog cocked its leg against the bold, black-lettered sign.

Part Two

CHAPTER FIFTEEN

HE was late and Ruth Larsen was frightened, her fear compounded by the first touches of winter – a wafer of ice on the lake that morning, the keen young wind coming off the mountains, the smell of cold gathering, the sky so pale that the evergreen trees looked black.

As always she dreaded winter, although when it arrived and settled she didn't mind it because of its finality, because, although you could freeze your lungs by breathing too deeply and suddenly, and the wolves came close, there was also a rarefied security, a togetherness, with the stove glowing and books to read and their son asleep in his cot. Tenderness and physical love were heightened as the wind piled snow against the outside of the cabin.

The absurd cuckoo on the wall-clock stuck its head out: it was six p.m. Richard had said he would be back by five-thirty after flying two wealthy Americans on a fishing vacation back to Anchorage. She opened the door of the cabin and stared at the pale sky, shielding her eyes with one hand. A hundred yards away the dogs in their enclosure started barking; they had been barking that morning, too, which made Ruth suspect that there were wolves in the vicinity.

In the distance she could see McKinley, or Denali, the Tall One, as the Koyukon Indians had named it. And, as she waited for her husband to return, she thought: What am I doing here? And she wanted an autumn that was red and gold and smoky, she wanted a Westminster chiming clock instead of an idiot cuckoo and, as the mountains began to recede in the late afternoon light, and the loneliness embraced her she began to cry for the first time since she had come to Alaska four years ago.

Long Island had been the transition. They had been married in London and she had arrived on the Island while Richard was being discharged and had stayed on with his parents while he was learning to fly with a Government grant in New Jersey.

She had settled down easily although it had taken time to accept the luxuries of the land.

Refrigerators, central heating, chromium-plated limousines. The stores with their well stocked shelves of canned food, the liquor shops with bottles stacked like shells in an armoury stunned her when she remembered her mother returning from Mrs. O'Driscoll's shop at the end of the street with a finger of butter, a morsel of cheese and a twist of tea.

At first her relationship with Richard's parents was a shy one. Her speech sounded affected. She had difficulty in persuading them that her stage career hadn't been quite the same as Gypsy Rose Lee's, although she noticed a quickening in her father-in-law's interest when she first said she had stripped.

Then she discovered that, whatever they thought of her, they were friendly because they wanted her as an ally in their campaign to keep Richard in New York. But this, she knew, was impossible because, like so many other young men who had returned from battle, he would never settle in the slot carved out for him in his youth.

The campaign didn't last long. The lean, restless man who had returned was a stranger to his parents. And they, so he told her, had aged dramatically so that the defeatism of middle-age was settling into acceptance. There had been a small scandal when his father had been convicted of allowing his shop to be used for betting; the disgrace had aged him, but it had also brought home to him the futility of trying to enlist his son into the business. They tried for two or three weeks until his father said: 'I guess I can't expect my son to go into business with a crook.' Then he sold the shop.

Richard Larsen's sense of guilt lifted. He wouldn't be deserting them: he saw them sitting on the lawn with their scrapbooks and albums of photographs of the days when he was a boy, memories of all that had been good open before them. This was a bonus of war, that the young had realized that they do not belong to the old and the old had realized it too.'

So the break was easy.

At first his parents had difficulty in comprehending that their son was going to Alaska. Before his departure there was a cere-monial lunch on the lawn with a turkey roast and pumpkin pie and jugs of Californian white wine. Then Richard Larsen picked up his bags and left his wife and mother crying at the door – 'You look like something out of an old Nelson Eddy movie,' he shouted, blinking his eyes.

He took the railroad to Seattle, then flew to Anchorage where he booked into a small wooden motel a block from down-town Third Avenue while he established himself before his wife arrived. He made a pilgrimage to the far side of town but the apartment block where she had lived had been torn down to make way for a depot with barbed wire on its walls. He read the girl's note; then he placed it deep in his wallet. *It's only now that matters.*

He bought an old Dodge and drove to Merrill Field to begin his career as an Alaskan bush pilot, to fly by the seat of his pants, to join the ranks of crazy men who took their stubby aircraft up in storms and white-outs and put them down on rivers and glaciers and mountain ledges.

Ever since he had watched aircraft lowering themselves from the grey ceiling over the Aleutians Larsen had been reading about Alaska's bush pilots. He knew them all as other men know the Red Sox or the Yankees.

And when he arrived at Merrill Field it was a photograph from one of the books he had read. Pilots with oil on their faces, engrained in their hands, leather-faced and wrinkle-eyed, wearing scuffed leather jackets and flying boots. Patching and sewing and feeding their old ships.

Richard Larsen, war-veteran and *cheechako*, stood and watched with awe and hesitated to approach these men who flew and crashed and flew again and somehow managed to stay alive. He walked into the photograph, there were the wooden hangars, shacks and stores, only the control tower was modern.

Yet at this airfield there were ten thousand arrivals and

departures in one month, more than La Guardia handled. He watched the little aircraft stumble across the field and take to the air where, in the autumn sky, they looked suddenly light and fragile, and come bouncing down, agile and waspish until their propellers were feathered and they were still. Larsen smelled aviation fuel and oil; and he wanted to be at the controls of one of these ships, looking down at Alaska.

He approached a small sandy man painting a red single-engined Cessna, applying the last few touches as carefully as a woman making up her face. He was humming to himself; there was a lot of red paint on his face and hands. He looked up. 'Hi,' he said, 'you want to fly?' He put down his paint brush. 'I can always tell a guy who wants to fly. They have that look about 'em.'

'I want to buy an aircraft,' Larsen said.

'So you want to buy a ship, huh? How do you fancy this beaut?'

'How much?'

'She's yours for ten thousand dollars and a bargain at that.'

'I couldn't afford that,' Larsen told him.

'I can arrange terms, boy. How does a hundred dollars a month grab you?' He wiped his hands on his leather jacket. 'How about a coffee? Do you fancy a coffee? God's drink, coffee. Then we'll do a deal, huh?' He took Larsen's arm. 'Do you play poker?'

'A bit,' Larsen said.

'Christ you got to play poker, boy, if you're going to fly in Alaska. That's all there is to do when you get holed up in some shack up north when the wind's blowing.' They went into a shack with a desk and two aeroplane seats either side of it; a telephone, a manual on flying and a fat dog simulating death on a rug. The sandy man who wore a pair of sun-glasses with one cracked lens stuck out his hand. 'George Mint's the name, known as Minty. Welcome aboard. You done much flying?'

'About sixty hours.'

'Sixty, Christ?' Mint sat down as though he had been struck. 'Sixty, Jesus! That's like asking a baby how long he's been walking and he tells you since yesterday. Sixty, Jeez.' He lit a cigarette and looked at Larsen. 'And now you're going to tell old Minty that you ain't never flown in Alaska.'

Larsen grinned. 'I ain't never flown in Alaska.'

Mint slumped in his chair at the second blow. 'And you want to buy my Cessna? Jesus, if I sent you up in that baby I'd be a murderer, that's what I'd be, dammit.'

'I wouldn't kill myself.'

Mint tapped ash onto his trousers. 'I wasn't thinking of you, son, I was thinking of that beautiful ship. That's what I'd be killing if I let you up in it. The beautiful bastard would end up like one of them.' He pointed at the photographs on the wall and Larsen noticed that they were all pictures of wrecked aircraft. 'I crashed every one of those beauts,' Mint said proudly. 'But you've got to know how to crash 'em and you don't crash 'em into the side of The Mountain. No, sir, you've got to learn how to crash. And *you*' – stabbing his cigarette towards Larsen – 'have got to learn how to fly all over again because flying in Alaska ain't like flying nowhere else in the world. Do you know how to crash a ship nice and pretty?'

Larsen shook his head.

'Well, I'll tell you how to crack up the easy way. If you're out of gas and you're coming down on a small field you've got to knock off your landing gear as you come in and take a slide on the belly and you got to let one wing take the force of the landing.' He picked up a pencil and burrowed in his ear with it. 'You ever flown with skis or floats?'

Larsen shook his head.

'Jesus! You almost make me speechless and no one's done that to Minty yet. So how would you take off from a small lake, son?' he asked as he poured coffee as black as night from a stained Thermos.

'I guess,' Larsen said slowly, 'that I'd go round and round it to get up speed and make a turn into the wind.'

'Pretty good,' Mint observed. 'Pretty damn good. I'll make a bush pilot of you yet. You've got to learn every goddam river and stream because that's the way to navigate. Follow the streams and avoid the mountains.'

'I've been studying the terrain with maps,' Larsen said.

'Yeah? You might as well study my ass as one of them navigational maps. Look, son, if you put Alaska on a map of the States it would stretch from Seattle to Miami, with the Aleutians that is. It's got thirty-three thousand miles of coastline and three million lakes over twenty acres, and it ain't no use trying to memorize them from maps. No sir, you've got to know her like you know a woman. A bend in a river, a geyser, the tilt of a mountain. These are what you navigate by. And you've always got to be looking out for places to land because one day you'll need 'em.'

Larsen had read that Alaskan pilots were laconic; another of the great misconceptions of Alaska, he decided as Mint paused to drink his coffee. He said: 'Sure Mr. Mint – Minty – but I've got to get up there to learn all this.'

'Sure you have. You want to fly now?'

'That would be swell,' Larsen said.

'Okay, we'll take the Cessna up. Your first lesson.' He stood up. 'How much money you got?'

'About four thousand bucks.'

Mint sighed. 'Okay I'll charge you ten bucks a lesson which will near as dammit break me but what the hell, I like to fly. Then we'll buy you a ship, a nice old crock so that when you have your first crack-up you can't do too much damage. Maybe a Stinson or an old Wasp Hamilton.'

They went outside and climbed into the red Cessna and taxied to the end of the field where Mint talked to the control tower as if he were talking to the man next to him at dinner.

Then they were bumping across the field until the lovely breathless moment when they were airborne. Soon they were climbing into the blue sky and the fields and town below were small and vulnerable and life was the throb of the engine. A sudden tilt of the wings, and they were climbing through shreds of cloud and the Cook Inlet was flat and molten behind them and the Chugach Mountains were the spine of the world and this was why he had come back to Alaska.

Mint jerked his thumb towards the mountains. 'As many bodies down in them ravines as you've had hot dinners. There's ships gone down there that we've never sighted.'

They flew over Knik Arm, picked up the railway to Fairbanks. 'Railways is for cattle,' Mint said. 'Planes is for people.' He banked and there was nothing beneath them except the green and brown land touched in places with early snow.

Mint said: 'Want to fly her?'

Larsen's hands were sweaty. He took over the controls. The Cessna wobbled. 'Relax,' Mint told him. 'You're flying like you were firing a gun for the first time.'

The Cessna settled. A great exhilaration came to Richard Larsen. I am in control. I am driving this beautiful red bird in the sky. We weren't meant to fly but I am doing it; I have conquered. He banked, he climbed, he dived. He wished Mint would stop talking.

'See that hill down there?' A hump in the endless land. 'I call that Senator's Ass. You know, we've had a few of those guys up here and they're all ass-holes in my book. There's landmarks in Alaska that you'll never find in any goddam books printed in Seattle. We named 'em – Windy Pass, Bullshitna Lake, Molly's tit . . .' He stopped talking and for a few moments there was just the sound of the engine. 'Hey, we'd better go down. Looks like that guy's in trouble,' pointing down.

Larsen looked down. 'I can't see anything,' he said.

'Ain't got your Alaska eyes yet. You'll see it as we go down.'

'You're going to land down there?' Larsen stared at the spruce forest and lacework of streams.

'I got to. There's a guy in trouble. See it now?' As he took over the controls he banked and Larsen saw a single word spelled out with logs in a clearing. HELP. 'That's old Marvin Winter. He's a trapper. It must be something pretty bad because he's a tough bastard.'

'I can't see anywhere to put her down,' Larsen said.

Mint peered down. 'Neither can I. But we'll find somewhere. There's always a field some place. But it ain't the getting down it's the getting up again that scares the shit out of me. The trick is to get your props flattened so's you get the lift. And never put down on ice till you've tested it or someone else has. Touch it, caress the goddam stuff with your skis before putting down.'

They were coming in low and the trees which had been pencil points were big and thick and still there was no landing ground and Larsen wondered if Mint might be contemplating putting his ship down on the tree-tops.

'They rely on us these guys, trappers, prospectors, screwballs. Boy, the flights I've made for these guys, me and every other goddam bush pilot in the territory. Sometimes the prospectors blow themselves up with dynamite and we have to fish 'em out, or what's left of 'em. I picked up a pregnant Indian girl once and her time was near but I didn't know how goddam near and when I looked round there she was – having the kid.'

The tops of the trees were just below the wing-tips. Ahead Larsen saw a narrow clearing where they'd been felling trees. 'There we are,' Mint shouted. 'There's our field.'

Larsen looked down in alarm. 'What about the stumps?'

'We'll have a look-see.'

Mint took the Cessna down below tree-top level to buzz the clearing. 'I think we can make it,' Mint said. 'A baptism of fire, son. Here we go. You know' – as the plane dipped over the trees – 'on the Outside' – as the Cessna sank towards the ground – 'they say they can always tell an Alaskan pilot' – as the wheels touched and they bounced once – 'because he always pulls short on a runway' – as they headed for a tree-stump – 'and now you can see why we get used to pulling up short' – as they stopped three yards from the stump.

They climbed out and walked to the trapper's log cabin and Mint told Larsen that getting the ship up again was going to be 'kind of tough' and the only thing for it was to dynamite the tree-stump in their path if Winter had any dynamite and that, even with the stump gone, it was going to be a bastard of a take-off.

'You'd do well on the airlines,' Larsen told him. 'You'd give the passengers confidence.'

When they reached the cabin the trapper was at the door. He was leaning on a stick and they could smell his leg as they got close. He was a bull-shouldered man with a sailor's beard, but his eyes were sick. He said to Mint: 'What kept you?'

They went inside the cabin where the smell was bad. Winter

told them that he had caught his leg in one of his own traps. The bandage, made from a sheet, was stiff with blood and pus. 'Going mouldy on me,' Winter said.

'Let's have a look,' Mint said. When he unwrapped the bandage the wound was full of pus and the flaps of flesh were turning yellow. 'Yeah,' Mint said. 'We'll have to get you to hospital if you want to hold onto that leg. What did you treat it with, paint?'

'Whisky,' the trapper said.

'Yeah, bad whisky.' He threw the bandage out of the open door. 'Ain't no point in keeping that on. You got any dynamite?'

'Nope. Spanish Joe has. Got a place downstream.'

'How far?'

'About five hours,' the trapper said, lying down on a heap of furs, his stinking leg sticking out as though it belonged to someone else.

Mint turned to Larsen. 'Better set off now, son. You've got yourself a ten-hour hike.'

'How the hell do I know where Spanish Joe lives?'

'Like the man said – downstream. Just follow the stream. We sure as hell can't get that ship airborne with that stump in the way. I do the flying, you do the hoofing, boy.'

It took Larsen four hours, walking beside the stream that pushed its way through forest, circumvented hills, nosed through soft earth. It collected sand-bars along the way, combed boulders and sometimes dropped down ravines before steadying itself in deep quiet pools where fish hung as dark as sharks. Beside him was the dusk of the forest and he wondered if there were bears there and what the hell he would do if there were because he had grown up a little and he understood that out here you had to kill to live and he had brought the trapper's Winchester. He would never kill for sport, he would never fly hunters to their killing grounds, but he would kill – to eat or stay alive – because here that was the law.

Once he saw a bald-headed eagle; it had been hunted almost to extinction in the States yet here it was, here in the Great Land, an arrogant refugee.

It was two in the afternoon when Larsen reached the cabin where Spanish Joe lived. Spanish Joe was dark with a Mexican moustache and yellow teeth; when Larsen arrived he was pulling porcupine quills from the muzzle of a malamute dog. He didn't look up. He said: 'I guess you want dynamite.'

'Well yes,' said Larsen who also wanted food. 'How the hell did you know?'

'There ain't no secrets out here. You can hear an old brown bear two miles away. You can smell a fire from three miles.' He held the dog's head firmly as he pulled out the needles with a pair of pliers. 'He's plumb stupid, this mutt. Third time this year he's stuck his nose into a porky.' The malamute wagged its tail. 'And when I saw old Minty's plane putting down I said to myself, "That Winter's in trouble and Minty's goin' to pick him up but sure as hell he can't take off with all them tree stumps" so when I heard you coming I said to myself. "He's coming for dynamite to blast one of them stumps." '

'And you were right,' Larsen said.

'Well he can have some dynamite. Tell him it'll cost him ten bucks.'

'His leg's in pretty bad shape.'

'Yeah? Guess he caught himself in one of his own traps again. Well tell him he'd better leave the money in his cabin in case something happens to him.'

'If you knew he was in trouble,' Larsen said carefully, 'why didn't you go and help him?'

Spanish Joe looked up. His eyes were dark and the moustache made him look mean. He carried a knife in his belt. 'I didn't know he was in trouble till I saw Minty's ship. That's why I didn't go and help him *cheechako*.'

'I'm sorry,' Larsen said. And then: 'Do you have anything to eat?'

'It'll cost you,' Spanish Joe said.

'I'll pay. I haven't got any money with me but I'll pay. But what,' he asked, 'happened to the Brotherhood of the Bush?'

'I never joined,' Spanish Joe said. 'I'll fry you up some beans and a bit of moose and you can tell Winter that he owes me another buck.'

With the sticks of dynamite in the pocket of his windcheater, rifle in one hand, Larsen set out for Winter's cabin half an hour later. He followed the stream again but the water seemed colder now with the sky turning green. The coldness came in from the forest, too, and there were movements in the green-black depths. Once he heard a noise which sounded like a short-sighted bear heading for the stream; he hid behind a crop of rocks but the noise receded.

When he got back to Winter's cabin the trapper was delirious and the smell of his leg was overpowering. Mint was pampering the Cessna which he had taxied to the far end of the clearing; he had also drilled a cavity in the tree-stump. He jammed the dynamite into the cavity, and retreated with the fuse. 'Ornery stuff, dynamite,' he observed as he lit the fuse. 'Never know which way the blast is going to go. Might knock the cabin down, might blow the Cessna up for the quickest take-off it's ever had.' The fuse spluttered and they ran for the cabin.

Silence closed around them. The explosion hurt their ear-drums, the blast rushed past them into the forest where it lost itself. Inside the cabin the man with the rotting leg screamed. But the tree stump had disappeared.

'Okay,' Mint said, 'let's go.'

'Isn't it too dark?'

'If we stay the night Winter loses his leg and maybe his life.'

They carried the trapper into the Cessna and laid him on a bed of skins. There were stars in the green sky.

'Still don't know if we can make it,' Mint said as the engine fired. 'Them trees look pretty high to me.'

They began their bouncing run. Mint pulled the stick back. The wall of trees came at them; Larsen wanted to shield his face with his arms but that wouldn't do, not in front of Mint who was humming to himself.

Larsen heard the tops of the trees brush the undercarriage, then they were climbing towards the cold stars.

Mint began to talk again.

'Now that Bob Reeve, there's a flier for you. Once he lands on a mountain and a williwaw hits him.' He paused. 'You know what those sons-of-bitches are?'

Larsen said he had experienced williwaws in the Aleutians; after that Mint treated him with more respect, but not much.

'Well this williwaw picks up his ship with him in it and tosses it over a precipice. So what does he do? Opens up the engine and tries to fly the bastard. But then they go into a spin bouncing off the sides of the precipice. Then, goddamit, he levelled out just above the ground flying like he was just taking off from some neat little strip.'

The sky darkened and the smell from the trapper's leg got worse while the trapper talked disjointedly in his delirium and Mint talked to Larsen and to the control at Anchorage.

They began to descend. 'Want to take her down?' Mint asked and Larsen replied. 'I'll leave this one to you.'

Then the airfield lights were streaking past them, then slowing, and an ambulance with a flashing red light drove up beside the Cessna.

They taxied to Mint's office where the fat dog was still asleep. 'That'll be twenty dollars,' Mint said as he began to write in the coffee-stained, cigarette-burned, grease-smeared, dog-eared volume that was his logbook.

Larsen heard later that the trapper's leg would probably be saved.

Larsen flew with Mint for six months and crashed twice in the asthmatic, single-engined Stinson he bought from another flier – once with skis trying to land on a frozen river with overflow; once when a gust of wind blowing through the Chugachs flipped him over as he tried to land on a snow-field. The impact started an avalanche so that they had to dig the ship out.

He cabled his father for a loan and bought a Piper PA-14 to go into business flying trappers, prospectors, climbers, fishermen. He also bought a cabin beside a lake north of Anchorage with the idea of flying expeditions to McKinley and the other peaks in the range.

Beside the cabin he levelled a strip and, with Mint's help, built a small hangar. By break-up of the following year he was in business with Larsen Airlines. He had memorized landmarks within a three hundred mile sweep of Anchorage; he had learned to read the sky so that he could take off in ground fog knowing that it would be clear and blue above; he memorized the twists of deep pass as a racing driver memorizes the bends in a track.

He had flown in the worst time of the year and now he was ready to establish Larsen Airlines in the awakening time. He installed a radio in the cabin, he rented office space at Anchorage and Fairbanks; he advertised in the Anchorage and Fairbanks newspapers; he waited. He played a lot of poker, drank a lot of coffee; he watched the other fliers with whom he now had an affinity, although he still felt an Outsider because he didn't want to fly hunters. He watched them fly out beefy men with guns and he watched them return with moose attached to their struts. He filled his tanks through a chamois strainer and practised landings on glaciers because that's what he was going to be, a specialist, a glacier man like Bob Reeve. And he waited.

The winter melted. Soon Ruth would be here. He was approached by two men in real estate from Seattle who were willing to pay him forty dollars an hour. They said they wanted to photograph game but when he went to pick them up at Merrill Field they carried guns, not just guns for survival, enough guns and ammunition to defend the Alamo. He refused to take them. They went to another flier who flew them for forty-five dollars; Larsen still joined the poker games but they shook their heads and grinned when he joined them.

Mint took him aside. 'Look, these guys like you okay but they think you're screwy. And so do I,' Mint said. The fat dog stirred, looked at Larsen through a milky eye, went back to sleep.

Larsen said: 'So I don't like to see animals killed for fun. Why does that make me so screwy?'

'Because here you're part of nature. Animals kill each other, herds have to be thinned out. We're part of that. We kill, we get killed. We're part of the goddam pattern and you can't live here and act like some dumb *cheechako*. If you don't like hunting you should have stayed in a zoo someplace. When in Rome, buddy . . .'

'Do you see anything heroic in shooting a beautiful animal with a gun?'

'I ain't talking about heroics. People need meat, people need furs. Herds have got to survive and they've got to be controlled. If you don't drop a bull moose with one nicely-placed slug then a wolf will and if you ever saw a pack of wolves kill a moose then you'd know which the moose would prefer. They take its nose and its hind legs and then they wait for it to lose its blood before they go in for the kill.'

'The laws of natural selection,' Larsen said. 'Leave it to nature.'

'Up here we are nature,' Mint said, 'and I'm beginning to wonder why the hell I taught you to fly.'

'Because I paid you ten dollars an hour,' Larsen said. He regretted it immediately.

'Yeah? Well you just lost yourself an office.' Mint turned and strode away followed wearily by the fat dog.

Soon after that Larsen got himself a client. The police asked him to fly back a prisoner from a village on the Susitna River but it wasn't until he was airborne with the cop who was to bring back the prisoner that he learned that three other fliers had turned down the commission. The prisoner was a criminal lunatic who had killed his wife with an axe. However, it was Larsen's first charter. I'm in business, he thought as he took off with the plain-clothes cop sitting beside him checking his pistol.

The prisoner was red haired, six foot three inches, two hundred and thirty pounds and there was caked blood on his clothes. The policeman suddenly looked small. Why, asked the cop as he saw the prisoner, hadn't they sent two cops?

They climbed into the Piper behind Larsen. When they were airborne the prisoner began to mumble to himself. His hands were in cuffs, his arms were bound with rope but he looked lethal. The cop unbuttoned his gun holster.

The prisoner suddenly shouted: 'Where's Jennie?'

The cop's hand moved to his gun. 'She's dead.'

'Who killed her?' the prisoner began to sob. 'Who killed her? I loved that woman.'

'I don't know who killed her,' the cop said.

They flew into a squall with the rain spattering against the windows. The Piper bucked while Larsen fought it.

Behind him he heard a snap. He glanced round. The prisoner had burst the ropes around his bull shoulders. He was shouting: 'My wife, my wife, some bastard killed my wife.' He beat his cuffed hands against the Perspex window.

The policeman drew his gun. He said: 'Cool it, buster.' The prisoner clubbed at him with his manacled hands. Larsen put the Piper into a dive but when he pulled out the prisoner was on top of the cop still clubbing at him. As the squall pulled at the plane Larsen managed to turn; he chopped at the back of the prisoner's neck. The prisoner loosened his grip. As he did so the cop banged him on the head with the butt of his pistol. The prisoner dropped. At Anchorage he was taken away in a strait-jacket lamenting the death of his wife whom he had struck thirty-two times with an axe.

When word of Larsen's presence-of-mind reached them the pilots' attitude to him became more indulgent. They always checked police charters before accepting them and they should have warned Larsen; but he had come through; he was okay even if he was a little crazy. He began to get more commissions; he even won a couple of pots at poker.

One day he stopped Mint outside his office. 'Minty,' he said, 'I'm sorry.'

They shook hands.

In the office Mint began to talk. The fat dog slept.

During the next five years Larsen became an established glacier pilot and by that evening in the fall when his wife waited for him outside their cabin and their son slept inside, he was breaking even.

What kind of a life is it, she asked herself, when a woman begins to go into mourning every time her husband goes to work? The fear which she had never learned to control ached inside her as she stared into the darkening sky, listening for the first throb, the first heartbeat, of his engine.

It's like being married to a pilot during the war, she thought, remembering the faces of women she had known when the telegram came. They didn't cry because intuitively they had known before the telegram arrived. And I won't cry, she told herself as an eagle swooped over the airfield and landed on the hangar. At the moment she hated this wild place which would soon be imprisoned in ice and snow; she was sure it had taken her husband as it had taken so many fliers. She hated the hostility of the land, the defensive toughness of the people. But she had finished crying; the fear had settled; she would no longer move to her husband's warm body at night when she awoke scared as winter tried to claw through the tripped spruce logs of the cabin. She would take their boy back to London, back to the security of a terrace of grey houses. The adventure was over, love had been taken from her.

The first pulse of the engine quivered in the chilled air. She was crying again as she ran to the edge of the lake. And she was still crying as the floats made their first touch on the water. The ripples reached the water at her feet. He waved to her and she tried to stop crying but the tears were still wet on her cheeks.

She cried as he put his arms round her and kissed her and stroked her hair and said: 'There, there, honey' and she wished that she had been beautiful for him instead of tear-stained.

That night, after he had played with the boy and the boy had been put to bed, after he had fed the dogs, after they had eaten stew and sourdough bread and sweetly sharp berries with ice-cream, after they had drunk a glass of wine, when he was bathing in the tin hip-bath behind the screen, when the stove was glowing and the wolves were howling, Ruth Larsen stripped off her clothes, tied up her long hair which she had allowed to grow since she came to Alaska, touched herself here and there with perfume, made a rug of furs in front of the stove and lay down to wait for him.

When he came from behind the screen he was naked except for a towel around his waist; his hair was damp, his eyes were very blue. She smiled at him with a sudden shyness that she had never experienced on the stage. She touched her breasts which were still fine, heavier since she had suckled the baby; the rest of her body was good, too, belly still flat, thighs firm below the thick, moist, curling black hair.

He let the towel drop and she saw that he was aroused. He lay down beside her, kissed her, kissed her breasts. They reached for each other and then she was beautiful for him.

CHAPTER SIXTEEN

SHE would always remember these autumn days as they were whittled away to leave only the hard nose of winter. This was a hurried time but it was being printed on her mind with lasting colours. Each day the announcements on Fairbanks radio eroded the daylight. Four minutes less, three minutes. Soon there would only be a thin ration of light. Soon it would be winter.

This was the time that Richard Larsen liked least, although as a child he loved the Fall. But he hated this late September time because he had to kill. He was an Alaskan and he had to kill to keep his wife and child.

He had already killed caribou in the autumns that lay behind them and each time he had been sick and, after the animal had been dressed, Ruth had nursed him as he twitched on the borders of sleep. Always he put off the day of the hunt although he knew that he had to kill before the great antlered animals began to live off their own fat and the taste of their meat became rancid.

Wearing an Eskimo parka and mukluks, carrying a ·270 rifle, he set out alone one day in late September when there was wood-smoke on the air and the caribou from the Delta or Nelchina herds were descending from the heights where they had escaped from the insects.

His wife and his son waved to him from the door of the cabin. He smiled but the smile was an act, he trembled inside himself, he loathed himself. He had discovered that he was a good hunter and this disgusted him. He skirted the lake where the ice was a quarter of an inch thick but melting and cracking in the midday sun, skirted a clump of willows, headed for a belt of spruce where he could hide and watch his quarry on the flat land, all the time re-affirming to himself that this was a necessity, this was an act of survival; at the same time doubting his sincerity because he could have flown in supplies from Fairbanks or Anchorage, then reminding himself that they needed fresh meat, that his son needed the meat and, in the cold, the fat.

He reached the spruce. He waited beneath the cathedral roof of branches. He sat on a deep mat of twigs and long-dead foliage. The rifle was across his knees. He drank coffee. He waited. Beyond the trees it was very bright, the peaks of the mountains floating in the distance.

Three hours later he heard the caribou. Ah, the honed instincts of the hunter! On two other occasions he had seen caribou and let them be, chickening out so that he had been forced to stay in the spruce belt until his body was chilled.

He peered into the light. There it was, a fine buck, pausing in its restless life to graze off reindeer moss, antlers lowered, feet so large that they looked as if a cobbler had shoed them. It moved to another patch of moss making the strange clicking noise that was supposed to come from the tendons in the legs; it looked, Larsen thought, noble and awkward, a king bowed down by a heavy-weight crown.

He knelt and lifted the rifle which was heavy in his hands. A bullet through the neck or shoulder was the best shot. There was the neck lined up in the sights. He stroked the trigger with his forefinger and he whispered to the caribou: Get the hell out of here, gallop as I've seen you gallop with all your awkwardness lost in speed.

But the caribou went on grazing. It was content. There were no insects to bother it. The moss was sweet and tender. Soon it would rejoin the herd and they would move on, always moving on, stopping only to feed or fight or rut.

And then it was dead. Blood pouring from its neck. And Larsen the hunter was slitting its jugular vein to hasten the bleeding. And sliding the knife down the warm belly to skin it before it bloated with gas.

After he had slit the belly Larsen vomited.

It was dusk before he had quartered and gutted the animal,

filled a sack with its offal, tongue and heart and signalled with a Very light to his wife to bring the outboard across the lake. Later they strung the meat high between two spruce trees and set traps beneath them.

Then they went inside the cabin where their son, Billy, demanded details of the kill; but Larsen was abrupt with him. That night Ruth fed the dogs while her husband drank whisky.

'But I have provided,' he told himself as he undressed and lay down on the bed covered with skins. When he finally drifted into restless sleep he talked about killing a squirrel but she didn't understand.

Next morning Larsen was pale but the killing fever had passed and he grinned across the table as they ate cookies which she had baked on the Yukon stove and told her: 'I've got a hangover.' He took Billy down to the dogs, huskies and mal-amutes, and then they went for a walk leaving Ruth in the cabin.

She made sourdough bread which they would eat warm with home-made jam; she baked more cookies. She washed her hair in lake water boiled on the stove; she played Glenn Miller on the gramophone; she read a Pearl Buck paperback; she peered through the double-glazed window at the fading sky; she saw a jay winging past the window, she saw the merganser ducks on the lake.

And again she worried as women always worry as they wait for their husbands and children. But whereas they worry about the overspent housekeeping, mortgages, infidelity, mumps and measles and overdue periods, her worries seemed bizarre. She worried about defects in aeroplanes, schooling for a boy in a desolate land, wolves and bears, her own sanity at this meno-pause of the seasons.

But mostly she worried about her husband.

Last winter she had come across his diary which he had left open on the table when he had taken off on an emergency flight to rescue a wounded mountain climber. She had passed it sev-eral times, each time averting her gaze. You do not peer into a man's soul because in every person there are secret territories:

it was never meant that you explore them: you touch and you fuse and you join but there are still those deep sanctums that are inviolate. And perhaps if you do peer inside you find shocks that can freeze your love; your time is the present and you have no right to disturb the chambers of the past.

So she walked past the diary three or four times. She closed it but it sprung open at the page on which he had been writing. And she happened to see her name.

She stood back but her eyes began to read.

It seems sometimes to me that this land which I sought is rejecting me. Not just the people because I expected that: they have as much right as I to their way of life. No, more than the people. Sometimes when I am flying I can feel the hostility rising from the land. And it is more than the bitterness of winter; it is a tangible resentment, a rejection. The blizzards, the white-outs, the cold – they seem to be reaching out for me. Go home Yank, go home before it's too late. Did I make a mistake? Was it ever intended that I should leave the safe haven where I was born? Should I ever have asked my beautiful Ruth to come to this place? To rear our son here? I love flying, the freedom, the escape, and yet these are the thoughts that assail me when I am up in the sky and the land is white beneath me . . .

Ruth closed the diary; this time it stayed shut.

She remembered the entry in the diary now as she waited for her husband to return. The diary was much thicker but she had never again sneaked into it, was ashamed of the one time she had. But she wondered what he wrote as he sat at the table after dinner when Billy was in bed and the Fairbanks radio station was transmitting messages from family to family, wondered as he frowned and sometimes sighed. At these times she knew that what mattered most to him – perhaps more even than his wife and son (although she never pursued this possibility) – was to come to terms with Alaska, not to tame any part of it but to become part of it; so it followed that this must be what mattered most to her.

Sometimes she stared at her hands, calloused and saddle-smooth from carrying buckets, from splitting firewood. She recalled the girl who had shown her body to thousands of men, the girl who had vaguely assumed that she would settle down in a small house, fussily neat with laburnum in the garden. These hands belonged to someone else.

When her husband and son returned, their cheeks burned red with the cold, she had dinner ready. They ate lustily like young animals returned to their mother. Stew made from the meat of hare and porcupine, berries and ice-cream and cookies and coffee. Afterwards father and son played chequers and threw darts at the board she had brought from London. While they played she looked at them over a copy of *John Bull* that her mother had sent. There was little of her in the boy, she decided, although some people said he had her mouth, her temperament. His hair was silky blond, his eyes the blue of glaciers, his body straight and sturdy. A Viking.

Father and son had a disagreement about chequers. To settle it they wrestled. Billy received an unlucky blow in the face. His eyes watered. He should have cried but he didn't. His father told him: 'Don't ever try to be brave, son, don't ever be ashamed of tears.' But the boy didn't understand. He stared resentfully at his father.

Soon he will have to go to school, Ruth thought. Soon he will learn to fight, to be tough because toughness is the code of Alaska. You've got to drink and fight and hunt, it's what's expected of us and by God we'll give 'em what they expect. But what will become of my son when they learn that his father won't hunt? Worse, what will my son think of my husband?

They put him to bed where he said his prayers, including a request to God to forgive his father for punching him in the eye.

Then they read while the antique clock on the wall ticked away the evening and radio issued its instructions. *Will Luke Salter from Bearpaw get himself to Fairbanks where there's a job waiting for him at a saw-mill. Can Mrs. Oats from Caribou hurry down to Summit where her mother's mighty poorly.* She listened as she read hoping there wouldn't be any emergency calls for Richard. *For Mr. and Mrs. Larsen – there's groceries on the way to be picked up from the railway at the usual place.*

He put down his book. 'Now why the hell have they done that? Don't they know I've got a plane?'

'Maybe,' she said, 'they were thinking of you. After all you've been flying with floats and it's almost freeze-up time and you yourself said it was too dangerous to take off and land on water. Maybe they don't know what the weather's like here. Maybe they don't know whether the snow's thick enough for skis or too thin and treacherous for wheels.'

'Okay, okay,' he said.

'You shouldn't be so ready to take umbrage,' she said.

'Take what?'

'Umbrage. You're getting testy.'

'I know it,' he said. 'I'm over-reacting, right?'

'Right,' she said.

'And I should quit feeling sorry for myself?'

'Right,' she said. 'In a way you're getting like them. You're coming out fighting – only from the other corner of the ring.'

'Well put, ma'am.' He yawned and stretched. She noticed the little webs of lines at the corners of his eyes formed by squinting into metal-bright skies and snow. 'Then I guess I'll put away my gun.' He fetched his rifle from the corner of the room, spread newspaper on the floor and began to clean away the oil with a rag because in the winter the oil would freeze. 'And good riddance to it,' he said as he wiped the bolt with gasoline.

'What do we do next, Richard?'

'When is next?'

'Billy will have to go to school next autumn.'

'Then I guess he'll go to school.'

'But where? The nearest village is forty miles away.'

'Maybe we'll decide that when the time comes.'

'I think we should decide it now.'

He dried the gun without love. 'Can you teach him a little?'

'I have,' she said.

'Maybe a couple more years? You know, reading, writing and arithmetic – the three R's.'

'I think he should go to school.'

'Okay,' he said. 'We'll think of something. Don't worry about it.' He looked up, touched her knee. 'Don't worry about it,' he said again. 'He won't want for anything.'

He opened the door and put the rifle in the closed-in porch with an air of finality. But she knew that nothing had been settled.

Next day they watched winter arrive. There had been several false starts, but this was it. Ice reached out from the fringes of the lake to meet in the middle and freeze downwards in search of the lake-bed. Snow falling hesitantly, fluffily, treacherously, covering the ground and the ice and staying. Snow too heavy for the grey sky to hold it any longer. Sound being stifled. Animals falling into deep snow-drifts of sleep.

By dusk the snow was a foot deep. Then it was blown against the cabin by a wind that sang cruel songs in the spruce trees. Dogs and wolves howled and the snow melted on their tongues. Mountain, plain, lake and river became one.

And now that the phenomenon they had been dreading had occurred Richard Larsen and his wife rejoiced.

The next day Larsen got out his sled and tried out the dogs on the airstrip. He had a team of nine. At first they got in a tangle and snapped at each other. But then the leader, Jake, an eighty pound malamute with a wolf's eyes and a white mask of fur, took over and they straightened themselves out.

Larsen wanted to mush as he had in other winters, to feel the wind rushing at his face as the frost formed on his eyebrows; to be alone with the yelping exuberant dogs in this great white beautiful land. But the snow was too soft. So he let them have a run, then took them back to their kennels. One day, he thought, I'll race them and I'll win, anticipating the expressions on the faces of the crowd as the Outsider who was soft about animals romped home.

With Billy tramping beside him on snowshoes, he checked out the Piper in the hangar and fetched the aircraft's skis from storage. Then they went down to the lake to check the ice: it was about two inches thick so it would be a week or more before they could clear a runway. Instead he cut a hole to draw water while Billy examined tracks on the snow – caribou, ptarmigan, wolf and the big prints of a grizzly.

They fed the dogs. They returned to the cabin. They dined and played and read. This was their winter routine broken only by a few flights in the Cub, a couple of visits to the village, one visit to Fairbanks – and one outbreak of Cabin Fever.

Life in an isolated cabin surrounded by snow and ice can have two extreme effects on people. The warmth from the stove, the kerosene lamp, can melt them together so that they become one, so that the union of marriage is a fusion, so that when they lie beneath hummocks of skins they reach for each other and, so it is said, share the same dreams. Alternatively the confines of the cabin can, after a month or so of winter, drive a couple apart snapping and snarling so that one or the other walks out into a blizzard and sometimes never returns and the body is found in the gurgling days of spring with tranquillity of sleep preserved on the face. There is an alternative for those who were neither born naturally to the wilderness nor sought it through perversity or lust for gold or furs: these people have sporadic bouts of Cabin Fever at which times recovery depends on the strength of their love. Nevertheless it is a testing time.

Cabin Fever attacked the Larsens just before Christmas. As in many quarrels the catalyst was of little consequence; in this instance a pair of Larsen's mukluks placed in front of the Yukon stove to thaw out; but before he placed them there Ruth had scrubbed the floor and the melting ice dirtied it.

Ruth kicked the boots aside. 'For God's sake,' she cried, 'I've just cleaned out this damned shack. Haven't you any consideration?' as women have demanded since they swept out the first caves.

Calmly, too calmly, Larsen replaced the boots and patiently, too patiently, explained that the boots had to be thawed and dried because in the morning he had to dust the snow from the gasoline cans marking the runway on the lake.

She kicked them aside again and their son crept away to his bed behind the partition to listen and wonder who would win.

They stared at the big fur boots.

Now Larsen's patience was tight and controlled. He said quietly: 'You're behaving like some nagging harridan in a West Side tenement.'

'I don't know the West Side,' she said. 'But whatever it's like I'd rather be there than stuck in this dump.'

'Then you shouldn't have come.'

'Shouldn't have come? That's rich. Who brought me? Who promised me the glory of the great outdoors?'

'I told you what it would be like,' he told her. 'I told you it would be tough. You chose to come with me, I didn't force you. And let me tell you this – you're free to go at any time.'

'Oh, so I'm free to go. Do you know what the temperature is outside? Minus twenty. And I'm free to go.'

'With the chill factor it's more like minus fifty.'

She picked up a cup of hot coffee and threw it at him.

He wiped the coffee from his sweater with a handkerchief but he couldn't get rid of the brown islands on the white wool. 'I suppose you'll be washing that,' he said.

'I'm finished with washing. Finished with cleaning.' She paused, weighing up the next words; he grinned and that did it. 'And I'm finished with you.'

'Good. We've had our run, now let's make the break. No more squabbling, a good clean break. When the weather clears I'll fly you to Anchorage.'

'Marvellous. And how in God's name do I get from Anchorage to London?'

'You fly, of course.'

Now she was searching for a way to hurt him. 'All right, you fly me to Anchorage with Billy. But supposing some hunters want to share the ride? I suppose we couldn't go then because of your . . . your ethics.'

He began to lose grip of his patience. 'Do you object to my . . . my ethics? Have you been putting up with them all this goddam time?'

'I'm sick of being an outcast,' she said.

It was then that domestic strife degenerated into Cabin Fever. He took her by the shoulders, shook her and pushed her into a chair. The walls of the cabin closed in upon them, the stove hissed, the wind cried in the rafters, wolfish faces pressed against the frost patterns on the window.

She kicked him. 'I've got to get out. Let me go.' He let her go and she stood up but he had to hold her because of the wildness in her eyes.

In the bed behind the partition Billy listened.

'Let me go,' she screamed, kicking him.

He slapped her face, she clawed him. The cabin was a tiny place now with no air to breathe, a cell with bars of cold outside. Only the stove seemed to increase in size as inanimate objects swell and take on life in nightmares.

'Look,' he said, 'I'll go. You stay here. I'll go.'

'Go,' she shouted. 'For God's sake go. One of us must go.'

He pushed her down again. She stayed there trembling. He put on the offending mukluks. He put on his parka with the wolverine fur trimming the hood. He got his rifle.

'Why do you need that?'

'Because,' he said.

The sun had made its shallow orbit of the mountains. It was mid-afternoon and it was night. The wolves called. He pushed against the door glued tight by ice. The cold and the night rushed in. Then he limped away.

She poured herself a shot of whisky and lit a cigarette. The trembling subsided, the walls of the cabin retreated. Billy came from behind the partition. She tried to gather him in her arms but he wriggled free and she thought: He doesn't love me, he wants his father. She wanted to cry, the beautiful release of tears, but not in front of her son.

I am alone, she thought as the alcohol reached her brain. *We* are alone. Deserted. Ah, that it has come to this. Was it predestined? Where would I be now if I had kissed a soldier a little longer in Trafalgar Square and the two sailors had found another girl to molest?

She drank a little more whisky. The boy began to piece together a jigsaw puzzle. A picture of Buckingham Palace! He said: 'You needn't worry, Pa will be back.'

'Why don't you call him dad?'

'Because he's Pa,' the boy said, fitting a bearskin onto the guard outside Buckingham Palace.

Her thoughts drifted until suddenly they changed current. He'll die out there. Alaska will take him just as he always feared it would. And I love him so. She ran to the door, opened it, swallowed freezing air, felt it bite at her lungs. She called out but her voice only carried a few yards.

I'm a bitch, she thought. I have sent him to his death. She began to dress to go and find him. But I can't leave the boy. She sat down beside the stove. She noticed that the pools of water from the mukluk had dried without staining the floor.

One hour, two hours. Then she heard a shot. Not loud, more like a branch snapping. But a shot. She went again to the door. It was moonlit outside and she saw him coming across the snow, rifle over his shoulder.

When he came inside there was frost on the fur of his parka and his eyebrows. 'A beautiful night,' he said. 'I thought I saw a bear back there. I loosed off a shot just to frighten him.'

He took off his parka, his mukluks. She took the mukluks and put them in front of the fire. 'I'm sorry,' she said and he said: 'So am I.'

The fever was spent.

Four days before Christmas she snapped off a branch of spruce; it was frozen hard so that it snapped cleanly and easily. She put it in a barrel which she wrapped with red paper. She and Billy decorated the spruce with the tops of tins, puffs of cottonwool, twists of ptarmigan feather that they had collected in the fall, cones painted gold and silver and last year's tarnished tinsel. They strung toilet paper dyed blue and red and yellow across the ceiling. They stuck tufts of spruce above the pictures on the walls and white tallow candles in saucers on the table. They fashioned Christmas cards to give to each other and told each other that it was just as pretty as Christmas in London or New York. But they were wrong: it was prettier, because they were encompassed by Christmas, by snow and spruce, and the caribou were reindeer and the stars were from Bethlehem.

On Christmas Eve Larsen flew back from Fairbanks. He brought with him the mail. Two sackfuls of it, tied with rope, bulging with mystery. The problem then was whether to open them then or leave them to Christmas Day; Billy opted for now and his parents were easily persuaded. Inside the sacks were smaller mysteries from London and Long Island, tied with shining ribbons with snow-scene stamps upon them because Christmas means snow whether you're in Alaska or the Sahara. There were plum puddings, two boxes of crackers containing indoor fireworks, a box of sticky dates, walnuts and Brazil nuts, a pack of disintegrating mince pies, a large stinking cheese, a box of cigars as dry as snuff, dried apricots and figs, sweets and chocolates and, from London, a sealed tin 'of authentic fog'.

Billy hung a pillow-case from the end of his bed and his excitement was the quintessence of all the world's children. They ate the mince pies that crumbled in their fingers, they drank wine, they sang a couple of carols and the wolves joined their anthem.

Then, when they drew the curtains, they saw Christmas decorations in the sky – the Northern Lights fizzing in red and green plumes.

Next morning they opened their presents.

From Richard to Ruth a wrist-watch set in a gold nugget – and a book on dieting.

From Ruth to Richard a book on wild life, an axe with a wicked blade and a home-knitted cardigan that he thought might make a waistcoat for one of the dogs.

For the boy a trumpet which he blew all day, a jig-saw puzzle, a Hornby train-set, a rifle that fired table-tennis balls, 14 candy bars, a painting-set, two packs of balloons, plasticine which he mixed into streaky mud, two annuals and an educational book on the universe which he hid and a Meccano set.

In the morning while Ruth cooked the ptarmigan and steamed the plum pudding, Larsen and his son put on snow-shoes and walked across the lake as night briefly lifted and the sun gleamed redly over the mountains. A handful of ptarmigan in winter plumage lifted and took to the sky; grey jays and ravens flew overhead.

When they returned the cabin smelled of Christmas, spiced and steamy. Ruth served the ptarmigan. They drank Californian wine and there were coins wrapped in silver paper deep in the plum pudding.

Afterwards they pulled crackers while Larsen lit a desiccated cigar and the air was fragrant with Christmas. They listened to the radio which was a personal thing here in the interior and heard Christmas greetings passing from shack to shack, village to village, the messages crackling with Yuletide static.

They ate nuts until tea-time, then cake from New York, thick and heavy with moist cherries hidden inside. The stove hummed with heat as they lay back, their hands over their distended stomachs. Then they passed the time until the next meal – Ruth with the *Saturday Evening Post*, Larsen and Billy dispatching the green Hornby engine with its coal truck and two coaches on circular tours of the room.

And now the next eating. Cold meat and mince-pies and coffee, the final test of digestion. Carols on the radio. Curtains opened for a few moments to see the moonlight on the snow. Billy's prayers, Billy to bed. Rumination, a couple of gentle belches. Each with the act of love as a completion on their minds.

They lay in front of the stove replete, content, together. And they were still thinking about making love as their eyes closed and they slept.

During the next month there was no sun.

One morning Billy got up and dressed before his parents were awake and crossed the snow to the kennels where one of the mamalutes was sick with hepatitis. The previous day Larsen had thawed out the engine of the Piper and flown to Anchorage for serum for the dog.

Billy put on his parka and his mukluks and his green woollen mask because the wind was blowing from the east creating a chill factor of around minus seventy. He remembered not to run because if you pumped air too quickly into your lungs they got frosted. As he walked, snow-shoes hardly leaving imprints in the hard snow, he regarded the white, moon-bright landscape without wonder because this was the world and big cities were in books. A wolf had investigated the caribou meat hung high between the spruces and there were tracks near the kennels which might have been left by a wolverine which Billy knew was to be feared more than a wolf if, that is, any animal was to be feared. If, between the ages of four and five, anything is to be feared except, perhaps, parental wrath.

The woollen mask was white with his frosted breath. His feet ached a little inside his mukluks. He had been told that in the far north it got colder than this; sometimes minus a hundred with the wind, his father had said, and he had been unimpressed because cold was cold so what?

The dogs were out in the yard. They jumped at him. They were black and grey and white, thick-furred with almond eyes and plumed tails; they laughed a lot although, according to some people, they weren't laughing but this Billy didn't believe. 'To hell with that,' he said aloud.

One of the dogs snatched one of his mittens off. He bent to pick it up but his attention was distracted by a clown of a dog running its nose through the snow like a plough. Billy patted him. 'To hell with that,' he said.

He stopped and went into the shed. The sick dog lay on a blanket. Its breathing was strained and there was pus in the corners of its eyes. Billy wiped away the pus. The dry-nosed dog gazed at him without interest. The dog knew it was dying but the boy didn't: he only associated death with guns.

He stroked the dog a couple of times, listened to the breathing that sounded like the pedalling of an organ before a note is struck. 'Poor boy,' he said.

He crawled out into the moonlight and began to walk back to the cabin. The light was shining, growing stronger under the door; his father was up, lighting a kerosene lamp. For the first time Billy wondered if he would be cross with him. His father didn't often get cross but when he did it was scary. Suddenly he decided that his father might be very cross. He spat a couple of times in a gesture of defiance and because he liked to see the gob of spit freeze before it hit the snow. His ungloved hand began to burn.

His father flung open the door. He looked very cross. Billy spat again, walked more slowly.

'Come back in here!'

Billy walked slowly towards the cabin, stopped as his father came running out. 'What the hell . . .' His father picked him up and ran back into the cabin where his mother was waiting, looking worried but probably about to get cross too.

'I went to see Bruin.'

'To hell with Bruin. I told you never to go out alone until spring.'

'Bruin's breathing is bad,' Billy said, waiting for his mother to get cross as well.

But they didn't reply. They were staring at his hand. Then he looked at it and suddenly felt sick because two of the fingers looked like wax.

'Oh God!' cried his mother.

His father said to his mother: 'Boil up some water.' He took off the boy's parka while his mother fetched a block of snow from outside and put it in a pan on the stove where it immediately melted.

His mother said: 'Is it bad?' She was shaking and this frightened Billy.

His father said: 'Nothing to worry about,' but the tone of his voice said something different.

Steam was rising from the water. His father took down the pan and put it on the table, testing the temperature with his wrist as his mother had once tested Billy's bathwater. 'Too hot,' he said, 'put some more snow in.'

When the sting had gone from the water his father told him: 'This is going to hurt but you've got to be brave,' just as he had said when he poured iodine onto a grazed knee. He picked up Billy's small frozen hand and immersed it in the water and when the pain came to the fingers Billy wanted to cry out but you didn't because, well, you didn't, although he remembered his father telling him not to worry about tears.

The pain ran down his fingers and back again, crept across the palm of his hand, a spreading stain of agony. He squeezed his eyes together, shaking his head so that the tears didn't run down his cheeks, feeling a strange sick-coldness flow from his head through his body . . . the familiar outlines in the room becoming blurred . . . His father kept his hand in the water at the same time pressing his head towards his knees so that a little warmth returned to his head, but the pain was still there in his fingers.

'Will they . . .?' his mother began.

'I don't know,' his father replied.

'Dear God!'

'Boil a kettle of water,' his father said, and when the kettle had boiled he poured a little of the steaming water into the pan and the pain grew worse although he hadn't thought that it could.

Then it began to recede. Now it was only an ache. His father withdrew his hand from the water. The waxiness was touched with pink. Back into the water. Another spouting gush of boiling water. Only the ache now.

Then the two fingers were pinker than the others. Billy regarded his hand. 'To hell with that,' he said.

Then they got cross.

Break-up.

In some places it arrives with cannon-fire, with dark wounds splitting the ice, with islands of ice taking off and hustling down a river, with soft snow on the mountains sliding into avalanches that shake the ground. And fortunes are won for the gambler who forecasts the exact time of break-up at a certain point.

But on the Larsens' patch it came insidiously with spiteful acts of treachery in the process. Now there are full three hours of direct sunlight and you wear goggles to shield your eyes from sun-blindness but you can smell the awakening, hear new

227

rhythms begin with the dripping of icicles, the pad of falling snow. Old ambitions are joined by youngsters, your juices flow quickly, you smell hope on the soft breeze. Next day there is a blizzard.

But finally at the beginning of May, spring arrives as soft and delicate as a moth emerging from a chrysalis. It preens itself in the sun and, as its white wings dry, dark patches appear. You can smell the soil and soon there are only islands of thaw-soiled snow under the spruce trees. The lake melts and fish send bubbles of air to the surface; new streams appear on the flanks of the mountains; the caribou herds get on the move to old pastures or, for reasons unfathomed by Man, to new ones; hunger awakes the bears and they move sleepily, blinking in the new light; shoots of grass probe the black earth and there are buds on the willow trees as soft as a puppy's muzzle; animals begin brief fierce courtships, star flowers are embroidered on the tundra, the air pulsates with the wing-beats of returning birds.

With the spring come new pests which, at first, are as nothing compared with the perils of winter. Flies and then the mosquitoes; and soon the mosquitoes with their homing whine and bloody bite are the plague, and frost-bite is just the kiss of winter.

But there are butterflies, too, and the fireweed is pushing through the earth and the sun is splintering over the mountains at 3 a.m. and the call of the loon is heard in the land.

And now it is summer.

On days when he wasn't flying, taking climbers, geologists, cartographers, photographers and city-faced pioneers to McKinley and its battlements, Richard Larsen took his wife and boy into the warm green country. They carried lunch-baskets and a camera with a long-focus lens and a pair of Zeiss field-glasses. In a blue exercise book they recorded sightings of birds – Arctic tern, jaegar, bald-headed eagle, golden eagle.

They smothered themselves with mosquito repellant. They cut swathes through the fireweed, they feasted off berries; they fished for trout; they grew brown beneath the sun that only dipped fleetingly before bouncing back.

And secretly without confessing it, idiotically and ashamedly, each found himself longing for the prickle of cold in his nostrils as he had longed, or believed he longed, for the warmth of the midnight sun.

During these quick months the Larsens did most of their socializing. They found that with Alaskans they either made direct hits or hopeless misses. The misses came from the Alaskans who made a Broadway production of their pioneering background, drinking heavily in mean bars, reminiscing, belching over thick steaks; the old men had creased faces and ratty ears and white hair curling from the tops of their shirts; the womenfolk knew their place; the young men were strong and white-teethed, inclined to be paunchy before their time.

These people resented the Larsens. The wife with her airs and her actress's voice, the husband with his cranky views on killing. They pitied the little boy handicapped by such parents.

But the friends that the Larsens had were good. They were mostly young people. Men like Larsen who had been transported to Alaska by war, returned to cities where they couldn't breathe and brought their wives back to the Great Land.

While spring was melting and freezing and there was still snow on the ground they went by sled to a village twenty miles away, stopping on the way at a cabin where a young man from California with Mexican blood in him had settled and married an Indian girl with a flat, watchful face, hair as black and shiny as coal and a figure that made men falter in their steps.

Here they spent the night. Ate spicy porcupine stews, played poker and reminisced about the war while the women discussed their children and the art of making ice-cream from caribou fat and, when the men were concentrating on the pot, about the free romancing days before marriage.

This couple had a baby girl, Indian and Mexican and Californian, as dark as Billy was fair. Its hair was thick and black and in its crib it lay quietly regarding the ceiling, smiling occasionally as it remembered the feel of the nipple, the warm flow of milk.

The Californian who wore a brigand's moustache was bitter

about Alaskans. Sipping his coffee after dinner he talked about antagonism to a mixed marriage.

'In the village it ain't so bad. But in the towns you'd think we were lepers. Even guys I flew up with dodge out of the way when they see us coming. We turned up at one of their goddam houses once and there was light on but they must have seen us coming because the lights went out and when we knocked on the door there wasn't no answer. I tell you, man, they're big-hearted people but they got little minds. Now the Indians are different. Yes, sir, they're different. Kind of suspicious to begin with and kind of sore if you take a good woman from them. But pretty soon they take to you. That's why I don't go much far-ther than the village,' the Californian said, wiping coffee from his moustache. 'But the Indians know how to live. They sure know how to live – if the white men would only leave them alone. Their marriages are good, they pick the right man and woman and they don't get hitched for convenience or money or position. No, sir, they get hitched because they're attracted to each other like magnets. And sex' – the Californian glanced warily in the direction of the kitchen where the women were washing the dishes – 'takes all your stamina to keep it up.'

When Larsen and his family reached the village they stayed in a small hotel that had been sunk a foot deep into the earth by the weight of many winters. It was wooden and warm with old, cigarette-burned chairs in the lounge where the sourdoughs gathered and gazed at the past through wreaths of tobacco smoke. They bought provisions at the only shop, visited the only church, had the sled repaired by the only carpenter. This was a mongrel village, white, Indian, a few Eskimos from the coast, even a couple of Aleuts; as usual they were accepted by some, patronized by the others.

The village, ankle-deep in mud, tired buildings steaming in the sun, brought home the necessity of decision to Ruth Larsen.

Billy was in bed in the bedroom upstairs. They were sitting with the sourdoughs listening to the radio. She touched his arm. 'Soon we'll have to move, for Billy's sake.'

And he knew it, although he was reluctant to concede. 'Let's give it a little time. He's learning a darn sight more than he would in any school. And in any case there's a school here.'

'No,' she said, 'we have to go.' Her face was flushed from the stove; her long hair shone. 'It's no good, Richard, he's got to grow up like other boys not as . . .'

'As a savage?'

'If you like.'

'He won't like it.'

'Does any child like going to school?'

'Only the crazy ones,' Larsen said.

'We must move to a town. To Anchorage or Fairbanks.'

He sighed. 'I guess you're right. I'll fly down to Anchorage and find us a place. But we'll have the summer. And I'll keep the airfield going and I'll rent some new premises at Merrill.'

'Yes,' she said, 'we'll have the summer. And we'll have other summers and Christmases and Easters.'

'I'll keep the dogs,' he said.

'And we'll take provisions up there and you won't have to shoot caribou,' she said craftily.

He smiled. 'I really am a crank, aren't I?'

'Yes,' she said.

'And you don't want Billy growing into a crank, huh?'

'One crank in the family's enough,' she said.

'A crank and a stripper for parents. What chance does that kid have?'

He wanted to ask her if she had any regrets about Alaska but he didn't ask because he feared the answer. 'I'll get an apartment,' he told her. 'Downtown some place. You'll be near the shops and movie houses and coffee shops and maybe we can get your mother out and she can start organizing a committee to provide bootees for poor exploited huskies.'

'She wouldn't come.'

'You could try.'

'And you could have your parents out too.'

Larsen said with certainty: 'The old man couldn't come and the old lady wouldn't come without him.'

Outside the evening was still bright. Ruth Larsen and her husband were silent. They had arrived at another point of departure and it was as though they were on the deck of a ship, sailing inexorably forward, and they were watching the wake as it churned and boiled and was then quiet so that the turbulence might never have been.

CHAPTER SEVENTEEN

GUTHRIE had a bachelor apartment off Fourth Avenue. Many girls had known it but none had stayed long enough to begin the insidious process of occupation. Guthrie loved women, especially fine-breasted, sleek-thighed women who were not in a hurry to return home at night, and he loved children, other people's children, but he saw no reason to combine the two.

He was always honest about his intentions. 'I guess I was born a bachelor,' he told the girls over martinis, over the meals he cooked with the single man's gourmet pride, in rumpled beds surrounded by flimsy female garments. But, of course, these assertions were taken as a challenge. He explained that his work took him away for months at a time, that fidelity was not his strong suit, and the girls smiled secretly, knowingly, and had to be restrained from pressing his shirts and re-arranging the furniture. Once when he awoke to find a naked blonde with scissors poised to trim his beard he threw her out, caught a plane to the North and only began to relax as the aircraft flew over the Arctic Circle.

Since the end of the war he had learned a lot about the wealth beneath Alaska's crust. He had studied at the university at Fairbanks and now he lectured there, wagging his pointed beard in the direction of the girl students with the best legs. But recently there had arisen within him a conflict of interests which bothered him a great deal because he had always been complacent about his imperturbable soul.

Guthrie knew the buried secrets of Alaska. He knew where there was iron at Klukwan, near Haines; he knew where there was copper, nickel, tungsten, mercury and long-fibre asbestos near the Canadian border. And he knew where there was gold which might one day come back into its own if the price rose on the world markets.

In short, Guthrie was in a position to cream a fortune from Alaska. But he preferred to act as a consultant, to make a living for himself and fortunes for others; to control the appetites of his clients so that they couldn't desecrate the land, mutilate that most delicate wafer of the earth's surface, the tundra.

This was how he felt until he got the taste of oil.

Now the taste was corrupting him. Oil, as any Texan will tell you, is habit-forming. Now Guthrie calculated in petroleum barrels; he saw the stuff oozing from the earth thick and black; he felt it as slippery as soap between his fingers; in his dreams he floated on a viscous sea of oil and in his nightmares he drowned in its heavy depths.

But it wasn't merely oil-lust that disturbed him: it was the attendant appetites. Everything about oilmen is big and Guthrie found that he was beginning to think big; in particular about big money, the sort of money that flows the way of Texan millionaires and Arab sheikhs.

Guthrie knew that he could make big money because he knew where oil was located.

But his principles had not yet been sunk in oil and this was the root of his conflict. He had travelled Alaska and he felt for these vast regions and he didn't want civilization to encroach, he didn't want the graffiti of pipe-lines, derricks and roads on its pristine surface; he knew how a gash with a pick-axe on the tundra can spawn a lake and he knew that a series of oil strikes could destroy the tundra and, perhaps, Alaska.

He lingered in pastures of fireweed surrounded by crumpled white peaks and watched herds of caribou on the move: he imagined the bewildered herds blocked by a pipeline, he saw criminals and camp-followers, he saw corruption and pollution and the disintegration of the land he loved.

But still he slavered for oil.

So, one day early in the Fall, he consulted Richard Larsen who was looking for an apartment in Anchorage. They travelled to one of the tributaries of the Yukon where, at the end of the last century, men had found gold in the white gravel, had made fortunes or died unmourned. Guthrie squatted on the bank of the tributary, issuing instructions while Larsen dug into the bed of the stream and sifted the gravel and mud.

'Turn around,' Guthrie said. 'I want to see your face when you see your first colour. I've seen other men when they strike gold for the first time. You can see it on their faces – the reasons for every war the human race has known. Greed, lust, cunning . . . Yeah, even on those wide-eyed features of your's.'

'Supposing I make a strike. A big one. Could I make a fortune?'

Guthrie shook his head. 'No way. You need capital and even then with the price gold's fetching you wouldn't be able to quit your job. You'd have to contact one of the big mining companies and they'd ask how many tons you'd dug out and you'd say nothing but a couple of nuggets and they'd say, "Forget it brother." Your only chance, if you haven't got the capital to buy drills and bulldozers, is to hoard what gold you've got and hope that the price will be hiked in the next few years. At the moment it's fetching a mean thirty-five dollars an ounce.'

Larsen, barefoot with jeans rolled up to his knees, stared into the pan. Nothing. He moved downstream a little and began again.

Guthrie said: 'No, if you want to make dough go prospecting for black gold.'

Larsen looked up. 'They don't seem to be having much luck up north.'

'Because they don't want to find it. Not yet awhile. But they will, mark my words. One day soon there'll be such a scramble for oil in this territory that the Gold Rush will seem like a school outing.' Guthrie scratched the black soil with a stick. 'What scares me is that I'll be there fighting and clawing with them.'

'Why the hell would you do that?'

'Because I guess I'm greedy like everyone else.'

'Not you,' Larsen said.

'Me,' Guthrie said.

'But they'll destroy Alaska if they hit it big.'

235

'I know it,' Guthrie said. 'And I'll be there with the demolition gangs.'

Larsen filled the pan with more gravel and silt. 'You'd better tell me about it.'

And Guthrie told him. About the smell and taste and feel of oil and the fact that he knew where it could be found.

'Then you'd better keep your knowledge to yourself,' Larsen told him.

'Yeah? What about when oil fever really hits this place? What do I do then? Sit back while all the other bums rip it apart? At least I could tell 'em where to sink their wells.'

'You know, of course, that you're kidding yourself.' Larsen sat on the bank of the stream feeling the water tug at his ankles.

'I know it.' He scratched self-consciously with the stick. 'That's why I've found a diversion and done something for this place. What's more it's time you got up off your ass and did something,' channelling his anger with himself towards Larsen. 'You're not a freshman any more. Time you graduated, boy.'

'What the hell are you talking about?'

'You aren't helping Alaska by refusing to kill furry animals. They just think you're some kind of nut. It's time you did something more than refuse to fly hunters to their killing grounds. You and me have got to help shape Alaska.'

'You mean Statehood?'

Guhrie pointed the stick at him. 'We're Alaskans now, you and me. America *uses* our land and denies us the right to vote for a President. We haven't got self-government like the other States, we don't have a say in Congress. And for why? Because the big boys Outside want to keep it that way, they don't want us to tax them on their minerals, their salmon, their furs . . .' Guthrie snapped the stick in half. 'And they won't want any self-governing state interfering with their next harvest which as sure as hell is going to be oil.'

Overhead a squadron of migratory birds headed south.

Guthrie went on: 'It's the lobbies we've got to fight. And by Christ they're powerful. Powerful because America doesn't give a monkey's toss what happens to Alaska. The lobbies are still making the same sounds they've made for decades. We aren't ready for Statehood, we're too far away, we can't afford it . . . But, by God, we were good enough to fight for America. Now we've got to fight again and we've got a good man to lead us – Governor Gruening.' Guthrie grinned. 'It's Gruening's Guerrillas all over again.'

Larsen filled his pan and peered in vain for evidence of pay-dirt.

'The hell of it is,' Guthrie said, 'that the enemy's got good men too. A guy named Bill Arnold on the canning side. He's got money, he's got influence and he's a fighter. Who do we have on our side? Sourdoughs, cheechakos, Eskimos, Indians . . . But we'll win, godammit, we'll win.'

Larsen sifted his dirt. 'Okay, count me in when we've got our apartment. What do you want me to do?'

'Lobby,' Guthrie said. 'Campaign. Raise dough. Maybe you could lobby on the conservation issue. You know, tell Washington that the exploiters from outside are knocking the hell out of the ecology. Fishing the rivers dry of salmon, killing off the polar bear.'

'Sure, why not? We protected Alaska once,' Larsen said and was about to say something more when a glint of yellow in the pan caught his eye and Guthrie said: 'I can see it on your face – you've sighted colours.' Larsen tried to wipe the greed from his face, tried not to think what he could do with gold at seventy dollars an ounce, or even a modest thirty-five, if there was a gold vein somewhere upstream. He touched the shining flakes with his forefinger, experienced the alchemy of the mind that the pioneers had once experienced, drooled a little, and smiled shame-facedly when Guthrie said: 'Now you know how I feel about oil.'

That autumn the Larsens moved to Anchorage to a two-bed-roomed apartment just on the right side of the tracks but not all that far across. Larsen rented a hangar near Mint's shack and did enough flying to pay the rent of the apartment; Billy went to a nursery school; they bought an old automobile that made rusty sounds when it hit a bump in the road; Ruth took a job teaching English at the High School.

Billy made no secret of the fact that he preferred the cabin, that he hated the school, as well as the children and the teachers, but Larsen and his wife told each other many times how well they were settling down, but it wasn't until freeze-up, until smoke and steam arose like white trees through the town that they began to settle, welcoming the cold as an ally.

They made several friends among the new Alaskans, not so many among those who had rooted themselves long ago.

The Larsens' principal friends were Guthrie and his girls and Ott and his wife who journeyed to Anchorage from Fairbanks to campaign for the Natives and for Statehood.

During the winter when flying was curbed Larsen tackled statehood as he had promised Ruth he would. He was fascinated by the graft and double-dealing involved and he decided to fight it. He became a fringe politician, a lobbyist.

CHAPTER EIGHTEEN

A FEW years earlier Charles Browning had become slightly involved with politics: he used a politician named Senator Joe McCarthy for his own purposes.

His involvement began one spring day in New York. He was staying with Judy and their son – her second pregnancy had been false – in his father-in-law's East side apartment. Thackeray was away in Texas and it was a beautiful time in New York (if you lived in those places where beauty still flowered) with daffodils in the window-boxes and a breeze skipping in from the East River. Love blossomed in Central Park and even the cops looked happy.

With Judy beside him, Browning sauntered down Third Avenue, wandered into the sixties to inspect the antique shops where the sun polished the copper kettles and brass bedsteads. While Browning thought about oil leases in Alaska, they talked about this and that.

With her fashionable clothes, coiffured hair and Bermuda tan Judy looked every inch the up-and-coming young executive's wife. Strolling beside her eager, spring-suited husband, she looked as if she was in league with beneficient gods and she was much admired and much envied.

While Browning's thoughts strayed to the neat buttocks of an airline stewardess he had met on his way to Anchorage the conversation moved to the post-war problems of the United States.

'I just can't understand them,' Judy remarked as they paused outside an antique shop to examine a fake Confederate musket.

'Nor can I,' Browning said. The agreement with the stewardess whose body seemed to spring from her tight uniform when he undressed her had been explicit: no emotional involvement, just transient physical attraction.

'You can't understand what?'

'How they can get away with fakes like this.' He picked up the musket, squinted down its phoney barrel. 'I can forgive people anything except amateurism.'

'That wasn't what I was talking about.' She walked ahead of him as he replaced the gun. 'Sometimes I wonder if you ever listen to me. Sometimes I figure our marriage is developing along classic lines. You know, the tycoon absorbed with his work, the wife managing the home. Two different lives, meeting occasionally in bed. It's kind of Victorian, isn't it?'

'You don't look particularly Victorian,' Browning said.

'We don't spend much time together, do we?'

'You knew what it would be like. It was just the same with your parents. It doesn't preclude . . . love,' he said it hesitantly, as though he were ashamed of the word. He caught up with her and tucked her arm in his and thought how much more beautiful she was than the stewardess. 'Now what was it you couldn't understand?'

'It doesn't matter.'

'Sure it matters. Now what was it?'

'I was talking about these crazy men who think Communism is the answer to our problems.'

'Ah, the red peril,' he said.

'I mean we fought a war to defeat a tyranny, to keep our freedom. Now the Communists want to change it all, to create another tyranny. Why?'

Browning shrugged. It was spring and it wasn't a time for politics. He said: 'You're right of course. But anti-Communism has degenerated into a witchhunt. It's a kind of madness. Innocent people are being branded for life.'

'Oh I know that.' She sniffed the smell of pretzels on the air. 'We had Reds at college. A few girls with boy friends who were flirting with Communism. But that's just a part of being a student, of being young,' she said. 'They grow out of it. I even remember my father talking about it. He said he was a Communist at college for all of two days – until he made his first buck,' she said, buying two pretzels and handing one to her husband and wishing they were students walking out for the first time.

Her husband took a small bite from the pretzel. He pretended he wasn't speaking because he was eating. A chord had struck inside him, an ugly vibration. It made him feel sick and excited. He told Judy he was expecting a phone call at the apartment. He escorted her to a café with tables and chairs on the sidewalk; he ordered her coffee and told her that he would only be fifteen minutes. He walked away, lowering his head so that she couldn't see the excitement and perhaps the ugliness on his face.

From a call box two blocks away he telephoned a firm of private investigators named Snowdon and Stopforth who undertook snide assignments for handsome fees and put aside a portion of their income to establish an atmosphere that reassured their clients that their requests weren't really so shitty.

He made an appointment to see R. G. Snowdon next day. That night, as he lay beside his wife, he explored his motives. For a while he tried to convince himself that it was in his country's interests to have his father-in-law's background investigated but, hell, he didn't have to bullshit with himself. Then he pretended it would be in Thackeray's interests to have his named cleared before McCarthy and his lieutenants hauled him in. But this was such transparent crap that he got out of bed and went to the kitchen where he made himself a cup of tea and admitted to himself that his motives were personal, that this was the law of the jungle, that this was the way Thackeray had clawed his way to the top. The old man was due for retirement, it was in the interests of the company that he should quit a couple of years ago before his faculties were dulled. This last sentiment Charles Browning almost believed.

Next morning he put R. G. Snowdon on the trail.

And while R. G. Snowdon, the rich man's shamus, peered among the dead leaves of a man's life, that man's son-in-law began to gather together the best button-down brains in the company. He tested their alertness, their ambition, their technical knowledge and that quality in business which has many

241

euphemisms but is, in fact, ruthlessness. The Army had taught him his lessons early in life: he didn't want desk-bound generals, he wanted Pattons.

He took the short list of candidates back to his home in Chicago; he met their wives and girls. He hinted at his plans but gave them nothing with which to betray him. Within six months he knew that he had seven men plus Trusz, the scout, who would follow him, a team that could take on the established oil industry.

At the end of that six months R. G. Snowdon came up with the goods. Such a savage indictment of treason. R. G. Snowdon had obtained three signed affidavits to the effect that, when he was a young man, Thackeray had attended a left-wing meeting and had signed a birthday card to Joseph Stalin!

Within the year Thackeray was arraigned before the House Committee of Un-American Activities. It took Thackeray only nine months to die after his enforced retirement. It took his wife three months longer. They left all their money and property to their daughter and son-in-law.

Shortly before Thackeray was arraigned Browning discussed Alaska with Trusz.

While Trusz pored over the *Morning Telegraph* in his small apartment off Rush Street, Chicago, Browning said to him: 'Nothing's moving on the North Slope of Alaska, right?'

Trusz made a pencil mark beside a horse in a race at Belmont track. 'That's right,' he said. 'The Navy's playing it down. Or rather the oil company men employed by the Navy are clamping down.'

Browning who had just been playing squash because he had seen too many businessmen sagging over their desks combed his hair in a wall-mirror beside a racing calendar. 'But there's oil in other parts of Alaska?'

'Oh sure. It's leaking with the goddam stuff.' He rubbed his neck where the stiff collar was rubbing it.

'Where are the biggest leaks apart from the North Slope?'

Trusz ticked another horse. 'A few places down the Canadian border. Bristol Bay . . .'

'We can forget that,' Browning said sitting down, squash racket between his knees. 'That's red salmon and I don't want my salmon polluted with oil.'

'You got a lot of interests, haven't you,' Trusz remarked.

'I like to spread myself.'

'Ain't it time you spread my payment a little?'

Browning twirled the racket. 'Don't get greedy.'

'Seems like you're a little on the greedy side.' Trusz put the pencil down. 'Seems like I'm only helping you to satisfy your greed.'

Browning said quietly: 'Don't threaten me.'

Trusz lit a cigarette, inhaled, blew out the match. 'Have you ever written scripts for B movies?'

'I'm warning you.'

'Maybe it's me who should be warning you. I mean, I could do you a lot of harm.'

'And I could break you. Have you ever heard of industrial espionage? The F.B.I. could become very interested in you, Trusz.'

'Sure they could. And they might be even more interested in the guy who pays me to spy.'

'You couldn't prove it.'

'Mud sticks,' Trusz said. He tapped ash from his cigarette with a neat-nailed finger. 'I figure it's a case of which of us would fall the harder. Me, I wouldn't fall very far. But you – it'd be like dropping off the Empire State . . .' He stubbed out his cigarette, picked up the pencil, and returned to the lists of runners. 'Now this is what I suggest,' he said turning the pages. 'You double my payment and you've got yourself a partner. Then there'll be no pussy-footing around, no double-crosses. I've got the know-how, you've got the dough. And I'm sure as hell not going to make you a millionaire for peanuts, Mr. Browning, sir.'

Browning picked up the racket, tested the strings as a man feels a thong before a whipping. Then he replaced it between his knees. He said softly: 'Okay, you got yourself a deal. Three hundred dollars a week above what the company pays you. The bookmakers will have themselves a ball.'

'Don't worry yourself about what I do with the dough.' Trusz made a pencil mark beside a horse in the last race. 'Now there's a funny thing,' he remarked. 'That's the first time I ever chose a horse because of a fancy. It's called Lucky Strike,' he said.

Next day Trusz flew to Alaska.

While Trusz was away, Browning, operating from his headquarters in Chicago, expanded his Alaskan interests. Salmon hauled from the sea, pink and bright and gasping, were stuffed into cans and shipped Stateside, without too many inquiries into the legality of the fishing. He joined forces with shrimp importers in New Orleans who had become aware of the seabed harvests off Kodiak. He exported red caviar to Japan and he got his claws into the king crab business. He entertained Alaskan businessmen in his Chicago penthouse where he discovered that good food and wine, cash inducements and girls were as acceptable to the men from the Last Frontier as they were to any city dudes with a concession to sell. With agents working on your behalf inside a territory you could plunder it from as far away as Chicago, London or Paris. Not that Browning considered it plunder: he was reaping a harvest. This was the way it had always been, always would be, and if he didn't reap the harvests then someone else would. Charles Browning always tried to be honest with himself.

At the same time he kept his word with the Japanese who had set him up in canning by pushing the oil lobby in Washington to keep up their campaign against statehood. Unlike most of the anti-statehood lobbyists – Browning suspected that the cause was a lost one. The new Alaskans were pushy, war veterans like himself; they had fought for their country and they were going to make damn sure that the territory they had chosen to inhabit had the same rights as the other states.

One day soon it wouldn't be so practical to gather the Alaskan harvest from remote cities. So, when Trusz called him to

244

report that the best oil prospects – apart from the North Slope – were in the south to the Gulf of Alaska, Browning flew to Anchorage. He bought himself an unobtrusive, four-bed-roomed, spruce-built retreat overlooking the city and went to meet the man who, according to Trusz, knew more about the black gold beneath Alaska than anyone else. His name was Guthrie.

Guthrie confirmed that there was oil along the Gulf. It was no great secret, he said, while Browning tried to remember where they had met before. 'There've always been seeps along there,' Guthrie said. 'In fact they've worked a few shallow wells. But there isn't much you can do about it,' he said, and Browning wondered at the hostility in his voice.

'Why not?' Browning asked.

'You should know all about that,' Guthrie said. 'You're in the oil business.'

Guthrie, Browning and Trusz were sitting in Guthrie's office.

Browning asked: 'Where have I met you before?'

'In hospital. A soldier named Larsen had just saved your life. You were going to get him a medal.'

'I remember you,' Browning said. 'You were the civilian.'

'Sure I was.' Guthrie pushed himself away from his desk and put his feet on it. 'Whatever happened to that medal?'

'If you want to know the truth—'

'What else?'

'I didn't do a damned thing about it. I should have done. But I'm being honest with you.'

'Now you're in Anchorage you can be honest with Larsen. He lives here.'

Browning's hand strayed towards the old scar on his belly. 'Maybe I will.' Surprise gave way to the old resentment which he didn't care to explore. 'What's he doing here?'

'Flying aeroplanes. He's made quite a name for himself as a glacier pilot. Maybe you'll fly with him one of these days.'

Trusz shifted in his seat. He played with a set of poker dice in his pocket. He said: 'Let's talk about oil. When you say there isn't anything we can do about it I figure you're talking about leasing terms.'

Guthrie nodded.

Trusz explained to Browning: 'He's talking about the limitations. One company can only lease 15,360 acres which isn't enough. It's something to do with conservation.'

Guthrie said: 'One of the few decents laws around here.'

'You don't want to get into oil?' Browning asked.

'I'll advise anyone about oil for a price but I don't want in. I like this place nice and clean. I don't mind advising because I know there isn't a goddam thing you can do about it.'

Browning gazed at him reflectively. 'What about the oil up north? Supposing there was a big strike and the laws changed . . . Would you be interested then?'

'Nope.'

'I wonder,' Browning said. He stared at Guthrie. Most people indulged a habit when they were lying. Guthrie began to stroke his beard. Browning smiled. 'I wonder,' he said again.

Guthrie pulled his hand away from his beard. 'That will be five thousand dollars, gentlemen. I'll tell you exactly where there's oil and that's my fee.'

Browning said: 'Cheap at the price,' writing out a cheque.

A week later in a suite in the Waldorf-Astoria Browning met one of the bright young men he had selected within the oil company. His name was Stanstead; he was tall and languid and he had brown eyes, but whereas most brown eyes have a softness about them this brown was like wet stone. Stanstead was good on land and leases; Browning had consulted him about the conservation laws in Alaska and Stanstead had found their loopholes and was eager to explain them.

He told Browning: 'We've got to form a company that will have power of attorney on behalf of hundreds of leaseholds. In other words we've got to interest hundreds of people in buying oil leases. Each of the purchasers will own 15,360 acres but they will all be in one vast block and they'll have to sign agreements that they're willing to let us act on their behalf. It's called unitizing,' he added.

Browning got some ice from the freezer and poured them

each a Scotch. 'We'll have to be pretty sneaky, I guess,' he said. 'I mean if anyone got to hear of what we're doing they could buy a strip right down the middle of the block.'

'Sure they could. But we don't have to broadcast our intentions. We know enough guys who will be willing to come in. We could end up with a holding of a million acres or more.'

Browning sipped his Scotch. 'Then what do we do? I mean what the hell's the use of a million acres or more if we can't drill it?'

Stanstead said: 'I figure we can if we play our cards right. You see, the Secretary of the Interior has the right to okay big developments regardless of acreage restriction if they are *in the common good or national interest.*'

'And drilling for oil and making lots of dough for the boys is in the common good?'

'Two gas deals have already gone through,' Stanstead said.

'You've done your homework.'

'I enjoy it.'

'And how do we persuade the Secretary of the Interior that this is in the common good or national interest?'

'We get ourselves a good attorney,' Stanstead said. 'Someone who knows his way round the department. And in any case' – he spread his hands wide – 'who says it isn't in the national interest. I guess it's more in the national interest to strike oil than to pretend it doesn't exist.'

Shortly after this conversation Browning quit the company taking with him Trusz and the other six young men of wolfish instincts. They formed their own company and canvassed for prospective buyers of leases on the Gulf of Alaska. In January 1951 Browning handed in several hundred applications for United States oil leases to the adjudicator of the Anchorage Land Office with the request that they be regarded as a single block.

The application was granted. The oil lease boom had begun. Charles Browning was in at the beginning.

The new company, Harvard Oil, now had to get permission

from the Department of the Interior to develop the land. It took two years but finally the development contract was granted and they started drilling in the company of such enterprises as Colorado Oil and Gas Corporation, Frankfurt Oil Company and Continental Oil Company *in the common good or national interest.*

Now that the regulations had been tamed other companies unitized and began to develop. Businessmen, real estate speculators, football players, movie stars, lottery winners, politicians grabbed tiny handfuls of Alaska. Wildcatters began to drill. Pin-pricks in the vast crust of Alaska. But a beginning. If the pin-pricks withdrew smeared with oil then wholesale desecration would be attempted.

In 1954 the possibility of this desecration was given a boost. The Federal Mining Leasing Act was changed and any one person or company was permitted to buy 100,000 acres of leases with options on 200,000 more. Speculators besieged the land office in Anchorage.

Harvard Oil continued to drill on the Gulf. They were one of the smaller development companies and before permission to develop was granted they had to prove that they were serious contenders. To do this they pointed to the barren ranch in Arizona where *fortuitously* they had just struck oil, making the strike with ease because they had known the oil was there all the time.

The chairman of the company was Charles Browning. Also on the board was Guthrie who shaved off his beard when he accepted Browning's offer.

Now Browning began to spend more time in Alaska although he didn't like the place. But every businessman has his penance and Alaska was Browning's penance. He tried to compensate. He went hunting, he bought a team of dogs and went sledding, he installed home comforts into his spruce-wood house including the stewardess from North West Orient Airlines.

He spent a lot of time on aircraft and he established two separate existences. At home he was the pillar of society, doting father, Saturday night lover. Away from home frustrated appetites were released. He wasn't ashamed of his dual life because no one suffered: it was a cliché of his way of life, it was business practice.

The girl was twenty-three, small, dark, plump-breasted. He assumed she was amoral with lovers in other cities where North West Orient Airlines stopped over and in the cockpits of their aircraft. But, like many amoral girls, he decided she was seeking, through a succession of testing grounds, ultimate security; when she found it she would become jealous and possessive.

Browning was afraid she was now reaching that stage in her search for completion.

He had returned to the house overlooking Anchorage on the sled drawn by eight dogs which he hoped to race. His cheeks were polished, he felt hungry and healthy. The brief day was sliding away in a red glow across the water. The heat inside the house struck him, he felt his face begin to melt.

She was waiting for him with a martini and was wearing a chiffon gown and high-heeled slippers. She wasn't wearing any make-up and smelled of bath-salts.

He struggled out of his parka, took off his mukluks, sat beside the log fire and enjoyed the atmosphere of the lounge which was both basic and luxurious and as phoney as an alpine chalet in Manhattan. She sat beside him on the sofa, legs tucked under her and he knew that shortly they would make love in front of the shifting logs of the fire and that afterwards she would slip a few remarks into the conversation that were the foundations of the security she sought and that soon he would have to terminate the affair.

'Well,' she said, sipping her martini, 'how was the great outdoors?' She had the husky voice that some Spanish girls possess.

'Exhilarating,' he said. 'But I'd rather be playing squash in New York or Chicago.'

'I could live here,' she said.

'Maybe you've got Eskimo blood in you.'

'Oh sure. With a father called Fernando and a mother called Maria.'

'Pretty hot-blooded those Eskimo girls.'

'Not as hot-blooded as the Spaniards.'

Her robe slipped so that he could see the curve of her breasts, he felt the stirring in his loins. And he thought: Maybe she loves me. And then: What if I had met her first and we had got married? Then he thought: Shit, what the hell's the matter with you? Where would you be if you hadn't married Judy? And then he thought about Judy and was suddenly, incongruously, touched by the loyalty of his wife. But that thought had no effect on the swelling in his loins.

He handed the girl his empty glass. He watched her while she mixed another cocktail. It was dark and primeval outside and you could smell the resin of the spruce logs.

She handed him his drink, resumed her place, looked at him with brown eyes that sometimes appeared black. He hoped she would marry and have kids and be happy; he hoped that her husband would never know the extent of the testing grounds of her youth because he knew that girls like this often destroyed that which they were seeking.

He had allowed the affair to linger too long, and yet he wanted it to continue. He wanted to be gentle about the parting and he wondered whether he should give her money.

She kissed him, mouth open. Perhaps she would agree to being a permanent mistress. But no, not these healthily sexual girls who enjoyed making love with any man who attracted them. Browning knew that, paradoxically, they only settled for marriage.

He slipped his hand inside her robe and stroked her breasts, feeling the nipples harden. She put her arms round his neck and kissed him again and the robe fell away from her shoulders; she withdrew a little so that it fell to her waist and her breasts were pressed against his chest.

They lay in front of the fire, feeling the heat against their bodies. Sometimes they took a long time before he entered her, but not tonight. The hunger was upon both of them and he was inside her and their mouths were together and he knew that he couldn't stop and that she didn't want him to and they came together swiftly and savagely and sweetly.

Afterwards, as they lay watching the ash drop into the grate, she kissed him gently and said: 'I know what you're thinking.'

'I love you,' he said, and was surprised.

'And I love you. Always remember that.'

Suddenly he was afraid. 'You sound as if you're talking in the past.'

There were tears in the corners of her dark eyes. 'I am,' she said. 'I'm leaving you.'

CHAPTER NINETEEN

THE love of Ruth Larsen for her husband was like the flame of a candle. Strong and steady but wavering occasionally in the wind of uncertainty that blew in from the cold, twilight streets when smoke and steam were trapped and frozen above the city. She felt then that she was an alien in the land, she sensed hostility in the eyes of the women towards her with her actress's voice, she longed to hear the sooty accents of Cockneys and to be walking from the rust-smelling railway station to the terrace house in London.

But for the most part the flame of the candle was steady and she rejoiced to see that, in the campaign for statehood, her husband was finding a new stature. He was becoming a crusader alongside other young, strong people, the new Alaskans who were emerging stridently from the defensive insularity of the sourdoughs.

The Larsens mortgaged a white frame house overlooking the flat waters of the Inlet where Ruth watched her son growing up sturdily, like a Viking, like an Alaskan.

She was still scared when her husband was flying but the sharpness of her fear was blunted. He drove to Merrill Field, he took off for the airstrip beside their cabin, he landed on lakes and snow-fields and glaciers tucked high in the Alaskan Range and, when he drove away, she managed to convince herself that he was off to work like any other husband with a job of work to do. Next to Don Sheldon who ran the Talkeetna Air Service, Larsen was reckoned to be the best glacier pilot in the territory. They said in Anchorage and Fairbanks that Richard Larsen could land on a snowflake.

After they moved into the new house Larsen borrowed money to buy a Super Cub with a 150-horsepower Lycoming engine. It was a beautiful little lightweight ship; it couldn't take the weight that a Cessna 180 could but it could nip into the air off a shorter runway than the 230-horsepower Cessna.

He also brought his dogs down from up north. He entered five races and won two. He was an Alaskan. An eccentric perhaps but, because he could fly, because he could race dogs, an Alaskan. And one day he wrote in his diary:

At last this territory has accepted me. For the wrong reasons, perhaps, because I don't want to conquer it: I want to become part of it. But no matter, it is the acceptance that matters.

With Ott and the new, clean-shaven Guthrie, Larsen flew several times, on scheduled airlines, to Washington to campaign for statehood. He put the case for conservation, Ott put the case for the natives and Guthrie who had become withdrawn since he had sheared away his wagging beard concentrated on politics which surprised Larsen because he thought Guthrie would have been strong on ecology.

They joined the Alaska Statehood Committee with Robert B. Atwood publisher of the *Anchorage Daily Times*, as chairman and Mildred Hermann, a lawyer from Juneau, as secretary and treasurer. With a recent Gallup Poll showing that Americans were eighty-one per cent in favour of granting statehood a bill was introduced to every session of Congress.

It should have been a cinch.

It wasn't.

Because the enemies of the bill had the needs of the American people at heart. They wanted to keep on supplying them with vitamin-rich salmon – (trapping them at rivermouths and destroying the runs); with lignite and anthracite coal and pulp timber from the hemlock forests of the southeast, and precious stones for the jewellers of Fifth Avenue. And they wanted to supply them with the oil that lay in great lakes below the surface, deep and still and thick, waiting to be tapped for the American automobile owner, but tapped nice and discreetly because, with a glut of cheap gasoline, the air over the cities would be polluted and the American motorists would run riot over the fair land killing and maiming each other. Like diamonds, you had to control the supply of gasoline for the good of the consumer.

And, of course, all these benefits for the forty-eight states suspended beneath the belly of Alaska had to be accrued without the burden of taxes imposed by a state government. So that was why statehood was opposed – for the sake of the American people.

These philanthropists were powerful and, because of this, statehood bills had been thrown out since the first one was introduced in 1916. Not merely for the benefit of the Outside: for the benefit of Alaska as well. *Not enough resources to be a State . . . too remote from Washington . . . population too small . . . not enough money to support itself . . .*

Among these philanthropists was Czar Ickes who, in the thirties, wanted reservations for natives and an eight per cent gross tax on gold production. And later W. C. Arnold, general manager of the Alaska Canned Salmon Industry, who was said to control the territorial legislature and was adamant that statehood could only harm the Great Land. And then Senator Hugh Butler of Nebraska, Chairman of the Interior and Insular Affairs Committee, who went to Alaska to assess feeling for statehood of the 'little man' and returned opposed to statehood despite a forest of banners proclaiming I'M A LITTLE MAN FOR STATEHOOD. And then President Eisenhower who failed to mention statehood in his 1953 message to Congress despite the overwhelming support of the American people for statehood for their last frontier.

Opposing these benevolent men, lobbyists, Congressmen and officials, were such figures as Ernest Gruening, Governor for thirteen years, Anthony J. Dimond and his successor, Bob Bartlett, Alaska's voteless delegates in Congress, Bob Atwood and his wife, Colonel M. R. 'Muktuk' Marston and many others who must surely have been in a conspiracy against the best interests of Alaska and the American people.

The anti-statehood lobby made several counter proposals. They suggested that Alaska become a commonwealth member like Puerto Rico, they suggested – for the second time – that

Alaska be partitioned (leaving prime salmon fishing grounds out of the deal).

No dice, said the *little men*. Men like Richard Larsen who had suddenly found their feet and their voices on public platforms and wrote tracts and letters to the Press. These people cajoled and lobbeyed and testified before Washington committees.

Every morning Larsen awoke with the scent of battle in his nostrils. In Alaska he had once learned about bravery and cowardice and violence in men; now he learned about more subtle nuances of behaviour. He learned, for instance, that not everyone railing about Outside interests milking the territory was absolutely sincere; many of them owned mines and fishing grounds and forestland; they traded with Outside interests and they were the tools, agents, minions of those interests.

In 1955 Alaska made its first really devious move to counter the deviousness of the anti-statehood lobby. Like an enemy making war without the prelude of a declaration they drew up a constitution for the State of Alaska without authorization from Congress.

Fifty-five delegates including Larsen, Ott and Guthrie were dispatched to the University of Alaska at Fairbanks to draw up the constitution. It took them seventy-five days, the same period of time that it took to draw up the Constitution of the United States.

Then came the next ploy which shook Washington. Resurrected from the archives it was called the Tennessee Plan. It was a simple strategy which had been used by Tennessee and several other territories prior to statehood. Alaska elected two senators and a representative and dispatched them to Washington *before* the reality of statehood.

The rebels then breached protocol by opening offices in Washington. Like the Japanese in 1941 they had struck without observing any preliminaries: they had arrived and could no longer be ignored.

In 1957–58 eleven statehood bills were introduced.

The anti-statehood lobby went on the defensive. The House Rules Committee, comprised largely of hard men from the south who thought to hell with liberal Alaska joining the Union, sat on the final bill for nearly a year.

It was during the avalanche of statehood bills that Charles Browning, Chairman of Harvard Oil, a leader against statehood, and Richard Larsen finally faced each other. Neither was surprised. It seemed that it had always been inevitable. And it seemed to each of them that they were the personification of the opposing forces and their armour shone.

The meeting occurred in a committee room on Capitol Hill. The long table was fashioned from rosewood. The air-conditioning was cold and smelled sour. There had been many such statehood committees and there were few people present. The chairman of the committee was a rumpled man with soft, snow-white hair and mauve cheeks; despite the air-conditioning he sweated a lot.

Browning testified first.

He spoke with eloquence and force that almost confounded logic but it didn't fool the lawyers and legislators who were on intimate terms with the various faces of truth, although they admired his style. And he answered a lot of questions. His main point was that by prematurely drawing up their constitution, by appointing two senators and a representative the people of Alaska were out of order. Moreover by such precipitous action they were proving that they were as yet unprepared for their own state legislature. They were in the adolescence of self-government and the federal government should wait until they reached maturity.

The white-haired chairman dropped cigarette ash on his creased trousers and stared with admiration. He didn't accept much of what Browning had said and he doubted if Browning did. But Browning was well set-up, persuasive, intelligent; it was men of this calibre that America needed even if this one was a little too smart, so smart that one day he might pick his own pockets.

He said: 'I believe you have some views on conservation, Mr. Browning.'

Outside interests – 'that's us,' Browning said with a disarming smile to the chairman – had the interests of conservation well in hand. For example, the old cut-and-move-on methods of felling timber that had devastated so much forestland elsewhere had been controlled and the great belts of hemlock and spruce would be preserved. The spawning grounds of salmon were being protected – and when oil was struck steps would be taken to preserve the ecology. It was doubtful if the young pioneers of Alaska had the resources to implement these measures and if a state government taxed Outside interests, the Outside interests would be unable to pour sufficient money into Alaska to 'protect that beautiful virgin land'.

The chairman nodded sagely. He had once shot a 1,000lb bear at Kodiak and when he returned there to hunt and fish he wanted to find it still beautiful and virgin. He almost wished he could believe this plausible young man. He felt like a member of a jury in a criminal trial swayed by a smart lawyer engaged by a well-heeled defendant. Now he had to listen to the small-time lawyer, the amateur, Richard Larsen.

Larsen admitted that Browning was correct when he made the point that Outside money was needed to preserve the 'beautiful virgin land'. He was grateful that he had brought this point to the committee's notice. But it was Federal money that was needed to protect the land that was one fifth the size of the entire Union. It was Federal money that was needed to implement laws that would conserve the wilderness of the Last Frontier. And the Federal Government could not be expected to pour money into a territory, a colony, a poor relation. Only when Alaska took its rightful place alongside the other states could its future be assured.

The chairman was surprised. The small-time amateur was out-smarting the pro. Had grabbed Browning's big guns and turned them around. It was stimulating and the chairman decided to give Larsen more ammunition. 'Can we be more specific?' he asked. 'For instance, what can be done to conserve the salmon?'

Larsen was grateful. He answered briskly. 'Mr. Browning only mentioned the spawning grounds. He failed to mention the prime cause of depletion because, perhaps, he is in the canning business and has a vested interest. At the moment traps are set at the mouths of rivers. These must be made illegal before the salmon are exterminated.'

The chairman smiled, polished his spectacles, gathered together his papers in an untidy heap and adjourned the hearing until after lunch.

Browning said: 'That was pretty smart.'

'I said what I believe,' Larsen told him.

They were walking down a marble-cool passage leading from the committee room to a flight of stairs that led to a lobby with a domed ceiling. The corridor was peopled with marble busts and oil paintings of politicians long dead.

'It was pretty smart just the same. You took my argument and used it. I call that pretty smart. I guess I had it coming,' Browning said. 'I never did anything about that medal. I guess,' he said, 'that if it hadn't been for you I wouldn't be walking down this passage today.'

'I didn't want a medal,' Larsen said.

'I always felt bad about it,' Browning said.

'Forget it,' Larsen said.

'Maybe I can do something for you now. I hear you're a bush pilot. Maybe I can put some business your way. Maybe I can inject a little money into your business.'

Larsen said: 'I don't want your money.'

They reached the top of the staircase. Beside them hung the chandelier suspended over the lobby below. There were rainbows in its pendants.

'It doesn't pay to be proud,' Browning said.

'But it's good to have pride.'

'I told you once that if things ever got tough you could come to me.'

'I don't accept charity,' Larsen said as they began to descend the stairs. He limped slightly.

'Just bear it in mind.'

Larsen didn't reply.

'But don't get the idea that I'm going soft or anything. We've got a fight on our hands.'

Larsen glanced at Browning. Hair still glossy and thick, a few shrewd lines on his face, figure still athletic, thickening a little at the waist. 'Sure we have a fight,' he said. 'And for once you're on the losing side.'

Browning smiled tightly. 'I'm never on the losing side,' he said.

'You know nothing can stop statehood now.'

'There's a hell of a lot more to this than statehood.' They were half-way down the curve of the staircase. 'This is a fight between progressives and reactionaries – conservationists like you. Alaska is there to provide food and fuel, to be mined and fished and tamed just as the whole of the world is being tamed. Throughout history there have been people like you who want to hold back.' There was a rasp now in Browning's voice. 'To stop people benefiting from what the world's got to offer because of eccentric obsessions.'

'You mean,' Larsen asked, 'that Alaska is up for grabs?'

They had reached the lobby where groups of men holding brief-cases were talking earnestly.

'I mean,' Browning said, 'that the land provides and a handful of crackpots are not going to stop Alaska providing.'

'I think you mean,' Larsen said quietly, 'that the land provides for Charles Browning.'

There was contempt in Browning's voice. 'Sure it does. And Charles Browning provides for thousands of others. Maybe hundreds of thousands one day. And what will you have? I'll tell you what you'll have, you'll have your ideals because that's all guys like you will ever have because you know you can't make your way in the world so you take to the pulpit.'

Larsen stretched out his hand. 'I hope the salmon are running for you,' he said. 'But don't bother to stock up with traps. This idealist reckons that the days of trapping salmon in the river mouth are numbered.'

He smiled and they shook hands and the shake was the seal of everlasting enmity.

The pro-statehood lobby now made yet another spectacular

political move. Two Democratic Congressmen, Wayne Aspinall and Leo O'Brien, dug up an old decision that a statehood bill is privileged: it can be debated without consent by the Rules Committee. Their case was upheld by the Speaker, Sam Rayburn.

The anti-statehood lobby was in disarray. They fell back. They adopted guerrilla warfare and they won a few minor clashes. For instance they retained control of the fisheries for the Federal Government so that, in a suite in a Tokyo hotel, the Japanese businessman named Nagata gratefully provided Charles Browning with food, drink, a Japanese girl with a tiny body and surprisingly full breasts and a contract to open another cannery with Japanese funds.

The anti-statehood movement also used delaying tactics including a demand for a referendum – the second – in Alaska. On May 28th, 1958, by a 208–166 majority the Alaskan statehood bill was passed in the House. The fight moved to the Senate. Then on June 30th a proposed filibuster melted like the snows of Alaska in summer. The Senate voted 64–20 for statehood. The news reached Anchorage at 2 p.m.

The roads were jammed with cars and the sidewalks were crowded with laughing, singing Alaskans and it was like St. Patrick's Day in New York except that everything was yellow and blue instead of green. At Fairbanks they dyed the Chena river gold with a dye used for air sea rescue and in Anchorage firemen lifted up Rita Martin, Queen of the 1958 Fur Rendezvous, to pin the 49th star on the American flag outside the federal building.

But the fight wasn't over. Although it was in its death throes. The anti-statehood lobby spread rumours across Alaska that natives would have to live on reservations, federal workers would lose their jobs. But the lobby had lost: the referendum was 5 to 1 for statehood and on January 3rd, 1959, Eisenhower officially proclaimed Alaska as the 49th state.

But by this time an event had occurred which would change Alaska more cataclysmically than any statehood bill. In 1957 the Richfield Oil Company struck oil in commercial quantities on the Kenai Peninsula forty miles north of Anchorage.

CHAPTER TWENTY

AND so it began.

From their first wildcat strike Richfield struck oil that flowed at the rate of nine hundred barrels a day. Then, in collaboration with Standard Oil of California, another strike was made a few miles away.

Oilmen poured into Anchorage and across the land to the Arctic Circle, the land of the polar bear. Nearly four hundred lease applications were filed daily. When four million acres of the Arctic were made available there were 7,406 applications for 1,320 parcels of land.

The hotels filled up with big drawling Texans. The price of real estate shot up. Membership of the Petroleum Club of Anchorage rose from a handful to one hundred and twenty-two.

Rotary rigs bit deep into the Alaskan Peninsula, Kenai, the Gulf of Alaska, the Matanuska Valley. Wildcat after wildcat, deeper and deeper beneath the crust, men snarling at the cold that can freeze flesh and blood, brushing aside the fat mosquitoes that can bloat your body with bites, challenging the bears that can take off your head with one tentative swipe, scrabbling and scrambling and scrapping as the bearded men had once done in their search for gold.

And maybe there was a little pollution. But nothing to worry about. Just a few spills in the Cook Inlet when they started offshore drilling. Some crude oil, engine oil and garbage in the lovely flat waters that mirror the clouds, a few hundred ducks killed, their feathers clotted obscenely with oil.

But still no commercial strike on the North Slope. The reservoirs of oil up there were big and deep, God knows how big and deep, perhaps as big and deep as the finds in East Texas in the thirties.

Charles Browning said to Trusz one day: 'Pretty soon some smart-ass is going to break this . . . this gentleman's agreement.'

Trusz who was shuffling a shiny new pack of cards said: 'You the smart-ass?'

They were drinking Scotch in Browning's house on Turnagain Arm. 'Maybe. Already production of crude oil in the United States is falling and one day soon we're going to have to go buying oil in massive quantities – and that means the Arabs. All of a sudden the Arabs are going to find themselves dictating terms. And boy, will they call high. Then there'll be a great howl for oil from the North Slope.'

Trusz slid the cards down the length of his arm and back again and looked pleased with himself. 'So you want me to go find it?'

'I want you to go and see our friend Guthrie. Sound him out. When the times comes I want to be in there drilling.'

And if I strike oil up there, Browning told himself, it will be for the good of the nation. He believed this. He sincerely believed it.

CHAPTER TWENTY-ONE

THE emergency call came over the radio at 11.38 a.m. on a blue and gold day in May.

While the fat dog, very old now, twitched in a shaft of sunlight and Larsen got his things together Mint enthused. 'Jeez what a break. So they gave you a hard time at the beginning but now you've arrived and for why? Because you had good training, the best, that's for why. You know, if it hadn't been for old Mint you'd have flown that first old ship of yours straight into The Mountain. Me, I'm not for the mountains,' Mint said, explaining why the call hadn't been for him. 'No sir. I'll put down in any goddam forest or river you like to name and I'll take off with floats from a puddle on Fourth Avenue but not mountains, not glaciers, not those mothers. Now you take care,' Mint warned as they walked to the Super Cub outside the office.

Larsen filtered gasoline into the tank through a chamois to get rid of any water which could freeze in the altitudes to which he was flying and choke a fuel pipe. Sunlight splintered on the frail silver body of the Cub – silver because Larsen had taken a tip from Don Sheldon and reduced the load by dispensing with paint.

Mint said: 'Hey, are you crazy or something? That ain't enough gas. Go on, gas it up some more.'

Larsen grinned at him: 'You stick to puddle take-offs.' He stroked the ship's warm silver body. 'This is mountain rescue, right?'

'Sure it's a mountain rescue,' answered Mint, chewing at a wad of gum.

'If I have too much I won't make it with a high altitude take-off.'

263

'And with too little gas you won't make it noways.'

'I've got to calculate it just right.'

'You're the boss,' Mint said. 'Boy, what a pupil I produced.'

Larsen loaded the plane as lightly as possible. First-aid gear, survival kit, ice-axe, rope, snow-shoes, snow-glasses, parka, mukluks, Scott's portable oxygen equipment. Then he went into the office and, stepping over the dog, telephoned Ruth.

Her voice sounded small, a long way away. He told her about the lucky break and his voice was proud.

'Do you have to go?'

He looked at the telephone. After a pause he said: 'Of course I've got to go.'

In the house overlooking the water Ruth felt the baby move, felt a ripple of pain. But it wasn't due for two months; she was being stupid. Just the same she said: 'There must be other pilots who can do it,' frowning and disliking herself for what she was saying.

'They don't seem to think so.' His voice was hurt. 'They seemed to think I'm the best guy for the job.'

'Then you'd better do what *they* want.'

'Look,' he said, 'what's got into you? I mean, what the hell's this all about? It's the break I've been waiting for and now you're knocking it.'

'If *they* mean more to you than—'

'Hell,' he said.

'Do you know what it's like waiting here? Year after year? Wondering if you're going to come home and knowing that one day you won't.'

'Now come on,' he said.

'It's just that I've got a feeling about today. A premonition.'

'Shit,' he said and then suddenly as the thought occurred to him: 'You're not sick or anything?'

'No, I'm not sick or anything,' as the baby moved again with a sharp pain.

'You're sure? I mean the baby's okay and everything?'

She thought: Why am I being such a bitch? If I have the baby prematurely there's nothing he can do so why am I acting like this, when he's got a break like this, the break he's waited for so long? And she thought: He loves Alaska and these people more than me because if he didn't he would understand, he would hear it in my voice. He's risking his life when I'm about to have his baby. You mean, morbid bitch, she said to herself.

Her voice softened. 'Yes,' she said, 'the baby's fine and so am I and I'm sorry I spoke like that. I suppose it's the pregnancy. You know, I'm a bit querulous.'

He smiled at the receiver. 'I know, honey, and I'm sorry too. I wish I could come back home now but, you know, this is quite an honour. They'd have chosen Sheldon but he's away up north someplace.'

'You go,' she said. 'But call me as soon as you get back. Radio the control when you've done whatever you've got to do and ask them to call me. What mountain is it?'

'McKinley,' Larsen told her.

'What's it like up there today?'

'Fine except that it's socked down with cloud at the top.'

'Don't do anything stupid,' she said, then amended this to 'foolhardy.'

'Don't worry. There's a good strip of snow near where this guy's lying.'

'What happened then?' she asked. 'How did he fall?'

'I'll tell you about it when I get back.'

'Okay. And don't worry about me. Premonition? It's this baby,' she said, touching the drum of her belly with her free hand. 'It makes me say things I don't mean. Premonition? Since when was I superstitious?' She laughed and made it sound natural. My stage training, she thought.

'I thought it sounded kind of crazy,' she said. And then: 'I love you.' And softly so that Mint couldn't hear: 'And I love that baby too. It had better be a girl,' he added.

'Don't say that. Supposing it's a boy, will you hate it?'

'Oh sure,' he said. 'If that kid's a boy I'll dress it in skirts.'

Mint slapped him on the back. 'Hey, there's a guy waiting for you up on that fucking mountain.'

Larsen held up his hand. 'I know.' And to his wife, wanting to kiss her: 'I'll call you as soon as I get back.'

'I love you,' she said.

'Me too,' he said.

He hung up and Mint said: 'The trouble with guys like you is that you talk too much.'

He embraced space. Blue, limitless space in which stars and suns and moons floated like algae in a shoreless ocean.

He climbed towards infinity, levelled out. He dived, he climbed, he waggled the wings of his little hornet; he breathed deeply and he laughed and he remembered the beautiful things and the sad that had happened to him; he remembered the girl in Anchorage who had loved him and left him to die but was still sometimes with him; he remembered the first time he had kissed his wife and the first time he had made love to her; he remembered the first sight of his son with his blue, uncomprehending eyes; he remembered jewels in the snow, sails across the Sound, the rustle of birch leaves, childhood . . .

Ahead lay McKinley. Clouds covered its crest. Now it was a mountain, soon it would be a wall above and below him and he had once chance, one chance only, to land, and if he didn't make it he would hit that wall or fall into its moat.

Premonition. Why had she said that? And why the hell do I care that she said it? What is superstition? It's fear but it's more than fear: it's a dog's hackles rising in a haunted house, it's the cats stopping meowing before an earthquake. And it's infectious. Some of the elation bled from Richard Larsen. He held the aircraft steady on course. He watched the dials. He stared through the Plexiglass windscreen. He found comfort in the smell of gasoline and engine oil. He glanced down at his territory, no for Christ's sake, his state.

Below he could see the dark green of spruce and small lakes like scattered hand-mirrors in the snow. He saw a trapper's hut, the trapper waving from a clearing in the spruce, a trail through the trees where in deep winter dog-sleds would bump and slither.

He gained altitude. Now he would really have to climb because the mountain was swelling into a wall of crags and turrets and battlements. Green and grey and crumpled in the foothills, then fingered with white where the blowing snow had lodged in crevices, then all white, glaring white, until you hit the strata of clouds that bandaged the summit. Behind those bandages lay the broken body of a Japanese climber.

There were many Japanese climbing the peaks of the six hundred-mile-long range of mountains these days. Seventeen years ago I was killing them now I'm rescuing them. In those days the Russians were our allies, now the Russians are our enemies and I'm trying to pluck a wounded Jap off a mountain and maybe he was the Jap who nearly shot my head off when I peered out of that goddam foxhole.

He climbed steadily to make his approach to Kahiltna Pass. He was clocking one hundred miles per hour. The spears of the approach mountains seemed to be reaching for the belly of the little aircraft. *Premonition?* It had to be the baby, the fear of birth, of its agony, spreading and encompassing other fears. Yes, that's what it was.

Larsen stared up at McKinley's peak. The cloud was still there which was good because it meant that the one hundred miles an hour winds that come in from the Pacific weren't around and, according to the met report, wouldn't be around for some time, except that you could never be too sure with met reports, especially around the upper reaches of The Mountain which made its own weather.

He was still climbing. He checked the oxygen apparatus. He stared across the peaks. 'Like looking out of the very windows of heaven,' according to Bradford Washburn, one of the first men to climb McKinley. Now he was flying through the 10,200 foot high corridor that is the Kahiltna Pass and the walls were on either side of him and there was loneliness and cruelty here in the cockpit. Then he was through, looking for the Jap.

According to the radio report the rope connecting the Japanese climbers had snapped and one of them had fallen down a crevice. They had got him up again but he was in a bad way, legs broken, breathing difficult, concussed with probable internal injuries. Twenty-four more hours in the cold without medical attention and he would be dead.

The Japs had given a fix and, if Larsen was correct, it was

right beside the glacier on which he had landed before. A fine glacier, with a good tilt to it to slow his ship down on landing so that it didn't career majestically over the lip.

Then he was in the cloud. This was the frightening part, mist pouring over your wings, driving at the windscreen, with only your instruments to fly by, and the feeling that the walls of the mountains are magnetic, drawing you to them. And you think of your son and the coming baby and your hands stroking the tight belly of your wife; you think of these things remotely while you concentrate on the flying but even now, when you think you see a gap in the cloud, the thoughts are still with you on the retina of your subconscious, but you don't think of death, there is fear but no thought of death, thoughts of life rather than death.

A gap in the cloud.

You are through. There is the glacier below. Relief oozes from you in sweat. Your bowels feel loose. But there's a lot of flying ahead.

The light wasn't good. Good for mountaineering, maybe, but not for gauging the surface of the glacier when you needed the sun at an angle to find shadows on the snow that indicate drifts and lips of ravines covered with a crust of ice and snow. And then there is the white glare that comes from staring at the glacier that distorts your sense of height. This is glacier flying, this and the business of putting the plane down and getting it up again. But thank God I've landed here before and I should know where to put down.

Then he saw it. A flash of light. Probably a mirror. He blinked and stared down. A trickle of smoke. So they must be burning some of their equipment because there was nothing else to burn. You had to hand it to the Japs, they were super efficient except, perhaps, when it came to buying good tough rope.

Larsen waggled his wings to show that he had seen them. He flew low over them and waved and they waved back. There were four of them and a tent.

Now for the landing on the strip of glacier that was safe if his memory was correct. He banked and began his first approach. As he flew over the snowfield he dropped branches of trees that he had brought with him. This was Sheldon's technique, with the dark line of branches down there you could overcome the distorted height perception.

He began his final approach. He adjusted the throttle. Airspeed and glide slope correct. He was coming down, searching for the snow with his skis, engine at full power which was tricky for a landing but essential here because he would be landing on an upward incline and he would need that power as he touched down. Ahead lay a ravine, a great wound between glacier and mountainside, and if the skis didn't touch snow soon he would be spinning down that wound.

The skis kissed the snow. The mountainside was coming at them as the Super Cub slowed. Larsen kicked the rudder and the plane slewed round. It stopped. He switched off the engine. The little plane sighed and groaned as the heat went out of it. Larsen climbed down and patted it as a jockey pats a winning mount.

Two of the Japanese were walking across the snow to meet him. They looked neat, precise, efficient. And, of course, they smiled. In death they smiled. They were very polite. They talked about their wounded colleague as Americans talk about the weather.

One of them was a doctor. 'How is he?' Larsen said.

'Fair,' said the doctor. 'Perhaps worsening.'

'I mean is he going to live?'

'You brought plasma?'

Larsen nodded.

'Then he will live if you get him to hospital. Get the plasma please.'

Larsen peered inside the orange tent. The wounded man's legs were splinted and there was blood on his mountaineering clothes. His face was calm, only his eyes looked sick. Another Japanese squatted in the corner of the tent.

Larsen returned to the plane while the doctor gave the wounded man a transfusion. The weather was still good. He breathed deeply and felt the cold prickle his nostrils.

The doctor called to him. 'Come please. It is necessary that you get him to hospital as soon as possible.'

'And you, what are you going to do now?'

The doctor shrugged his shoulders. 'We hope you will return.'

Larsen stopped outside the tent. 'What the hell are you talking about?'

'We have another casualty.'

'Another?'

The doctor shrugged apologetically. 'He has altitude sickness. He was very brave and he didn't tell us.'

'Very stupid,' Larsen said.

'Perhaps, but he will die if we don't get him to a lower altitude.'

'Then get him to one.'

'He is very bad. We cannot get down quickly enough.'

'Let's have a look at him, for God's sake.'

The Japanese squatting in the corner of the tent looked up with eyes as sick as those of the man with the broken legs. There was a bluish tinge to his skin. Larsen had seen it before; he knew the man could die within a few hours.

He said to the doctor: 'I can only carry one man.'

'I know.' The doctor nodded thoughtfully. 'I know that.'

'Which one shall I take?'

'You must take the man with the broken legs. He bleeds inside. If the bleeding isn't stopped he will die.'

'So will your other friend.'

'I know. But it was his fault. He was too proud. You have oxygen, perhaps?'

'Yeah, I've got oxygen but it won't last forever.'

'You can leave it here?'

'I can leave it, sure, it's portable.'

'That will help him,' the doctor said, 'for a while.'

'Can't you get him down after he's had oxygen?'

The doctor massaged his hands together, murmuring: 'They are very bad these cases. Once they have breathed the air with little oxygen they are very weak.'

'But it's not all that goddam high here.'

'Too high for a man like him,' the doctor apologized. 'Too high for a man in his condition. It is very cold, too, at night. His hands have a little frostbite.'

'Surely to Christ you've got sleeping bags.'

'He must have slept with his hands outside.'

Larsen kicked the powdered snow viciously. 'Is he crazy or something?' he asked, turning and heading towards the Super Cub without waiting for an answer.

The doctor followed him. He said: 'I don't know whether he is crazy but he has money. He put up the money for this expedition. He will pay you well,' he said as they reached the plane which looked bright and cold and self-sufficient in the splintering sunlight.

'He'd better,' Larsen told the doctor.

Some of the blueness left the altitude-sick Japanese as he sucked down oxygen. They laid the wounded man on a stretcher and hoisted it into the plane.

'You'll come back?' the doctor asked.

'I'll come back,' said Larsen thinking that two landings and take-offs on a glacier was chancing your luck. 'Now you can help. You and me and what's left of your expedition had better start trampling a strip. You got snow-shoes?'

'Of course,' said the Japanese.

'Of course,' said Larsen.

It took them an hour to trample the snow into a surface on which the 1,000lb Super Cub could reach an airspeed that would get the lift before it reached the crinkled snow where the crevices lay.

'We're very grateful to you,' the doctor said.

Larsen who was thinking about Ruth and the baby said: 'Damn right.' He climbed into the cockpit, fired the engine, stuck up his thumb. 'Here goes boy,' he said to himself as the ship accelerated.

He figured that in this starved air he would be losing about forty per cent of his power. Come on my little sparrow, he prayed, my light-feathered little sparrow.

They were gathering speed, but not enough, not enough yet to get the lift. *Ruth I love you.* And then the tail was up. He eased the stick back and the eyes of the Japanese stared at him with trust as though he were Buddha or someone.

Then the nose was up and they were airborne and the glacier was beneath them and the Japanese smiled.

Larsen put down at the Summit airstrip where the wounded Japanese was transferred to a six-seater Cessna. He was on his way to Anchorage while the Piper was still being fuelled.

Larsen got a mechanic to call Ruth and tell her that everything was okay and that he was on his way back because, if he called her, she would hear the lie in his voice because that's the way they were with each other. He remembered the kick of the baby against him when he was lying close to Ruth.

Then he climbed into the cockpit, climbed into the lingering light of the afternoon and headed for the glacier.

After the call from Summit she concentrated her attention on the game of Monopoly and tried to stop her son buying up all the prime areas. Relief suffused her like a drug.

'Was that Pa?' Billy asked.

She said it was.

'You sure look happier now.'

'I am,' she said.

'Will he be here when the baby's born?'

'I hope so.'

The baby was quieter now and the pains had stopped.

'I hope it's a boy.'

'Your father wants a girl.'

'Yeah, well he's got some screwy ideas.'

'Perhaps he thinks that one of you is enough.'

The boy grinned and she saw her husband grinning. The same eyes radiating blueness, the same hair only Billy's was crew-cut. He wore jeans and sneakers and a striped T-shirt and he was straight and strong. She wondered what he would have been like if he had been reared in London. She tried to imagine him with a Cockney accent; he would be the same boy and yet he would be different because you judge people from the outside.

Rattling the dice and spilling them on the table, he said: 'Do you reckon he'll let me go hunting?'

She shook her head. 'You know he won't.'

'Not even if I don't do any shooting?'

She said: 'Stop trying to work on me while your father's away.'

'A lot of the guys at school think he's weird that way.'

'Do you?'

'No,' said the boy but there was doubt in his voice. He heard it and said: 'No, of course I don't.' He paused. 'All the guys think he's great. You know, one of the best bush pilots in Alaska and pretty good with the dogs, too. But they don't understand this thing about hunting.' The boy examined the fallen dice. 'And I'm not sure I do either.'

'Your father doesn't like unnecessary killing. Why kill a beautiful animal just for sport?' She threw the dice. *Why had the call been made from Summit?* 'If you want to be brave, if you want to pit yourself against wild animals why not photograph them?'

'Aw come on,' the boy said in disgust. 'You've got a grizzly coming at you and you pull out your camera and pop off a picture?'

She counted the dice. She went docilely to jail. 'You can get away in a jeep. You can take photographs of other animals.'

'Hell—'

'Don't say that.'

'Well – that's what I meant to say – the other guys, my buddies, say their fathers reckon animals have got to be killed to control them.'

'Maybe but not killed for sport.' *He had said he would get control at Anchorage to call her.*

'If you've got to kill 'em why not have some sport at the same time?'

She looked at her son again as he shook the dice, whispering to them like a craps player. He's Alaskan, she thought. He's tough and strong and assertive. She wondered if he would develop the defensiveness that often lay behind the assertion. She wished that there was more of her in him. Then she thought with surprise, perhaps there is. Perhaps there's more of me in him than there is of Richard. Perhaps it's just his looks that are Richard's because he has instincts that are alien to his father. Perhaps those instincts are mine. After all, she hadn't known much about ecology, wild-life, hunting until she met Richard. Perhaps I'm a huntress!

'Come on,' he said, 'it's your throw and the way you're playing you'll soon be broke.'

And he should be landing at Anchorage now. Calling from the airfield. Driving back.

The old fear returned. She sold a couple of properties. The baby moved. Girl or boy?

'Look,' he said, 'you've blown it. It's not me that's going broke. Why don't you quit?'

'All right,' she said. She opened the window. There was a smell of balsam on the late afternoon air. The sky was blue and as she stood at the window she could feel the sun's warmth on her body. The baby moved again as though alert to her fear. Another twist of pain. Oh God, she thought, it's coming and I want him here.

She said to the boy: 'You all packed?'

'Sure I'm all packed. You packed for me.' Such blueness radiating from those eyes.

Now she saw the plane crumpled against the mountains, his body, trapped in the cockpit. *But he might still call from Anchorage. And this is crazy because he's hardly overdue and I don't know how long the rescue took. You're a crazy woman, Ruth Larsen.*

'Come on,' she said, 'I'll drive you over to Guthrie's place.'

'Is it coming? Is the baby coming?'

'Soon,' she said. 'She'll be here soon.'

'He.'

'He or she.'

She wanted her mother but her mother had died a couple of weeks ago, had anticipated death and made all the arrangements. Ruth heard the chiming of the Westminster clock and she wanted to be going by taxi with her mother to an old, ether-smelling hospital with dusty plane trees outside.

Her son stared at her belly. 'Can you feel him coming? I mean can you actually feel *it*?' making the baby neuter to please his mother.

'Get your case,' she said.

They went down the stairs to the old Volkswagen he had bought her. The temperature was in the low sixties and the breeze blowing across the water was clean and full of promise. *O God, bring him back.*

'Hey,' said Guthrie, his naked face grinning, 'so it's really on the way, huh?' He took Billy into the kitchen and poured him a Coke and left him there while he talked to Ruth. 'Where's our intrepid pilot?'

She told him.

'Of course he's overdue,' Guthrie said. 'You don't pick up wounded Japanese on glaciers and hand them over and keep to a schedule as though you were transporting vegetables to Fairbanks. Maybe he's doing a little hunting at the same time,' beardless face grinning.

'But why the call from Summit?'

'Why not? If he had to refuel why not call from Summit?'

'But why would he have to refuel?'

'Search me. But I guess if he was going to make a high altitude landing on a short strip he'd take as little fuel as possible.'

Ruth sat down, refused a drink. 'I hadn't thought of that.' A pulse of hope as strong as a movement from the baby. 'That could be the answer.'

'Sure it could. Now what do you want to do? I suggest you leave your car right out there and I'll drive you to the hospital.' He gazed at her anxiously and she knew he was hoping nothing was going to start here in his apartment.

'That would be fine.' A sharp pain that made her gasp. 'I think we'd better be on our way.'

She kissed Billy. 'Call home in an hour,' she told him, 'and tell your father what's happened.'

'Sure and give my love to *it*.'

She was in a private ward and the two nurses were very efficient. They bathed her and shaved her and talked about the impending birth as though it were something off an assembly line and they commented on her accent – or lack of accent, whichever way you looked at it – and one of them asked: 'Are you British or Australian?'

The pains were subsiding.

The nurses looked at each other, shook their heads.

'Not for some time yet,' one of them remarked.

'I'm sorry—'

'No need to be honey. Happens all the time.'

It was because those first pains were false, because it was six hours before the true labour began, because in those six hours she heard nothing from her husband that she knew that something had happened to him.

He was flying towards the wall of the mountain again and it was only the wall he could see, no sky, just the wall of snow and granite and the only comfort was the warm oily smell of the cockpit and the purr of the engine.

He found the snowfield on the glacier by its marker line of branches. He flew over it once, banked and began his approach. The engine was sweet, the strip looked good and flat, polished by the sun.

The wind hit him as he was thinking how easy it is once you know how. As easy as driving an automobile down Fourth Avenue, he was thinking as the wind pushed him sideways and downwards; he fought the stick, kicked the rudder; maybe he tried to put her down when he should have tried to get her up again, but there was the wall in front of him, and so he tried to put the plane down because at the moment of decision he could only imagine the plane smashing into the wall.

The wind pushed him down.

And then when he just might have made it, when he was waiting for the song of the skis on the polished snow, the wind slapped him sideways so that it was his wing-tip that hit the snow first. The wing came off as easily as a fly's wing and the plane lay on its side with the other wing sticking up like a monument. Joyously the wind drove at this wing and bowled the plane over so that it lay on its back like an immobilized beetle.

Larsen hung upside down. He wasn't aware that he was upside down. Blood was dripping from his scalp and he was unconscious.

There were no exploding stars, no distant murmurs, no indistinct impressions of unconsciousness. Unconsciousness is nothing.

'There,' they said. 'You'll be all right now. You had a rough ride but you'll be all right now.'

She could smell anaesthetic, could see a kidney bowl on the table beside her in case she vomited. One of the nurses was wiping her forehead with a towel. And she felt empty.

'Don't worry,' they said. 'It's all over now.'

They were all white and pink and she was empty. And the pain had moved; it was in her chest: she couldn't breathe.

She tried to sit up.

'There, there.' Strong gentle hands pushing her back. 'It's a natural reaction. Nothing to worry about. You'll be just fine.'

The voices faded. She was cold and there was a fly buzzing inside her head. Then they returned. Looking down at her. She could see the slackness beneath their chins.

She felt for the emptiness but she couldn't move her arm.

'How—'

'Don't you worry . . .'

'Is it—?'

'Just you get some sleep . . .'

'A boy or a girl?'

They didn't reply for a moment. She could see their eyes swivelling. And she knew then. It wasn't a boy or a girl. It was just . . . it was just . . . it.

CHAPTER TWENTY-TWO

THE first gusts of wind had been coy. They had merely tipped over an aeroplane. They were a tease. Soon they gained power.

The gusts tugged at the three Japanese trying to free Larsen, tried to send them skimming across the glacier and drop them down one of the deep slits in the side of the mountain.

The Japanese seemed very small as the wind pulled at them.

They managed to open the upside-down cockpit and cut Larsen free and pillow his body as it slumped headfirst. One eye was closed, the other open; there was a little blood seeping from the corner of his mouth.

The doctor said: 'It doesn't look good,' but no one heard him because the wind took his words with it.

They could feel the wind shifting the aircraft as they pulled at his body, trying to be gentle with his head. They winced at the sting of the blowing snow.

They shook their heads, they clapped their mittened hands, they stamped their big-booted feet and they wondered what had happened to the fair weather that had been forecast.

The aircraft shifted a few feet. They held on to the body of the pilot. And this movement of the aircraft helped them because the wind was *peeling* the aircraft from the man.

Then they had him and they were staggering towards the tent, burrowing into the wind, feeling it inflate their cheeks if they opened their mouths, thrusting into their nostrils.

Soon the wind velocity must decrease. But it increased and it took the new, silver-bright lightweight not-yet-paid-for Super Cub with it, dropping it down one of the deep slits where it lay broken and dead.

It was difficult to breathe out unless you turned out of the wind and then it sucked your breath with it. And the flying snow was creating a white-out where all dimension is lost and, although the wind was howling with strength, the air was weak, and the three Japanese toiling with the pilot felt life leaving their limbs, being replaced by cold. They wanted to breathe, they wanted to lie down but still they made their way towards the orange tent, or made their way to where they believed the orange tent was.

But were they making any progress at all? The wind was a snow-plough shoving against them. Once they dropped him, paused a moment while they got a fresh grip, grateful for the pause.

They tried again.

Suddenly the wind was a tease again; the flying snow subsided; they could see the lustre of the sky.

And there was the tent. As bright as a flame.

They laid him down beside the Japanese with altitude sickness. The doctor tested his breathing with a mirror, listened to his heart, peered into the open eye and then, lifting the lid, into the closed eye. He felt his body, found the scar on the thigh and said to one of the others: 'Maybe we did that.'

They had a Primus stove in the tent but it was running low on fuel. They slid Larsen's body into the spare sleeping bag.

'I think he will be all right,' the doctor said. 'He's concussed. Maybe a hairline fracture of the skull.'

'But the blood,' queried one of the other climbers.

'He bit through his tongue,' the doctor said.

'And what about him?' asked the third climber, built like a wrestler, pointing at the sick Japanese. 'Now that the oxygen's run out?'

'He will die,' the doctor said.

They hadn't believed that any wind could be stronger than the one that shifted the aircraft but they had been wrong. This was a McKinley wind and there are intrepid men who have travelled the dust-bowls and ice-caps of the world who will tell you that there is no sound, no assault on the senses, like it.

Larsen blinked. He thought he was in a train passing through a tunnel. He tasted blood; he felt pain on his tongue but immediately that was erased by the noise of the wind. He tried to move his head but it was weighted so he moved his eyes and saw the Japanese and remembered making the approach to the glacier. So I crashed. I really crashed. And that beautiful little plane that I haven't paid for ... He tried to move again, to speak, but no words came.

He looked at the Japanese and he thought: Christ that's funny. They try to kill me, I try to kill them, I rescue them, they rescue me. He grinned and the doctor looked at him inquiringly, indicated with his hand that he should be calm.

Am I badly hurt? He didn't think so. He tried to assess the situation. As soon as he was overdue they would mount a search, weather permitting and as sure as hell the weather wasn't permitting up here but, knowing McKinley as he did, it was possible that down below it was as balmy as a fine May day on Long Island, but that didn't help them any. *That beautiful little plane.*

He beckoned to the doctor. The doctor came close and Larsen shouted (although he whispered): 'What about the plane?'

The doctor shook his head. Made a thumbs-down gesture. Waved the other hand. '*Kaput,*' he shouted.

As he lay there waiting a terrible sadness came to Richard Larsen. The plane was wrecked and he was broke and in debt. He told himself, Alaska has done this to me, has rejected me because I am not the stuff of the Great Land, because this is a cruel and brutal place and it is cruel and brutal men that it needs, so that they can pit themselves against each other. I was never wanted here, I am a soldier fighting on the wrong side. Oh Christ this is all muddled but the pain is real, I am in the wrong place, I always have been.

And then he thought of the baby.

How long had he been up here? The premonition! Perhaps she had felt the baby beginning its escape from the womb. Hadn't told him because she knew how much he wanted this flight. Perhaps now she was in the middle of the agony.

Richard Larsen groaned but, against the wind, the groan was the call of a lemming against the roar of a lion.

The doctor was tending to the sick climber, bending over the bluish face protruding from the sleeping bag.

Larsen managed to look at his wrist-watch which had remained intact. It was 10.15 p.m.

It was at that moment that his wife was delivered of a still-born child.

It was at that moment that the Japanese with altitude sickness died.

It was at that moment that the wind snatched away the orange tent and left them in the white-out like blind puppies abruptly left by their mother.

They huddled close and ducked inside their sleeping bags and they all knew that they would die if the wind didn't let up. The snow spattered them like lead-shot. The snow buried the dead man. He wasn't the first to be buried on The Mountain. Others lay beneath the snow, beneath glacial ice, embalmed for eternity.

The progression towards death was pain, then numbness, then indifference. Larsen was becoming numb but he could still feel the snow stinging his cheeks. He remembered Robert Service's poem:

> *This is the law of the Yukon, and ever she makes it plain:*
> *Send not your foolish and feeble: send me your strong and*
> *your sane—*

Good old Robert Service. He knew about guys like me. And I don't care and this is the indifference, this is the slide to death, because I have made a fuck-up of the whole thing and I should be selling the *Times* and the *News* and the *Post* and sticks of fruit-flavoured gum in the family store and getting paunchy, or maybe managing a card shop selling mitzvah greetings and silver wedding cards and risqué cards with drawings of pregnant women – *Ruth, my love, how are you?* – instead of which I am lying here freezing to death, because

Robert Service got it all right and I got it all wrong which no longer bothers me, I don't give a shit because I'm going to die, odd that you don't care, except perhaps about what you've left behind – *Ruth, the boy, the baby* – and none of it's the way you imagined it because with illness the fear of death is a stench but when it's inevitable you don't give a shit, no, really you don't.

He noticed that the Japanese were trying to pile the snow around him. He remembered survival instructions. *Use the elements. Snow insulates, use it.* But I don't give a shit. The doctor pointed at the snow, Larsen freed his arms and scooped a little around him.

You're strong and you're sane.

So where did I go wrong? The best pilots in the world could have been fooled by a skittish wind that turned into a hurricane; McKinley has fooled better than me. At least I'm wearing several layers of clothing and thermal underwear and mukluks with liners and double mittens and a parka with a wolverine ruff and I've kept the clothes clean because dirt cuts down insulation. But wasn't there something about not wearing too many clothes inside a sleeping bag to avoid sweating because the sweat freezes and causes frost-bite? Ah, to hell with it, you can't think of everything.

He wondered what the chill factor was with this unbelievable wind. And why was he regaining some of his morale? Thinking constructively. Maybe that was the final trick; maybe you came to the conclusion that everything was worth while just before you kicked off.

I love you Ruth.

He couldn't feel his cheeks. Never rub frostbite. Rubbing as a remedy was an old wives' tale and many an old wife must have been mutilated that way. Larsen put his mittened hands to his cheeks to give them body heat and was astonished at this sudden desire to live. It must be the last throes, the last spasms of some big game shot by an intrepid white hunter in a Hollywood movie.

Yes, it was the last throes because now I can feel the sleep feeling its way through my body and I don't care except that I would have liked to see a little more, taken the journey a little

282

farther – *and now life was in reverse and the grenade was exploding and the squirrels were playing on the trees in the garden and he was on his way back from whence he came –* except that there was a brightness somewhere, penetrating his closed eyelids, a brightness that halted the reversing images and, bringing him back to the present, caused him to blink and shake the snow from his face.

There was no sound. Above, the sky was blue. He could even feel a little warmth.

The doctor's voice came to him, distorted by his frozen lips. 'It stopped just like that ... like a train crashing. Silence and now the sun ...'

Larsen stared into the pale blue feeling the snow melt around his eyes. He couldn't move, he didn't want to move but it came to him then that he was going to live, that he had almost crossed the border, that if he had retracted beyond childhood he would be dead, he would know all the answers. But now he would have to wait because the peace after the noise of the wind had startled his senses as abruptly as a sudden noise, because the touch of the sun, however light, had infused life.

They stayed there quietly because there was no point now in trying to take any of the precautions that the manuals prescribe. They were too sick to move; they had been brought back from death and all they could do was wait for help.

The buzzing came from far away. It grew louder. It was above them somewhere. They searched the sky with sore eyes. They saw two helicopters, two great dragonflies. But the pilots couldn't see them and Larsen realized that they were covered by snow and the Piper Cub and the branches had been blown away. He tried to sit up but he couldn't. But the doctor was moving, slowly, slowly, emerging from the chrysalis of his sleeping bag, searching with slow hands in the pockets of his parka, finding matches, trying to set fire to the sleeping bag, finding that the material wouldn't burn.

The doctor looked at Larsen and he looked at the other two men and he looked away and he set fire to the dead man, to his clothing, and a stem of grey smoke rose into the thin air and the helicopters began their descent.

CHAPTER TWENTY-THREE

THE valley is salad green in the early days of the fleeting summer and rich green later and rich gold and brown in the last days before the frost.

It is only ten miles by sixty miles and is but a tiny oasis of fertility in the Great Land.

The valley is named Matanuska and it owes its fecund presence to The Depression when the Federal Government helped some two hundred midwest families, lean and hungry-faced, to leave their own lands and try to cultivate this valley just north of Anchorage where the old sourdoughs grew stringy radishes and potatoes.

The farmers from the midwest did to the valley what the Jews have done to Palestine. They made it blossom. No, they did more: they made a mockery of those who claimed you couldn't cultivate the hostile crust of Alaska. They produced cabbages weighing sixty pounds!

And they did more. Behind belts of cottonwood, willow and spruce they reared dairy cattle and horses, grew oats and barley that is rippled and dented by the late summer breezes before the combines fist their way through.

The valley became famous and scientists who dislike *a phenomenon* analysed it and decided that the fertility was due to the nightless days of summer and the lower angle of the sun's rays which meant they travelled longer through the earth's atmosphere which filtered the ultra-violet. Which was fine for jungle growths of vegetables but not so good for fibre content and when you tried to ship the vegetables they bruised as easily as ripe peaches.

The valley, flat and green with a great hump in the middle, was reminiscent of the green patchworks of England which was why Richard Larsen sometimes drove his wife there when the nostalgia was upon her.

But these days there was more than nostalgia between them. Much more since the loss of the baby, since his weeks in hospital after the accident which had left frost-bite scar tissue on his face, hands and feet. There was lack of money, there was despair and there was something more: Alaska was between them.

Perhaps it was a mistake to bring her to the valley because when she gazed upon it he knew she wanted to go home.

He parked the car near a field where the breeze pushed slow brown waves across the barley. In the distance they could hear the busy sound of a combine.

They walked beside the barley. They plucked whiskered fingers of grain, rolling them between their hands, blowing away the chaff and nibbled the grain.

'You want to go back home, don't you,' he said because it was difficult for her to say it.

She stopped, the breeze tugging at her skirt. Her face had been tired recently, her eyes seeing beyond immediate things, but now there was a longing in it from which he turned away.

'I want to be with you,' she said. She took his hand but her touch was cold.

'But not here?'

'Perhaps I could go away for a little while. Perhaps we could all go ...'

But she didn't know how broke they were, so he said: 'No, I've got to get the business going again' – *With what?* – 'but why don't you go away?' knowing that she would misinterpret this.

'You've been here a long time. Can't you leave it just for a little while?'

'No,' he said, 'I've got things to do.'

They were deliberately talking themselves apart. Each could have adjusted their words so that they moved closer; but some force was propelling their speech; not just pride, not perversity, some guiding force of destiny.

'You've got things to do!'

'I've got to buy another plane.'

'We both need a rest,' she said.

'You go,' he said. 'Take a vacation in England. Take Billy with you.'

'He's an Alaskan,' she said. 'He doesn't care about England.'

She asked: 'What has this place ever done for you?'

'It's given me a purpose in life.'

'Which is more important than your family?'

'I didn't realize there was any contest.'

She started walking again. Picked up a stick and switched at the long, pollen-dusted grass beside the road. She walked ahead so that he was able to observe the fine swing of her body; naked, her body was still firm and supple, although her breasts that had filled with milk for the baby looked tired, as though they missed the small sucking mouth. For some time now she had been physically well enough to make love but he had waited, waited for her to come to him. He was ashamed of his desires, ashamed of the way his body betrayed him, but still he waited and the longing became a tide pushing against a dam when he remembered the healthy abandonment of their love-making before. They didn't discuss it but he knew she believed the baby would have been born alive if it hadn't been for the shock of knowing that he was missing: the baby would have been alive if he hadn't taken off that day. The baby girl.

The combine clattered busily.

She said: 'In a month's time this' – gesturing at the bowl of gold and green scooped from the mountains – 'will be winter again. I hate this place,' she said, turning and heading back towards the car.

'That's not true,' he said.

'It's true,' she said.

'Did you hate it when we lived in the cabin?'

'I hate it now.'

'Have you always hated it in the house?'

'I tell you I hate it now.'

'What's changed you?' he asked, knowing.

'You know.'

'Would I ask?' *And still they were pushing against each other. Why?*

'There should have been four of us now,' she said as she switched off the head of a fireweed.

'Maybe there will be one day.'

'And maybe when we're about to become four again you'll fly away to rescue an Eskimo or an Indian or an Aleut.'

'The baby would probably have been born dead anyway. Isn't that what they said?'

'They said it might have been. They didn't know.'

'But there are three of us. We're a family.'

'I know,' she said, and she was crying. 'I can't help it. I can't help it,' she said, turning and allowing him to put his arms round her so that for a few moments he thought everything was all going to be all right. 'When the baby was dead and I thought you were dead I wanted to die, too.'

'But the boy—'

'I know. Our son. But I wanted to die.'

He stroked her hair. 'That was only natural. That was only natural,' he said again.

'But now, I don't know . . .'

He lifted her head. 'Do you still love me?' He waited, waited.

'I love you,' she said.

The relief was as warm as blood.

'But—' she began.

'But what?'

'I don't know. I can't explain.' She searched for a handkerchief, found one, dabbed the corners of her eyes. 'I need a rest,' she said. 'Something happened when the baby . . .' She began to cry again. 'Perhaps if I went to England and got things arranged about the sale of my mother's house.'

'I understand,' he said, but he resented her wanting to leave him, although he knew that she wouldn't if he told her how broke they were. But he didn't tell her, so he was responsible for his own bitterness.

'You don't mind?' she asked.

'I suggested it, remember?'

287

'And when I come back everything will be all right again.'

'Everything will be all right,' he soothed her.

'And maybe we'll have another baby.'

'Sure,' he said. 'Why not?'

She kissed him, gently, gratefully.

They were quiet on the drive back to Anchorage. He guessed that she was thinking of London in the fall. He was wondering how he was going to pay her fare, find the next payment on the house and buy another plane. But he knew the answer, all the time he knew the answer.

Judy Browning found out the conventional way.

The trace of perfume that wasn't hers, the red-daubed cigarette butts in the ashtray of the car, the indiscreet letter in his desk in the study.

The letter was very physical. She read it with detachment. I am, if anything, saddened, she decided, as she folded the letter, replaced it in the envelope and put the envelope back into the desk. Saddened at the goddam conventionality of it all; the girl was a secretary (aren't they all?) who thought Charles was a great lover and expected him to leave his wife.

But what did I expect, she wondered, as she stared at the sheafs of papers, receipts and notebooks in the desk. From the start there had been this tacit understanding. We've kept up the partnership because that's all our marriage ever was.

She began to flip through a sheaf of typewritten papers with her long tanned fingers. Were we ever capable of giving more? If we had met other partners? I doubt it, she thought, and was further saddened.

She scanned a sheet of typewritten paper with the names of Snowdon and Stopforth on the letterhead. It was a report on an investigation into the un-American activities of her father.

They were on the roofgarden of the penthouse in Chicago. The lights were bright beneath them, the car headlights moving slowly down the streets, neon lights blinking. There was a smell of chrysanthemums on the air, a scent of impending autumn.

She said: 'You killed him.'

'For Christ's sake,' Browning said. He sipped some brandy and picked a grape from the fruit-bowl on the table.

'Why? Why did you have to do it?'

'Do what, for God's sake?'

'I read the report from the detective agency.'

'I'll have to change the locks on that desk,' Browning said.

'You killed him. Why?'

'I happen to go along with the idea that anyone with Communist leanings should have no part in a capitalist society. Not just because they may be undermining our system but because it's so goddam hypocritical. And I did not kill him,' Browning added.

'Bullshit,' she said. She lit a cigarette; her hand was shaking. 'You married me to help you up that little old ladder. Right, I accepted that. And maybe my motives weren't so shining bright either. But I always figured you were honest. Not with me, not with your business associates but with yourself. But this crap about Communism, stop kidding yourself.'

He was silent, staring at the linen, the crystal glasses, empty plates.

'Okay, I guess I'm lying to myself. But I didn't know it would kill him.'

'You didn't think retirement would kill a man who's spent his life grafting?'

'Men retire. Live a long time. Have a long, happy retirement.'

'Are you still lying to yourself?'

'I don't know,' he said. 'I don't know.'

'Was it so important to get him out of the way?'

'It was—'

'I know – business practice.'

'It's been done before.'

'Most shitty tricks have been done before.'

He poured himself more brandy. 'Not so shitty. He was get-

289

ting on. The old have to go and if they won't they have to be hustled a little.'

'Oh Christ,' she said.

'I'm trying to be honest.'

She poured herself brandy in a balloon glass. Swirled it around and drank. Grimaced as the brandy burned her stomach. 'Un-American activities,' she said and laughed.

'Whatever I say sounds phoney so I might as well keep my mouth shut.'

'Boy,' she said, 'this is one hell of a marriage.'

'So, what do you want to do about it?'

'I don't know yet.' She knew he wouldn't plead with her. 'I guess I'll go away for a while.'

'A good idea,' he said. 'Go to the Bahamas, get some sun. Work things out your way.'

She swallowed more brandy; it didn't burn her stomach so badly now. She thought her husband looked very self-sufficient for a man who had just been accused of killing his father-in-law. He had stopped lying to himself; his strength reached her.

He said: 'Maybe I should explain about myself.'

'I know everything there is to know about you,' she said but he shook his head, 'I doubt it because I don't.'

'I don't want to know anything more,' she told him, pouring more brandy into her glass.

'You're getting drunk.'

'Yes,' she said.

'I don't like to see drunken women.'

'Neither do I,' she said, rolling the brandy on her tongue, thinking how much more dramatic a female drunk was if she was tall and slim with gold on her wrist and Italian silk at her throat.

He shrugged. 'I was going to try and tell you about my values.'

'And you will. You will.'

'I'm not defending anything. Nor am I doing the ruthless tycoon bit. Nor am I claiming to be immoral, or amoral or whatever. It's just that I don't see a damn thing wrong with the way I operate. I operate through strength, I employ clever men and they give employment to others. Business has always been like this and it's only the guys who don't make it – who know they can't so never try – who yell about graft, corruption, screwing the little guy. The way I operate produces maximum efficiency, that's the way the great corporations of the United States have been built up. That's the way the United States has been built up, if you like. And every other goddam empire there's ever been.' He took another grape. 'I saw inefficiency in the army and I saw bullshit. I saw men in command of men who shouldn't have been in charge of a peanut stand. They're the guys who should be crucified: the muddlers, the Bullshit Brigade, the guys who can bring a company to its knees through their stupidity and throw thousands of men and women out of work. You've got to climb over those people, weed them out because they're the criminals, not us.'

'I'm going to enjoy being a lush,' she said, swallowing more brandy.

'Somewhere along the line accepted ethics got mixed up—'

'You got to believe,' she said.

'—so that ambition became a crime and inertia became a good Christian attitude. All I'm trying to say is that I believe in what I am doing. I really do.'

'So did Al Capone.'

'You don't understand,' he said, leaning back in his chair.

'Sure I understand. I understand you killed my father.'

'He died. Is all. He died.' Now he was talking more to himseld than her. 'Pretty soon they're going to be hollering about Alaska. Why, for God's sake? The world was given to us to harvest. Grain, gold, timber, meat, fish—'

'Oil,' she said.

'Sure, and oil. Man multiplies and he has to go to the treasure chest, the power house, that is this earth. It was never supposed to lie there fallow. Take the Bible—'

'You take the Bible,' she said.

'The parable of the Prodigal Son. That's the one the idealists never quote. The one guy who failed ' – he hesitated – 'in the eyes of God was the one who did nothing with his sovereign, just kept it, nursed it . . .' He asked her: 'What's the matter?' as she stood up, holding the edge of the table.

'I think I'm going to throw up,' she said.

She ran water from the faucet. She gargled with a pink mouthwash. She looked into the mirror and saw the pallor beneath the tan, the redness of her eyes; she looked beyond this and saw that her face was beginning to age; no wrinkles, no bags under the eyes, nothing like that, just subtle changes in texture, expression, a loss of elasticity.

She dabbed her forehead with cologne and she remembered how it had first been with the hard-muscled, ambitious young man she had married; how she had hoped that something more rare than a partnership might develop from the marriage.

But he is what he is and I always knew it. It is my fault as much as his.

The floor tilted. When she closed her eyes colour began to spin in diminishing circles. She wanted to cry. She bit into the flesh on the inside of her lip, she tasted blood.

The bastard killed my father.

What have I got to look forward to? Pretence, photographs in the snob magazines. A gigolo or two as you get older – expert body erect and satisfying enough but the eyes scornful as he works with his body only; tea-parties, dinner-parties, charity work, Paris, Rome, Mexico . . .

She stood back from the mirror. You're still young, Judy Browning. Tall and sharp-hipped with a fine bone structure in your face. And you have a fine son. Why are sons always *fine*? A *fine* son just like your husband, athletic, not brilliant academically but bright and pushy. And with our money he will have the best education in America. But will he want me? With a father like my husband will he ever want me?

She closed her eyes. Catherine-wheels of colour. She opened them, opened the door of the cabinet above the washbasin, looked at the boxes of tablets blue, yellow, white. A handful of tablets – white ones, more discreetly lethal – a glass of water, fill the bath, lock the door, no more problems Judy Browning, toast of the Society photographers.

She picked up a box of barbiturates. She took off the top. She cradled a handful of tablets in her hand. Sleep and warmth and not caring any more. Another conventional, predictable, sordid cliché. Is this all you've managed to produce from the seeds of your birthright, Judy Thackeray, golden girl?

She poured the tablets into the sink, turned the tap and watched the spout of hot water push at the tablets until they dissolved and slid away like wet white sand.

She ran a bath. Tipped in pink bath-salts and smelled the sandalwood scented steam. She took off the Italian silk at her neck, took off her blouse and skirt and underwear and climbed into the bath with the gold handles; the water scalded, soothed; she sank into the scented steam.

She didn't know if she was crying. The steam was scented and the moisture ran into her mouth. She sank deeper into the water.

She knew he wouldn't come down to the bathroom to find out what had happened to her. Because he knows that we will continue. That, in a way, we are the same. Ah yes, we are well matched. Well coupled. Well partnered.

She pulled the plug and the water gurgled away.

CHAPTER TWENTY-FOUR

I'M going to win, Charles Browning thought, because I have to. There was only one team ahead, an Eskimo musher with nine Siberian huskies.

Browning shouted to his own team of huskies. The wind pushed against his goggles, frost sparkled on his clothes. The countryside was lonely white, the silence thick except for the barking of the dogs, the song of the sled.

But where is the bastard? Browning wiped frost from his goggles, corrected a swing to the right that could have plunged the sled into a drift. The dogs slowed down to sniff at some moose droppings; Browning shouted at the lead dog, the dogs took off again.

It was then that he noticed one of the dogs was flagging. He should stop, release the dog, but hell, they were almost there and the Eskimo was still ahead.

Then he saw the Eskimo. In a drift, his dogs in a tangle. He waved and his own dogs strained forward and a great exultation came upon Browning as they crossed the finishing line and he heard the cheering of the crowd.

He waved and they waved back, the people of Fairbanks, his own oilmen, kids from the university, children with cold pink faces framed by the hoods of their parkas. And there was Larsen staring at him with those blue eyes of his . . .

He was slowing down when the dog that had been flagging died.

Larsen said: 'You should have stopped.'

'Maybe. But that dog wanted to win. If it had a bad heart it would have died anyway. Better for it to die in harness, better to die winning.'

The rest of the dogs jumped at him, licked him, nosed excitedly in the snow outside the kennels on the outskirts of Fairbanks.

Larsen bent down and examined their paws. Gently he began to remove the sharp wedges of ice between their pads.

A kennelman brought tin mugs of sweet black coffee.

Browning gulped coffee, took off his fur hat, touched his cheeks which were beginning to burn. 'You guys will never learn, will you? You think that everything has to be done your way. You think you know what these dogs want better than they do. You *know* what other people want when the odds are that's exactly what they don't want. God save us from missionaries,' Browning said, throwing the dregs of his coffee onto the snow, 'they've caused enough trouble up here already.'

They left the dogs still drunk with victory, tongues lapping, volpine eyes blinking, and went into the kennelman's hut. The hut was part of old Alaska, iron stove in the middle, sprucewood chairs, table covered with faded oilcloth, unmade bed in one corner.

Steam arose from their bodies, they drank more coffee laced with rum. The kennelman left them to attend to the dogs. Browning took off his sealskin boots and rubbed his feet inside his thick grey socks.

Larsen told Browning that he wanted help. 'I tried everyone else first,' he said.

'And of course you saved my life once.' Browning held up his hand. 'I'll say it before you do.'

'I wasn't going to say it.'

'But you've said it anyway. Just by being here.'

'Okay, so I saved your life. Now I want a job instead of a medal.'

'You should have had a medal,' Browning said, feeling the hot coffee warm his whole body.

'Screw the medal,' Larsen said.

'What sort of a job?'

295

'Flying.'

'But you crashed your aeroplane, didn't you?' Browning paused. 'Wasn't it insured?'

'The insurance ran out the day before the crash.'

'Tough shit,' Browning said. 'So how can you fly without an aeroplane?'

'I want a year's advance on my salary to buy a new one. I'll pay you back with interest.'

'You want a lot,' Browning said.

'And I don't want to panhandle for it. It's yes or no.'

'What about everyone else?' Browning was interested. 'All your buddies, your do-gooders. All the guys like you who decided to become Alaskans. Couldn't any of them help?'

'They hadn't got the money,' Larsen told him. 'And some of them I didn't like to ask.'

'But I'm a soft touch, huh?'

'You're the hardest,' Larsen said.

'Look,' Browning said, 'I'm staying at a motel on the edge of town. Let's talk about it while we drive over there.'

He pulled on another pair of boots and they went out to Browning's rented car, cream and brown station wagon with heavy-duty tyres, engine still running to stop it freezing up. It was late afternoon but already it was night.

'Tell me about yourself,' Browning said, as they turned into Second Avenue.

'I didn't expect to be interviewed.'

'I'm interested. I really am. Why the hell does a guy like you decide to settle in this Godforsaken dump?' He stopped the car at a red light suspended above the street; snow was falling lightly, pink feathers in front of the light.

'What the hell do you expect me to say? One man's hell is another man's heaven?'

'It hasn't done much for you,' Browning said, as the car moved off and the flakes of snow turned green.

'But it's done okay for you, huh?'

Browning shrugged. 'I don't live here. God forbid. I've got a base here, sure. But now, you know, you won the day and Alaska's a state and I have to be seen around, I have to be a part of the place, so while I'm here – which is as little as possible – I make a show of it. Like winning dog-sled races.' He laughed.

He drove the station-wagon into the parking lot of a square-built motel, its outlines softened by snow.

They went into the bar which was crowded with men from the outdoors; men with creased necks and rough cheeks; lonely men working the interior of the Arctic in a hurry to make friends. A few girls sat at tables, tapping their cigarettes, taking bird-sips from their drinks, soft-skinned and full-lipped, as predatory as falcons.

The barman was loud and cheerful, but he never smiled. 'Good evening, Mr. Browning, had a good day?'

'Fine,' Browning said. 'How are things with you?'

'Can't complain. Doing good things, thinking bad thoughts.' He dried a glass. 'What can I get you gentlemen?' throwing up a bottle of beer, catching it, yanking off the top and handing it to a big man with a deep southern voice.

They ordered Scotch on the rocks. 'So,' Browning said, 'tell me about yourself.'

'It doesn't matter about myself,' Larsen said.

After the third whisky Browning said: 'You know there's something about you. It gets under my skin. I don't know why the hell it does and I don't like things I don't understand.'

'That's it,' Larsen said. 'You don't understand me. Do I get the job or not?'

'I guess so,' Browning said.

'And the advance?'

'Why not? But you're not the sort of guy who's going to enjoy being in debt.'

'Perhaps it will make you feel better about me.'

'Maybe, I like to win things.'

'You won't own me, buddy. You don't own a guy just because he owes you a few bucks.'

Browning ordered two more whiskies. He stared at Larsen. 'Do you know what I'm doing up here?'

'Looking for oil like everyone else, I guess.'

'Yeah. Like everyone else except that I'm going to find it. Not just a dribble like the Kenai strike. No sir, I'll have a commercial strike that will change the face of Alaska.' He tapped Larsen on the chest. 'What do you think about that?'

'I don't think anything about it,' Larsen told him.

'Sure you do. You don't want oil spoiling the fair face of Alaska, now do you?' One of the girls smiled at Browning but he ignored her. 'I hear you've joined the Sierra Club.'

'You checked on me?'

'Sure I checked on you. And I'm curious about you. How can a conservationist want to work for a guy who's going to spill oil all over the countryside? You might have won the statehood stakes but you'll never beat the oil lobby.'

'If it's inevitable then it won't make any difference whether I work for you or not.'

'Damn right,' Browning said.

'You sure know how to make someone grovel, don't you.'

Browning stared into his drink. 'Not really. It's just that ... Hell, I don't know what it is. I'm sorry but you've got the job, okay?' He frowned. 'Maybe it's just your breed that gets under my skin. You think we're going to desecrate Alaska. Well we're not, just a few scratch marks. But the oil *is* there and it isn't there to be left stagnant. Alaska was never meant to be inhabited: it was meant to be milked.' He grinned suddenly and waved. 'And here's the guy who will confirm it,' he said as Guthrie entered the bar, and to Guthrie: 'I believe you two know each other.'

Guthrie said: 'We do,' feeling for the beard that wasn't there, and asked Larsen: 'What brings you up here?'

Browning said: 'He's going to work for me.'

'Work?'

'Fly. He's going to fly you up north looking for oil.'

Guthrie looked away from Larsen. He ordered a Martini. He tasted the drink, grimaced. Without looking at Larsen he murmured: '*Et tu Brute.*'

Larsen put down his glass. 'You mean you work for Browning?'

'Sure he does,' Browning said. He lowered his voice. 'He's our prospector. He knows more about what's underneath Alaska than he does about what's on the surface.'

'Yes,' Larsen said, 'I know.'

Guthrie said: 'So we're both in it now, Richard.'

'I didn't know you were,' Larsen said.

'I told you how I felt about oil.'

'And what about all that crap about statehood. Did you believe in that?'

Guthrie said: 'You just don't understand.' He turned to face Larsen. 'It's got nothing to do with statehood. Of course I believed in that. But the discovery of oil in commercial quantities can only be good for Alaska.'

'And good for Guthrie?'

Guthrie leaned back against the bar, there was a rasp to his voice. 'Now cut out the horseshit, Richard. Pull the chain on those fucking ideals of yours. I'm doing what's best for Alaska.' He stabbed the air with his forefinger. 'You ask any Alaskan what they think's best for them. Preservation of the wilderness or banner of burning oil, banners that will proclaim a new deal, prosperity.' He smiled shakily. 'Anyway, what the hell, we're on the same side, for Christ's sake.'

'You didn't always think that way,' Larsen said to Guthrie, turning as Browning said to him: 'Now cut it out, Larsen, like Guthrie says, you're both on the same side. Oil is going to be the lifeblood of Alaska. Either you want Alaska to be a Great Land or you want it to remain what it is, a great big nothing.'

'I want it to be a big *beautiful* nothing,' Larsen told him. He turned to Guthrie. 'At least I had a reason for coming to Browning. You had nothing, not a goddam thing because you were doing all right without leading guys like this to their oil.'

'Now you look here—' Guthrie began.

Larsen dug in his pocket, picked up the tab. 'I'll get these.' He put a couple of bills on the bar. He said to Browning: 'I think you mentioned that medal.'

Browning looked at him quizzically.

'Know what you can do with that medal *and* your job?'

Browning opened his mouth to speak.

Larsen held up his hand. 'You can shove them,' he said. 'I don't have to tell you where.'

The barman slapped the change on the counter. 'Have a good day,' he said.

Outside the cold reached his lungs. He didn't care; he breathed deeply, staring at the sharp chips of the stars, at the glow in the sky to the north; he grinned and then he laughed as the depression lifted, as defeat lifted, and he leaped in the air and it seemed to him that the man who had come grovelling for a job from Browning was a stranger.

He took the railroad back to Anchorage. Next day he sold the white-frame house at a profit. He borrowed some cash from Mint and he bought a Piper Cub, not a Super but not so shabby. He painted LARSEN AIRLINES in red letters on the fuselage and he cabled Ruth who was in England COME BACK ALL IS FORGIVEN, adding I LOVE YOU.

And she came back.

And for a long time they were happy. It wasn't the first careless rapture, nor was it the contentment that is sometimes supposed to succeed the early passions of marriage. No, they were happy with each other, they shared; and in the bedroom of their rented apartment they made satisfactory and uninhibited love.

Larsen Airlines increased its fleet to two small aircraft. The Larsens moved out of their apartment and mortgaged another neat house beside the water. Ruth got a job teaching. Billy played for his high-school basket-ball team.

Men continued to climb McKinley and its neighbouring peaks and Larsen flew them there.

Larsen, Ruth and Billy grew older together. Indefinably, nothing was ever quite the same as it had been in those first years in the cabin in the wilderness; nothing was quite the same since the loss of the baby.

But they lived, in happiness, not contentment, until Alaska made its next move.

CHAPTER TWENTY-FIVE

THE first warning came from the cats. They started to miaow and howl and their noise was eerie in the snow-calm of the evening. The first shock came at 5.36 p.m. Houses shivered, the earth rippled. Alaskans accustomed to small 'quakes sensed that they were about to experience a terrible phenomenon; that forces were about to be released that spoke of the beginning and the end of everything man understands.

Eighteen miles below the thin surface of the world, two rock masses had collided and their reverberations were creating the strongest earthquake ever recorded in North America, the second most powerful in the world; a disturbance two thousand times stronger than the biggest nuclear device exploded.

Buildings thrashed backwards and forwards, some snapping like bones. Chasms opened; the firm earth was a sea on which there were waves of soil; houses collapsed and, with their structures exposed, bathrooms and bedrooms naked, revealed the vulnerability and fragility of human achievement.

At Valdez to the east the 'quake flattened much of the town and the *Tsunami*, the attendant tidal wave, swept away the dock. At Seward a cannery, warehouses and storage tanks slipped into the sea while other tanks exploded in flames. At Kodiak, home of the big bears and king crabs, the *Tsunami* swept away buildings and tossed boats into the main street; Kodiak was the worst hit.

In Anchorage, downtown streets dropped thirty feet and the roof of the foyer of the Denali theatre was suddenly level with the sidewalk. The control tower at Anchorage airport collapsed; the Four Seasons, shortly to have been the city's most exclusive apartment block, fell apart; J. C. Penny's new store was wrecked; houses were tossed around, bent, torn apart, telescoped together; and yet only one hundred and seventeen people died because, at 5.36 p.m. on this Good Friday evening, most people were on their way home, or at home away from the worst-hit areas.

Billy Larsen was on his way downtown to meet his girlfriend, Marion Davenport when his car went out of control; for a moment he thought it was the steering, then he saw other cars sliding around, smashing into each other like dodgem cars at a fairground. He hit a wall, stopped and climbed out; beneath him the earth bucked; he could feel a rumbling power, harnessed when the earth was born, trying to escape. A naked woman carrying a baby ran screaming into the road just before her green-painted, wooden house collapsed.

Billy looked at her helplessly as the street rolled beneath him. He walked towards her as a fissure opened where he had been standing. She waved him away, still screaming. He held out his hands but a neighbour came out carrying a blanket which he put round her shoulders.

He thought: I must find Marion. He found her on Fourth Avenue near C Street; she was holding onto a telegraph pole with a notice on it urging poeple to HELP KEEP ANCHORAGE CLEAN. She was in a state of shock, staring at a section of the road that had subsided taking automobiles with it. The buildings beside the cars – the Scandinavian Bar, a pawn shop, Pioneer Loans – were angled like teeth loosened by a fist.

The shocks continued.

Billy took her hand and ran south, with a vague idea that they should get away from tall buildings. As they ran he shouted to her that everything would be okay and felt her hand tighten on his.

Richard Larsen was driving up to the house when he felt the car sliding out of control. He peered through the windscreen and saw his house slipping away towards the sea, riding the snow-covered ground like a ship; *floating* on the soil. He braked, cut the engine, jumped out onto the heaving ground and saw his wife outside the house that was moving towards the sea.

He shouted to her. Her hands were at her face. He began to run towards her but he wasn't getting anywhere. Across the street a clapboard house reared up on one end, the roof fell away and he could see old Will Herbert climbing *up* the living-room.

The earth moved again, the shoulders of a great animal trying to shake off insects. A chasm opened where Ruth had been standing. He could see her crumpled on an outcrop ten feet below the surface. And he was screaming and he loved her. There had only ever been the two of them because they were one and he wanted to get down there to her, to be with her, to die with her, but his feet wouldn't take him because of the bucking of the earth. Then suddenly he was moving forward, as the chasm closed up again . . . Ruth saw her husband. Her fear was replaced by a great choke of compassion. And this was crazy because here she was in the middle of an earthquake with the house sliding towards the sea. But there it was, this great sob inside her because over there, trying to reach her, he looked small and weak and all she could remember was his tenderness. She was sprawled on a rock down the side of a precipice, but there was no fear, no pain, only regret as she saw the opposite wall of the chasm driving towards her and then there was a chiming, the sound of a Westminster chiming clock, and she thought: I will wait for him.

Part Three

CHAPTER TWENTY-SIX

First it was furs – in the eighteenth century the Russians massacred the Aleuts as they hunted sea otter and seal; then it was gold – and the legacy of the prospectors was disease, alcoholism and crime; now it was oil.

In 1968 oil was struck on the North Slope, an ocean of black gold; by comparison the 1957 strike at Kenai was a puddle.

Oilmen swarmed north and such was their eagerness to reach that layer of sandstone, two hundred and twenty million years old, and pump up the oil for their countrymen facing an energy crisis that they didn't have time to clear up their litter. Oil drums, garbage, the empty boxes of the seismic exploration teams stayed preserved in the deep freeze. And, such was their haste, that they carved up the tundra; dug pits for the mud spewed up by their drills; laid airstrips for the big transports which flew up from Fairbanks; hauled the rigs across the skin of the North Slope leaving it to bleed.

And oh how tender is that skin. In the winter it is covered by snow and ice but in the transient summer it is a beautiful sponge, honey-combed with patterns of lakes and ponds, hummocked with hills filled with ice; stitched with Lapland rosebay, purple monkshood and dwarf dogwood under which larvae hatch in the warmth of the Midnight Sun, while ptarmigan change their feathers, the Arctic fox his coat, and the hum of insects is a kind of silence.

Scratch the tundra and the insulation that has kept the permafrost frozen as hard as concrete is removed. The permafrost melts, the scratch becomes a lake or a canal. It is progressive and cancerous; the waters are dark and deep and there are those who believe that the whole face of Alaska could be changed by these malignant scratches.

One driver of a bulldozer decided to put these theories to the test. With the blade of his bulldozer he carved the initials of his company, Geophysical Services Inc., in two hundred foot-high letters on an expanse of green tundra. His experiment proved the theorists' point: the letters became ditches eight feet deep in places.

The first North Slope strike had been made by Atlantic Richfield, with Humble as a partner in July of '68; eight months later British Petroleum made a strike. Others followed. Then the State of Alaska, needy for cash, put up more land for sale in its northlands and the rush became a stampede of giant names, Shell, Standard, British Petroleum, Gulf, Philips, Mobil ... 1,105 bids for one hundred and seventy-nine leases in the Colville River delta ... thirty million dollars offered for a single lease.

What chance did the virgin land stand? What chance the predatory polar, the whistling swan, the wandering caribou, the rivers of grayling, whitefish and char, the tundra with its unhealed wounds still bleeding? What chance the Last Frontier when there is believed to be billions of barrels of oil beneath its surface?

The wells were sunk. Two billion dollars was sunk. Three thousand men were put to work, while the oilmen planned the final rape.

The need for a pipe-line was simple: somehow the oilmen had to get the oil to the gasping American people. So a consortium was formed and it drew up blueprints of a pipeline joining Prudhoe Bay in the north to the ice-free port of Valdez in the south where tankers could ship the oil to the West Coast of America.

But most of the pipeline carrying the hot oil will be buried. The heat will thaw the permafrost. The pipeline may bend and break. Hot oil will pour into the tundra. And what of the earthquake zone? One good 'quake and the pipe will snake and spurt black gold onto the sparkling snow. And what, pray, of the herds of caribou whose passage will be blocked by the pipeline?

Fuck the permafrost. Screw the caribou.

The laws of supply and demand must be obeyed: our country

needs oil. The biggest private enterprise of its kind in the world must get under way.

So in comes the pipe. A hundred million dollars worth of it from the old enemy, Japan.

But wait, a phenomenon has occurred in the swinging sixties. It isn't all long hair and pot and promiscuousness, love-not-war and flower people. Words have been resurrected: environment, ecology, conservation, words which send the critics of young people scurrying for their dictionaries. *Pollution.* Many young people with long hair and flowers stitched on their jeans are concerned that this sweet world of ours is becoming polluted – the air by chimneys pouring out smoke and automobile exhausts exhaling carbon monoxide; the rivers and the sea by factory waste and oil and sewage; and the land . . . ah, the land, what better example of pollution than the Alaskan pipeline?

Simultaneously with this phenomenon the politicians realize that conservation is fast becoming a power in the land. So they, too, are heard preaching the cause of the environment and, in 1969, the National Environment Policy is enacted by Congress.

The pipeline planners confer uneasily.

Then yet another phenomenon, this time in Alaska itself. The natives lay claim to the land. In fact they have been laying claim since 1912 but suddenly there are fresh notions of equality abroad as the sixties swing into the seventies. Eskimos, Indians, Aleuts, these descendants of the very first settlers, want a slice of the pie and their demands embrace the land upon which the pipeline is to be laid.

The pipeline is threatened with impotence.

CHAPTER TWENTY-SEVEN

ROSA CARELLI, 28, extravagantly built but a little heavy in places due to a hunger for pasta took the $200 from Ernie Trusz – she had expected $100 – and began to undress.

Before coming to Fairbanks Rosa had been a croupier at Lake Taho. Then she had read about the money the oilmen made in Alaska, she had read about the money a girl could make from the oilmen who were isolated in the Arctic for weeks on end and she had calculated that up there she could in one year save enough for a down-payment on a health farm in California. If you charged a hundred bucks a time – which was the going rate according to the magazine – you could make a thousand a day which was 7,000 a week which was over 300,000 dollars in one year.

Of course it hadn't worked out quite as neatly as that. There was a lot of competition and you had to be quick to grab the men as they piled into town from the north, as hungry for women as caged animals for their feed. Pick them up, pop them in the old Winnebago and be off. If you didn't scoop them up as soon as they had landed then forget that hundred bucks because, second or third time round, they had become careful, remembering the promises they had made themselves to lodge fat sums in their bank accounts. And with some of them you had to be careful: they had been without women too long, they had been in the dark days too long, and sometimes they were a little crazy and which was why Rosa carried a small weapon loaded with gas cartridges. Sometimes she settled for fifty dollars but never less: when a hooker starts settling for less then the writing is on the wall – of a motel room with a bed and a jug of water and squashed insects on the walls. Rosa had no intention of degenerating like that: she would have her health farm although it might take two years with the competition, the high cost of living and the occupational hazards – the gangsters and pimps and conmen who, like her, had come north for the oil pickings.

To her surprise she liked Ernie Trusz making love to her, liked the feel of his hard, hairless body; after a little while her responses were no longer mechanical.

She said candidly: 'I like being screwed by you.'

'Can't you speak decently?'

'So what's wrong with screwing? Screwing is screwing. I think you've got a little kink up here' – she touched her head – 'when it comes to words. Words, they never hurt no one.'

He lay naked on the bed, hands behind his head. 'I don't like bad mouths in front of broads, I don't like broads with bad mouths.'

'So, that word broads, that's a nice word to use about a lady?'

'Broads are broads,' he said.

'Screwing is screwing.'

He glanced at his watch. 'You must be some broad,' he said, turning the radio control beside the bed. 'I almost forgot.'

'Forgot?'

'The lottery. If I win I'll take you to Hawaii.'

'Oh sure,' said Rosa who had heard many promises. 'You mean it?' she asked, remembering that no one else had ever given her two hundred dollars. 'And what lottery is this?' she demanded.

'The break-up lottery. You pick the right time the ice breaks up on the Tanana river and you win a lot of dough.'

'And you got a ticket?'

'Sure I got a ticket.'

Music issued from the radio. Then it stopped. An announcement said: 'Nothing definite yet, folks, but we sure can hear the ice. And, like I told you before, a beautiful great hunk of ice broke away just below the radio station this afternoon. It can't be long now so stay tuned to this station to see if you've got yourself a winning ticket. If you've won yourself a small fortune – enough to take you to Hawaii.'

The music returned.

Rosa: 'How can the ice be breaking up? It was snowing outside.'

'Just a few flakes,' Trusz told her. 'Ain't got nothing to do with it. It's been thawing for days now. Break-up will be tomorrow.'

'How do you know?'

'Because my ticket says so.' He opened the drawer in the bedside table and took out a ticket. 'It will break up at 11.35 a.m.,' he told Rosa. 'At 11.35 you and I will be in a position to take the next plane for Honolulu.'

She ran her hand down his chest and belly. As she did this her big breasts moved lazily. The movement reminded her of the growing swell of her stomach. She bit Trusz's ear. 'Tell me about this lottery,' she said.

Trusz explained that in 1917 a group of railroad workers at Nenana had organized a lottery on the time of break-up with a six hundred dollar pool. Now each of the eleven winning tickets bought for a dollar was worth thousands of dollars. Tickets weren't sold to Outsiders. 'But I ain't an Outsider no more,' Trusz said as though this pleased him, as though he liked belonging somewhere.

He explained the machinery of determining break-up. The free ice pushed against a pole – and this pulled a wire running to a clock-house on the bank. 'The wire trips a meat cleaver, would you believe, and this cuts a rope which triggers some sort of mechanism that stops the clock.'

'I don't believe it,' she said.

'You will at 11.35 a.m. tomorrow.'

'Do you really mean it? You know, about going to Hawaii?'

'I said it, didn't I?'

'Sure you said it . . . I know you said it . . . but . . . Can I have a bath?' she asked him.

'Two hundred bucks *and* a bath?'

'I like bathrooms in joints like this. Nice deep baths and soap that smells good and pretty tiles. I like to bath when it becomes a pleasure like eating canneloni or spaghetti . . .' She swallowed.

'By the way,' he said, 'you're putting on weight.'

She looked at him sadly. 'I know it,' she whispered. 'You don't have to tell me.' Her voice rose. 'I know I am . . . plump. A gentleman wouldn't point that out.'

'By the way,' Trusz asked, 'how much do you usually charge?'

'I told you.'

He slapped her buttocks through the sheet. 'How much?'

'You think you paid too much?' There was a blade in her voice.

'I paid my price. I just wondered what the other guys got it for.'

'None of your damned business.'

'A hundred bucks?'

'You pay for what you get.'

He grinned. 'I just had a thousand bucks' worth.'

Suddenly there was softness in her voice. 'You mean that?'

'Sure I mean it.'

The announcer broke into the music. 'Nothing yet, folks, but it's got to be soon. There's a big ice jam across the river and it's got to be soon. Anyone got 11.30 a.m.? That's always one of the favourites because, as you know, it was was 11.30 on April 30, 1917, when the break came on that first historic lottery. And tomorrow's the thirtieth . . . Stay tuned to this station . . .'

Later Rosa Carelli took a bath. Trusz lit a cigarette and lay back on the pillows reflecting that there were many ways in which he could make money quickly and none of them was honourable.

The most obvious way was to sell Browning down the river. He was known to be one of the best scouts in the business; he had received offers since joining forces with Browning. He knew where there was oil in Alaska. (He knew there would be more auctions, more strikes.) But Browning had always been straight with him; Trusz didn't want to double-cross him; you didn't want to double-cross a man who was quite capable of having anyone who cheated him killed.

He could threaten Browning. *Are you crazy, Ernie Trusz?* He had never known Browning to be violent, but there was violence in his make-up, a controlled, civilized savagery; and the shackled violence of the worst kind, the violence of the man who believes right is on his side.

The music on the radio was interrupted again by the announcer, but he hadn't got anything further to report and Trusz, replete and naked on the bed, smoking steadily, gazing at the blind eye of the TV, listening to the girl who was a noisy bather and a noisy lover and probably a noisy eater too, pondered on the inexorable force that was Charles Browning.

Trusz and Guthrie had been able to tell Browning where there was oil under the North Slope. Thus Browning had been able to buy selectively when the leases on the tundra were first put up for bids in 1964, '65 and '67.

So, long before the first strike, the scramble and the big auction, they had got the land. All that had remained in their way was the gentleman's agreement.

In a suite in Chicago's Blackstone Hotel Browning had told Trusz and Guthrie and his other lieutenants, middle-aged but still lean and hungry, what should be done with the agreement.

'Forget it,' he had said. 'Walk all over it.'

Guthrie had said: 'But, hell aren't we cutting our own throats if we do that? The whole price structure which is supported by state production controls will collapse if we tap Alaskan oil now.'

Browning, sitting at the head of a long mahogany table, poured himself water from a carafe. There was a bottle of Haig on the table but during business hours Browning rarely touched liquor.

He stood up. 'The fact of the matter,' he said, 'is that this gentleman's agreement – which owes nothing to any gentleman – isn't worth the paper it was never written on. It was drawn up to soak the American people and it's about to become extinct. Because,' Browning said slowly, head turning as he addressed each man individually, 'we are on the brink of a world shortage of oil. Everyone knows it but no one has the guts to do anything about it.'

He drank some more water. Trusz poured himself a small Scotch and regarded the man. Trim, hardly any paunch, hair needled with grey. How old was he? In his late forties but still vital in the pursuit of his beliefs, still moulding others' weaknesses into his own strengths. Unprincipled? Trusz didn't think so: Browning merely had his own set of principles.

'And soon,' Browning went on, 'the Arabs are going to call the tune. You know it, I know it, the whole damned oil industry knows it but no one moves. Already the Saudis have screwed something like two hundred million dollars out of Aramco and put Yamani on their board. But that's just a beginning. There's a revolution under way, the old order changeth ... The Arabs, who we think of sitting in their tents eating sheeps' eyes are on the ascendancy: we are on the decline. The Arabs are cramming our technology, while we stand back and watch. What the oil states of the Persian Gulf are after now is participation and they'll get it gentlemen, they'll get it. Maybe a quarter, maybe more. But there will be worse to come.' Browning stabbed his finger at his audience. 'One day oil will be used as a weapon against Israel. The Arabs will turn right around and put out an ultimatum to the States: stop supplying the Jews with arms or we'll stop supplying you with oil. And without Middle East oil, gentlemen, this country of ours is dooméd. Unless,' smiling boyishly, 'we tap other sources. Unless, just for starters, we start drilling for oil on the North Slope.'

Guthrie swallowed some whisky. He said: 'But supposing none of this happens for a few years? Supposing we go it alone on the North Slope? All we do is invest a fortune, crack the price structure and make a lot of enemies.'

Browning stared at him, Trusz sensed the antagonism. 'It's a risk,' he said, his voice tight. 'Everything in business is a risk. But I believe it's a calculated risk.'

Trusz said: 'Sure it's a gamble but the odds are in our favour. All we need to make a killing is a shortage of oil in the West.'

'At the very least,' Browning told him, 'the Arabs will hike the price.'

One of the lieutenants, dark and watchful and beak-nosed, spoke. 'So when do we start exploratory drilling?'

'Soon,' Browning told him. 'Very soon. As you know the

State sold 900,000 acres of leases for a mere twelve million dollars. After the first oil strike the next lot, a fraction of the size, will be sold for a hundred, maybe two hundred, times that price. But we'll be sitting pretty, we'll be sitting on an ocean of oil.'

Trusz felt for the dice in his pocket. He was getting bored. He jingled them, feeling for the dots on their smooth sides. 'How much do you figure drilling one well is going to cost?'

Browning said: 'A lot of dough.'

The lieutenants looked uneasy. 'How much money?'

Browning said: 'In Texas they reckon between fifty to seventy thousand dollars.'

'Well, that isn't so bad,' said the beak-nosed lieutenant.

'In the Arctic I reckon it's going to cost anything up to four million bucks.'

The silence was now immediate, as if it had been switched on. Ice tinkled in a drink. Down the corridor a door slammed, a jet passed overhead.

'Jesus,' said one of his lieutenants.

'Can we afford that sort of dough?' another asked.

'We can afford it,' Browning snapped. 'If we can't raise that sort of money we might as well throw our hand in.'

'Okay, we can afford it,' the lieutenant said. 'But supposing we don't strike oil first time. Supposing it takes us a couple of years. Can we afford that sort of investment?'

Browning's fingers drummed the polished wood. 'Like I said, it's a calculated risk. In any case, what the hell, we've got other interests. For Christ's sake let's be pioneers, let's get up there and get that oil. Let's lead, let others follow.'

Guthrie said: 'There's just one other thing.'

A muscle played on Browning's jawline. 'What?'

'How the hell are we going to get that oil out of the Arctic Circle?'

Browning said: 'There's only one practical way and that's a pipeline to an ice-free port in the south. It'll cost a billion dollars maybe' – he held up his hand – 'but by that time the big boys will be investing. They'll build the pipeline. A billion dollars.' Browning sat back, arms folded. 'Do you realize that even if there's only twenty billion barrels of oil under the slopes and it's sold at say eighty cents a barrel in Chicago that's profit for the oil companies of at least sixteen billion dollars?'

They realized it. They savoured it, they digested it. They fed on it and they relaxed and their eyes blinked lazily.

Lying in the motel room waiting for Rosa Carelli to finish bathing, Trusz remembered how they had punctured the flesh of the North Slope looking for the black veinous blood below.

Browning's rig wasn't the only one.

Other leases had been sold. Atlantic Richfield merged (ARCO) and, with Humble, spent 4·5 million dollars drilling a test hole that turned out to be dry.

But when ARCO finally made their strike Browning was oddly philosophical about it.

Probably because he had respected the man who had beaten him to it. Robert O. Anderson, ARCO's chairman.

Browning didn't seem to mind being beaten by men he respected, men of his own ilk.

Smart men, ambitious men. The sort of men who had built America. Without them reforming zealots, Marxists, conservationists, revolutionaries who found a cause instead of a livelihood wouldn't even have inherited a battleground.

Browning had adapted as he always did. Whatever happened he used it. He turned defeat into victory. While the oilmen streamed north he went on drilling and lobbying in Juneau and Washington where, it is said, the oil lobby is the fourth arm of government.

The first hole that Browning drilled was dry. Browning sold two companies, borrowed from a couple of banks. Once again down through permafrost, through gravel and silt. Nine thousand feet, ten thousand. Nothing. Had Guthrie and Trusz been wrong?

The oilmen drilled on, illuminated by floodlights in the darkness that lasts from mid-November till the end of January. Faces masked, bodies clumsy with insulated clothing, the Arctic wind gumming down their eyelids with ice, burning their lungs with cold if they moved quickly. The derrickman on the platform working in a blizzard was only able to stay up there for the time it takes to stack one joint of pipe. Metal shattered as the cold changed the structure of molecules.

Thirty days since this second well was spudded. Still nothing.

Once Trusz flew up with Browning, it was midday, dark with a wind blowing in from the frozen Beaufort Sea. The illuminated rig was a piece of theatre; it was an intruder.

As they reached the drilling floor the supervisor grabbed a lever. The machinery stopped. Trusz said to the supervisor. 'The bit busted?'

The supervisor nodded. 'Up she comes again.'

Trusz said to Browning: 'He's good that guy. He heard a noise. He knew.'

'Did you know?'

'About the bit? How the hell would I know?'

'Are you sure you were right about there being oil down there?'

Trusz said: 'Guthrie knows his stuff.'

'And you know your stuff, don't you, Ernie?'

'There's oil down there,' Trusz said. 'You know this game as well as I do. You don't necessarily strike it the first time or the second. And don't act the heavy with me,' Trusz said, breathing too deeply and feeling the cold lay its finger on his lungs.

They flew back to Anchorage in silence.

At 11,000 feet they struck oil. One well that would probably produce 10,000 barrels a day. A daily net profit of 8,000 dollars. And there would be many more wells. The land upon which Browning had set his sights twenty-five years ago was finally paying up.

It was 11.20 a.m. The radio was on. Light slipped in through the curtain in furtive shafts. Beside them lay two trays with empty dishes on them. Trusz lay on the bed, wide awake, listening to the radio; Rosa Carelli slept with her head resting in the crook of his arm snoring slightly.

Trusz imagined he could hear the grinding of the ice in Nenana where the crowds would be gathered. He glanced at his wrist-watch. 11.22. He woke Rosa.

11.28.

The voice of the announcer was becoming excited. 'Any minute now, folks.'

'Seven minutes to be precise,' Trusz said. 'Now, baby, you've got to co-operate.'

'Hey,' she complained as he pulled her down in the bed. 'What's the idea?'

'Just a premonition. You know, us gamblers are kind of weird about these things.'

Trusz looked at his watch as they made love. The second hand jerking round the dark green and silver dial was twenty-five seconds off 11.35. 'Now,' he said urgently.

The announcer was shouting. 'That's it. Eleven thirty-five. Anyone with 11.35 is in the chips.'

Trusz rolled off. He lay back. He grinned foolishly.

Rosa Carelli looked down at him: 'You made it,' she said, shaking her head in wonderment. 'You really made it. In more ways than one,' she added.

CHAPTER TWENTY-EIGHT

In the beginning the battle was clear-cut and had many precedents. Man versus Nature — it was as old as that — and there was little doubt that man in his need would finally win; he would be harassed and bloodied but finally he would win as he always has done; finally he would take the oil from the Arctic and pump it down to his factories and his automobiles, would go on taking it until the land was defaced by the ugly scrawl of his signature.

But after the first exchanges this battle became diffused. New combatants emerged, combatants who had been waiting a long time, since the first slum festered in a fair city, since the first slag heaps grew on green grass. Now, when men and women disgusted by the malaise among themselves turned once again to the land for salvation. Now was a time of hope and its testing ground was Alaska.

The antagonists were those who wanted to *keep* the land and those who wanted to *use* it.

And it might have been thought that those who wanted to *use* it, to tap the oil and drain it south through seven hundred and ninety miles of pipeline, would have had the money and the brains and the guile and the influence in high places to trample all over the conservationists. But it was not to be so. This time the idealists had clout. They had guile. They had a message which ordinary people believed in and suddenly they had influence in high places. They had brains, they had money, they were winning.

Permission for the pipeline was delayed in Washington ... the Department of the Interior now led by Alaska's Walter Hickel set up a task force to study developments. President Nixon asked Hickel to enlarge the task force's scope (this was how big environment suddenly was), the Department laid down rules that the oil companies would have to follow, the Senate and House committees gave their approval for the pipeline, the Interior Department again postponed the permit.

The oil companies who had once greased the corridors of power groaned at the injustice of it all. Hadn't they agreed not to pollute the land and water, not to use certain pesticides, not to block the passage of game, not to carve up the permafrost, to clean up oil spills and, goddamit, to stop work when wildfowl were nesting or caribou were migrating or fish were spawning! Hadn't they agreed to all this, and instigated much more themselves, just to get the oil flowing to their countrymen who would soon be sorely in need of it? Hadn't some of the Arabs already threatened embargos after the Israelis had beaten the Arabs in the 1967 war?

And, then there was the Lachenbruch geological report. According to Arthur H. Lachenbruch the heat from the pipeline could create underground rivers of mud which would pour over the pristine surface, could cause conditions where the stress margin of the pipeline could be exceeded once every mile. Hot oil spurting out over the tundra, over the sleeping valleys of the Brooks Range: the pipeline was the Interior Department's Vietnam: permission was withheld. By January 1st, 1970, it was still withheld and the stacks of pipeline were growing high in Valdez.

And what about earthquakes? At Capitol Hill where conservation, ecology, environment, were now snowwhite crusading banners, the men in power winced at the possibilities, the scandal, even though the possibility of a break in the pipeline was said to be slight.

And it was not only the conservationists who were blocking the pipeline permit. The natives were agitating about their land claims. It was the age of the idealist, the minority. It was ridiculous.

On March 26th, 1970, three conservation groups charged in court that the pipeline didn't meet the standards of the National Environmental Policy Act of '69. That it would harm the 'last great wilderness in the United States'. Next month they were granted a temporary injunction once again stopping the Interior Department from granting a permit.

Far away from Washington the moose and caribou wandered freely and the snows melted and tundra flowers budded and blossomed and died and the berries ripened for the bears to eat and the timber wolves mated while the whistling swans from Chesapeake Bay flew high over the melting land on their way to the North Slope.

Watching the bearded young men digging in the dark soil with their trowels, Charles Browning shook his head in disbelief. Here they were on the route of the pipeline; but instead of watching roughnecks gouge open the tundra he was watching students pecking around for artifacts.

At first Browning had been philosophical about the delays. The oilmen had been too hasty in the first place. They had needed a restraining influence such as the conservationists. Because of the restraint they would have a better pipeline.

But now, more than two years after the first strike, the permit was still held up. Browning couldn't understand how the oil lobby that had helped to rule the Union had suddenly had its teeth drawn.

One young man called excitedly to the other two. 'I think I've got something.'

It was touching, Browning thought. It was highly commendable. But, hell, was this more important than pumping oil into a fuel-thirsty America?

'Looks good,' said one of the young men.

They worked gently with their hands, craftsmen who love the materials with which they work. They wore blue denim shirts and crumpled jeans and heavy boots. Their hair was long and their beards full; they were absorbed with their work and Browning, the intruder, leaning against the fuselage of a helicopter, envied them.

He had tried to understand the young. Not out of compassion but because he had to understand. And he believed he did: the revulsion over Vietnam, against graft, against the hypocrisy of the old morals. Yes, he understood the clothes, the hair, smoking pot, free love; but there was something about the young he could not forgive and that was their refusal to try and understand the middle-aged and the old and their values.

The young men from the University of Alaska and the Alaska Methodist University burrowing in the soil were employed by the pipeline companies to search for archeological sites along the route. A committee drawn from the Arctic Institute of North America would report to Washington about their discoveries.

Reverently the young men laid aside small, soil-encrusted objects. The one who had made the find held up a sharp stone. 'This is really something,' he said. The other two gazed at the object in his hand. 'Do you know I reckon this site could be anything up to ten thousand years old?'

Browning strolled across to them. 'Can I see?'

They looked up in surprise, they had forgotten him. 'Sure,' said the first young man. 'But it won't mean much to you. Now I've seen a few like this elsewhere in North America and they're reckoned to belong to the Clovis or Folsom cultures and, hell, they're at least ten thousand years old. I don't think anyone expected to find anything that old up here,' the young man explained.

Browning didn't think he had ever seen his son so animated and at that moment he was proud of him.

When Robert Browning's excitement faded the old expression returned, alert and wary and telling his father nothing.

Once there had been vivacity on his face. When Browning came home from work, when they went on vacation together, at Christmas and Easter and Thanksgiving. Browning remembered the hand of a small boy tucked in his and he turned away from the young man with the shuttered features.

What had he done to deserve his son's contempt? Browning slapped a mosquito on his cheek. He remembered his own contempt for his father. But that was different. It was contempt for a snob, a hypocrite; he had sniffed out his father's weakness beneath the mannered ways. But there's no hypocrisy about me; I have worked and gambled and I have won.

The remoteness had come to the boy in his mid-teens.

Browning signalled to the pilot of the helicopter to hand down the picnic hamper and the beaker of Martini.

They sat on the tundra where, if his son was right, men and women had sat ten thousand years ago.

Browning had always believed that he got on well with young people and he had never really accepted that he was growing old. Now he talked brightly but he was aware of himself. He knew they were waiting for him to go. It hurt.

They stroked their beards, they drank water from the stream instead of Martini, they nibbled the chicken, and made polite conversation.

Browning prided himself that he hadn't forced his son into a way of life that he resented. He often boasted to conservationists that his son was an archeologist at the University of Alaska, saying: 'Now you realize how I see both sides of the argument.'

An archeologist for Christ's sake!

He poured himself a Martini in a plastic cup and said: 'You realize, of course, that you wouldn't be able to do this work if it wasn't for the pipeline.'

His son looked at him impassively. 'It's an ill wind,' he said.

'You don't sound too grateful.'

'We're grateful,' his son said. He bit the end off a chicken bone, sucked the marrow and said: 'But would you have cared if they hadn't stopped the pipeline?'

Browning said: 'The fact remains that we care now. We care about the views of botanists, biologists, geologists, ornithologists, zoologists, entomologists ... you name them, we care about them. And I admit that's the way it should have been in the first place,' he added.

They digested this placidly. It was this dreamy serenity that also angered Browning about so many of the young.

'Do you think the pipeline's a good thing, Mr. Browning?' One of the young men asked in a soft deferential voice.

324

'Naturally I do. I have an investment in it.' He slapped another mosquito.

'Sure I know that. You know, a capitalist can have an investment in a coal-mine but that doesn't necessarily mean he thinks a slag heap improves the scenery.'

'Look,' Browning said, his voice louder, 'every goddam thing that can be done is being done to protect the ecology. We're even conducting experiments to re-seed areas where the tundra's been broken up. The way the industry's been thinking,' Browning said, 'they'd divert the pipeline to avoid breaking a spider's web.'

'Still seems a pity though,' one of the young men said. 'You know, the last frontier, all that. This pipeline is just the beginning.'

Browning tried not to sound patronizing. 'Well,' he said, 'I guess you know that Mobil put an ice breaking tanker, the *Manhattan*, through the north-west passage to see if they could get the oil out that way but it just wasn't practical. And I guess you know that a lot of people think a trans-Canadian route would do the trick. Well, it might – but it would take anything from two to six years longer to construct and we'd have to go through all the birth pangs we've suffered here all over again. The Canadians would probably want access to the pipeline and by the time it got going we could have shifted something like three and a half billion barrels of oil to the West Coast. So you see the pipeline has to go through Alaska.'

'I realize that, sir,' the young man said, 'but is it necessary?'

'I thought I just answered that.'

His son said: 'My friend wants to know whether it matters a goddam whether the oil gets through or not.'

'You would think it mattered a goddam if you hadn't got any heating in your apartment and gas cost you five bucks a gallon.'

'Maybe, I don't know. I guess we could always dress up warm. I guess we could always walk. I guess the air would be cleaner.'

Browning stared at his son and thought: I am a reasonable man, but this is the talk of children. He said: 'I just don't understand you.'

His son looked at him with his brown eyes and there was no expression in them. He didn't reply.

'No offence,' said one of the other young men, pulling up a stem of cotton grass and nibbling it, 'but I know what Robert means. You know, there isn't any need to keep hustling, pushing. What the hell if we haven't got any gas, we'll survive.' He shrugged. 'Maybe we'll start civilization all over again and maybe make a better job of it this time.'

Browning felt tired. You couldn't answer their illogical statements. He changed his talk, 'And what will the world gain from your excavations?'

His son spoke. 'Do you really want to know?'

'I asked.'

The shutters were lifted briefly. 'Well for one thing they could change the current theories about the origins of Eskimo culture. You see,' he said, rocking backwards and forwards on his haunches, 'it's generally thought that Eskimo culture began in the west and north-west of Alaska and across the ocean in north west Siberia. But we're finding ancient Eskimo sites much farther south and what's more some of the tools appear to be Indian. As the sites contain Eskimo *and* Indian artifacts we think maybe there was a common origin of northern Indians and Eskimos or maybe even an Eskimo culture with an American-Indian derivation.' He stopped and gazed at his father. 'Does that mean anything to you?'

'It means what you just told me.'

'But you're not interested?'

'I didn't say that.'

'That's right, you didn't.'

'Look,' the father said to his son, 'I think it's fascinating. I really do,' he said awkwardly. *And I'm proud of you*, he wanted to say. 'Look, I realize that we think differently . . .' He wished the other two weren't there. 'But that doesn't mean I don't admire what you're doing even if I don't really get the point . . .'

'The point?'

Browning listened to himself – it was coming out all wrong. 'I mean I don't understand what difference it makes to anything whether the Eskimos came so far south or whether there was an Indian derivation . . .'

'You don't understand what difference it makes?'

'Well, what difference *does* it make?'

His son blinked his eyes, the old expression returned. 'I wouldn't know,' he said. He stopped rocking, lay back on the cotton grass, hands behind his head, gazing at the clouds riding the sky.

The pilot called from the helicopter. 'Hey Mr. Browning it's a quarter after two.'

Browning waved his hand. 'Well, I guess I'd better be off.'

His son's friends stood up. They stuck out their hands. In their gentle voices they thanked him for the lunch and said it had sure been nice having him up at the site. His son said: 'Be seeing you.'

Browning lingered for a moment. Then he strode to the helicopter. When he looked down through the Perspex the three young men had begun to excavate again.

Below the helicopter it was all greens and greys with lakes and pools firing silver light at the sun. The helicopter was so low, its shadow following them on the tundra, that Browning could see life: a moose with its calf staring up at the clattering machine, a handful of ptarmigan taking off from the edge of a pool. Looking down on the land, softened and melted by summer, Charles Browning wondered if perhaps there was oil there too.

The young men conversed in soft voices as they explored the black earth. Their limbs were brown and, beneath their denim shirts, their bellies were flat. They wore a few beads and elephant hair bracelets. The one with the softest beard and the slowest ways had scars on his chest and back from a Viet Cong bullet.

'You're pretty hard on your old man,' one of them said to Robert Browning.

Robert Browning shrugged as he felt the soil, imagined the hard bedrock of permafrost beneath. 'Yeah, it makes him cry at nights.'

'I don't know, he doesn't seem such a bad guy. I mean, why are you so anti, man?'

'Would you like being called Robert Browning?'

The young man with the scars said softly: 'Would I fuck but that isn't what's bugging you. I mean he's been pretty decent to you and brought you up like a good American boy so why treat him like he was shit? You know, he did what he thought was right.'

Robert Browning extracted another sharp stone from the soil and put it with the others. 'I guess because he represents everything I detest.'

'But it can't always have been like that, not when you were a kid.'

'Maybe I sensed it.' He dipped his hands in the soil as though washing them. 'I remember we used to go on vacation and he would go hunting and then he'd skin whatever he'd killed and there would be blood on his hands and then he'd cook the meat over a fire and I'd have to eat it and then I'd go off some place and throw up.'

And he remembered his father's casual infidelity which he had hardly bothered to hide. Maybe because they were man to man.

The other young man said: 'He brought you up the way he thought right. You shouldn't be so tough on him, man.'

'Look,' said Robert Browning, 'he's my old man and I'll treat him just how I think I will so let's knock it off, shall we?'

'Okay,' they said mildly.

'For Christ's sake,' Robert Browning said, 'doesn't it bug you that he's one of the guys who wants to ram the pipeline right through Alaska? He's one of the guys who wants to drill offshore up in the Arctic. I mean, have you guys forgotten Santa Barbara?'

'He's entitled to his viewpoint,' the young man with the scars remarked. 'You don't have to fight because you don't agree with a guy's point of view.' One hand strayed to the circle of puckered skin on his chest. 'And in any case he's losing.'

328

'Want to bet?'

'Well, put it this way, no one's going to win.'

The other young man said: 'Hold it.' He lifted an object from the soil, brushing it lightly with his fingers. 'Looks like some sort of tool,' he said. He peered closer. 'Indian by the look of it.'

They examined the tool. They were intent upon it. Their voices were muted but their bearded faces were keen. They had forgotten Robert Browning's father and it was only this tool dug from time that mattered.

Two days later Charles Browning sat in his study in the Chicago penthouse gazing angrily at a magazine open on his desk.

There was a knock at the door and his wife entered with coffee and biscuits on a tray. She smiled at him and he thought how good she looked in her forties, slim and tanned. She was a fine wife, he was very fond of her, and as she put the tray in front of him, he squeezed her arm and looked up at her smiling.

She sat down on a leather easy chair. She crossed her legs, good legs. She looked at him with her blue eyes for a while and then she said: 'You look tired.'

'I am tired. This damned Alaskan fiasco.'

'They have a point.'

'Sure. They *had* a point and they won it.'

'Never mind,' she said, dropping a sweetener into her coffee, 'you'll win in the end.'

He nodded. Her confidence pleased him. He stretched his arms above his head, feeling his stomach tighten. He patted his stomach, lately it had become a little slack. He would have to start playing squash again and when the pipeline permit was finally granted, they would take a holiday somewhere, maybe Europe. He said: 'It's not just me, I'm small fry in this game.'

She said: 'But you'll win, you always do.'

He said: 'When I'm fifty-five I'm going to quit. Then we can enjoy what I – what we – have worked for.'

She frowned, one leg swinging. 'That will be nice,' she said.

'You don't sound very enthusiastic.'

'Don't I? I didn't mean to sound unenthusiastic. You look as if you need a holiday right now,' she said. 'You look so tired.'

'I'll be all right. Someone's just pulled a fast one on me. It came as a shock I guess.'

'Business practice?'

He stared at her for a moment. Then laughed. On an impulse he crossed the room and kissed her. Her lips were dry and closed but she smiled at him as he stood up. 'What was that for?'

'For our . . . our partnership.'

'I'll drink to that,' she said, finishing her coffee.

When she had gone Browning picked up the magazine. It was published by one of the environmental groups. On its jacket was a coloured photograph of an oil rig on the North Slope. The snow around the rig was criss-crossed with tracks and small craters and fouled with cans and garbage The headline read CAN YOU REALLY TRUST THE OILMEN? The rig was the first one built by Browning's company.

As Browning gazed at it the anger returned because not only was the photograph an unfair tactic – the oilmen had long since cleaned up their sites – but it represented an act of betrayal.

The photograph had been taken from a Company helicopter. It had been in Browning's private papers and it had been stolen and handed over to the enemy.

Who could have done that? Browning considered the men close to him. Each was capable of a stroke like this, but not against their own interests. The only possibility was Guthrie with his conflicting loyalties, his greed and his guilt and his hypocritical devotion to the virgin lands of Alaska.

Perhaps Guthrie and Larsen were conspiring. Once again it seemed to Browning that all conflict resolved itself into the conflict between the two of them.

CHAPTER TWENTY-NINE

JUDY BROWNING went back to her room, took a sheet of notepaper from her dressing-table and began to write.

Dear Charles,

I came to your study just now to talk to you, to tell you that I intended to leave you, but somehow I couldn't bring myself to say the words, perhaps because you looked so tired, perhaps because I am a coward. But I am convinced that there is no point in the continuation of our 'partnership'. It has served its purpose. By this I do not mean to imply that it was a marriage of convenience merely from your point of view. I went into it with my eyes open and you have fulfilled your part of the bargain. You have been a good husband (partner) and I have tried to be a good wife. It is hard to say whether I ever wished it any other way, it is so long ago. Perhaps I hoped that during the years we would tread greater depths, swim out beyond the shallows of convention of our respective backgrounds, but this was not to be and, because I too sought the advantages of marriage, I had no right to expect more. But now there is nothing to keep us together. Our son is grown up and like so many sons today has gone his own way. You are no longer the bright young man on his way up who will profit from a presentable wife (the boss's daughter?). I want to have a few years to myself before this short experience is over (sorry to sound morbid). I don't think our relationship – doesn't that sound ghastly? – has ever been quite the same since the day I discovered what you had done to my father, but don't reproach yourself any more – if I had really wanted to find those deeper depths then I should have left you that day. I thank you, Charles, for giving me what we agreed you should give. That there was nothing more is

*neither of our faults. I wish you well in this next period of your
life, I do not fear for you because, as I just said, I know that you
will win.*

She signed it with a flourish and began to cry. For what?
Self pity? For what might have been? For her own cowardice
over the years? For the waste?

She stopped crying and picked up a photograph of her
husband taken in the fifties, studio lights finding the sheen of
youth on his face, youth snared and pinned inside a silver
frame. *And even then I knew but I did nothing.* And a photograph of their son when he was ten and staring out of the frame
with trust in his eyes. *Did we betray that trust?* She placed both
photographs in a suitcase.

One by one she took the suitcases to the elevator. She
stopped outside her husband's study and listened; he was on the
telephone shouting. Something about the Middle East. She slid
the envelope containing the letter under the door. She hesitated, remembering the first time she had come to Chicago to
meet his parents.

Anything had been possible then.

But I didn't understand.

She ran to the elevator. She went to the underground garage
and stacked her suitcases in the red MGB that her husband had
bought her for her birthday.

Then she drove south.

CHAPTER THIRTY

THE Eskimos came from miles around to drink at Bethel. In summer they came by boat down the Kuskokwin River or across the lakes, or they walked. In winter they came by dog-sled or snowmobile.

They came with serious intent and premeditation. They came to Bethel (population two thousand, five hundred) because it was the city; they came with the money the white men had paid them, maybe as much as six hundred dollars a year, to spend in the bars and liquor store the white men had provided. They came for the pool room, for the girls and perhaps shelter for the night in a shack made of tar-paper, they came to get as drunk as skunks.

They drank neat vodka through a straw or beer from cans. They became joyously intoxicated, they became tearfully intoxicated; they robbed and they fought and they beat up their wives and they lay down to freeze to death in the streets.

In their villages they left behind the old people to fish through holes in the ice. They left their walrus-skin boats, suspended on drift-wood frames. They left behind values that had changed as slowly as glaciers until the white men brought salvation.

In return the Eskimos brought prosperity to the white men: six hundred and fifty thousand dollars in one year from the liquor store; one thousand dollars a night in either of Bethel's two bars. The town had once tried to control the natives' drinking by introducing prohibition, but it was no more successful than national prohibition had been. The bootleggers moved in and the Eskimos went on drinking, so the experiment was dropped, and the Eskimos continued to get loaded, committing the occasional rape, the occasional homicide, falling in the road in their beautiful parkas with the fur-trimmed hoods.

Of course some whites got drunk, too. Holding their liquor better, tossing back their bourbon with a more experienced hand, bending to the first drink of the day rather than picking it up with shaking hands, never passing out in the street when the temperature was too far below zero.

One of these white boozing men was Richard Larsen.

He had started drinking a year after Ruth's death at about the time that he heard that his father had died, closely followed by his mother's death. He had never fooled himself that he was drinking just a little at lunchtime, at the cocktail hour, to take the chill off his loneliness; he never said to himself, 'Just one more,' or 'I can knock it off whenever I want to.' He drank deliberately and suicidally; he could feel the alcohol destroying his brain, softening his body, and he didn't give a damn. He didn't drink steadily every day: he drank in great bouts of oblivion two or three times a month. Nor did he seek a cause of his drinking: he knew it: he had capitulated and he was in full alcoholic retreat. Alaska had won, he told himself, as he sat in hopeless bars in Anchorage, Alaska has rejected me.

He crashed one of his two aircraft when he was drunk. He sold the other and closed down his company. He heard that Mint had been killed in a crash and he thought: Alaska has claimed another victim. He sold the land where the house had been before the earthquake and moved once again into an apartment. He worked for the environmentalists, in particular the Sierra Club, but without enthusiasm, and he helped Ott with his paperwork for the native land claims. He kept his dogs and sometimes rode with them into the Interior when the country-side was grey-white and bleak. He got a licence to drive a cab and never drank when he was driving passengers; but he got a name for it just the same. Wasn't he the crank who had once refused to fly hunters up north? And wasn't he the guy who had rescued a Jap once from the slopes of McKinley? Well, that must have taken guts, but to come to Alaska from the Outside and start laying down the law about hunting when men had been hunting since time began, well, that was a bit strong. It was his son they felt sorry for, they said. He was strong and husky, a fine tackle, fearless ice-hockey player, a first-class shot, a good Alaskan, a shame that he should be shackled with a father like that.

Four years after Ruth's death Billy came in to see his father while he sat reading in the lounge of the apartment. It was apparent that Billy had come to make some sort of announcement. Larsen put down the book he had been reading; it was the diary he had kept until the earthquake. He had never written in it again and he had been reading the last entry:-

Like the Phoenix I have arisen. I have a beautiful wife, a fine son, a prosperous business. I have not beaten Alaska, nor is Alaska the victor. I know this is fanciful but it seems as if this country wanted a fighter; I fought and now at last it has accepted me.

Larsen looked up at his son. He looked very big and healthy and he had shed his teenage clumsiness. How old was he? Nineteen, going on twenty. He looked very confident, very strong, very Alaskan.

Larsen who was on his third Scotch and water motioned towards the sofa. 'Sit down. Have a drink.' He pushed the bottle towards his son who shook his head. 'Let's hear what's on your mind.' He wasn't yet drunk but he had to think before he spoke. He retrieved the bottle. 'No, I guess you don't drink much. Sensible at your age.' Did he already reek of whisky, was it oozing from his pores? Surely not already; he hadn't taken a drink for ten days and this was only his third ... well, his fourth, as he poured a finger of Scotch into his glass and added ice and water.

His son sat down; he didn't seem as self-confident as usual. He just sat there in his winter sports clothes looking like an instructor from the ski-slopes.

'What's on your mind?' Larsen asked again. 'Anything I can do?'

'No, there's nothing you can do,' his son said thoughtfully. 'I just thought you should know the way things are working out.'

Larsen nodded encouragingly, sipping his drink. It was

extraordinary how quickly alcohol reached the brain. Even when you were used to it. 'Shoot,' he said.

'Well, it's like this.' Billy massaged one fist as though he had just hit someone. 'I know how you feel about conservation and everything. About keeping the virgin land pure.' *Was there a touch of sarcasm there?* 'Well, as you know, not everyone feels that way. Not everyone in Alaska, that is. In fact a hell of a lot of people think it's bad for the State. They've just struck oil and for once Alaska is in a position to get in there among the chips. If your people do anything to stop the pipeline then it will be Alaska that will suffer.'

'They don't understand,' Larsen told his son.

'Sure they understand. They're in for the main chance and they don't want it spoiled by—'

'A lot of cranks?'

'If you like, I didn't say it.'

'Have you any idea what offshore drilling could lead to?'

Billy shrugged, poured himself a glass of water.

Larsen said: 'They reckon that an oil spill in the Arctic would spread over thousands of acres of ice. This would absorb the sun's heat that is normally reflected from the ice and the increased heat could melt the polar ice cap.'

'Do you really believe that?'

'I didn't say I did. But you've got to take all the risks into consideration.'

'They said steam-trains would make cows run dry,' Billy said. He watched as his father poured himself more Scotch. 'Do you really have to have another?'

'Does it bother you?'

'I don't like to see anyone let liquor get hold of them.'

'It got hold of me a long time ago,' Larsen said.

'I don't buy that. *You* got hold of *it*.'

'Anyway, what did you come to tell me?'

Billy stared at him and Larsen felt his contempt. 'Just that I'm going over to the enemy camp.'

Larsen said: 'What the hell are you talking about?'

'I'm going into oil.'

'Marion Davenport's old man?'

'That's about the size of it,' Billy said.

'Doing what?' Larsen asked dully.

'I don't know yet. I've got to graduate first at Fairbanks, then Mr. Davenport is going to fix me up with some sort of job on the North Slope.'

'Doing your bit for Alaska, huh?'

His son stared at a photograph of McKinley on the wall, the slope where his father had made that crazy landing. He remembered how proud of him he had been and how it had given him status at high school.

He said: 'Yes, as a matter of fact. That oil will bring prosperity to Alaska. You know, you and your generation campaigned for statehood. Well, we reckon that oil will do as much for Alaska, maybe more. Now they've struck oil in the north the state will be able to sell the rest of the leases at fantastic prices and take a royalty on the value of the oil. Then there are filing fees, drilling permits . . . they reckon all in all they'll make up half of Alaska's general fund budget.'

'Who's *they*? Mr. Davenport?'

'He knows what he's talking about.'

'I'm sure he does,' Larsen said.

'But it's not just that.' Billy leaned forward making a last effort to convince his father. 'There'll be good jobs to be had for everyone – natives included,' he said quickly, 'and money will pour into the state from Outside. Alaska will become one of the richest states in the union and I can't see much wrong with that,' he finished.

'Maybe it won't be worth living in.'

'You mean the countryside? That's all crap,' his son said, his features tightening.

'They've got to get the oil south. The only feasible way's a pipeline. That could change the whole, the whole' – he searched for the word – 'the whole ecology of Alaska.'

'Bullshit,' his son said. 'Like I said, not many Alaskans go along with this conservation thing. Sure they want to keep the place beautiful but they're realistic about it. The oil's there and it's got to be got out. And they resent interference from cranks in the Lower Forty-eight.'

'And in Alaska?'

'Maybe,' his son said.

'I'm not very active these days.'

His son didn't reply.

'I know what you think,' Richard Larsen said, hearing the self-pity in his own voice.

His son glanced at his watch: 'I'd better be going. I'm meeting Marion in twenty minutes.'

'A beautiful girl. She reminds me of your mother.'

Billy Larsen started to speak, stopped.

'What were you going to say?'

'I guess it's none of my business.'

'Go ahead.' Larsen stared at the almost empty glass wondering whether to fill it up now or wait until his son had left. 'We are father and son.'

'We used to be,' Billy said.

'And what the hell's that supposed to mean?'

'I don't know how to put it but well, you know, my mother's been dead a long time . . .'

'Yes?' Larsen's voice was tense now.

'And I figure you should have gotten over it by now. I don't mean forgotten her or anything because she was a wonderful woman . . .' He stood up. 'But, hell, you just gave up,' pointing at the bottle. 'Do you think that's the way she would have wanted it?'

Larsen poured more whisky into his glass. He drank. He said: 'You were quite right, it isn't any of your business.'

'But it's pathetic. Driving a cab, getting drunk . . . I mean, why give up just like that?'

'It's my privilege,' his father said. It was an effort to enunciate. 'Now go and meet your girl.'

'There's just one other thing.'

His father looked up at him blinking. 'Yeah, what's that?'

'I shan't be staying here next vacation.'

'That's your privilege.'

'I'm going down to Seattle to see how Mr. Davenport's operation works down there.'

'You're going to go places,' his father said, slurring his

words. 'Do you know something? You remind me of a guy I once knew. Married the boss's daughter. Very sensible thing to do. A guy named Browning, Charles Browning.'

'He's a pretty big operator,' Billy Larsen said. 'Did you really know him?'

'Sure did. He was going to give me a medal.'

His son looked puzzled. 'I don't understand.'

'He was going to give me a medal. Then he was going to give me a job. I told him to stick his job.'

'I don't understand,' his son said. 'And I'm not marrying Marion because she's the boss's daughter. I didn't give a damn what her old man did when I fell in love with her.'

'You'll go places,' his father said, 'marrying the boss's daughter.'

His son moved quickly to the door. He opened it and when he spoke his voice was hard. 'Maybe I will go places. But you aren't going any place, you're all washed up.'

He closed the door and was gone.

And maybe I should weep, Larsen thought, pouring more Scotch into the glass, not bothering with the ice. The whisky did its work, soothing and muddling and numbing and opening up lockets from the past. This was what he liked at these times, when the liquor opened these lockets and the past tumbled out more real than the present.

He frowned as a squirrel ran towards him, its body mutilated by lead shot, and he poured himself more whisky, drinking it quickly so that the alcohol would open up another locket, and the knuckles of his fist shone white as he pulled at the heavy bleeding body of Charles Browning and he smiled gently as he kissed a girl with no name, smiled more broadly as he lived again with his wife ... the earth rippled, the house slid towards the sea, the jaws of the earth opened up ...

He poured what was left of the bottle of whisky into the glass and drank it in one gulp.

And he went on drinking and soon alcohol was part of his system. It guided him as much as hunger or fatigue and it showed in the colour of his eyes and skin, and in the lines on his face. It showed in the way he dressed, in the way he talked, hesitantly, feeling for words, conscious of them and wondering if they were right. In drink he was sometimes maudlin, sometimes blearily hostile; when he wasn't drinking he smelled of drink and his body shook in the mornings and he jumped as the wind stirred the curtains. When he gazed into a mirror and saw what had become of the Viking he was no longer shocked.

When Ott wanted some research done in Bethel it seemed right that he should go: Bethel with its unrelenting poverty and alcoholism was a cradle for men like Larsen.

He flew there one day late in 1970 as the mud was beginning to freeze and a cold wind was blowing down from the Kuskokwin mountains and the dull sky was shedding a few flakes of snow. He took a room furnished with a bed, a cupboard, a chair and a honeybucket. He lay on the bed for a few minutes until his skin began to itch. Then he went down to the liquor store and bought a bottle of Scotch which he stuffed in the pocket of his torn jacket and made his way unerringly to one of the two bars.

As he arrived they were throwing out an Eskimo. No one took any notice of what was after all a common enough spectacle. They left the Eskimo propped up against the wall. He was in his late forties but he looked older; his short hair was grey and his eyes were almost closed; he was unshaven and there was spittle on his lips.

Larsen glanced at him, paused. He bent down and stared at the lolling face.

A man standing at the door of the bar said: 'Don't waste your time with him, mister, he's been like that for a week.' He noticed the bottle in Larsen's pocket. 'Come on in but don't drink your own hooch, that way we go broke.'

Larsen continued to stare at the Eskimo. Snow was settling on his shabby parka and he looked very sick. Larsen said: 'We'd better do something for this guy, he looks like he's dying.'

'Yeah, he don't look so good. Maybe we should get him up to hospital.'

They got a taxi and Larsen went with the Eskimo to the hospital run by the federal Alaska Native Service. The Eskimo's head rolled with the motion of the taxi while Larsen stared at him and tried to place him. For some reason the Eskimo stirred in him a feeling of guilt. He knew it was important to him to find out who he was.

When they reached the hospital a woman in her thirties was just leaving. Her face was framed by the hood of her parka and she had the cheekbones and eyes of an Eskimo; she looked attractive and feminine and competent.

She saw Larsen and the cab driver pulling the Eskimo out of the cab. She came across and said: 'That was quick.'

The cab-driver looked up. 'What was quick, lady?'

'He was only discharged this morning.'

'You work here?'

'I visit.' She touched Larsen's arm. 'Wait, I'll get a stretcher.'

She came back with two orderlies carrying a stretcher. 'Jesus,' one of them said, 'not him again.'

'Why bring him here?' the other said. 'This ain't a home for incurables.'

But they took him inside and the woman said to Larsen: 'That was good of you to bring him here,' eyes straying towards the bottle in his pocket, taking in the shabby clothes and the lines on his face. 'Mind if I share the cab with you?'

'Please,' he said. When they were inside the cab he said: 'That Eskimo, what was his name?'

She told him that it was Taluk.

'You see,' he said, 'I knew him a long time ago. He had come south to try and live with white men. He nearly died on the way but he made it and he was very proud and he had every right to be because it was a courageous thing that he did, leaving his village, coming all that way by himself. He was in the same hospital ward as me. He was eager to learn and to get out of the hospital and start a new life with us civilized people. I wonder what happened,' said Larsen, sitting awkwardly in an easy chair holding a cup of tea.

She had said to him: 'You don't look much better than the patient, you'd better come in and have a cup of tea,' and here he was in her apartment which was a neat place, smelling faintly of lavender, with Eskimo carvings on the table and Eskimo paintings on the walls. It wasn't too warm but it had a snugness about it, perhaps because of the grey, white-flaked day outside.

She said: 'What happened to him? The usual I guess.'

'What do you mean – the usual?'

'There are all sorts of phrases for it. Failure-to-adapt is as good as any. Or failure to be adopted by the white man,' she said in a more cynical voice, stirring her pale tea.

'We can't judge,' Larsen said. 'Alaska is a tough country. Look at me.'

She said: 'We can guess. Maybe he was good with his hands, a good engineer. You know, Eskimos *are* good engineers. Maybe some white man gave him a job and when it was done paid him off, left him with his pockets stuffed full of dollar bills in Anchorage or Fairbanks, some town which was as alien to him as the jungle would be to you.'

He began to shiver.

She said: 'You look in pretty bad shape.'

He nodded. He took the bottle out of his pocket and placed it on the polished table beside a vase of everlasting flowers. He stared at it and licked his lips.

'Maybe you're right,' he said. 'But maybe you're over-simplifying. Perhaps something happened in his life to make him this way. Not just the usual thing – rejection unable to adapt – maybe there was some sort of tragedy . . .'

'As there was in your life?'

'Maybe.'

She said: 'You need help.'

'We all need help,' he said.

She told him that her name was Theresa Williams and she was a government welfare worker and that she had asked for the Bethel assignment so that she could lose herself in its gutter poverty and alcoholic escape. 'My husband was a pilot,' she said. 'He died in a crash two years ago.' She was making a

342

study of the Bethel problem; if she came up with any answers then they could be applied all over Alaska, wherever Eskimos or Indians drank their wages.

'And have you come up with any answers?'

'A few. But they don't help, not really.' She put down her cup, pointed at the bottle. 'You want a drink of that?'

He nodded, ashamed.

'It's killing you, you know that?'

'We're all dying from the moment we're born.'

'All right, I'll pour you a drink. A nice hot one with some cinnamon, how about that?'

He said that would be fine and when he drank the hot spiced whisky it seemed more like medicine than a drink. He felt the whisky reach his stomach; it felt like molten lead. He sat still with his mouth full of hot spiced whisky. He recalled the ward in the military hospital thinking that there had only been four of them there and it was a hell of a record that fifty per cent of them had ended up alcoholics. For the first time since he had started drinking he felt ashamed. He swallowed the mouthful of whisky. When he reached across to put the half-empty glass on the table he felt faint; sweat started on his forehead.

'Put your head between your knees,' she said.

'I'm sorry.'

'Don't be, I've seen it all before.'

'But in your home—'

'Between your knees.'

There was fire in his belly and ice in his skull. He stayed with his head between his knees until the sick cold retreated as the blood rushed to his brain.

She knelt in front of him and put a match to a newspaper, *The Nome Nugget*, under the dry spruce logs in the grate. Flames leaped around the logs, then they caught and he smelled the bonfires on Long Island in the fall.

She asked him: 'When did you last eat?'

'Yesterday,' he said.

'Would you like something to eat?'

'I'm not hungry.'

'Well you can try. I'm going to eat. Don't worry, not raw

343

fish.' She laughed again. 'Here, drink up, you can't stop drinking just like that.'

'Who says I'm going to stop?'

She shrugged. 'You'll be dead in a year if you don't.' She went into the kitchen and he heard the clatter of dishes, then the smell of fat frying. It made him feel sick. He drank up the rest of the hot whisky. He considered splashing another finger of cold whisky into the glass. 'Go ahead,' she said as she came back into the room carrying a tray.

'You psychic?'

'No, just experienced in these things.'

'Do you drink?'

'Sure, pour me a Scotch. I like to take a drink while I cook.'

The meat she cooked was moose. With canned peas and potatoes followed by Eskimo ice-cream and coffee. Larsen ate a little; he didn't drink any more whisky.

Then they sat by the fire as fingers of ash fell into the grate and flames flapped around the remains of the logs.

She asked him where he was staying and when he told her she said: 'That's a flop house. I've got a spare room. Would you like to stay with me?'

He said he would.

He collected his case from the room and returned to the apartment.

He asked her what was to be done about places like Bethel. She threw another log on the fire and they watched the flames feel for it.

'I don't know,' she said. 'You either start a full-scale programme of rehabilitation or you leave the Eskimo alone. You do one or the other, you don't have half measures like we've got now. A lot of the villages round here are pretty primitive. You know, many of them have never even heard of native land claims. Can you imagine what it's like leaving a sod hut where you've lived on raw fish all your life, maybe never tasted alcohol, and arriving here, the Big City. Does it surprise you that they follow the white man's example and go straight to the nearest bar and drink themselves stupid?'

Larsen said: 'It doesn't surprise me.'

'I'm sorry,' she said, 'I didn't mean you.'

'It was a good point,' he said.

'But the white people who sicken me are the ones who point to an Eskimo lying in the street and say, "Another nigger who can't hold his liquor" – and go into a bar and get plastered. Of course Eskimos can't drink. Nor can Indians or Aleuts because they don't know how to. They come here from some little fishing settlement and instead of eating they drink vodka as though it were water and pass out on the street. And then they get a taste for it,' Theresa Williams said sadly, 'and one day they pass out when the temperature's minus thirty and they die.'

She went into the kichen and made some more coffee. When she returned she said: 'The transition's got to be slowed down. Some of the natives can take it and some can't. People have got to be patient. And they've got to know their stuff before they come up here preaching, reforming, educating. I mean some of them don't know one Eskimo from the other. An Inupiat from a Yupik. An Athabascan Indian from a Tinglit. They're all just *natives*, to these people. A sickening word, isn't it?'

'Maybe, but I guess it's well-meant,' Larsen said.

'Perhaps,' she said without conviction. 'But what about the Eskimos and Indians in the universities of America, in business, in politics – are they *natives*? Or are they Americans? What about the authors, painters, sculptors? What about the mechanics? In Canada they say they can train an Eskimo to be a jet mechanic in a fraction of the time it takes to train a white man. Are they *natives*?'

'I don't know,' Larsen said. He felt very tired. 'I guess not.'

'You'd better get to bed, you need sleep. You need help.' She gave the logs a last kick and sent plumes of sparks streaming up the chimney. 'You know, there's something familiar about you. Richard ... Richard what?'

'Larsen,' he told her.

'The pilot?'

'The ex-pilot.'

'You used to be a bush pilot. Used to land on McKinley like Don Sheldon.'

He nodded warily.

'You used to be one of my heroes.'

He was embarrassed. 'I was just a pilot, ma'am. Nothing uncommon about that in Alaska.'

'I remember when you rescued a Japanese from McKinley and went back to get another.'

'But I didn't get him off,' Larsen said as if it summed up his life.

'And I remember reading that you wouldn't fly anyone who was going hunting and I thought "Gee there's a guy with ideals, I'd like to meet him." And here you are drinking coffee in front of my fire.'

'And you're wondering, "What the hell happened to those ideals?"'

'I think you tried to drown them,' she said.

'I'm doing a great job.'

'And proud of it.'

He held up his hand. 'No lectures.'

She was angry now. 'Do you think I'd bother. I think someone like Taluk is worth bothering about. You know, a *native*. But not an educated white man like yourself.'

'Thank God for that,' he said. 'And now I think I'll go to bed.'

But he twitched in his sleep, jumped awake as he flew a plane into a precipice. Once he awoke and his cheeks were damp after a dream in which he had been trying to establish what had happened to the young Eskimo with the sleek, tough face he had once known. What had happened in the lost years . . . and his cheeks were damp because in the dreams those lost years were his own.

When he awoke at 7.30 a.m. he wanted a drink badly.

Larsen stayed at the apartment for a week and visited Taluk in hospital every day. Each day the Eskimo seemed weaker and he didn't recognize Larsen.

Larsen was drinking less – less than half a bottle of Scotch a day – and eating more, although his tongue still itched for alcohol. He asked what hope there was for Taluk and the doctors shrugged; they would do their best but it didn't seem to matter because Taluk didn't want to live.

In fact Taluk wanted to join his ancestors. He had been wrong to leave his village and seek the white man, but he had been driven by restless spirits. Perhaps he should have resisted them, perhaps they had been bad spirits; but he hadn't known, now it was over.

Occasionally there were moments of lucidity. Then Taluk spoke of the white man who had journeyed north with him and asked him to show him where he had found the oil which he had brought south with him in the Coke bottle. They had flown in an aeroplane and Taluk had lost his sense of direction; this had angered the white man who had promised Taluk a lot of money if he took him to the spot where the oil oozed thick and black.

'Who was this man?' Larsen asked as he sat at Taluk's bed-side.

'I do not know,' Taluk replied and then, his eyes sly, 'Have you any drink with you?'

Larsen said he hadn't and the Eskimo fell back on the pillows and talked no more. On the next visit Taluk talked a little more.

Who was the man? Taluk shrugged. Just a white man who was willing to give an Eskimo a fortune for information because to the white man it wasn't a fortune at all, just a few weeks pay.

'And did you find the oil for him?'

'Yes,' said Taluk, he had found the oil and the white man had been very pleased and had given him more green bills than he had ever seen before and when they had got back to Anchorage he had got very drunk.

Larsen asked: 'Had you ever seen the white man before?'

Taluk nodded. 'A long time ago . . . in hospital.'

'And did he have a beard at the time?' Taluk nodded, wagging his chin slightly, while Larsen thought, 'That sonofabitch,' wondering how he had ever been deceived by Guthrie, then reminding himself that the thirst for oil and the money that follows close on its heels is only a weakness, no worse than a thirst for liquor.

Taluk had continued to drink, he told Larsen, and he had married an Eskimo girl who had been very pretty and passionate. They had rented a tiny apartment where they had lived quite happily, except at certain times, like early April, when he was restless because he knew the ice would be moving in the north and *agvik* – the whales – would be swimming through the leads in the ice. And he hungered for the taste of raw fish at the ice camp and he remembered the exultation as a harpoon speared a baluga or bowhead and the smell from the butchered carcass as the sun set over the jagged ice of the ocean.

All had been well, with Taluk working as a mechanic, until the discovery of oil at Kenai. Then, when the oilmen came to town, his wife began to change; she bought fancy clothes and cosmetics and, when Taluk remonstrated with her, she became angry, saying that he had wanted to join the white men and all she was doing was acting like a white girl. One day he saw her in a bar on Fourth Avenue talking and laughing with two white men who had arms as thick as thighs and there was such intimacy about them that Taluk realized where she had been getting the money for the clothes and cosmetics. He contemplated killing her, but instead he left the apartment and got drunk at the end of Fourth Avenue where it wastes away into small bars with pool tables and pornographic book shops. He never returned to the apartment.

After that he worked a little and drank a lot and that's how it had been until he moved from Anchorage seeking salmon-filled rivers and blue skies and space; but he had met some Inupiat Eskimos from the north who travelled by snowmachine and when they told him about Bethel the thirst returned and he paid his fare to Bethel where he realized that, just as summer withers and freezes, so it was his time to die.

'But you can't just give up like that,' Larsen urged.

Taluk stared at him calmly. He could hear death calling him. He remembered the church in the village and smelled burning tallow; he tasted Eskimo ice-cream and there was a harpoon in his hands that became a fishing rod over a round black wound in the ice and he heard the voice of his teacher and he smelled the walls of the sod-hut and felt its oily heat in the winter and

348

he heard the grinding of the ice-floes and he dreamed again of his Great Adventure that was somehow painted in white and gold and it was at that moment that he died.

Two weeks later Larsen returned to Anchorage and Theresa Williams went with him. He tried to stop drinking altogether but the alcohol had been in his bloodstream so long that his body needed it as it needs nourishment. He taught himself to despise himself; he trained himself to imagine the contempt that would have been in Ruth's eyes; he sought the help of Theresa Williams who gladly gave it; but still he drank, when his tongue thirsted, when his limbs shivered and his muscles jerked and he knew that liquor would quiet them. At times like these he kept himself from other people, from Theresa, from his son on the few occasions when he called. But the bouts of drinking were spaced at longer intervals, and it was during these intervals, when he began to feel clean, that he looked back upon himself with disgust; and that was why, when he was drunk, he hid.

Once Billy came to the apartment when he had poured only one drink. After a long interval it only needed one drink to blurr his reactions and he wished he hadn't opened the door because of the expression on his son's face.

Billy twirled a tennis racket. He asked: 'Where's the native woman?'

Larsen stared at him. 'You mean Mrs. Williams?'

'If that's her name that's who I mean.'

'I'd be grateful if you didn't talk about her like that.'

'Nothing wrong with the word native,' Billy said. 'Nothing derogatory, nothing racist.'

'Yes there is,' Larsen said. 'You're just playing with words.'

'Well, I didn't know her name so how should I refer to her?'

'With respect,' Larsen said. 'She's educated, cultivated, intelligent.'

'So if she's all those things I mustn't call her a native? Now that's really racist. That's saying that every Eskimo who still fishes through a hole in the ice is a native but anyone who's been to college isn't.'

'It's the inflection,' Larsen said. 'Anyway now you know her name you can use it.'

'Okay,' Billy said, 'so where's Mrs. Williams?'

'She's around,' Larsen said, drinking the last of the Scotch in the glass.

'So I've heard.'

'And what's that supposed to mean?'

'Whatever you want it to mean.'

'I think,' Larsen said slowly, 'that you ought to leave.'

'Don't worry,' Billy said, 'I hadn't reckoned on staying.'

'You're thinking of your mother, aren't you?'

'I'm thinking of Mrs. Williams.'

'Your mother would have understood.'

'Would she?'

'I think she would,' Larsen said.

'An *Eskimo*! Does that sound better than *native*?'

'She's a nice woman,' Larsen told his son. 'You'd like her.'

'*I* don't need a nurse,' Billy said. 'Or whatever she is . . .'

'I think you'd better go,' Larsen said tiredly, regarding his son with compassion, not really blaming him, because a lot of people felt this way about Eskimos and Indians and sincerely believed that they were getting a good deal, resented handing over land and money to a people who had contributed little to the development of Alaska.

'Take care,' Larsen said.

Billy shrugged and left, leaving Larsen alone with the whisky bottle.

Once Theresa took him north to her village. It was in the fall and the mists were gathering, the sea freezing, the sun dipping low in its orbit; soon winter would be sniffing over the rim of the world.

They planned to stay a couple of months hoping that the cold would help cleanse Larsen's body of alcohol; they talked about his craving for liquor as if it were a third person and it seemed to help.

Theresa's people lived in a modern frame house equipped

with electricity and a chemical toilet. But it was crowded so Larsen and Theresa were allotted a hut made of plywood and tin covered with caribou skins, equipped with a chair and a few tables, a kerosene stove and a honeybucket.

They slept beneath skins, sweating from the heat from the stove as the winds from the polar cap piled the snow against the walls outside. At these times Larsen remembered the hut beside the lake, Ruth waiting as he touched down with his Super Cub, and when Theresa undressed to go to her bed he turned his head away.

Alcohol was banned in the village and for a while Larsen was tortured by the knowledge that there was no way to slake his thirst. He suffered bouts of cabin fever aggravated by the craving for liquor and at these times, when he might have fled into the night where he would have frozen to death in half a minute, Theresa comforted him. He felt the warmth of her body and sometimes the touch of her small breasts against his chest.

The cure was drastic; there wasn't a drink to be had and that was it. Soon his sleep grew calmer and he only woke with a jerk when he dreamed that he had taken a drink. At these times he awoke with sweat pouring from his body and it took Theresa several moments to explain where he was, that he hadn't touched any liquor. Then he smiled and returned to sleep, his breathing steady.

The dreams grew less frequent, the craving diminished.

They walked a lot in the quick hours as the sun made its low flight across the horizon. In the evenings they joined Theresa's parents in their home.

Her mother had grown very old, but her father still looked strong and virile; his face was broad and flat. He knew that Larsen and his daughter weren't married but he told no one because he wasn't sure how the Presbyterian Church would react.

Her father was the headman. He had seen the village change as the white man appeared. One of the first changes had been wrought in his daughter who had gone to the University of Alaska and then to the Bureau of Indian Affairs in California.

As they ate caribou and drank coffee he told Larsen: 'Once

the white man came only to prey on the Inupiat. They took our furs and our women and they killed our animals and we knew hard times but we survived.'

He lit a pipe which he lodged between a gap in his teeth. 'Now they are good to us. Maybe they have stolen our land but they are good to us. They have built us a school, in the winter when we grow thin through lack of fish and meat they drop supplies to us. But they have changed us and sometimes I wonder if this is good.' He sucked at his pipe. 'Maybe it is, maybe it isn't but it must happen, that I know. It was written that it would happen when the first white men landed in this country.'

Larsen asked: 'In what way have your people changed?'

'We have grown soft. In the old days we would have found ways of getting food in the winter. Now we just wait for the welfare' – he nodded towards his daughter – 'to drop food.'

Theresa said: 'And in the old days your hunters would have died looking for food.'

'Death?' Her father shrugged. 'Many died, it is true. But it was always that way and we had our independence. Now we have the school. We used to travel many hundreds of miles, but now we cannot because our children have to attend the school.'

'What my father says is true,' Theresa said. 'The native Eskimo is suspended between two ways of life and we don't know yet which way he will swing. The white man killed us, now he cossets us. But he must be patient with my people. If he suddenly cut off the welfare then my people would die because they are losing the skills of survival. Soon they will be given land and money beyond their comprehension. It is then that they will need help most.'

'*Given* land?' The old Eskimo who spoke with a young man's voice put down his pipe. 'It was not their land to give, it was ours.'

Theresa said to Larsen: 'The land where they are drilling for oil belonged to the Arctic Slope Eskimos. The State sold the leases to the oil companies.'

Larsen asked how the land and money would be handed over when the claims were settled.

'Quickly,' said the old man, the pouches round his eyes breaking with lines of laughter. 'We have waited long enough. Now at last it is us who make the demands. And why is that?' The lines splintered into a laugh. 'Because the white man has educated us to do this. For that we thank him.'

Theresa told Larsen that the hand-outs of land and cash would probably be handled by various native corporations. The villagers would be given shares of stock in the corporation, but they wouldn't be able to sell them for twenty years.

'And will they get what they're asking for?' Larsen asked.

The old man said: 'Not everything, they don't expect that. But they will get a lot because the oil people want the claims settled.'

'And,' said Theresa, 'that means that Washington wants the land claims settled. In 1966 the Secretary for the Interior put a freeze on all land claims to make sure it wasn't all grabbed before the native demands were settled. Which means that the freeze won't be lifted until the claims are settled – so there won't be any pipeline until that happens.'

As they walked back to their hut the night was bright and hard and as cold as pain; behind them the Northern Lights filled the sky with green curtains; their feet kicked up sparkling snow.

She took his arm. 'Well, now you've seen a different sort of Eskimo to the Bethel breed,' she said.

'I think I could live here,' he said.

'No you couldn't. And' – sadly – 'nor could I.' They passed the school and the log church and the post office.

She opened the door of the hut and they went inside.

For several days now he had been free of the thirst and that night, with his belly full, with the heat from the stove and the intimacy of their confinement thick about him, he didn't look away when in the light of an oil lamp she undressed beside him.

And her face was suddenly beautiful and he wondered why he hadn't noticed this before. In her face was everything that she had spoken about, the wild past and the present of which he was now a part. Her smile pushed at her cheekbones and her almond eyes looking steadily at him were dark in the lamplight.

And when she came to him the thirst that had been with him for so long was replaced by a hunger that he had thought drowned.

Two months later they were married in Anchorage.

CHAPTER THIRTY-ONE

OTT smelled trouble.

My old Indian instincts, he thought.

He stared at the audience from the wings of the stage, narrowing his eyes as he looked for the trouble-makers. There they were for sure – three young men with athletes' bodies and pugnacious good looks.

Ott sighed. He was nearly sixty and this was his last battle and he didn't want trouble. He knew what the young men wanted to say; they had a right to say it and he would let them speak. But he wanted no violence.

The young men joked and punched each other. They smoked a lot, betraying nervousness or excitement, and stared round at the Indians who had come in from the bush to the hall at Fairbanks to hear about the land claims.

Intuitively Ott knew their views about natives.

Young men such as these needed only the breath of a cause to create trouble; as soon as the trouble began the cause was forgotten. These young men would start a fight at a ball game, they would rip through a cemetery on motor-bikes, they would desecrate the flowers beds in a park where old people dosed and smelled the roses.

Young men such as these boys were not the sole property of Alaska. They grew up in New York and London and Paris; they felt their inadequacy without being aware of it and they compensated with violence.

The Indians sat with folded arms staring at the empty stage as though a miracle might occur. A reporter arrived from the *Tundra Times*, the crusading native newspaper edited by the Eskimo, Howard Rock; this evening there might even be a reporter from the Fairbanks *Daily News-Miner* present.

These days, Ott thought, we Indians and Eskimos and Aleuts are news. We are going to win our fight against the State, against big business, against all opposition; everyone knows this and it is just a question of how much we win by. But still the enemy tries to hold back as much land and money from us as possible.

Of the three hundred and seventy-five million acres of Alaska, the natives have full ownership of FIVE HUNDRED ACRES.

How can such injustice exist? Ott wondered. Why should we have to plead and haggle and cajole and demand and threaten for what is rightfully ours? It was the humiliation that affected him; when the claims were settled he knew what he would do.

Ott, his hair thin, his face and neck creased, turned away from the audience and addressed the Athabascan Indian waiting with him in the wings. He was young, this Indian, one of the young braves who had arisen to fight the white man at his own game; but he also understood the old Indians, their reverence for land where their ancestors had fished and hunted, and he didn't despise them as some young Indians did.

Ott said: 'Looks like there's going to be trouble out there,' pointing at the young men.

The Athabascan shrugged. 'There are three of them, many of us.'

'Maybe that's what they want. Maybe they will accuse the Indians of beating them up.'

'And scalping them,' the Athabascan said. 'They would make good scalps,' he added, looking at the long thick hair of the three young men.

'Perhaps they have others waiting outside.'

The Athabascan gave a Hollywood Indian sign with his hand. 'Then me send smoke signal with old blanket and our warriors will ambush them and we will take their women and ravish them. It's at least twenty-four hours since I ravished a white woman,' added the Athabascan who wore a grey worsted suit and had his own law practice in Seattle.

Ott envied him his youth. He had never adapted to his own ageing. He didn't like to look in the mirror; he preferred to look at a photograph of himself, a cigar rammed in his mouth, bottle in hand, taken by a boy named Richard Larsen.

Nor did he like the way he thought: he fought old battles as generals relive their victories. He was an embittered historian when all that mattered was the living present.

But he couldn't help it: the injustice of the past had burned him and the scars were still livid.

When he addressed audiences he told them that the first land claim to be settled was started by a Tinglit Indian – 'I am a Tinglit, ladies and gentlemen,' – named William Paul who had campaigned for the return of Tinglit and Haida land that had been encompassed by the Federal Government in the Tongass National Forest. It was more than forty years before the Indians were paid for their land. They got seven and a half million dollars.

And all the time the humiliation. The degradation. The restaurant signs years ago NO DOGS OR NATIVES ALLOWED. But even since statehood the native claims had been treated with terrible arrogance. The State had been given one hundred and three million acres; they had taken part of the Indian village of Minto, they had planted a survey stake in the centre of the village of Tanacross and, of course, they had taken Prudhoe Bay where, until there was the smell of oil in the air, only the Eskimo had lived and hunted and fished.

He told his audiences about the real beginnings of the present native agitation that had been inspired by an act of white arrogance. In 1958 the Atomic Energy Commission had decided to excavate a harbour at Point Hope on the remote coast of north-west Alaska. They intended to make the excavation with a nuclear explosion without taking into consideration the fact that eight hundred Eskimos lived here – although they did offer to evacuate them.

Eskimos of twenty villages, supported by the Association of American Indian Affairs, banded together to repel the atomic invaders. From that movement the *Tundra Times* was born. The harbour project was cancelled: the natives flexed their muscles.

By 1966, with the native claims to Minto largely ignored, the movement had really come alive.

The land claims became an avalanche until the whole state was patchworked with them and the land freeze was imposed.

Before he became Secretary of the Interior, Governor Walter Hickel promised the Senate Interior Committee under Senator Henry Jackson that he wouldn't lift the freeze without Senate and House consent.

As Governor, Hickel had not only fought the land freeze but had tried to settle the land claims; offered ten million acres of land in response to their demand for eighty million; then compromised with forty million acres plus fifty million dollars as part settlement . . . But the bill got nowhere.

There were other bills and at one stage it became plain that no one had any idea how many natives there were in Alaska . . .

'By God,' Ott said to one of his audiences, 'did any of this matter when we enlisted to fight for the United States in the war?'

But no one seemed sure what war he was talking about.

Then came a report, five hundred and sixty-five pages long, on the natives. It concluded that they had 'a substantial claim upon all the lands of Alaska by virtue of aboriginal occupancy.'

'Which meant,' Ott told his audiences, 'that our claims were all right, were okay. And by September 1969, when the oilmen handed out nine hundred million dollars for leases on the North Slope it was plain that we were in for a big slice of the loot. Like maybe forty million acres and five hundred million dollars in cash over nine years and maybe a two per cent royalty to be taken from the State's twelve and a half per cent? And what were we offered? A mere twelve and a half million acres plus five hundred million dollars spread over twenty years – and no damn royalties . . .

'For domestic reasons the Interior Committee's deliberations got delayed until February 1970, by which time we had a good counsel, Arthur Goldberg, a former Supreme Court Justice, and a lot of help from people like former Californian Senator Thomas Kutchel and Ramsey Clark. And we were strong and we insisted on forty million acres and five hundred million dollars over nine years and a percentage of the royalty.

'But time was running out,' Ott said, 'because the land freeze expired at the end of 1970 and then the State would be in for grabs again. But we had fresh support now – oil people who had paid nine hundred million dollars for a few frozen acres of land. They wanted to see everything settled so that they could stick their pipeline through our country. And then we knew we were going to win. It's just a question of how much we were going to get. How much we've been cheated out of over the years . . .'

Ott was once again speaking about injustice in the hall in Fairbanks. And, as always, he was surprising himself. He had said it all so many times that it was a recitation, but always his anger burned through.

To douse the anger he paused. Looked at the three young white Alaskans. Looked at the passive Indians. Looked around at the other speakers on the platform.

He started to speak again and the anger returned.

It was warm in the hall this spring evening and it had a classroom smell about it – the stripped spruce walls, the dust from the floor, the sweat.

Ott told his audience about the time that the Department of the Interior had asked native groups to agree to the lifting of the land freeze on the route of the pipeline. In return the pipeline companies had promised work for the natives and contracts for native companies.

'Did they get them? Did they hell!' Ott stared again at the three young men, no longer worried by what they might do. 'Once again,' he shouted, 'the natives were cheated. They signed waivers authorizing the building of the pipeline and the oilmen promised them preferential treatment. As a result the Department of the Interior amended the land freeze on the route of the pipeline and the oilmen applied for a right-of-way. But,' said Ott, 'the natives got no contracts, very few jobs. And so a group of Athabascans decided to sue the pipeline for forty million dollars damages.'

Ott grinned fiercely at his audience. Now, he thought, we have power, we are a force to be reckoned with. We are as clever as the white man. 'And then we got injunctions stopping

Wally Hickel, Secretary of the Interior, from issuing permits for the right-of-way for the pipeline. In effect we told the oilmen: "We will not be cheated. We have the same rights as you." '

The other speakers clapped; they were followed by some of the audience. The white Alaskans sat with arms folded. And it was then that Ott realized that there was something familiar about one of them. He frowned and narrowed his eyes but his eyesight wasn't so good these days.

He hurried on. He covered the natives' legal rights to ownership of land, which some politicians claimed was only a moral right, and the opposition to granting the natives royalties on oil.

He tackled the proposed settlement of the native claims which the Senate Interior Committee had announced a few weeks earlier.

Ott said that Senator Henry Jackson, 'our friend – and we have many friends in Washington,' believed the bill to be a good one. He had said that it gave Congress 'the chance to provide the native people of Alaska with justice, hope and opportunity and to end a hundred years of less than benevolent wardship.' He had said that the bill would be 'the last chapter in the sad history of the United States' relations with Alaska. Indian, Eskimo and Aleut people will have a just, generous and honourable closing.'

Ott spread wide his arms. 'Just?' His voice rose. 'Generous?' The anger broke through. 'They propose to give us five hundred million dollars over twelve years and two per cent of the royalties on minerals not patented to the state and four million acres of land.' He punched the palm of one hand with the knuckle of the other. 'Four million, ladies and gentlemen, FOUR MILLION.'

He took a drink of water. The Athabascan Indian touched his arm and said: 'Take it easy.' Ott brushed his hand aside. He turned to his figures. 'There are three hundred and seventy-five million acres of land and we who once owned them ask for forty and are given four? Is that just? Is that generous?'

The audience murmured angrily. Ott held up his hands. His mouth ran with saliva, he knew the power of the hot-gospeller.

'And the pay-off? What about the pay-off? All right, with the royalties we might end up with a billion dollars. Yes a billion,' as some of the Indians whistled with awe, 'and I know that sounds a lot. But you just work it out. They're paying us one billion dollars for what's left of Alaska's acres after we've received our four million acres. That's one billion dollars for three hundred and seventy-one million acres . . .'

He drank more water. Sweat trickled down his face. His head ached with his figures. He went on: 'Don't forget that the oilmen have just paid nine hundred million dollars for their leases – only the leases mind you – on a mere four hundred and fifty thousand acres.' He flung wide his arms. 'I ask you – is that just? Is that generous?'

He sat down wiping his face with a handkerchief, mopping at the sweat in the creases in his flesh. The Indians were applauding frenziedly. I have become a rabble-rouser, goddamit.

One of the three young white Alaskans was on his feet. The Indians were quiet. It was the boy whose face was familiar to Ott.

He said in a loud, clear voice: 'The answer to your question is Yes, it is generous.'

Wariness descended upon Ott, the passion was spent; he was as he had been before there had suddenly been hope, in the days when he had sought the cause of animals because there seemed to be no hope for Indians or Eskimos or Aleuts. What was it about this boy that was so familiar? He reached for his spectacle case on the table and said: 'You'd better explain yourself.'

'Sure I'll explain myself.' Ott realized that he had been wrong about this boy: he wasn't here just for a fight. 'You speak about the land as if it were all yours, every damn acre of it. Well I tell you this – it isn't. This isn't the Lower 48. Neither the Indians nor the Eskimos nor the Aleuts were ever tricked out of their land here. We have as much right to it as you. It's the white Alaskans who built the cities, who developed the fishing, the mining and timber forests. And,' said the young man slowly and deliberately, 'it was white men who struck oil.'

Even the voice . . . Ott stood up. 'What's your name, young man?' he asked, although by now he knew.

'Does it matter?'

'Sure it matters. It's always good to read a signature to a letter.' Ott smiled at him. 'But I think I know your name anyway.' *He stood in the zoo in Central Park* and he said to the young man in the spruce-wood hall: 'It's Larsen, isn't it?'

Billy Larsen nodded. 'How did you know?'

'Your voice, the way you stand. The *belief* in your voice.'

'Belief?'

'Sure, belief. I figure you believe what you're saying just as I do. You see,' Ott said, putting on his spectacles and looking at the finely-built figure of the boy, 'I knew your father.'

'Oh.' The boy seemed to shrink; Ott who knew about Larsen's drinking understood; he thought he would talk to the boy after the meeting.

Ott said: 'I met you a long time ago when you were small . . .'

One of the other young men stood up. He was chewing gum and smoking at the same time. He said: 'Let's knock it off shall we and get down to business. We all know about old man Larsen.' The third young man sniggered.

Billy Larsen looked down at them, fists clenched. Ott thought he looked very lonely. He came to his rescue: 'So you're saying the proposed settlement is generous and just?'

'Sure I am. More than generous.'

'Did you know that even five thousand million dollars stretched over nine years wouldn't give the natives half what white Alaskans earn?'

One of Billy Larsen's companions said: 'The natives don't earn it,' and the other said: 'Should keep 'em in liquor for a while though.'

'What do you think?' Ott asked Richard Larsen's son.

'I think it's a ridiculous comparison and I suspect you do too. How can you compare the salary a white man needs to exist in a city with the money a native needs in a village?'

'I take your point,' Ott said, ignoring the murmurs of dissent from the other speakers. 'But maybe if they'd been given a decent wage fifty years ago then they'd be living in the cities, in a downtown apartment in Anchorage with a couple of automobiles.'

One of Larsen's companions said: 'And eating blubber on the fine new upholstery.'

Billy Larsen turned to him. 'Knock it off, will you,' he said and the boy who had spoken worked the muscles in his jaw and said: 'I thought we'd come for some fun.'

Outside the bird still sang in the tree.

'What I mean is,' said Billy Larsen, 'that maybe the natives should never have left village life. Maybe they were happier that way. Maybe giving them a whole bundle of money is going to do them more harm than good.'

'Not if it's handled properly,' Ott replied.

'*If* it's handled properly,' said the third young man.

Billy Larsen turned and looked around him; the Indians stared back with hostility. He noticed that the two reporters at the table beneath the platform were writing rapidly in their notebooks.

He swallowed and said: 'What I came to say is this. The discovery of oil and the pipeline is just about the most important thing that's happened to Alaska. It shouldn't be stopped either by land claims or conservationists.

'Maybe in the first place they tried to rush the pipeline through too quickly. But now the natives have been offered a decent settlement and, as for conservationists, they've got everything they asked for.

'I believe,' said Billy Larsen, 'that like Senator Jackson said, the natives have now got a chance to own their homes and their lands, to get decent education, to be healthy and "an opportunity for individual identity and pride". I believe that oil is the life-blood of Alaska, maybe the whole of the United States, and I believe it should be allowed to flow freely. I believe that you' – pointing at Ott and the other speakers – 'are stunting our economy and betraying Alaska.'

He sat down abruptly.

The audience looked to Ott to reply, to destroy this loud-mouthed interloper. Ott, who knew the tricks of debate, asked casually: 'You don't have any interest in oil to declare, do you, son?' and wished he hadn't when he saw Billy Larsen's embarrassment. But there was no going back. 'Well, do you?'

Billy Larsen said: 'Not real interest.'

Ott sighed. 'Do you or don't you?'

One of Billy's companions shouted: 'What goddam business is it of yours?' And to Billy: 'Don't you tell the nosy bastard.'

Billy Larsen stammered. Then he said: 'Not interests. I'm engaged to a girl whose father's in oil, that's all. But that's got nothing to do—'

The Indians shouted him down. Ott called for order but the Indians went on shouting. The Athabascan lawyer murmured: 'Jesus, he's in the pants of some chick whose old man's made a fortune from oil and he preaches about not giving the goddam natives too much bread.'

The Indians were still shouting as one of the other young whites stood up and turned round, his arm hitting two of them across their faces as he got up. 'Sorry,' he said and he grinned and squashed his cigarette butt with his shoe.

But one of the Indians held onto his hand. There was a little blood oozing from the Indian's nose.

'I said I was sorry,' said the young white, body tensed.

Ott shouted from the platform: 'Now cool it, this is the sort of publicity we don't want, no one wants.' The two reporters scribbled busily.

The Indian twisted the young white's arm. The third member of the trio stood up.

Ott shouted: 'Please, I appeal to you.'

The third white broke the Indian's grip on the other's hand.

Ott was pleased to see that Larsen was appealing to them not to fight.

Ott said to the other speakers: 'Okay, let's go,' noting with surprise that the Athabascan lawyer was taking off the jacket of his Brooks Brothers suit and hanging it on the back of the chair. He grinned at Ott. 'Maybe I can settle a few old tribal scores.'

It was a good fight while it lasted, the whites chopping and ducking and weaving and, when they were on the run, picking up chairs and wielding them as they did in movie bar-room brawls.

Larsen was fighting and fighting well, classic stance, fists bloodying noses, parrying blows. But defeat was inevitable.

Finally they went down but not before they had inflicted a lot of damage. One by one they were tossed out of the hall.

Ott went outside to talk to Billy Larsen who was sitting on the grass, one eye closed, nose bleeding, feeling a loose tooth with his tongue.

Ott said: 'You knew that would happen, didn't you?'

'I guess so.'

'It was stupid.'

'I wanted people to know how the young feel about it.'

'Most people already know.'

'I wanted them to know that we aren't just anti-native – it's Alaska we're bothered about,' feeling the tooth with his fingers.

'And your friends?' He pointed at the other two licking their wounds.

Billy tried a smile. 'They were just my bodyguard.'

Ott said: 'I'm sorry about that oil interests crack. It was a diversionary tactic. I didn't know about your girl . . .'

Billy Larsen said it was all right.

'It was dirty,' Ott said.

'No it wasn't.' Billy touched the tight mauve flesh that had closed up around his eye. 'But those figures of yours were dirty. You know, they were irrelevant, they were out of context.'

'But they were true.'

'Maybe, but that isn't the point. You can manipulate figures and that, Mr. Ott, was what you were doing.'

Ott said: 'At least we both believed what we're saying. You know, maybe we're both right. If that's so how the hell can this ever be settled?' He thought about it. 'By compromise, I guess, the no-man's land between two truths.' He stuck out his hand and Billy Larsen stood up and shook it. 'I knew your father when he was younger than you.'

But at the mention of his father Billy Larsen seemed to withdraw from Ott and there was a wariness on his battered face. He said: 'I guess I'd better be going, Mr. Ott.' He turned to his two companions. 'Come on you guys.' He nodded to Ott. 'It's been a pleasure, Mr. Ott.'

Ott said: 'Give my regards to your father. Tell him to look me up, I haven't seen him in years.'

But it was no good. Billy Larsen had his back to him and he was walking away.

Ott looked at the three bruised young men and he looked at the Athabascan lawyer whose face was bloodied and bruised and he thought: What the hell, we're all savages, the whole goddam lot of us.

Nineteen months later, in December 1971, Ott finally relaxed. He got drunk for the first time in many years. He laughed a lot; he shook strangers by the hand in the street.

The natives had won. The symbolic forty million acres was theirs. Congress had voted them this acreage plus four hundred and sixty-two and a half million dollars from Federal funds and another five hundred million dollars from the state's revenue from Alaska's mineral resources.

It remained to be seen what the natives would do with it. Ott believed they would invest it wisely.

He intended to take no part in this investment. He had played out his part in history. He had one last call to make before doing what he planned to do.

He parked his car outside the apartment block where Richard Larsen lived with his wife. He hesitated outside the door, rang the bell, and felt the scrutiny through the spy hole; then the door was flung open and they were pumping each other's hands and slapping each other on the back.

He was introduced to Mrs. Larsen and he shook her hand and grinned and said: 'You did well, Richard. Only one thing – you should have gotten yourself an Indian, preferably a Tinglit.'

While Theresa prepared a meal in the kitchen Larsen poured drinks. Ott watched him and Larsen, sensing the surveillance, said: 'Don't worry, I'm off the juice.' He poured himself a tonic water and gave Ott a large Scotch on the rocks.

They sat down, looking over Anchorage, its lights glimmering coldly and Ott said: 'Well, Richard, happy?'

'What do you think?'

Ott studied him. The stains of his boozing were still there, in his complexion, in the slight tremble of his hands as he poured the drinks; but he had the composure that is the partner of contentment. His blue eyes were healthy and there was a lustre to the thick hair greying at the temples.

Ott said: 'It looks good.'

'It is good, we're very happy.' Larsen pulled the drapes shutting out the bleak night. 'So you're a conquering hero, huh?'

'We won,' Ott agreed. 'It's taken more than two hundred years but we finally made it.'

'Congratulations,' said Larsen inadequately.

They were awkward together because they were strangers. Ott had known a different man to the one sitting opposite him; over the past decade they had chosen different paths and now all that was left for them was, *'Do you remember that time . . .'*

But Ott had wanted this last connection with the past.

He asked: 'What are you doing with yourself these days?'

'Nothing much,' Larsen said. 'Working for the Sierra Club. Carrying on where you're leaving off. Making sure some of the wilderness is left.' He leaned forward and whispered so that his wife couldn't hear: 'I'm also learning to fly all over again.'

'That's great,' Ott said.

'And I've started racing my dogs again. Maybe one of these days I'll come up against Browning.'

'Ah that Browning,' Ott said. 'That sonofabitch. But I guess he's taking a beating over these pipeline hold-ups. So is Alaska,' he added.

'You mean you want the pipeline to go ahead?'

'Sure I do. We're in for a cut of the profits, remember?'

'And you don't care about the environment?'

'I care,' Ott said, 'but I figure everything that needed to be done has been done.'

'We're going on fighting,' Larsen said.

'Fight on,' Ott said. 'But don't get cranky about it.'

'Talking about Browning. His son has gone over to the other side. Our side,' Larsen said.

'Jesus. And your son—'

'Has gone the other way.'

'I'm sorry,' Ott said.

'You don't have to be. He's entitled to his own opinions. He's marrying into oil. Just like Browning did,' Larsen said.

'He'll go far, that boy,' Ott said.

They didn't know what to say to each other. Larsen poured Ott another Scotch, topped up his own tonic water, grimacing as he sipped it and explaining: 'I used to drink whisky.'

'I heard,' Ott said. 'Do you miss it?'

'Not now. I think I'd throw up if I touched any.'

'Don't ever try,' Ott said.

Theresa came in and poured herself a gin-and-tonic. She smiled at Ott and said: 'That's a good job the Federation's done for us.'

'We had a lot going for us in the Lower 48,' Ott said. 'We were America's conscience. The last lot of natives that they could really do anything for.'

While she laid the table Ott examined Richard Larsen's new wife. Her watchful face with its flat nose and the dark eyes, the neat, small-breasted figure clothed in skirt and dark green cocktail blouse. She looked very sensible he thought; mature enough to live as an American *and* an Eskimo.

Whereas I never learned, he thought.

They ate shrimp cocktail followed by steaks and while he and Theresa drank wine Larsen drank some sort of concoction dyed pink with bitters.

Ott felt the togetherness of his hosts and was glad. He was glad that the boy with whom he had sat on the beaches of Long Island staring at the birds wheeling in the sky had surfaced again.

Over coffee Larsen asked: 'What are you going to do now?'

That was simple now that he had finished what he had set out to achieve. It was simple but it was difficult to explain.

'I'm quitting,' he said. *But it is much more than that.* 'I'm going back to the lands of my ancestors in the south east.' He smiled at them. 'You remember when we first met?'

Larsen said: 'Of course I do. I'll never forget. You as drunk as a bastard threatening to let out the polar bears . . .'

Ott cut in: 'Yeah, I guess I was a little wild in those days, but the point is all I ever talked about was animals, right?'

'And girls,' Larsen said.

'I was a dog,' Ott said to Theresa Larsen.

'I'll bet,' she said. 'And probably still are,' which was kind.

'Anyway,' Ott said, 'my scene was really animals as Richard here will tell you.'

'Already have,' Larsen said, smiling.

Theresa poured more coffee.

'And then,' Ott went on, 'the war came and everything changed and then I began to get the idea that the natives might become something. You know, we were at a time in history. So I took up the cudgels, the crusade . . .'

'And you won,' Theresa said.

'Sure we won. But now I wonder whether I wasn't diverted. You know, I kind of prefer animals to humans, present company excepted,' Ott said, smiling over the top of his coffee cup.

Larsen asked: 'What are you leading up to?'

'I'm going back to animals.'

'You're going to let the polars out of Central Park Zoo?'

'No,' Ott said. 'I'm going back to the forests where my people come from. I'm going to live in the forest like one of those weird old trappers you used to pick up. And I'll have the animals and birds all around me.' He hesitated because he suspected it sounded crazy. He made a joke of it. 'I guess I'm going native.' No, he wouldn't tell them that sometimes the legends and the superstitions and the raven on the totem were more real to him than, say, this apartment with its central heating and TV in the corner.

He had said it all badly but he was glad he had said it. He looked at his watch. He exclaimed in disbelief. 'I'll have to be off,' he said.

Yes, he thought as he walked to his car, ice crackling under his feet, I'm glad I saw them. He felt serene and content. As he drove away a raven swooped down into the glare of the streetlights. Leading me home, Ott thought.

CHAPTER THIRTY-TWO

ROBERT BROWNING was smoking grass. Sharing a joint with the girl who lay naked beside him. They had just made love and the love-making had been slow and beautiful and the feeling of it had spread right through his body.

He laid one hand on her breast. He could feel its texture as though each nerve-ending at his fingertips was searching like the tendrils of a sea-anemone. They spoke to each other with their eyes as he passed her the joint.

He lay back on the rug in his apartment. The furniture in the room glowed. Outside in the garden the greens, yellows and reds glowed.

He was the centre of this glow, of this music of colour. And slowly, like oil on water, the music and colour changed form, became a fusion of currents which idled past until they changed direction and became a fountain that was as slow as lazy waves, and from the fountain, slowly-spouting, came ideas that were his own, that he could touch and feel and examine, ideas that had a new dimension of importance.

Sometimes as the perspective changed he *was* those ideas; part of their brilliance and originality; sometimes problems issued from the fountain and he solved them immediately.

As always at these times the thoughts and the problems concerned whatever had been on his mind before he smoked. He had been thinking about Alaska: the pink flash of leaping salmon, a lake in the tundra with a shoal of silver light on its water, white-fronted geese alone on a burnished sky ... Without moving his lips he told the girl: 'I have helped to preserve all this and I am content,' and she smiled back at him, ran her hand down his chest and his belly and his groin and let it lie there.

370

Now the fountains became rockets exploding in a dark sky, but the explosions were thick and soft and their stars dripped from the sky. He thought of his father, without violence because that is the way with grass, and how he had out-manoeuvred him, how deliciously easy it had been; he gave a great sigh of contentment while the stars dripped into a painting on a canvas. The painting was a question. What should he do next?

And, of course, the answer was in the painting too.

The sweet, brutal land will stay as it is. He saw his father's fortune sinking into thick black untapped oil.

And while Robert Browning, who had the body of a prizefighter and the face of Christ, lay there beside the naked girl in his apartment in Fairbanks, suspended in blurred colours and soft chimes, snow began to fall again on the great piles of pipe that had lain undisturbed throughout the summer.

On the North Slope where the three thousand men had once laboured only three hundred remained, guarding the hulking equipment against marauders – thieves, wreckers, spies, grizzlies . . .

The pipeline was stalled, the oilmen had gone home leaving behind the historic aftermath of grabs for riches – unemployment, bankruptcy, queues for welfare.

Alaska already stood to lose nearly one billion dollars in oil revenue; the next budget would need one hundred million dollars, deficit financing; the nine hundred million raised from the sale of the oil leases was wasting away.

The halcyon period for the state was all screwed up because of one commodity the planners hadn't considered – idealism.

At about this time, in the winter of 1971–72, there was a small oil spill from a well that lay idle at Prudhoe Bay.

The well was owned by Harvard Oil.

Immediately Browning flew up to Deadhorse airfield in a Wien airlines jet with Trusz and a couple of advisers.

The Arctic was in the depths of the night which would last for fifty-six days. They stared at the dark stain on the ice and Browning said: 'First we find the leak then we clear up this mess because if any of these conservation characters get to hear about it they'll crucify us.'

As they took off for the return flight Browning peered down at the languishing rigs and said to Trusz: 'You know this is a crime.'

'Don't worry,' Trusz said, 'you'll make your millions, you'll get your pipeline. I read the other day that the gas and oil down there is worth sixty-four billion dollars which means that before tax the oil companies will rake in about one billion a year.'

'Yeah, but it could be laid now. I reckon it's going to cost four billion bucks by the time they get started. And five hundred million of it in the interests of the environment. But, hell, we'll never get that pipeline until *all* the big companies want it. Okay Atlantic Richfield want it badly. But not the companies with other big sources of oil. They want the North Slope oil to come out nice and slow so the market isn't depressed. You know, nothing's changed.'

'That sort of thing never changes,' Trusz said.

At Anchorage airport Browning warned Trusz and the two advisers not to tell anyone about the oil spill.

Three weeks later Richard Larsen had a typewritten document reporting the oil spill in his hands.

He said to Guthrie: 'Why?'

'My conscience, I guess.'

'Selling Browning down the river isn't in your interest.'

'I quit,' Guthrie said.

'Quit or changed horses?'

'Okay, I joined another company.'

'With interests in the North Slope?'

'Of course.'

'But if the news of this spill holds up the pipeline any longer it can't be in your interests.'

'Oh yes it can,' Guthrie said, 'you don't know just how shitty I can be. In fact,' he said, 'I'm feeling a little better these days, I've finally acknowledged my shittiness.'

'I don't understand,' Larsen said.

They were sitting at the bar of the Top of the World above the Westward Hotel. Below them lights twinkled, aircraft climbed into the dark sky like fireflies. Guthrie was drinking a vodka and tonic, Larsen was sipping an orange juice. Ella Fitzgerald was singing *San Francisco* on a tape.

Larsen hadn't spoken to Guthrie since confronting him with Taluk's story about their expedition up north.

'I'll explain,' said Guthrie, watching a girl with long blonde hair sitting at the other end of the bar. Guthrie's hair was grey and his face looked old, but some of his bounciness had returned. There was stubble on his chin and Larsen realized that he was starting to grow a beard again. 'I wonder,' said Guthrie, 'if a guy like you can ever realize how devious the sort of people I've been associating with can be.'

'Sure I can guess, you found your niche.'

'Now don't give me a hard time,' Guthrie said. 'Hell, I've brought you this report.'

'And now perhaps you'll tell me why.'

Guthrie swirled the ice in his glass; he smiled at the girl but she ignored him. 'I figured you and your buddies in the Sierra Club or the Wilderness Society or the Friends of the Earth could use information like this.'

'Maybe, but I still don't understand your own motive. You're not the sort of guy who cuts his own throat.'

Guthrie grinned. He touched the stubble. 'That's why I've stopped shaving.' He ordered two more drinks. 'But you're right, of course, I don't have any suicidal tendencies. You see there are some people in oil, some of the big boys, who are in no hurry to see this pipeline laid. They've got a big stake in the North Slope and they can afford to leave it there.'

'And you've gone over to one of these . . . big boys?'

'That's right.'

'And they would be quite happy to see more delays?'

'They wouldn't lose too much sleep.'

'And of course this spill which you've so decently reported to me could hold up the permit.'

'That's what *you* want, isn't it?'

'For different reasons,' Larsen said.

'This game is full of contradictions. Robert Anderson of ARCO for instance. He wants the pipeline like crazy and yet they say he contributes money to the conservationists because he really believes in what they're doing.'

'Did your new boss tell you to do this?'

Guthrie shook his head. 'But I might just reveal how helpful I've been to him.'

'But that isn't all of it, is it?'

Guthrie smiled at the girl again but she looked haughtily away. Guthrie sighed. 'She thinks I'm one of her grandfather's buddies.' He paused. 'No, that isn't all of it. I'm hurting Browning. That's something you should appreciate.'

'Sure I appreciate it. But I wouldn't feel too proud of the way you've done it.'

'That's fine then,' Guthrie said, 'you needn't act on it.'

'You really are a shithead, aren't you,' Larsen said.

'At least I've found myself.'

'Tell me one thing – how did you get hold of this?' tapping the typewritten sheets of paper. 'I can't see Browning sharing the secret with you.'

'It was given to me,' Guthrie said.

'By who?'

'That would be telling. There's the report. Do you want it or not?'

'Yes,' Larsen said softly, 'I want it.'

They were joined by a smart, middle-aged woman in a tailored costume, hair and face expensively cared for, rings heavy on slender fingers.

Guthrie said: 'Richard, I want you to meet my fiancée.'

Larsen stood up and, after the introductions, asked: 'Are you by any chance in oil?'

Guthrie interrupted, 'She's not just *in* oil, Richard, she's a vice-president of an oil company.'

Larsen burst out laughing. 'One of the big boys?'

'One of the biggest,' Guthrie said.

Browning put down the telephone in his study in his house in Anchorage and said to Trusz: 'Do you know who that was?'

Trusz shook his head.

'Larsen, the bastard.'

'I can't figure why you feel so strongly about the guy. He's a lush, isn't he?'

Browning said: 'He knows about the oil spill,' watching Trusz's reaction.

'He does? Well I'll be damned. How in God's name—'

'I don't know,' Browning said. 'But I mean to find out.'

The obvious suspect was Guthrie. Guthrie was weak, greedy and vain and Browning would be glad to be rid of him. But Guthrie hadn't known about the spill, hadn't had access to any correspondence about it. Unless he had an accomplice . . .

Browning tried to think logically but his reasoning was distorted by anger. Larsen who eighteen months ago had been a drink-sodden bum had just called him and talked to him as though he was the chief of police. One of these days there would be a showdown.

He paced the study and looked at Trusz. Could the neat little Pole who never seemed to age have betrayed him? Trusz was living with an Italian whore. Perhaps they were going to go into business together; perhaps they needed capital and Trusz had sold out . . . No the conservationists wouldn't pay the sort of money he would ask.

Trusz said: 'I know what you're thinking and you're wrong. Why the hell would I double-cross you?' He examined his manicured nails and then said: 'By the way I'm quitting.'

Browning stopped pacing. 'You're what?'

'I'm resigning. You know, it's been great – and I really mean that,' Trusz said in an embarrassed voice. 'But now I'm settling down.'

Browning sat down, shook his head. He began to doodle on his blotter with a ball-point. 'What the hell has settling down

got to do with anything? You can settle down and go on working for me.'

Trusz shook his head, ran a finger round his stiff collar. 'No
way. I'm going to California. I'm going to open a health farm.'
The last words spilled out in a rush.

Browning said: 'I don't believe it. And I suppose you've
given up gambling?'

'That's right,' Trusz said.

'Jesus H. Christ! Is there any way I could make you stay?'

Trusz shook his head. 'I was a scout not a businessman. This
isn't my scene any more and I'm getting too old for scouting. I
mean, if they ever struck oil in a civilized part of the world,
okay. But jungles, deserts, frozen nowheres . . . No, a nice little
patch in California will suit me fine . . .'

Browning stared at the doodles on the blotting pad. He found
he had been signing his name over and over again. He asked:
'How did this come about?'

Trusz told him about the lottery win. He had decided then
that his luck had changed. So, he had put the whole lottery win
on a horse that romped home at 6–1. Then a couple more big
bets without her knowledge. 'And now I'm worth a hundred
thousand bucks,' Trusz told Browning. 'How about that?'

'Supposing the next horse loses?'

'There won't be a next horse. Like I told you, I'm cured. And
you're invited to the wedding,' he said in another rush of words.

Browning ripped the sheet of blotting paper off the pad and
tore it up. 'Tell me I'm dreaming.'

'So you'll come?'

Browning grinned. 'I'll be there.' He took out his cheque
book. 'We've been together a long time, huh?'

'Seems like always.'

Browning wrote out a cheque for fifty thousand dollars.
'Might buy you a couple of rowing machines.'

The little Pole stood up. His eyes were wet. He began to
speak but none of it came out right.

Browning cut him short. 'Just one last job before you quit,
okay?'

'Okay.'

'Get up to the North Slope and do what has to be done before Larsen gets there.'

After Trusz had gone Browning roamed around the big house; from an upstairs room he could hear the throb of his son's record player; it was the sound of youth and he didn't understand it. He felt alone and he felt the hostility of the land pushing at the warm house from outside. He thought about the erosion of his money on the North Slope, he wondered who had betrayed him. Guthrie for sure, but who else? What papers had there been? Only the report from his foreman at Prudhoe Bay.

He seemed unable to concentrate on the problem of the betrayal. Was it age? He was fit enough, still playing squash and racing the dogs – he had just won a race at the Fur Rendezvous – and yet he felt his brain was slowing up. He associated it with the stagnation on the North Slope. When the hot oil began to gush south through the tundra, through the Brooks Range, across the Yukon, then his own juices would begin to flow again.

But I have made no mistakes, he thought. Every step I have taken has been carefully calculated and the calculations have been correct. I have used other people's weaknesses and that is how it should be.

No, it was an unpredictable quantity that had upset his calculations, a factor that he couldn't possibly have made provision for. It was the new clean thinking of the young that had been obediently followed by their elders.

He would always be a rich man because, ever since the strikes in the north, the giant oil companies had been seeking mergers; if he couldn't get his own oil flowing soon then he might have to sell out; but that had never been what he wanted; he wanted quite simply to be another Getty, another Hughes.

He finished his drink. He forced his mind back to the act of treachery within his organization. The papers about the spill had been locked every night in the safe in the company's new offices near the BP headquarters. Every night? No, once he had brought the report back here in his brief-case. Had left them spread on his desk in his study in a pool of light from a reading lamp.

The throb of the guitar reached him from his son's bedroom.

He hurled his empty glass against the wall.

He began to climb the stairs.

CHAPTER THIRTY-THREE

RICHARD LARSEN got permission from the conservation people in Anchorage to fly to Prudhoe Bay to check the oil spill.

He had lost their confidence during his drinking period. Now they trusted him again.

He didn't know if he was totally cured of drinking. Is any alcoholic ever cured? But had he been an alcoholic? Or just a potential suicide? Without Theresa he would have drunk himself into his grave.

There was a great warmth between the two of them. If he became depressed, if he felt the faintest need for liquor, he sought her warmth and it healed him. He had only loved two other women and he knew that his feeling for the Eskimo woman would never be the same; but that didn't matter, their love was merely a different precious metal.

He took a Wien flight to Fairbanks. From there he flew in a Super Cub on which he had paid a deposit with money Theresa had lent him after he had told her that he was taking flying lessons again. She was understanding about the flight. 'You've got to do it some time, why not now?'

But he was trembling as the little aeroplane accelerated down the strip. Then he was up and the ground was a long way below and, for the first time in his life, he had the feeling that he was up there with nothing to support him and he thought: I mustn't panic, but the fear was deep in his belly as he remembered the wild tugs of wind that had pulled him off glaciers in the old days, as he remembered the disorientation of a white-out, as he felt the engine of the Piper straining to take him higher into the late winter sky. He smelled the old familiar smells of oil and fuel and he used his feet and hands to remind himself of his control over his ship but for a while, like a novice climber glued to a precipice by fear, he didn't look down, just stared into the sky, trying to become part of the plane. When he banked he looked down and it was then that the confidence began to return as he looked at the spears of the trees and the grey braids of a river in the snow: it returned the way it had when he had first flown, when the conquering spirit assailed him.

Larsen checked his instruments and relaxed. His love for the land spread out below him returned. And he sang to himself as he drove his little ship through the sky.

But when he reached the well there was no spillage. And the jagged ice was smooth in places as though it had been melted. Larsen knew that he should have flown north before calling Browning.

He returned to Deadhorse and saw Trusz lining up to check in for the Anchorage flight. He tapped Trusz on the shoulder. 'What brings you up here? No one's working, there's nothing to spy on.'

Trusz turned, grinned. 'I've been doing a spot of cleaning up,' he said.

When Larsen got back to his apartment Robert Browning was waiting for him. He was drinking coffee and he had a black eye.

Larsen pointed at the eye. 'What happened?'

'My old man socked me.'

Larsen poured himself coffee. 'Why did he do that?'

'Because he thought I was a spy.'

'I see.' Larsen thought about Guthrie. 'And are you?'

'I guess so. I got that report about the oil spill for you.'

Larsen sipped his coffee. 'And now what?'

'It's like this,' Robert Browning said. 'I've left home and I'd like to work with you for the conservationists.'

Larsen stuck out his hand. 'Happy to have you on board,' he said, not proud of the elation in his voice.

CHAPTER THIRTY-FOUR

WHO is to say who won? In the case of the pipeline no one won and no one lost.

By May 1972, it seemed to be all over for those who love the untrammelled land and that which grows wildly upon it and the clean air and broad skies above. After publication of a statement on *environmental impact*, nine volumes long, a smiling six feet seven inches tall Kentuckian named Roger C. B. Morton gave his verdict. Morton, the new Secretary of the Interior, gave the oilmen the go-ahead 'in our best national interest' and said of those who had precipitately encouraged the rush for black gold: 'They got oil fever in Alaska and the tracts were sold without the foggiest idea how to get it out.'

The secretary had spoken and it was all over. Like hell it was said the hard-liners of ecology.

To all oilmen, most Alaskans and some conservationists these hard-liners were fanatics, nuts: everything they had sought had been granted – ocean and tundra and mountain, bird, beast and fish were protected.

Sorry, said these hard men of a gentle cause, our crusade is simple: we don't want *any* pipeline graffiti on the map of Alaska. And, with skills that bewildered the oil and state heavyweights, they fought back with law suits and injunctions and, by February 1973, had them reeling with a U.S. Court of Appeals decision that Secretary Morton didn't have the authority to grant the permit. How could this be? The conservationists had studied the Mineral Leasing Act of 1920 and there, in Section 28, was their killer punch: the pipeline right-of-way violated the width restrictions of the act.

There had always been an alternative – a pipeline through Canada which would take the oil to the Midwest where the fuel crisis was more acute than down the West Coast. But that would entail years of planning and litigation. No, it had to be Alaska and soon the battleground shifted to Congress.

By the summer of '73 feeling in Alaska against the conservationists was bitter. Hell, wasn't it the old story all over again? Interference from Outside; 1906 all over again when Teddy Roosevelt had banned coal mining. What did the crusaders of the Lower 48 really know about Alaska where the cost of living was thirty-seven per cent higher and unemployment averaged 9·6 per cent? Okay, the conservationists had won most of their points. Now for pity's sake let's get on with the pipeline: we want a piece of the pie and we're not going to be denied it by a bunch of do-gooders based in New York, Washington or San Francisco.

Alaska had already offered to build the pipeline road itself. The then Governor, Keith Miller, had sought one hundred and twenty million dollars from the State on the understanding that the pipeline companies refunded it within five years at seven and a half per cent interest. But the companies had refused.

Now frustration hissed like steam. The hell with the meddlers from the Lower 48. Let's cut ourselves free from the United States that has bled us since the day it bought us for less than two cents an acre. Independence for Alaska! Soon a sixty-year-old real estate developer named Joe Vogler had eleven thousand signatures demanding a break from the U.S. Said Vogler: 'We're a different people with different circumstances and we're tired of being treated like a warehouse and a vacation preserve.'

The people directed their anger at the conservation groups. In particular the Sierra Club which symbolized those who stood between them and progress. Hadn't they delayed construction of highways, stopped the building of a pulp mill near Juneau, forced logging companies to produce impact statements before felling the forests of the Tongass National Forest?

On the bumpers of automobiles there appeared a rash of stickers. INDEPENDENCE FOR ALASKA. SIERRA GO HOME. LET THE BASTARDS FREEZE IN THE DARK.

One morning Richard Larsen found the tyres of his car slashed and bumper stickers pasted over the windows. There were ugly telephone calls and once in a supermarket a woman turned on Theresa and began shouting at her. 'Listen you Eskimo bitch, tell that husband of yours to get the hell out of our country.' She pointed at the handful of groceries in her trolley. 'That's all I can afford because my old man's on relief because of Sierra. Have you got kids?' She pushed the cart at Theresa's legs and when Theresa shook her head shouted: 'Well, I have and they're both starving because of you cranks. Has anyone in Sierra ever been on relief? Well, have they?' thrusting the trolley forward. She looked around for support but the other women looked away, their faces locked-up. The woman who had a thin, hopeless face turned her anger on them. 'You're scared to speak up but you're thinking the same.' She turned back to Theresa who was lining up to pay. 'Take him back some blubber, honey, that's what bastards like him should be eating.'

Larsen wasn't surprised by the anger directed against him.

When Theresa told him about the incident in the super-market he put his arm round her and comforted her and asked her if she believed in what he was doing.

She looked at him, eyes dark with wisdom, and said: 'I believe in you.'

'And what's that supposed to mean?'

'I am your wife, I believe in you.'

'Which means you think I'm wrong?'

'It doesn't matter what I think.'

He became angry. 'I thought we felt the same way about it.'

'We do. But I know there's nothing more you can do. Don't you see, you've won? They've given in to every demand you've made.' She stroked his chin. 'No one on this earth can stop that pipeline now. There's too much commitment up there, too much money sunk beneath the ice.'

And he knew she was right but he refused to concede. 'We've got to go on fighting. No one ever believed we'd get this far. They thought they could brush us aside like insects. We can't give up,' Larsen said, leaving her on the chesterfield and sitting opposite her, staring into her eyes. 'Even if Nixon signs a compromise pipeline bill we've got plans. The Wilderness Society, the Friends of the Earth and the Environmental Defence Fund are going to claim that any Congressional finding in favour of the pipeline is unconstitutional . . .' He paused. 'Do you think I'm crazy?'

'I told you, I believe in you.'

'But not in what I'm doing?'

She smiled at him. 'That doesn't matter. If you were a nuclear scientist or a racing driver I might not believe in what you're doing but I'd believe in you.'

He spread his arms, let them drop to his side. 'I guess you're right. I guess you're always right,' he said, shaking his head. 'But there will be other incidents.'

'We Eskimos can handle ourselves,' Theresa said.

The telephone on the bookshelf rang. Larsen picked it up. 'Hallo,' he said, looking at his wife with affection.

The voice was male, educated. 'Is that Mr. Larsen?'

'That's me.'

'Mr. Richard Larsen?'

'Yeah.'

'I've got a message for you, Mr. Larsen.' The caller cleared his voice. 'We would like you to leave Alaska. We would like that very much and we would like you to do it within five days.'

'Who is that?' Larsen asked, trying to keep his voice calm as Theresa looked inquiringly at him.

'I represent a group of people who want Alaska to prosper. To do that we've got to get rid of its enemies and you're one of them, Mr. Larsen, you're definitely one of them.'

'And what if I stay?'

The voice thickened. 'Then you're dead you sonofabitch.' The caller hung up.

'Who was that?' Theresa asked as he replaced the receiver.

'Another crank.'

'What did he say?'

'The usual garbage.'

'You said to him, "What if I don't?" '

'He wanted to run me out of the country.'

'Don't hide things from me, Richard.'

'He was a nut,' Larsen said, going into the kitchen and pouring himself a glass of milk.

She followed him. 'Did he threaten you?'

'They all do.' He kissed her. 'Now let's go and watch television, have a game of Scrabble. For God's sake don't let them spoil our lives.'

They played Scrabble and she won.

No one tried to kill Richard Larsen. Perhaps because the caller was merely a crank, perhaps because he realized that the world was in revolution and Larsen's cause was being swept away by events on the other side of the globe.

The age of the Arab was dawning.

In the United States the energy crisis was acute. The Arabs had hiked the price of oil and, throughout 1973, King Faisal of Saudi Arabia warned that if the U.S. didn't force Israel to withdraw from Arab territories he would slow down production. Can it really be *us* who are dependent on *them*? the State Department pondered wonderingly as they began to seriously consider the desire of a sixty-eight-year-old King to pray at the Dome of the Rock of Jerusalem, Islam's third holiest city, without treading ground occupied by Jews.

By August 1973, the Senate and the House of Representatives had changed the right-of-way law relating to the Alaskan pipeline.

In October of that year Egypt and Syria attacked Israel. Within ten days the Arabs and Iranians had increased their take from a barrel of oil from 1·99 dollars to 3·44. Then, angered by continuing U.S. military support for Israel, they imposed an oil embargo and cut their output by twenty-eight per cent.

On November 16th President Nixon authorized construction of the Alaskan pipeline.

Faisal helped Secretary of State Henry Kissinger to reach an interim agreement in the Middle East War. The Arabs continued to hike the price of oil. They became incalculably rich –

it was estimated that within ten years Saudi Arabia could buy out all the companies on the New York Stock Exchange – and were passionately courted by the powers who had once patronized them. Oil was their weapon and with it they dislocated the international monetary system, pushed countries into recession, changed the values of civilization.

The protests of the conservationists withered. On April 29th, 1974, five years after ARCO had struck oil on the North Slope, work began on the pipeline road from the Yukon River to Prudhoe Bay.

No one had won, everyone had won. Oil, black and hot and dangerous, would flow across the Great Land; but never again would the rich and powerful presume to trample across a virgin white carpet wearing dirty boots.

Part Four

CHAPTER THIRTY-FIVE

PANIC stirred inside Billy Larsen as he lay on his bunk in a cabin at Coldfoot, north of the Yukon, north of the Arctic Circle. Stirred, stretched itself and demanded to be let out, it wasn't only in his mind; it was physical, too, a terrible impatience that stemmed from the crotch and spread to his limbs, forcing him to move.

He climbed out of the bunk and paced the floor of the prefabricated cabin. There were photographs from *Playboy* on the walls, girls with breasts like melons and great tufted pubes which stirred the hunger of the men without women on the pipeline. On the table were a few paperbacks, some writing material, half a bar of chocolate. The cabin was clean and neat, incongruous in this mountain setting where by rights men should have been grouped round a red-hot stove drinking rum-slugged coffee, brawling and boasting.

The man on the bunk across the cabin put down his paper-back. 'Knock it off will you,' he said. 'Pacing around like that – it gives me the creeps.'

His name was Ted Holder and he was full of guilt. He had come north from Minnesota leaving behind a wife and two children. He earned seven dollars an hour cleaning and had calculated that, with time and a half and double time at weekends, he could earn forty thousand dollars a year; in two and a half years he reckoned he could save sixty thousand dollars – if he didn't blow it every time he escaped to Fairbanks.

He was about thirty-five, with thin, tough muscles beneath a freckled skin, hollow-eyed, sandy-haired. His ears looked as if they had been nibbled by a rat.

Billy Larsen returned to his bunk and lay down with his hands behind his head glancing occasionally at the rat-eared man reading *How to Make a Fortune from Investment*. On his last visit to Fairbanks Holder had been rolled, lost all his money and returned with a dose of gonorrhoea; at night he had awoken calling out the names of his wife and children.

Holder was fast becoming a pipeline casualty. In one year there had been twelve deaths according to the company, which (said the company) was a lower rate than in general industry (even if other sources calculated that forty had died.)

Billy Larsen tried to equate the casualties with the clean blade of progress. Surely it was accident, not harassment, that caused the mechanics to pour jet fuel into the tanks of a prop-driven DC-6 which crashed in Happy Valley; surely there had been no negligence when an air hose broke away at Pump Station 7 and killed a man. Surely the Wien stewardess had been wrong when she described the bleeding, bandaged workers who were regularly flown back to Fairbanks and Anchorage.

Larsen felt the panic rising inside him again. I have been here too long, he thought. But I can't quit, he thought, as the cold beckoned him wickedly from outside.

He lit a cigarette and blew a jet of smoke that flattened against the ceiling and told himself that it was surely a joke that the Bechtel Corporation had fed a computer with statistics from the first year's construction to estimate the total death toll. The computer's reply – two hundred and seventy-three.

And, hell, the figures for heart attacks ... the guys who keeled over were overweight anyway, pigging the rich food in the canteens, chain-smoking, not taking enough liquid. These guys would have fallen greasy-faced on the floor of any factory in the United States.

As for the mugging, armed hold-up, murders, gambling and drunkenness in the towns, well for Christ's sake, this was a boom, a bonanza. What did they expect? Puppet shows and picnics? And the prostitution – wherever there were men without women, men with wallets stuffed with money then there would be prostitutes. And was that such a bad thing? If a roustabout with three months pay in his pocket was prepared to pay a hooker one thousand dollars for twenty-four hours of her time then it was his business. Although Larsen conceded, it was a little sad to see Eskimo girls hustling.

As for the hungry-faced men who lined up outside the hiring halls of the Teamsters' Union and the other unions, well, they had been warned enough times that there weren't enough jobs to go around. Whose fault was it if they flew, drove, hitched to Alaska only to find themselves No. 1,000 in line for a job? Larsen had heard that it cost five hundred dollars to grease a palm to get a job; he didn't know if this was true. He did know that the construction companies honoured their promises: an electrician could earn twelve hundred dollars a week: you can't bad-mouth an organization that pays that sort of money.

He heard a wolf howl. He wanted to join in. He wanted to embrace the cold, to feel it clutch at his lungs. I'm crazy, he thought. Outside it was dark, but it had been all day; his existence was timeless, disorientated. He glanced at his watch, 11 p.m. He should have gone to the movies, but he had gone to the movies every night this week. He said to Holder: 'Maybe we should get some sleep.'

Holder said: 'You get some sleep. I want to read.'

Larsen lit another cigarette. 'So you're going to invest your money?' he said to Holder.

'Betcha ass,' Holder said, turning a page of the book.

'Bad luck getting rolled.'

'It won't happen again,' Holder said. He turned his back on Larsen.

But it would happen again. Holder was a loser. He shed money like the leaves of a dying tree. When the cardsharps in Fairbanks saw him coming they smiled at one another, flexing their fingers; when the pimps saw him coming they nodded to their girls who thrust out their chests and composed their smiles. Holder also drank from a bottle that he hid under his bedding. Larsen had considered reporting him because drink and drugs and guns were banned, but informer wasn't part of the role he was playing.

Larsen began to think about Marion. The thoughts became sexual and he felt himself stiffen. He imagined her warm and soft and scented lying beside him. He had been away from her for more than three months now; when he was with her his thoughts occasionally strayed to other women; he enjoyed women's company and liked to watch girls with long soft hair and arrogant movements stepping along the sidewalk; but when he was away from her he thought only about her; he thought about her with longing and affection and slavering lust. He was happy that it was this way after three years of marriage.

Holder dropped his book beside his bunk, switched off the light and lay on his back. Soon he would be tossing in his sleep, snoring, murmuring, waking with the names of his family on his lips, the dream always the same – the children caught in the machinery of a threshing machine on the fields of the small, stony, unpaid-for, farm in Minnesota.

Larsen closed his eyes and tried to sleep. Perhaps he did, he wasn't sure, but the panic returned. The wolf called to him, the melancholy and beautiful call of the wilderness. And a wind had got up, whining through the construction camp, seeking to blow away the intruders.

I have to go out.

He put on his insulated clothing and mukluks. He didn't bother to put up the hood of his parka. Softly he opened the door and walked down the corridor of the complex. Out into the night, aware of his madness, not caring.

In the occasional shaft of light the wind-driven snow had a Christmas sparkle about it. He breathed deeply, felt the cold bite at his lungs. Already his ears were aching. He went to pull the hood of his parka over his head but somehow he couldn't be bothered. As the ache spread to his hands he realized that he hadn't put on his mittens and he thought: I'm going to die, and he didn't care, he wanted only escape. He began to walk in the direction of the old Indian burial ground that had been pre-served by the construction crews.

The wind pasted the snow against his face. If he turned now he would still be in good shape. But he walked on through the starless, wind-whipped night, remembering other roughnecks, as tough as teak, who had suddenly left their cabins, afflicted with the lonely fever, and walked into the cold; some of them had never been seen again, others had been found, bodies as hard as deep-frozen meat.

He was near the airstrip, packed snow like marble, when the security guard in the pick-up saw him. The tyres skidded as the truck pulled up beside him. The guard shouted to him. 'Hey fella, just where the hell do you think you're going?'

Larsen shook his head. He tried to speak but his lips wouldn't move.

The guard gripped his arm, pushed him into the passenger seat. 'Another five minutes and you'd have been dead meat.'

The guard drove to the canteen where soup and coffee flowed throughout the night. He sat Larsen down at a table and got him a mug of coffee. He examined his face and hands. 'You'll live, I guess,' he said. 'No frostbite, no nothing. But you go and see the medic in the morning because you've got cabin fever, son, and it's time they shipped you out for some R and R.'

The guard was a big man, kindness reluctantly stamped on his rough face. He had been a patrolman in Fairbanks earning sixteen hundred and twenty dollars a month but when the crime-wave had started he had taken a job with the pipeline at a thousand dollars a week.

He fetched Larsen some hot soup. 'Where you from, son?'

Larsen's lips had begun to prickle. He said: 'Anchorage.'

'Well you get back there. And my advice is stay there. There are some guys who can take this life, others who can't. And it ain't nothing to be ashamed of if you can't. I've seen real toughies crack up in these conditions. You know, the guys who came here strictly for the bread.'

'Isn't that why everyone's here?'

The guard sucked at his coffee. 'Sure, but to some guys this sort of life comes natural. You know, the real oilmen who've always worked in the ass-holes of the world. The others, well they're trying to make a fast buck, quit working for life, pay off their debts . . . Some of them have got worries back home and they just can't take it up here.'

Larsen said: 'But I'm an oilman.'

The guard stared at him closely. 'Like fuck,' he said.

'Why do you say that?'

'You don't look like an oilman. What's your job, son?'

Larsen said: 'Okay, I'm a materials handler.'

'Odd job man at nine hundred bucks a week, right?'

'I guess so,' Larsen said.

'Well, take my tip. Get the hell out of here. Go back to odd-jobbing in Anchorage at a quarter of the money.'

Larsen felt the soup scald his throat. He screwed up his face, he shook his head. He liked this guard, he revived his faith. But he shook his head and he told the guard: 'No, I can't quit now. I can't go soft.'

'Nope? Well maybe I'll have something to say about that.' The guard's face hardened but the kindness wouldn't be erased. 'My job's security and when guys get sick like you they're a liability.'

Larsen saw the kindness and used it. 'Listen,' he said, 'I've got a wife and kid back in Anchorage. I'm behind on the mortgage and the kid's sick. I've got to have the money.'

The guard sighed. 'Fat chance that kid will have when the wolves have finished with his old man's body.' The guard leaned across the table. 'Listen, I've been a cop all my life. I know people and I know you're not for this type of work. And anyhow,' he asked suspiciously, 'how come you speak so pretty? What are you, some sort of college drop-out?'

'Maybe I am,' Larsen said. 'But that doesn't change anything. I've still got a wife and a sick kid to support.'

The guard held up a fist like a ham. 'Okay, okay, I won't report you. But I tell you, this isn't your scene. There's going to be a lot of grief before this pipeline's finished. It's building up nicely right now. Graft, corruption, thieving. The Mob are moving in, the Teamsters are taking over.' He stood up, towering over Larsen. 'I sometimes wonder what the hell Alaska did to deserve this.'

There was an edge now to Larsen's voice. 'It's getting what it deserves,' he said. 'It's getting a new deal. It's getting prosperity.'

The guard rasped his hand across his chin. 'Boy oh boy, you really believe that stuff?'

'Sure I believe it.'

'Then you're crazier than I thought.' The guard began to walk away. Then he turned and said: 'Make sure you see the medic in the morning. If you don't I'll have you run off the site.'

Larsen, rising star of his father-in-law's oil company, had come to work on the pipeline because he didn't want to be an office-bound executive ruled by barrels and dollars and politics.

He wanted to get out and see for himself. See the mammoth drills boring into ocean-bed and tundra, get the taste of oil, mix with the men who drilled for it. He wanted to see for himself how the big cats cleared the path for three hundred and sixty-one miles of gravel highway from the Yukon to Prudhoe Bay; he wanted to witness the laying of the great pipe that would one day carry two million barrels of oil a day over mountains, across rivers, under bedrock, sand and gravel.

He wanted to see his beliefs confirmed. He wanted to know that he was right and his father was wrong. He wanted to see the Great Land produce and he wanted to see that it was treated with the respect the oilmen had promised.

To achieve all this he had to travel incognito otherwise he would be a spy, an informer and soon an informer with a busted nose and a mouthful of broken teeth. He used the Davenport name only to get work permits.

'If you've got to go then you've got to go,' said his wife as they drank a cocktail and watched the sun flame out behind the mountains across the water from their neat home in Anchorage. 'But don't think I like it because I don't.'

'I won't be away long,' he promised, looking warily at the watchful, spirited girl he had married.

'How long?'

'I don't know. Maybe three months.'

'But you'll be able to come home from time to time?'

He studied his drink. 'I guess so.'

'But you don't know so?'

'Well, it's only a couple of hours on a 737 from Prudhoe Bay.'

She said: 'But you haven't answered my question,' and waited.

'I'll see how it works out,' he said.

'Are there any girls in the construction camps?'

'One or two,' he said. 'And a few thousand guys.'

'Are you going to see your father before you go?'

'If I meet him in the street.'

'That's pretty childish,' she said.

'Maybe. But he never gives up, my old man. He's got himself a job checking that all the environmental requirements are followed. He buzzes up and down the pipeline route in his little plane and if he sees a blade of protected grass trampled down then he puts in a report.'

'That can't be bad,' said Richard Larsen's daughter-in-law. 'You know something? I admire your old man.'

'Yeah? Well you know something? I'm ashamed of him.'

'He's got his standards.'

'He's got those all right.'

'You still haven't answered my question.'

'I thought you'd forgotten it.'

'You know me better than that.'

He gazed at an icicle outside the window hanging like a sword. The orange light from the dying sun was imprisoned inside it. 'Don't worry,' he said without telling her anything, 'I'll be back.'

But he knew he had to stick it out, he had to test the life without the privilege of slipping away to a comfortable home.

He worked first as a truck driver on the snow-packed gravel road the drivers called the Kamikaze Trail. From the air it was a tranquil ribbon stitched across the land; at ground level it was brutal, carved through brutal necessity. Sometimes the big yellow trucks, hauling north equipment and the eighty-foot-long lengths of pipe, slid off the road killing and maiming driver and mate. Some of the drivers refused to use the road any more and the Alaskans jeered at them. 'What the hell does a Texan know about driving in these conditions?'

Then he flew north to Prudhoe Bay, seeing for the first time the oil rigs spiking the skyline like black, frostbitten fingers. And he felt the rejection of the land and frozen ocean which were one, the intrusion of Man spiking holes in the crust, sucking out its black juices. On his way to the BP-Sohio operations centre – the Prudhoe Bay Hilton – he noticed a snow-covered hump off the track. He asked what it was and the driver told him it was a DC-3 which had crashed there a few years back with stolen equipment on board.

'Then why don't they shift it?'

'Because they can't,' the driver said. 'The permafrost has got a grip on it.'

Larsen looked with awe at the operations centre which, raised seven feet off the ground by steel pilings, floated like a ship on a white sea. He worked as a cleaner at the centre which had single bedrooms, a swimming pool, a recreation centre, a glassed garden with a pine tree and some birches, a lounge with picture windows, a dining-room where good food was served against a background of psychedelic paintings that were supposed to help strong men from going crazy. The buildings had been streamlined to minimize the winds that could push the temperature down to minus a hundred and fifty degrees; the steel platform structures had been built in Houston and shipped by barge through the Panama Canal to Seattle where the prefabricated buildings had been built; the whole structure had been brought by barge to Prudhoe Bay during a summer thaw.

If men could achieve all this, Larsen wondered, why couldn't they shift one small DC-3 stuck in the permafrost?

But the operations centre wasn't for him. He hadn't come to the Arctic to live in a Hilton. So he moved a little south to Pump No. 1 station, the first of the twelve pumps which one day would move the oil south.

He got a job as a maintenance man and it was at breakfast on his first morning there that he experienced his first trouble.

He sat at a table alone with his orange juice, coffee, eggs, ham and sausages, toast and marmalade. Outside it was dark and bitter.

He was joined by three hulking men. One of them was black, six foot four, around two hundred and twenty pounds, with muscles that moved visibly beneath his chequered shirt. The other two were white, bearded, big-bellied, with pasty faces and mud-coloured rings under their eyes.

One of the white men said: 'Hi there, stranger, you're new around here ain't you?'

'I arrived yesterday,' Larsen said.

'My, you talk pretty,' said the second white man.

The black man said: 'Where you from stranger?'

'Anchorage,' Larsen said, sipping his orange juice.

'My, a real Alaskan.'

'Where are you all from?' Larsen asked.

'Well,' said the black, slicing into a steak that covered his plate, 'I'm all from Georgia. I'm one of Governor Wallace's black boys.'

'And you?' Larsen pointing his knife at the two whites.

'Don't point that fucking knife at me,' said one of them. He had a scar under his lower lip where a wound had been badly stitched and a twitch in one eye.

Larsen shrugged. 'Sorry.' He cut into an egg and watched the yolk spread across his plate.

'Don't take no notice of my buddy,' the other white said. 'He's been here too long. He's got the fever, poor bastard.' This man had a fleshy pitted nose and blackheads on his cheeks.

The black man said: 'We've got a problem and we figured maybe you could help us with it.'

Larsen nodded, chewing.

The white man with the blackheads said: 'You see my buddy here reckons he saw you driving a truck down south on the gravel road.'

Larsen drank some coffee. On the next table a girl – there were five here among hundreds of men – sat down with a truck-driver's breakfast. She smiled at Larsen who smiled back.

The white man with the scar spread mustard on a chunk of steak. 'What's your name pal?'

'Larsen.'

'What you doing here?'

'Maintenance.'

'Then how come you were driving a truck down south?'

'I wasn't,' Larsen said.

'Then your twin brother was.'

Larsen shrugged.

'But it wasn't no twin brother.'

Larsen said: 'Did you speak to this guy?'

'I didn't speak. But I saw you driving a big yellow truck loaded with machines.'

Larsen turned to the other two and appealed. 'The guy says he saw me down there. I say I wasn't.'

The black man said: 'Yeah, go ahead Walt. Give the guy a break.' White teeth flashed. 'Down Georgia we respect justice.' He laughed and hit the table with his fist.

They looked doubtful.

'I tell you I wasn't driving any truck down south.'

The man with the blackheads said: 'Okay, maybe you wasn't.' He prodded his fork at Larsen. 'But you was working up at the BP centre.' He picked some steak from his teeth. 'I know because I seen you.'

The three men waited. All around the sounds of eating, knives and forks scraping on plates, the murmur of conversation. The girl had been joined by another.

Larsen said: 'Sure I was. Temporary. On my way down here. Same union. So what the hell?'

'Seems like an awful lot of coincidences,' the black man said. 'My buddies here reckon you're some sort of cop.'

'Or a company man,' said the man with blackheads.

'Or a Sierra snoop,' the man with the scar said. 'Maybe we should look through your things. You know, we don't like any creepy fucking snoops round here.'

Larsen pushed away his greasy plate, started on the toast and marmalade. He finished the mouthful, washed it down with coffee. 'Over my dead body,' he said quietly.

The black man laughed. 'It could be just that friend.'

'No one touches my gear.'

'Why, what you got there? Company papers? Sierra crap?'

'I got private things,' Larsen said. 'No one touches them.'

The black man said: 'There's only one of you man and there's three of us.'

'So?'

'We could knock the shit out of you, you dig?'

'You could try.'

'Fighting talk, man.'

'Yeah,' Larsen said, 'fighting talk.' Larsen felt the quick thump of his heart.

They gazed at him, finishing their meals.

The blackheaded man said: 'Maybe we should meet a little later when it's real dark. Behind the huts some place.'

'Okay. Mind if I take you one by one?'

'Nope,' the scar-faced man said. 'Why that's only fair.' He wiped his mouth with the back of his hand.

The black man said: 'I don't know.'

The other two turned on him. 'What do you mean you don't know?'

'Well it's like this,' the Negro said. 'I'm picking up a thousand bucks a week, right?' They nodded. 'I don't want to lose that, man. I got a lot at stake.'

'So?'

'If they catch you fighting you could be run off the site. No more work on the pipeline. No more pockets stuffed with green-backs.' The black man looked a little ashamed of himself. 'You know, is it worth it?'

They thought of the money and they were silent. They lit cigarettes. They inhaled deeply and they stared at Larsen. And they thought about the money, more money than any of them had ever dreamed of earning.

Finally the man with the scar spoke, the scar flickering beneath his lip. 'Okay, no brawling.' He blew smoke into Larsen's face. 'But don't be surprised, pal, if you meet with a little accident. They ain't uncommon, now are they. Why only yesterday a guy got slowed up by the cold so much that he got his hand crushed.' He dropped his cigarette butt in the dregs of his coffee. 'Keep a weather eye open, pal. You wouldn't want to lose a hand now would you?'

On the wall was a notice. NO MATTER HOW CUTE THEY LOOK BEARS AND FOXES ARE DANGEROUS.

Everything here was dangerous, Larsen thought. The marauding bears that could kill you with a gentle cuff, the foxes that gnawed the insulation of the wires and could spread rabies.

But the endemic danger was the cold. There were warnings about it everywhere. And instructions. *For deep frost-bite immerse the affected area in water at 105 degrees F for 20 minutes. Then rest in a room at 72–78 degrees.* NEVER RUB THE AFFLICTED AREA.

Always travel in twos, said the warnings. When Larsen had been driving trucks one guy had taken off by himself. He had run out of gas and tried to walk back to camp. His stiff dead body had been found one hundred yards from the camp.

He headed for the living quarters. Here too was danger, the danger of fire, feared by the knowledgeable even more than the cold. They had installed smoke detectors which could react to the smoke from a cigarette, heat detectors that triggered mechanisms that shut all doors with fifty pound magnets.

He went into his room. Tidy with yellow carpet and two single beds covered with Army-style blankets. Pete Wolkonsky was playing himself at chess.

He looked up. 'Fancy a game?'

Larsen shook his head. 'Too goddam tired.'

'That would give me an edge,' Wolkonsky said.

'Maybe later when I'm rested,' Larsen said.

Wolkonsky was a middle-aged man. Educated, soft-spoken, thinning hair, hands blistered by work. He had owned his own real estate business in South Dakota. He had gone bust. And he had come to Alaska to start again at the age of forty-five. Now he didn't want to go back. He exulted in the conditions; he had shed a skin and found within himself an inner toughness that he had never realized existed. He believed that his bankruptcy had been his salvation.

Larsen lay down on his bed and wondered what sort of accident the three men at breakfast might arrange for him. Probably nothing. But I'll have to watch it, he thought. That is if the bears don't get me, or the cold, or maybe a fire.

He dozed a little. Then he gave Wolkonsky a game of chess. The real estate man played arrogantly, greeting every move Larsen made as though he had anticipated it.

Larsen envied him his delight in everything. As Wolkonsky swept a bishop off the board with his rook Larsen asked him if he had left any family back in Dakota.

'Sure,' Wolkonsky said, advancing a pawn with a queening gleam in his eye. 'Two grown up boys who've got themselves jobs and a cute little wife aged thirty.'

Larsen moved a knight towards the advancing pawns. 'What about the cute little wife?'

'I sold a farmhouse to a guy who ran a chain of hamburger joints up north. Real pretty it was. Four bedrooms, a couple of baths and a cute veranda where you could take a cocktail and watch the sun go down. Three weeks after I sold it to this guy my wife moved in with him.'

'Gee,' Larsen said, 'that was tough.'

'Yeah,' Wolkonsky said. 'Tough on him. She was a bitch. I'd have knocked twenty grand off the price for him to take her off my hands.'

'Don't you ever get the urge to go back?'

Wolkonsky moved another pawn. Larsen didn't seem to be able to get among those pawns. 'Never,' he said. 'Hell, I should have moved up here when I was a kid. But I don't fret about the wasted years. No sir. I just get on and enjoy what I've got left.'

Larsen didn't know what Wolkonsky did at the camp. He asked him and Wolkonsky told him: 'Sewage.'

'Christ,' Larsen said.

'Ain't nothing wrong with it. Why, when we're finished with the stuff you could drink it. Maybe you'd like to see round the disposal plant?'

'Sure,' Larsen said. 'Maybe I could take in the morgue at the same time.'

'You needn't knock it,' Wolkonsky said, pushing a pawn to within one square of reincarnation as a queen. 'It's as clean as a clinic. Maybe the cleanest place in the camp. Maybe the most important with the conservation inspectors sniffing around all the time. Hell, those guys could stop work here if they saw an empty Coke tin lying in the snow.'

'What do you think of those conservation guys?' Larsen asked, resigning as Wolkonsky queened his pawn.

'You've got to hand it to them,' Wolkonsky said, hastily setting up the pieces again. 'They saved Alaska. You know, all that crap the oil people handed out about the pipeline being just a pencil mark across a football field. Well, that's one way of looking at it. But how about a slash with a knife across a Rembrandt painting? At least the conservationists are making sure the Rembrandt's restored.'

'I guess you're right at that,' Larsen said, moving a pawn to King Four and thinking about his father buzzing up and down the pipeline route, thinking about his wife and how he should take a break and go down and see her but knowing he wouldn't because he had to see this thing through.

Twenty-three moves later Larsen had lost. Wolkonsky was setting up the pieces again but Larsen waved his hand in defeat. He lay on his bunk and wrote a letter to his wife.

It was early afternoon and it was dusk. It was primeval and beautiful, winds coming in from the ocean and smoking the snow. Larsen wore a woollen mask but the cold crisped the moisture in his nose. The men worked short periods before quitting to thaw out.

Larsen was mending a door to the living quarters. Nearby a man worked with an acetylene welder. The sparks, mauve and yellow, fell thick and soft. Larsen felt strong and keen. His tools were beside him in a wooden box, screwdrivers, hammers, screws, nails. He was attending to a broken strip of wood that had broken free when he was joined by another man, bulky and masked and anonymous in his Arctic clothes.

He squatted beside Larsen. 'Jesus,' he said, 'but you're sure making a fuck-up of that.' He held nails in his mouth in the way of carpenters at work and his voice was indistinct.

Larsen shrugged. 'Looks okay to me.'

'Well it ain't.'

The newcomer inspected the work, tapped a protruding nail experimentally. He handed Larsen the hammer. Then some nails and when Larsen went to take them in his free hand the newcomer said: 'For Chris' sake hold them in your mouth like any self respecting handyman.'

Larsen held the four nails in his mouth.

The newcomer raised his hammer. 'Now give me one of those nails. What sort of guys are they sending up here these days?'

Larsen took one of the nails from his mouth. With the frozen nail came a strip of his tongue and flesh from his lips. He cried out with the pain of it and the newcomer said: 'Go and tell Sierra about that you sonofabitch.'

Wolkonsky said: 'Someone was sure gunning for you.'

Larsen didn't answer. There was a raw weal down his tongue and his lips were crusted with dried blood.

'The other guy must have had warm nails in his mouth,' Wolkonsky said. 'You've only got to put your hand on bare steel out there and it takes the skin off.'

Larsen didn't feel angry but he was filled with hatred as cold and implacable as the night outside. He had been told that the two bearded men shared a cabin. He had been told that they had liquor hidden there and that by eleven at night they would probably be loaded. He waited.

Just before eleven he sat up and wrapped some lead strips round the knuckles of his right fist.

Wolkonsky said: 'You sure you know what you're doing?'

Larsen patted the lead with his left hand and nodded.

He opened the door and went into the corridor. He knocked on the door of the cabin where the two bearded men slept.

A voice came back: 'Who the hell's that?'

'Security.' Larsen didn't bother to disguise his voice: it was thick from the wounds. 'Just a routine check.'

'Jesus, wait a minute.'

Larsen guessed they were hiding the bottle.

The door opened. There were cards on the table and the smell of liquor on the air.

'What the hell—' said the man with blackheads as Larsen shoulder charged him, knocking him to the floor.

The man with the scar grabbed a glass, broke it on the table, menaced Larsen with the jagged edges. 'Why if it ain't the snoop. Got a sore mouth, pal?'

Larsen took him with a judo kick, hearing his breath rushing out of his mouth as he fell.

Larsen crouched as the other man came at him. He anticipated the knee in the groin and the head butt; as the man's knee came up Larsen swayed to one side, got his hand behind the man's knee and jerked him back. He fell hitting his head on the floor.

He turned to the man with the scar who was standing holding his big barrel belly. 'You fucking bastard,' said the scar-faced man, gulping down air. 'Oh you fucking bastard.'

Larsen feinted with his left, smashed his lead-knuckled fist into the man's mouth. Teeth broke and blood ran down his chin.

He clubbed at Larsen with his right. Larsen swayed and pulled his arm so that the momentum of the punch carried the man forward. He staggered and tripped over the other man who was unconscious.

The need to maim and mutilate, to kill, was strong in Larsen. He stood over them clenching his fists. He tried to control his own breathing, control the animal inside him.

After a while he said in his strange thick voice: 'Don't ever try anything like that again. Next time I'll kill you.'

He stepped over the bodies. Closed the door. When he lay down on his bed he was shaking. He had met a stranger he didn't know existed and that stranger was himself.

The black man ordered chicken noodle soup, baked spare ribs, potatoes, salad and chocolate. He sat down opposite Larsen.

Larsen was drinking soup. It was all he could take and it burned his wounds.

The black man said: 'Jesus, man, you sure took care of those two.'

'Did I?'

'Well didn't you?'

'I don't know what you're talking about.'

'Don't give me that shit, man.' He dipped a spoon into his chicken noodle soup. 'Well, I don't figure they'll give any more trouble.'

Suddenly Larsen wondered if the man who had knocked his head was dead. He said: 'Why, what happened?'

'Don't bullshit with me. They were shipped out this morning.' He glanced at his wristwatch. 'By now I guess they're back at Fairbanks. Maybe Anchorage.' He looked slyly at Larsen. 'Seems they had a fight. Some nice guy looked in their cabin and reported them. Seems they had booze in there too. Not nice guys to have around, huh?'

'They had it coming,' Larsen mumbled through his swollen lips.

'Boy oh boy,' the black man said. 'What did you hit Walt with? A rock?'

'I don't know what you're talking about.'

'Okay, okay, I dig. Now let's you and me make a pact, huh.' He tapped his teeth with one finger. 'I don't want to lose any of these.' He grinned. 'No baby, I don't want to lose them. Now how would it be if I got you another cup of coffee?' He stretched out a hand and took Larsen's mug. 'Okay?'

Larsen grinned and winced as the grin pulled at the healing flesh of his lips.

Billy Larsen worked on a rip on the North Slope before the sun set for the winter and discovered the subtle beauties of desolation. The sun skimming the horizon, lighting the sky with yellow and orange washes but barely lighting the ocean ice-pack or the snow-covered tundra which was shadowed and secret in the fall. The lonely flight of birds and the creak of ice and the sparkle of powdered snow suspended in the air and, before freeze-up, the olive polygon patterns of permafrost and dewlaps of underground ice and the silver ocean riding with ice floes like an armada of invading whales.

With the pride of the owner he observed the efforts of the oilmen to preserve this land. The disposal of waste, the great balloon wheels of the trucks which could pass over a man without hurting him, the care not to disturb animal life.

Everyone had animal stories. The grizzlies that were using petrol tanks as trampolines; the bears were tranquillized and dumped miles away, but within a few days they were back bouncing away. The giant mosquitoes refuelled at Deadhorse airfield. A polar bear stalked up to a roughneck on a rig on the Beaufort Sea. Unarmed, all the roughneck could do was the recommended ploy – rattle a tin filled with stones. 'And what happened?' 'Well, the polar didn't eat the tin of stones.'

By the time Larsen arrived at Coldfoot they had begun to lay the pipe.

How could anything go wrong? Larsen asked himself. The migrating caribou were catered for and the Dall sheep were not to be disturbed during lambing and streams were being diverted and the tundra was being preserved and valves and computers would check any spills.

Just what could go wrong?

Larsen didn't go to the medic the morning after the attack of cabin fever because he knew that if you displayed withdrawal symptoms they shipped you out for rest. And the security guard didn't check him out.

They symptoms of the lonely panic receded. This was once again adventure: men drilling and digging for their incredible pay-checks; the clean, sugar-white, bear-prowling, eagle-swooping mountains all around . . .

And it wasn't until he moved to Five Mile Camp near the Yukon River that cabin fever returned.

CHAPTER THIRTY-SIX

'OH sure,' said the young man with the soft beard who was planning to blow up the new bridge across the Yukon, 'the pipeline has brought great benefits to Alaska. Untold riches,' went on Robert Browning who was a little high on pot but not so much that he wasn't aware of the need to watch his words.

He looked through the helicopter floor at the milky waters of Port Valdez and it seemed to him that he was on the crest of one of the white mountains gathered around the fjord and it was a long time ago and glaciers were pushing aside the land and seals lazed on the rocks and the waters were ice-free which then only meant that the fishermen could pull halibut and red snapper and herring from the depths and scoop the crabs from the bottom.

Ice-free. This was the penance of Valdez for its undisturbed past (undisturbed until the 1964 earthquake swallowed much of it and its people built a new town on another site). And soon, simply because Valdez was *ice-free*, he would look down from the mountains at mushroom beds of tanks and new docks, watch great tankers gulping down crude oil to ship to the refineries on the West Coast. And maybe he would see slicks of oil floating on the water.

The man sitting beside him, a tall bony *cheechako* lawyer who spoke as though he were giving testimony, clicked his tongue against the roof of his mouth. 'I can't understand you Alaskans. One minute the pipeline is the greatest thing to hit the state since the Gold Rush. Next moment you talk about it like it was a sewage pipe.'

Browning's voice was dreamy. 'You don't understand – it's all those benefits it's bringing us. You know, the unemployment, the crime, the high prices in Valdez market, the housing

408

shortage. Did you know a small apartment in Valdez – *ice-free* Valdez – costs sixteen hundred bucks a month?'

'No I didn't,' said the lawyer. His name was Smith and he worked for the pipeline company. 'For God's sake can't you people look to the future? You've got enough oil here to supply the States with a quarter of its needs, enough natural gas to supply the U.S. for eighteen years. You're sitting on a boomer.'

'And don't think we don't appreciate it,' said Browning who was hardly listening. He was packing explosives at the elephant feet of the bridge being built by the State across the Yukon. He was waiting on the banks for the explosion. Watching girders lift into the sky in beautiful, slow-motion arcs.

If you were going to blow up anything make it a bridge. There was poetry about blowing a bridge and any explosive expert would tell you the same. During war everyone blew bridges and this was war, undeclared, underground. When you blew a bridge the destruction was clean and the break was complete; and when the smoke cleared and the sound of the explosion rolled away he would see the debris being carried away by the Yukon.

It had to be the bridge over the Yukon. The Yukon was Alaska. Put a road and a pipeline across it and you made Alaska weak. And if the road was used by tourists there would be beer cans on the tundra, and fires, and hearts carved on the bark of spruce, and all the shit that men brought from the cities.

It had to be the bridge over the Yukon. And it had to be done before the oil flowed because you couldn't spill *their* pollution into such a river.

'. . . and they're taking care of unemployment,' Smith was saying, 'by implementing a regulation that anyone wanting to work on the pipeline must have lived in Alaska for a year.'

'That's great,' Browning said.

He listened to the scything of the blades as the helicopter wheeled over the waters sprinkled with salmon scales of sunlight.

'Are you listening to me?'

'Sure I'm listening to you. Do I have an alternative?'

Smith said: 'I don't know. You seem sort of detached.' He hesitated. 'Are you on anything? I mean—'

'You mean do I smoke?'

'Well—'

'Sure I smoke. But I'm not high at the moment if that's what you mean. And if you make a report about it,' Browning said pleasantly, 'next time we're up here I'll pollute the water with your body.'

'Do you enjoy what you're doing?'

'You mean carrying out these inspections?'

Smith nodded.

'Like they say, someone's got to do it. And yes I do enjoy it because I love Alaska and if I see any sonofabitch down there stepping out of line then we have them by the balls.'

'You amaze me,' Smith said. 'Do you realize that if the oil had been flowing years ago it would have been the equivalent of the oil cut off by the Arabs?'

'Jesus, is that so? And what wouldn't that have done for the smog over Los Angeles.'

'It's no good talking to people like you,' Smith said.

'That's right,' Browning said. The helicopter was descending. Browning pointed down. 'Before the earthquake there used to be a bar down there called the Morgue. It was a mill once.'

'So why did they call it the Morgue?'

'Because in the winter they used to stack bodies there until the ground was soft enough to bury them.'

Next day Robert Browning made his weekly report to Richard Larsen. Larsen who was preparing to make an inspection flight up the pipeline route looked tired. He was working for the Sierra Club Alaskan Task Force keeping a check on the construction; he was also helping the Club to ensure that millions of acres of land now owned by the State were preserved as parks and reserves and refuges and helping them in their fight to stop construction of a gas pipeline that would cut across the Arctic National Wildlife Range. He was happy working with Sierra; he was happy that Republican Jay Hammond had won the election for governor because it meant that Alaskans had voted for the environment. He was also flying commercially, he was exhausted, lately his old wound had been aching and he had experienced pains in the chest.

Browning thought he looked ill.

He left Larsen poring over a paper-littered desk, head cupped in one hand.

That night Browning attended a meeting of his group.

They were all young and fierce with protest. They were Alaskans, Eskimos, Indians, a Negro from the South. Only two of them knew about the plan to blow the bridge, Browning and a fat, red-bearded man named Diamond.

Diamond was the pro. He had been an agitator since the days when he organized student revolt on the campus. He was wild and sincere; he was concerned with overthrowing the conspiracy of power that he believed ruled the States; he was angered by the arrogant assumptions of that conspiracy; his beliefs grew strongly in the manure of Watergate.

After the meeting he talked with Browning in the studio apartment he rented in Anchorage. They drank coffee and smoked ordinary cigarettes because Diamond didn't believe in grass or anything that impaired action.

As he talked he played with an old World War I hand grenade, a metal egg with a cubed surface, that he carried around with him as a good-luck talisman.

He said to Browning: 'When?'

'When it's finished, I guess,' Browning said in his quiet voice. 'There's no sense in destroying a bridge when it's only half built.'

'When will that be?'

Browning shrugged. 'Anyone's guess. They're having some hang-ups. The deliveries of special rigs and parts for the drills for the supports for the overhead pipe have been delayed. They tried using conventional rigs but they seized up in the frozen subsoil.'

'I need action,' said Diamond, tossing the grenade from one hand to the other.

'Don't worry, you'll get it.'

411

'Yeah? Well I can't wait too long man. I'm not like you, I can't sit around waiting for the action.'

'I have a placid temperament,' Browning said.

'You mean you smoke too much. Why don't you knock off the shit? It slows you up and one of these days when you're high you're going to shoot your mouth off.'

Browning shook his head. 'No way. It's not like alcohol. It's beautiful, just beautiful.'

Diamond tossed the grenade into the air and caught it. 'Well, it ain't for me. And I sure hope that you don't foul anything up by smoking that stuff.'

'I won't,' Browning said, and then: 'What made you choose Alaska?'

'Because it was a classic example of assumption by the privileged,' Diamond said. *We've got to get our sticky little fingers into that oil and make ourselves a few more billion bucks so we'll shove a pipeline right through Alaska and fuck anyone who protests.* You know, I'm not a Maoist or a Trotskyist or a Marxist. I just reckon it's time the old order changeth and I aim to hustle it on its way. You know, it's got to the point where a politician is outraged – genuinely outraged, goddammit – if he's arraigned on a graft charge because it's a way of life and everyone's doing it and *why the hell should they pick on me?*'

'So you protest about everything?'

'I protest about everything that outrages me. Well, almost everything. Vietnam? Well, I figured other guys were making enough noise about that particular obscenity. Me, I reckon that maybe I should concentrate on the way the privileged are fouling up our land and our sea and our air. And, by Christ, we've achieved a lot and don't let any mother in industry ever tell you that they would have brought in all these precautions and safeguards if it hadn't been for guys like you and me stirring the crap. No sir, no way.' Diamond tugged at his red beard, clenching the grenade with one strong, fat hand.

Browning said: 'I'm a love-not-war freak.'

'Oh sure. That's why you want to blow up a bridge.'

'That will be beautiful,' Browning said. 'Just beautiful.'

'You know something? I think you're a bit weird.'

Browning smiled beautifully. 'That *is* love not war. It's love for Alaska. It'll be love when I see those pieces of bridge sailing slowly through the air and falling in the Yukon and being washed away.'

'Who said they'll sail *slowly* through the air for Christ's sake?'

'They will for me,' Browning said.

'But this is only a protest. They'll build another bridge.'

'Maybe. But we'll hold up construction. The oil won't flow for maybe another year. The cost will go up – and they figure it close on seven billion now. Maybe a few guys will pull out. Maybe the big boys will say to hell with it.'

No way,' Diamond said.

'Then when they've built another bridge we'll blow that.'

'If we aren't in jail.'

'Then we'll get some other guy to blow it.' Browning took the old and toothless grenade from Diamond and weighed it in his hand. 'Aren't you scared that they'll finger you as soon as we blow it? I mean, you've got a record.'

'Oh sure they'll finger me. But they'll find me clean.'

'They could beat it out of you.'

'Not me. I've got connections, I'm bad news to the cops.'

Diamond got up and strolled round the room. He shuffled a pile of copies of *Time* and *Newsweek* and Sierra Club bulletins. He tore the tab off a can of Budweiser and drank from the can. He crammed a handful of peanuts into his mouth. He belched.

He said: 'I sure wish we had gotten some action now.'

'Don't worry,' Browning said. He rolled the grenade across the floor. 'Within three months we'll be blowing that bridge.'

Later that evening Diamond walked a block to a hamburger joint. The man who had been waiting in an automobile parked across the street gave him fifty yards before following.

CHAPTER THIRTY-SEVEN

AND so the road opened up the north and with it, like a probe, came the pipe, so big that a man could crouch inside for shelter.

In the winter, when the winds from the North Pole tried to dislodge the invaders, the roughnecks cursed this bitter place; but in the summer, when the temperature hovered in the eighties in Happy Valley, when the mosquitoes sucked their blood, when the tundra became thick mud beneath their feet, they longed for the winter and the cold seemed like a friend.

And as the Bechtel construction crews threaded their great needle across the land they treated it with the care of an old lady tending her roses. They reseeded grass, they planted trees, they skirted nesting birds and, at a site near Delta Camp, they left a gap in the pipeline pad because a bear was asleep there for the winter.

Occasionally they erred. In the Dietrich River Valley, for instance, they diverted a river into a narrow channel; in the spring it flooded and damaged a forest of white spruce.

But, as the pipeline grew, so did the cost. Estimates are always quaint commodities, good for a laugh by those who submit them; but this was a historical pinnacle in the charts of estimates: it doubled, trebled, quadrupled: what had begun at less than one billion dollars was now expected to break seven billion.

And in their boardrooms the oil barons who formed the Aleyska consortium building the pipeline – British Petroleum, Sohio, Atlantic Richfield, Exxon, Mobil, Phillips, Union and Amerada Hess – brooded darkly. To dispel the gloom they consulted other estimates – the profits that would one day flow through the pipe. And then their faces lightened.

And all the time the Sierra watchdogs kept the construction under surveillance. From the ground and from the air.

Richard Larsen, who was nearly fifty and looked older, peered down through the snow for the ribbon of the pipeline route. Nothing. A whiteout. Below, ahead, overhead. He gripped the controls of the Piper, stared at the instruments, seeking sanity from the altimeter.

He wondered if this was how his life was to end with half a century behind him, most of it in Alaska. He wasn't scared and it seemed to him that this was how it *should* end, his wreckage a snow-smoothed gravestone deep in the country he loved.

He began to descend, searching the whiteness for the spike of a spruce tree, the familiar bend of a river.

He knew he was somewhere near the Yukon and that the nearest landing strip was Five Mile Camp. He headed north watching the altimeter as he nosed down through the whiteness that had no dimension. He barely noticed the pain in his chest.

Three thousand feet. Lower, Whiteness. Then he saw the bridge and the men working on it and the shining ice of the Yukon. He levelled out and five minutes later he was touching down on the packed snow of the airstrip at Five Mile.

The project engineer brought coffee in the canteen. 'You say your name's Larsen?' he asked.

Larsen nodded. 'Why?'

The project engineer stirred his coffee. 'You got a son?'

'Sure I've got a son.'

'Could he have been working here?'

'Maybe. He's been working up north getting the feel of the pipeline.'

'Why the hell would he have been doing that?'

'Because he's in oil.'

The project engineer was silent. Then he said: 'Name of Bill?'

'Yeah, he's called Billy. What's this all about?'

The project engineer described Larsen's son. 'Is that him?'

'That's him,' Larsen said as fear stirred. 'Why, what's happened to him?'

The project engineer looked into his coffee as he spoke. 'He took off this morning. Nothing's been seen of him since. We've been searching all day.'

'What do you mean, he took off?'

'Just walked off the camp as far as we know. You know some of the guys get like that if we don't spot withdrawal symptoms first.'

Larsen stood up. 'How long's he been gone?'

The project engineer looked at his watch. 'About four hours I guess.' His voice was quiet. 'It's pretty cold out there. A guy doesn't stand much chance when it's as cold as that . . .'

Larsen said: 'He can last out if he knows how to take care of himself.'

'Sure, but when they're like that maybe they don't want to take care of themselves.'

'I'll find him,' Larsen said.

'I can't let you go,' the project engineer said.

'You can't stop me,' Larsen said.

'But it's a white-out.'

'I'll find him,' Larsen said. The project engineer drove him to the airstrip.

Billy Larsen came to his senses a mile and a half from the camp. He stared around like a man who has suddenly wakened in a strange room. He wondered at the craziness that had led him from the camp. He was scared but there was still pain in his flesh so there was hope. He was scared mostly by the whiteness that robbed him of all sense of direction. If I go on walking, he thought, I could be heading further into the wilderness.

He walked round in a circle, picking up his footprints, as he tried to work it out. He adjusted his snow goggles and the hood of his parka because he was an Alaskan and he knew about the cold: knew that if your head is unprotected you can lose half the heat production of your body. He was thankful that he was wearing mukluks and mittens.

He repeated his name to himself. And his address and telephone number because as hypothermia, the lowering of body heat, crept through you, your brain seized up: you couldn't remember ordinary facts, you couldn't co-ordinate your limbs. He wondered if he had shivered much as he walked in his lonely fever; if the first shivering had passed and the paroxysms of shaking were about to begin then he was in worse shape than he thought.

At least he knew what not to do. You don't eat snow to quench your thirst, you don't rub frostbite. He touched the flesh of his face with a mittened hand; he could just feel the touch of the mitten.

He stopped walking to cut down the movement of muscles which hastened the loss of body heat. What he needed was shelter where he could conserve his energy until the white-out cleared and the search parties could find him; and he needed wood with which to build a fire so that they would see the smoke.

The whiteness closed around him. He thought he heard an aircraft but the sound must have been inside his skull. He felt the touch of the vulture wings of death; he began to shiver.

Use your brains, he told himself. Find insulation with which to pack your clothes. Don't expend energy and create sweat that will lower your heat. Before he had left, he had eaten a big meal and drunk a mug of coffee so he had supplies of energy. There was still hope . . .

He didn't try and stop the shivering as his muscles sought heat. He started to walk again, seeking woodland. He felt as if he were walking into a white-washed wall. He didn't want to die and he raged against his own stupidity that had made him stay too long on the pipeline.

The pain was less severe now. Soon the shivering stopped and he knew that this wasn't good, that soon the body would resort to violent fits of shaking to create heat and that this would be near the end because a man can die when his body-heat drops as little as six degrees.

He almost walked into the tree, a spruce pasted thick with snow. He bent down slowly and scooped at the snow. His movements were slower than he had intended and he knew that the numbness was reaching his brain. He walked on a little because where there was one tree there must be more.

And there were. He noticed some humps in the surface of the snow. Ponderously, he excavated around one of them. He found some sticks and he made a small platform of them and dug around looking for twigs; he found a few beneath the snow and he managed to pull some bark from one of the trees.

The most difficult action was pulling a few scraps of paper and a box of matches from the pockets of his parka. His hands felt heavy and swollen; as though his hands were objects that he was picking up. He stuffed the paper beneath the twigs and bark and tried to strike a match but he missed the striking surface and dropped the match.

Name, address, telephone number . . . he flunked the phone number. And he thought: Why me? Dear God, why me? And he prayed to God for the sake of his wife thinking: Why should God answer a man who only prays when he faces death?

He went to strike the second match but his body was seized by a paroxysm of shaking as adrenalin and blood sugar surged in his veins. He dropped the second match.

His movements were unco-ordinated now and so were his thoughts. There was no pain. He wanted to sit and dream.

He managed to strike the third match. He applied it to the scraps of paper which burned with thin wings of flame. Another fit of shaking. The flames caught the twigs which hissed as the heat found the frozen sap. A stem of smoke rose, disappearing in the whiteness above as though it had disappeared through a chimney.

He squatted down beside the fire. He looked into the small flames and he saw death. The white-out lifted and he didn't notice it. He looked into the flames seeing himself as a child, seeing his mother running to the airstrip as his father landed beside the lake; and when the Piper touched down beside the belt of woodland and his father came running towards him he thought it was still part of his childhood.

They lowered him into a tub of hot water, they fed him hot soup, but it was some time before he fully realized what had happened.

His father sat beside the tub, his face moist from the steam.

When they told him what had happened he turned his face to his father and said: 'Thanks.'

Richard Larsen nodded but he didn't speak for a while because the expression on his son's face reminded him of the expression on Charles Browning's face when he walked into the hospital ward that day in Anchorage. So he just nodded and smiled and then he said: 'Just don't promise me any medals.'

On the day that Robert Browning was due to travel to Five Mile Camp to check an archeological site on the pipeline and make final preparations for blowing the bridge over the Yukon, police raided Diamond's apartment.

They took away papers and when Browning walked past on the opposite side of the street two detectives were helping Diamond into the back of a police car. Diamond saw Browning and shook his shaggy head slightly. He was driven away seated between the two detectives.

Browning walked back to his own small apartment in a shabby block on the outskirts of the town. Smith the lawyer was waiting for him outside. He said: 'I thought maybe we could have a little talk.'

'Why should I want to talk to you?'

Smith showed him his F.B.I. identification. 'That's why.'

Browning shrugged. 'Then I don't have much choice.'

'Not much. Supposing we take a little drive,' Smith said pointing to a tan Chevrolet with the state slogan NORTH TO THE FUTURE on the number plate.

Smith drove out of town, down Highway 1 towards Seward. It was a fine bright morning with big clouds sailing over the mountains. Smith drove well and his personality had changed; he wore a thick grey suit and a blue shirt with a button-down collar; he seemed lean rather than bony and his speech was clipped and direct.

They drove beside Turnagain Arm where Captain Cook had once turned because there was no through passage. The channel was humped with a frozen silt and the white mountains were folded in silence.

'Beautiful, isn't it,' Smith said.

'I guess so.'

'I can understand people wanting to keep it that way.'

'I didn't know you were so sensitive.'

'But blowing bridges isn't going to help anything. That's just plain stupid.'

Browning didn't say anything.

'And I don't think you're that stupid.'

'I don't know what the hell you're talking about.'

Smith shook his head wearily. 'Look, I've been through this scene so many times I could recite what you and me are going to say to each other so let's cut it out.' He jerked his thumb towards a black attaché case on the back seat. 'I know everything there is to know about you. I know about your association with Diamond and I know you were going up to Five Mile Camp to plant explosive charges under the Yukon Bridge. I'm levelling with you, I do have the evidence to put you away. But I don't want to so let's just talk like a couple of adults.'

Browning thought about it. Then he said: 'Okay, what do you want to know?'

Smith said: 'Maybe you and I want the same things.'

'You mean you want to blow up the bridge?'

Smith chuckled and said in his new, crisp voice: 'Maybe we both want to clean up this pipeline.'

'Wrong. I want to rip up the goddam thing length by length.'

'No one can stop that pipeline,' Smith said. 'There's too much muscle behind it, too much investment.'

'We can continue to protest.'

Smith sighed. Jesus! no more protest, the sigh said. 'Look,' Smith said after the sigh, 'leave the protest to your buddy Diamond. He's going to jail as sure as God made little green apples and he can do all the protesting he wants there.' He overtook a yellow truck, glanced at the side of a hill where there had been a recent avalanche. 'Look,' said Smith, 'I want to make a deal and I want to tell you about it so just listen, huh?'

'I'm listening,' Browning said in his soft voice.

'There's going to be a lot of shit flying on this pipeline.' He corrected himself: 'There *is* a lot of shit flying but there's going to be a hell of a lot more.'

Smith catalogued the graft, corruption, theft and extortion associated with the pipeline. Camps were losing ten thousand dollars worth of tools a day, two hundred trucks had vanished. The F.B.I. was investigating a prostitution ring in the camps near the terminal at Valdez.

'Ice-free Valdez,' Browning said.

'Nothing moves without the say-so of the Teamsters.'

'Maybe I should join,' Browning said.

'Do you know anything about welds?'

'I hear the X-rays need X-raying.'

They passed an expanse of frozen mud left more than a decade ago by the tidal wave that followed the earthquake. Grass was sprouting between the dead trees. A garage was still sunk deep in the land.

Smith told Browning that a lot of welds were faulty. That eventually President Ford would have to order an investigation.

'Is that a case for the F.B.I.?'

'Maybe,' Smith said. 'It looks like records of the X-rays were falsified. In some cases the X-ray of a good weld was substituted for a bad bastard. It looks like there could be a case for criminal proceedings. But that's only a part of it,' Smith said.

'A part of what?'

'Of the whole dirty scene that we're investigating.'

'We?'

'You don't think I'm running this show by myself, for Christ's sake,' Smith said as he parked the Chev across the ice from Portage Glacier.

They stood and stared across the frozen melt lake of the glacier and at the white avenue of the glacier and at an ice-berg becalmed in the middle of the lake with children sliding down its blue flanks. Browning thought of oil spilling from faulty welds on the pipeline, staining the snow.

'So what do you want me to do?' Browning asked as they drove back towards Anchorage.

'You people have got information on the pipeline, right?'

'Sure, we get reports from time to time.'

'I want them to do a little investigating for me. Like I said, we both want that pipeline to be as clean as possible. So what do you say?' Smith asked when they stopped for a drink at a sawdust-floored bar called the Bird House on the way back.

'I'll think it over.'

'You do that,' Smith said. His voice hardened. 'And let me know by tomorrow.'

'Otherwise I'm under arrest?'

'I don't think you're that stupid,' Smith said. 'Just misguided.'

Smith dropped Browning outside his apartment block. Browning thought about Diamond in a cell and he thought that what Smith was asking him to do was just as dirty as the graft on the pipeline and he packed a few things, locked up the apartment and drove to Anchorage police headquarters where he gave himself up.

CHAPTER THIRTY-EIGHT

In Anchorage, as in all cities, there are the very rich and there are the bums. But here the very rich differ in some ways from the very rich of other places; there is still in their character the stamp of the pioneer and it is reflected in the celebration of their riches – in the rugged opulence of their homes, in their open-air recreations. They are conscious of these differences and they cultivate them zealously. Their hand-clasps are strong, there is a flinty challenge in their gaze, their clothes are simple – even if they were bought at Abercrombie and Fitch – and the dude who arrives from the Outside in a brass-buttoned blazer, Gucci shoes and Pierre Cardin jersey is made instantly to feel ill at ease.

They are warm-hearted and suspicious: they are friendly and clannish: they are proud of their isolated independence and they are quickly on the defensive.

They meet formally for the gala dinners and balls of their many societies in big hotels like the Captain Cook and the Westward. But they prefer to meet in their homes where, in the summer, the plate-sized steaks spit and sizzle over flowing charcoal in their gardens; or, in the winter, in front of blazing logs that shift with comfort while they mix cocktails that burn holes in the stomachs of *cheechako* guests.

They play a lot of tennis, they ski on the slopes of Mount Alyeska, they fly their own aeroplanes, they shoot animals whose heads they stick on the walls of their dens, they take vacations in Hawaii.

Their sons are strong and sporting; their daughters are long-limbed with Californian good looks when they emerge from their parkas.

These well-heeled Alaskans of Anchorage are fast becoming more cosmopolitan because it is difficult to be otherwise in a city which has an airport that is often described as the crossroad of the world, where itinerant strangers walk the streets on the lookout for igloos and stray moose, where the lobby of the Royal Inn might be the lobby of a Tokyo hotel as the Japanese air-crews cluster round reception and the gift shop. But they still regard foreigners with distrust.

When they meet they talk about hunting and holidaying and tennis and real estate and inflation. They talk more about Alaska than the people say of Nebraska or Wyoming talk about their states; they talk about the recession and the boom because they see it both ways and this leads them to oil as surely as a hazel twig leads a diviner to water.

'Oil has brought disaster,' says an accountant who has been analyzing the shrinkage of the nine thousand million dollars plus interest that the state received from the oil leases while the tent-manufacturer whose sales have increased six-fold stares at his hands and the official of the National Bank of Alaska whose deposits rose by nearly a half in one year says: 'In ten years we'll be the richest state in the Union.' They all gloomily anticipate the next budget – maybe they'll have to sell more leases at Prudhoe Bay – and they drink up and agree that the economy is in a pretty bad shape but it can only get better and they brighten visibly.

They discuss graft and corruption, some of them guardedly, and the ingratitude of the natives (unless a prosperous Eskimo or Indian is present) who have been given a plethora of riches – land, cash and jobs on the pipeline. And more than likely one of them will recently have seen a drunken Eskimo driving a snow-mobile at hazardous speeds.

The clan is exclusive and entry is limited as Charles Browning discovered. He was Outside Interests; what's more he had never succeeded in disguising his hostility to the land and its people.

But today he had engineered himself an invitation to a party at a big house at Turnagain. He had arrived on an Alaska

Airlines *Pipeline Express* flight from Houston, and had booked into the Captain Cook Hotel.

He shaved and showered and regarded his naked body in the mirror. Belly bulging a little when he forgot to pull it in, hair thinning at the crown. But still an attractive man, he decided, as he remembered the raven-haired, full-breasted woman he had left asleep in the hotel room in Houston.

He massaged after-shave into his cheeks which only sagged slightly at the line of the jaw. He lifted his head and the sag lifted. He dressed carefully making sure that he didn't look too much of a dude. He ordered a Scotch on the rocks from room service.

He didn't delude himself that younger women still went to bed with him because of his physical attractions: he knew that his life style, his Cadillac, his pack of credit cards and his mannered assurance were powerful aphrodisiacs, as strong, perhaps, as youthful sexuality.

He ordered a cab and, as it took him towards Turnagain, he examined his achievements and he was content with them. The delays on the pipeline were aggravating but soon oil would flow south; soon he would be a millionaire several times over because, since the environmental hold-ups, he had expanded his interests in Texas, Las Vegas and Los Angeles. The future of oil now lay under the sea and he had done a deal with the Greeks exploring the Aegean. Also he still worked closely with the Japanese who were now in business in a big way in Alaska.

My intuition was right then, Charles Browning thought as the taxi stopped at traffic lights. I have plundered this hostile, barren place and now perhaps the time is right to get out and take my loot with me.

Only one thing marred his mood: his son was in jail convicted of plotting to blow up the bridge over the Yukon. He was there because he had joined forces with Richard Larsen and it seemed to Browning that Larsen was the only man who had never succumbed to him.

It was almost the fall. The sky was blue and the hillsides

425

were covered with red berries and golden lichen. Browning told the driver to hurry up. He was impatient to get to the party because he had revenge in his heart and Richard Larsen would be there.

Richard Larsen had accepted the invitation because he thought Theresa would enjoy the party. He was now accepted as an Alaskan but not as a member of this set. He had attended other parties such as this and it was his experience that he was invited either because the host was a genuine conservationist or because he enjoyed controversy at his gatherings. This particular host was in timber so it looked like controversy.

The party was held on the terrace of the house. Paths led from the terrace into woods of spruce; below, sunlight lay serenely on the water; the charcoal in the barbecue glowed deep red, the first steaks were spitting.

Larsen was drinking some sort of non-alcoholic fruit punch. He resisted efforts to make him take liquor and he exchanged smiles of understanding with Theresa. He was happy because she was proud of him and he was happy that the men looked at her with desire and the women with envy.

They moved from group to group. They encountered friendliness, hostility, a few attempts at ridicule. Larsen handled everything easily because he had learned to manoeuvre. He saw Browning arrive and experienced a moment of unease. They nodded at each other. Browning joined the group surrounding the host and the moment passed.

It was an hour before they spoke to one another. Larsen and Theresa were standing beside the wall of the terrace. Browning came up to them holding a heavy crystal glass of whisky. He was a little drunk, face flushed, voice loud.

He said to Theresa: 'Your husband and me once fought together. Did he tell you that?'

Her dark, knowing eyes looked him over. 'Yes,' she said, 'he told me. You were his officer, weren't you?'

'I was *an* officer,' Browning said, drinking from the glass, spilling whisky on the terrace. 'Not exclusively your husband's.' He swayed a little. 'Your husband saved my life. Did he tell you that?'

'Yes,' Theresa said, 'he told me that.'

'Should have recommended him for a medal. Never got round to it.'

The unease returned to Larsen. 'Let's not talk about that,' he said. He sipped his fruit drink. 'How's business these days?'

'Pretty damned good – despite you guys.'

'We did what we thought had to be done.'

'We got a better pipeline because of what you did. We're very grateful.'

Theresa said: 'A better pipeline except for the welds.' She smiled at him.

Browning considered this. 'Don't you worry your pretty self about those welds,' he said after a while. 'They'll get them fixed.'

What the hell does he want? Larsen wondered, saying: 'I hear they're talking about selling some of the oil to the Japanese. Odd when you think we were fighting them.'

'If you can't beat 'em join 'em,' Browning said.

'But we did beat 'em,' Theresa said.

'Oh yes,' Browning said, 'we beat 'em. Your husband and me – we beat 'em.'

There was a pause.

Then Browning said: 'I guess you heard about my son.'

Larsen said: 'It was bad luck.'

'Not bad luck, Larsen. If it hadn't been for you he wouldn't be there.'

'That's hardly fair,' Theresa said.

'Oh yes it is, Mrs. Larsen. I'm sorry but it is.' He swallowed more whisky. 'He joined up with you because he knew it would get at me.'

'Bullshit,' Larsen said. 'He was a conservationist, that's all.'

'Yeah, but he didn't want to conserve that goddam bridge.'

'I didn't tell him to do that.'

'No? Well maybe you didn't but I wouldn't put anything past some of you freaky guys.'

Larsen said to Theresa: 'Let's circulate,' but Browning put a hand on his arm and said: 'Just a minute. I've got some news that might interest you.'

'I doubt it,' Larsen said, lifting Browning's hand from his arm. And to Theresa: 'Come on, let's go.'

Browning stood in front of Larsen. 'It's about your son.'

Larsen hesitated. 'What about my son?'

'He knows the oil business pretty well. You've got to hand it to a kid who sweats it out on the pipeline.'

'So?'

'It's like this,' Browning said. 'I made him an offer and he's accepted and he's working for me.'

The challenge came later. Larsen was talking to one of Alaska's leading dog-sledders who had raced last year in the Iditarod, the toughest dog-sled race in the world, from Anchorage right across Alaska to Nome on the east coast.

Browning handed Larsen a glass of Scotch. 'Here drink this. Or maybe you'd like a glass of milk . . .'

Larsen put down the glass of Scotch on a table. 'Sorry, I don't touch liquor.'

'So I heard. One taste and Alcoholics Anonymous have lost another patient.'

Larsen drained his glass and faced Browning and said: 'Just what the hell do you want?' and the other guests were silent and the hostess whispered to her husband: 'What are we going to do?' and her husband said he didn't think there was much they could do and maybe it would blow over.

'For the last time,' Larsen said, feeling the tight grip of Theresa's hand on his arm, 'what do you want?'

'You've got dogs,' Browning said, belching. 'And I've got dogs. I was listening to what our friend here was saying' – pointing at the dog-sledder – 'and I thought to myself why don't I have a shot at this race.' He took another gulp of whisky. 'And then I thought to myself, Say, why doesn't old Richard Larsen have a shot? And then I thought, Why don't we have some bets on who gets to Nome first? You know, we'd both probably get licked by the young bloods but we could make it a private thing between us. How about a hundred thousand bucks say I get to Nome first?'

Theresa whispered to Larsen: 'Don't take any notice of him. Let him kill himself not you.'

Larsen said: 'I haven't got a hundred thousand bucks.'

'So what the hell have you got?'

'An aeroplane,' Larsen said quietly.

'You're on,' Browning said, staggering and clutching hold of the table.

'And maybe if I get there first you might pin a medal on my chest,' Larsen told him.

The other guests looked at each other, because they didn't understand. The host and hostess eased them away from the terrace, the guests made their way towards their cars. Then Larsen and Theresa left and, as they drove home, Theresa sat stiff and silent while Larsen explained that there was no way he could have refused, that it seemed as if this had always been written, but when they arrived outside their apartment block she told him that no, she didn't understand, and Richard Larsen wasn't so sure that he did either.

CHAPTER THIRTY-NINE

THE names are beautiful and they tell the tale of Alaska. There is gold in those names, poverty and desperation, endeavour and achievement, and the letters are the spray of mountain streams and the flakes of a blizzard and there is native blood in some of them too. Finger Lake and Rainy Pass, Farewell, Salmon River, Bear Creek, Poorman, Ruby, Shaktoolik and Koyuk, White Mountain, Nome.

And in March, as men and dogs stream out of Anchorage heading for these checkpoints on the Iditarod, they take up with the past which is in a locket round every Alaskan's throat. And as snow covers their beards and frost gives them old men's eyebrows they return to that past, handing out the mail to prospectors, riding shotgun on a Wells Fargo sled heavy with gold.

The cold hasn't changed on the trail, nor the rivers running with overflow, nor the wolves and the wandering moose, nor the avalanches and white-outs, nor man and dog. True there are bullet-nosed snowmobiles to be seen, and small aircraft overhead but they are intruders from the present and, when night falls in Ptarmigan Pass, with the light from a miner's lamp cutting shafts in the loneliness, with the runners of the sled singing, the machines are lost.

The race is pure Alaskan. Whereas other people excavate the past with pageants and banquets, strangling cities with bunting, stuffing old cannons with gunpowder, the Alaskan chooses hardship. Certainly there is fifty thousand dollars in prize-money and a lottery paid out to the punter who forecasts the winner's time but that is not the point: the point, as the frost-bitten mushers will tell you as they arrive in Nome at the end of their one thousand mile journey, is that the old Iditarod Trail still lives.

The dogs were fat and they moved slowly but they were sure-footed and willing and Larsen believed that they would endure longer than the other teams bred for sprints and he wasn't concerned that Browning was ahead of him.

He spoke to the dogs as he rode the sled or ran behind or pushed it up hillsides or braked down slopes, and the dogs, huskies and malamutes, laughed into the wind.

Soon man and dog were one which was how Larsen had planned the race, as an animal, as Ott had once explained animals to him, using his senses to feel the moods and messages of the land, like a moose seeking willow or birch. He laughed with the dogs and he rejoiced at the bright light on the glare ice, the blue of the sky on the snow, the clouds of powder snow that the wind picked up and bowled away. And, as he rode the sled, as shadows filled the hollows, he thought: Now at last I am part of this land.

With his animal intuition he smelled the real cold before it descended. He was near Rainy and Ptarmigan Passes and he hoped to reach shelter before the cold bit deep. But that night the dogs tired early so he stopped and fed them with Purina and beaver tallow and put up his tent while they curled up in the snow. He lit his camp stove and drank coffee and ate good fatty meat; then slipped into his sleeping bag.

Before he slept he thought of Theresa standing in the stadium at Anchorage. He slept as the wind blew up, pushing the temperature down to minus a hundred degrees, shaking the frost from the roof of the tent onto his sleeping bag.

She had stood there at the stadium, dark-eyed and pure Eskimo in her parka, wishing him back at home, with thoughts in her mind that would not become words, thinking of everything that had been left unsaid since they met. And she had thought that he was a beautiful man as he stood behind his sled, snow goggles on his forehead, smiling at her. Since Browning's challenge in the dying summer of last year she hadn't protested. She had planned it with him, helped to train the dogs, waited for him as he sledded through the snow to bring back youth to the muscles of his legs which, after a long haul, can seize up so that a man can barely stand. But she had never told him of her fear which mounted as the months passed, assailing her at waking moments in the night. Now the fear was in every part of her body but, as he moved away, all she did was wave and then turn away so that he couldn't see the tears that were cold and wet on her cheeks.

When he awoke the muscles were stiff in his legs and the sweat on his forehead had frozen. His sleeping bag was covered with the frost that had dropped from the ceiling of the tent. Outside in the dark the wind drove through the pass.

He went outside and the wind hit him. There was a touch of light in the sky so that he could make out the rims of the encircling mountains. He made himself coffee while the dogs slept in the snow.

When he had first arrived in Alaska, war veteran and *cheechako*, he would have denounced the race because of the suffering of the dogs. But now he knew better: this was their life and the good women who attacked the race were well-meaning but wrong, as they would know if they had mushed with a healthy team of huskies across the heartland of Alaska, witnessed their quivering enjoyment. If you wanted to be cruel to a husky or a malamute stick him in front of a fire all winter and feed him soft foods so that by the spring he is overweight with rotting teeth and fur as lifeless as dead pine-needles.

The sky brightened but the wind still came through the pass like a train through a tunnel. He packed up the tent and Arctic sleeping bag and loaded it onto the sled alongside his rations, snow-shoes, axe, first-aid kit.

The dogs looked at him, fur-masked faces intent, but they refused to face into the wind. He stroked the lead dog, Jessie,

432

who had been with him for three years; she was a fine dog, intelligent and resourceful, with the ice-blue eyes of a Siberian husky. He tried to think as she was thinking and he knew it was no good: they wouldn't turn into that wind.

He camped through most of the day by which time his rations were getting low. He decided not to try and make the Rohn River checkpoint; instead he would return to Rainy Pass Lodge and radio for food.

The dogs ran happily with the wind behind them. When he reached Rainy Pass he found other mushers waiting there for a break in the weather. At least, he thought, I'm not running last. But now the gap between him and Browning was greater. Still he didn't worry.

The other men greeted him with friendliness that shared hardship induces.

The next morning was calm and, after food supplies had been dropped, they set out together because the race doesn't really start till you reach Ruby and sled down the frozen Yukon.

Browning's dogs were running well and he was riding in the company of some of the best mushers in the land.

He was past the Rohn River checkpoint running through the bed of a valley deep in ice. The wind had blown away the red ribbons that blaze the trail but he was following two veterans who reckoned they knew where they were. They were heading for Farewell Lake; the temperature on his sled thermometer registered minus ten degrees but it was warming up with a gentle breeze from the south.

Browning thought: I'm beating this country and when I'm through I'll quit. He sensed hostility from the other mushers but there was respect there too. He didn't expect to win the race, he didn't expect to make the first ten of the thirty-five teams: he did expect to beat Larsen and he was pleased that bets were being laid on the outcome, and that he was favourite.

He was riding the sled over the ice as the Eskimo Jakey

Onalick passed him. He waved but Onalick didn't wave back. The dogs strained and the sled runners sang with speed.

An hour later, with the temperature above zero, he came to a stretch of iced mud. He pushed the sled behind the dogs until they came to a frozen creek. Jakey Onalick was there staring ahead. When Browning's dogs saw the ice they leaped ahead; the ice cracked and the lead dog fell into the black water followed by the other dogs.

As the sled slid towards the water Onalick ran up and held it and shouted to Browning: 'Unhook the line,' and then as Browning tried to unhook it: 'Get moving if you don't want to lose your gear.'

The dogs were struggling in the water, the ice cracking around them in long black veins. Then they were free paddling towards the firm ice on the far side of the creek.

Onalick said: 'You'd better pull the sled upstream and take it across where the ice is thicker. It's funny land here,' he said, 'the mud back there . . . I don't know why it wasn't froze.'

Browning stuck out his hand. 'Thanks,' he said.

Onalick looked at his hand; he didn't take it, saying: 'That's okay, we help each other on the trail. But you've got to know how to take care of yourself out here.'

It was an accident, Browning thought, that could have happened to anyone. Don't patronize me, you sonofabitch, he thought, withdrawing his hand. 'Well thanks anyway,' he said as he began to haul the sled upstream.

He crossed the creek with the ice creaking at his feet. He rejoined the dogs and took up the trail heading for Farewell Lake and then the Kuskokwim Mountains.

As he ran behind the sled the old wound in his belly jabbed him and he thought: If Larsen hadn't rescued me that time I wouldn't be here trying to lick him.

He shook his head at the irony of it as the soft wind blew from the south with its own brand of treachery.

CHAPTER FORTY

THE old wolf named Yellow Eye sniffed the trail bordered with fluttering red ribbon and remembered easy kills in the past. Dogs curled in the snow who had whined as his pack advanced in the darkness but hadn't been prepared for the final howling assault.

Yellow Eye's tail switched and his mouth ran with saliva. The pack was hungry and a few hours ago the second-ranking male who wanted to mate with the first-ranking female had challenged his authority. Why hadn't they eaten for so long? Why hadn't they attacked the bull moose they had surrounded, taking it by the nose and back legs and hanging on till it became weak from loss of blood? Was Yellow Eye scared of the kicking front hooves of the moose? If so it was time he handed over authority – and the first-ranking female – because he was too old to lead.

While the two male wolves stared at each other on the playground of trails crossing and recrossing each other outside the den, the top-ranking female lay in the snow, head between her paws, watching. She had mated with Yellow Eye for four years, but the second-ranking male was big and strong with no smell of age in his thick grey fur.

If Yellow Eye won this battle for authority then she would mate with him perhaps one more time; and she would do it with pleasure and pride because authority was essential in the pack, more important to her than the youth and virility of the second-ranking male.

If Yellow Eye lost then he would retire without bitterness, take his place among the elders of the pack which was a family. But that didn't mean he wouldn't resist the attempt by the younger wolf to usurp him.

435

So she watched with curiosity and pleasurable anticipation as the two males faced each other in the clearing among the snow-covered spruce trees. There would be no fighting, merely the exertion of wills until the moment of submission.

Many years ago Yellow Eye had lost one eye when he incautiously investigated a porcupine. A female had pulled the spike from the eye with her teeth but the eye had died, milky and opaque. Far from impairing the young wolf the loss of the eye had been his strength; the good eye gained power and glowed with yellow radiance and it had brought about the downfall of his predecessor five years ago. It seemed that two good eyes were a weakness when it came to staring into one good, shining yellow eye: it put the contest off balance as far as the two-eyed wolf was concerned.

The tails of the two wolves were raised high. They glared at each other, holding their ears erect, baring their teeth, furrowing the fur above their eyes.

They howled and they growled and they barked and they whimpered. The yellow eye of the leader gleamed. Infinitely slowly the head of the second-ranking male turned so that he was staring into this single orb. His tail began its descent of submission; he crouched; it was over.

But now, sniffing the trail, Yellow Eye knew that he had to find meat. If he didn't he would be defeated the next time he faced the second-ranking male. And, because he knew his powers were waning, it had to be an easy kill with which the pack could fill their bellies and congratulate him on his cunning.

The scent that he remembered grew stronger. Saliva dripped from his jaws onto the snow. He took up a position on an observation bed on a hillside beneath the spruce and waited.

A mile away Larsen's team was tiring. He decided to pitch camp and make an early start.

He stopped on the fringe of a belt of spruce, fed the dogs and took off their protective boots. He had scores of these boots on his sled because during a previous Iditarod supplies had run

436

short and the dog-lovers of Anchorage had cut and sewn hundreds of boots which were flown over the trail and dropped at checkpoints.

After they had eaten the dogs lay down, but they seemed uneasy. Larsen decided they were over-tired. After he had brewed coffee and cooked himself a meal on the stove he climbed into his sleeping bag inside the tent.

Outside, the huskies whimpered in their bed of snow.

The wolves approached cautiously. Their stomachs ached with hunger but they didn't abandon the elements of hunting. Their tails switched as Yellow Eye surveyed the prey curled in the snow outside the tent where the man was sleeping.

He had surveyed the huskies earlier as it grew dark, looking for signs of weakness – the scent of blood from a wound, the smell of sickness, a limp of an infirmity. But the dogs had seemed healthy; Yellow Eye had decided to wait till their bellies were full and sleep had taken them.

And so they had waited patiently just inside the border of their territory staked out by urine from the top-ranking male and female.

When Yellow Eye gave the signal to go they followed him. Still with caution. The huskies slept and from the tent came the sound of snoring.

It was Jessie who awoke just before the final assault. Into her sleep came a signal of danger so sharp that she was barking as she awoke; then the other dogs were struggling from sleep barking with fear.

Inside the tent Richard Larsen awoke. He scrambled from his sleeping bag and peered out of the tent just as the wolf pack began its attack, howling and barking, moonlight glinting on their eyes and their white, bone-crushing teeth.

Larsen grabbed the rifle which the *cheechako* Larsen would never have carried. By the time he reached the huskies the wolves had taken one and were mauling a second. The huskies fought back but they were heavy with food and sleep and they were no match for the wolves.

While the leading wolves attacked, the others dragged the bodies of the two huskies away. Larsen raised the rifle. He hesitated for a moment because of the danger of hitting a husky.

Then he pulled the trigger. Light and sound seared the night and man and dogs and wolves were frozen there for a fraction of a second in black and white.

Then the wolves were away into the trees. Richard Larsen went to the dogs who were sniffing the body of the wolf he had shot.

Larsen pushed them aside and knelt beside the dead animal whose teeth were bared in the snarl of death. It was then that he noticed that it had been blind in one eye.

The days melted and froze into the entity of the journey. How many days had they been on the trail? Eight, ten, twelve?

Browning pushed on towards McGrath on the far side of the Kuskokwim Range. Still it was warm, a few degrees above freezing, and when he reached McGrath, Browning put warm-weather plastic runners on his sled.

At McGrath he heard that Larsen was two checkpoints behind him. 'Poor bastard,' one of the mushers said. 'Got his dogs mauled by wolves.' He turned to Browning who was gulping down coffee. 'That please you?'

'He should have looked after his dogs better,' Browning said. 'It's the same for all of us.'

'I don't like to hear of wolves getting a man's dogs,' the musher said.

Browning looked at his dogs. They looked fit and were eager to be off. 'His dogs were too fat,' he said. 'He should have gotten himself fitter dogs.'

'Maybe yours are a mite too fit.'

'Yeah? What sort of horse shit is that?'

'Maybe you'll find out,' the musher said. 'And maybe you should put some boots on them dogs of yours.'

'There's nothing wrong with their paws,' Browning said. 'And anyway I doctored them with Coppertox.'

'You got boots?'

Browning shook his head. 'Here take some.' The musher handed him a bundle of dog boots. 'Not because I want to see you make Nome before Larsen but because I like dogs.'

Browning loaded the boots onto his sled. Then he set out for Ruby via Ophir, Bear Creek and Poorman. Half-way there the weather changed and the wind brought powder snow and cold from the north.

For a while he camped in a white-out. He heard an animal nearby but he couldn't see it in the whiteness. He fired his rifle into the air and a moose came running at him. It veered away and disappeared into the white veil.

Five days later when he reached Ruby the ache had returned to the old wound and the dogs were beginning to look tired. He changed sleds and left two dogs behind to be picked up.

When he set off down the long haul along the Yukon Larsen was still far behind.

Larsen had ten dogs left. Two had been killed by the wolves and he had to shoot a third which had been savagely mauled. He buried the dead huskies beside the one-eyed wolf in the snow.

With fewer dogs he had to push the sled more frequently. After a long period of pushing, his limp more pronounced, he was forced to stop by stabs of pain in his chest. He knew it was madness to be out here in the wilderness racing against a man whose life he had once saved but he knew that he had to continue.

He reached Ruby a day behind Browning with all but two of the competitors in front of him. He waited while a doctor from the U.S. Air Force checked out his dogs.

The doctor said: 'The dogs are in good shape. You've looked after them real well.' He stared at Larsen. 'But you don't look so hot. Want me to take a look at you?'

Larsen shook his head.

The doctor shrugged. 'It's up to you fella. But the going's really tough from here on. You know, the other guys are really

439

racing. Aren't you the guy who's got a bet with that dude Browning?'

'It's a private thing,' Larsen said.

'He's way ahead. No sense in killing yourself for a wager.'

'I'll catch him.'

'Yeah? Well, he looked like he was going pretty good.'

'And his dogs?'

'They were a little tired, I guess.'

'Then I'll catch him,' Larsen said.

'Have it your own way but don't say I didn't warn you.'

Larsen thanked him. Then he was away onto the frozen Yukon, riding the sled behind the barking dogs as the wind and the powder snow whipped down from the north and the temperature dipped at night to minus forty degrees.

Sometimes he even dozed on the sled. He dreamed fitfully of the relays of dog-teams that fifty or so years ago had rushed anti-diphtheria serum to Nome. He remembered the statue in Central Park of Balto, the lead dog on the final burst into Nome. He remembered Ott threatening to release the polar bears in the zoo.

At times he passed through overflow on the ice but it didn't bother him because his boots were warm and water-proofed. It wasn't until he reached Kaltag that he felt the numbness in one foot and it was then that he found the rent in one of the boots.

He tried to remove the boot but the overflow had entered the rent and frozen inside. He felt sick as if the cold had found a rent in his body and crept inside.

He thawed the boot with hot water. When he managed to pull it off his foot was swollen, suet-coloured and stiff. There were two other mushers there, the three of them bringing up the rear of the race.

One of them looked at the foot and said: 'You stay right here and radio for help. With that foot you don't go nowhere if you want to keep it.'

Larsen said: 'I need another boot.'

'You mean you aim to continue?'

Larsen nodded.

'You're crazy.'

'Maybe.'

'Just to beat this guy Browning?'

'You don't understand,' Larsen said.

'So you beat him and end up with one foot, maybe one leg. Is that worth it?'

'Do you have any spare boots?' Larsen asked.

'Sure I do but—'

'I'll buy them from you,' Larsen said.

'You're crazy.'

'Okay I'm crazy but can I buy your boots?'

'I guess we're all crazy at that,' the musher said. 'Here take 'em, they're a gift -- and good luck,' the musher said as he took off behind his sled.

Larsen left Kaltag last.

Browning's sled flipped along the trail where it runs parallel with Norton Sound where the Bering Sea bites into the west coast of Alaska.

His dogs picked up the scent of a wild animal and went after it, tangling their harnesses, snapping at each other in a confusion of legs and bodies.

Browning swore, running after them, as the sled swung round, smashing against a boulder and turning over, spilling equipment.

When he reached the sled he found that one of the runners had been broken. He heaved the sled upright but, as he did so, he felt a tiny pain like an incision with a razor-blade behind the old scar-tissue in his belly.

He reached the next checkpoint but there were no other sleds available. He felt weak as though his energy was bleeding away from him behind the scar.

He made the next checkpoint with the broken runner and was able to change sleds. But he felt terribly weak. If he continued like this Larsen would overtake him. The only course to take was to rest, although he had already taken his compulsory twenty-four hour break.

He lay in his sleeping bag while the dogs rested and again

he thought about the irony of the old wound but this time he thought how ironic it would be if it was this wound, inflicted just before Larsen dragged him to safety, that gave Larsen victory.

Except that I shall win.

When he left Solomon on the last lap of the race Browning, revived by his rest, was about two miles ahead of Larsen. From time to time there was a razor of pain behind the scar, but it felt as if the bleeding had stopped and with it the seepage of energy.

He and Larsen were now the only two left in the race, lagging twenty-four hours behind the last musher to enter the little gold-rush town.

Larsen, barely conscious on the runners, was catching up Browning. The pain from his chest filled his body but stopped at the top of one leg; the leg was now quite numb, the foot that had been immersed in water swollen and grotesque.

But I am catching him, he thought, as the crowds who had stayed to see the end of the personal duel came out from Nome on their snowmobiles. Vaguely he heard them shouting encouragement and this pleased him with a warm fluid pleasure that soothed the pain a little, pleased him because they were encouraging the freak who had once refused to fly hunters, and he shouted to Jessie who would surely take her place in Iditarod history, as he closed on Browning until there was only a few hundred yards between them; but there was only a few hundred yards between Browning and the finishing post. He shouted again to Jessie without knowing that no words were issuing from his mouth, unaware that his dead foot was trailing in the snow, while the faces of the crowd, looming, smiling, fading, were the faces of his wives, of his son, of an Indian, of a girl . . .

Browning was thinking that the bright, fast snowmobiles were there to greet him like the standard-bearers of progress when one of them, ridden by a drunken Eskimo, drove into his sled fifty yards from the finishing line. The sled tipped over and the dogs tangled as Larsen passed him.

They reckoned Larsen been dead on his feet as the sled

crossed the finishing line. When they checked his possessions they examined the contents of his wallet but no one noticed a scrap of paper, creased and transparent with age, stuck together with tape, blow away. If they had they would have seen a message written with a young hand in old, rust-brown ink. It read: I'M SORRY MY LOVE. YOU WERE MY FIRST LOVE, MY ONLY LOVE. NOTHING WILL CHANGE THAT.

But they didn't see it and the wind carried the scrap of paper away from the little town along the Iditarod trail towards the heart of Alaska, where it belonged.

THE END

TOUCH THE LION'S PAW BY DEREK LAMBERT

A COOL £14,000,000!
It would be the biggest diamond robbery ever. A king's ransom in uncut gemstones. It would take a year to plan. The action would range from Antwerp to New York, by way of London, Florida and Spain. The underworld's best brains would be involved. Security was said to be impenetrable but to Johnny Rhodes, mastermind of the operation, NOTHING was impossible . . .

By the author of 'The Yermakov Transfer'.

0 552 10345 4   75p

The Trans-Siberian Express left Moscow carrying the most powerful, most closely guarded man in the Soviet Union . . . and also the man who planned to kidnap him . . .

THE YERMAKOV TRANSFER BY DEREK LAMBERT

Tension aboard the train was at a maximum. The KGB had checked and double checked. Doubtful passengers had been removed and those allowed to continue their journey had authority from the highest levels of the Kremlin. But as Vasily Yermakov, the Soviet leader, tried to sleep on the first night in his cabin, he had an uneasy feeling that something was going to go wrong . . .

'A timely and gripping thriller . . .' – *Publishers Weekly*

'Hugely entertaining.' – *The Guardian*

0 552 09866 3   60p

THE YEARS OF THE HUNGRY TIGER BY JOHN GORDON DAVIS

Hong Kong ... crossroads of East and West, city of teeming streets and crowded harbours, of rickshaws and coolies and markets and girlie-bars.

Hong Kong ... where Jake McAdams, a successful young British policeman met Ying-ling, a Communist schoolmistress – a union as dangerous as it was unlikely and as beautiful as a sunrise over the Mountains of the Nine Dragons ...

THE YEARS OF THE HUNGRY TIGER is a poignant love story and an exotic journey through the last decade of Hong Kong's history. Against a background of savage typhoons, killer rains, espionage, riots, unlawful sex and the shock waves of Mao's Cultural Revolution, McAdams and Ying-ling fight for their love and Hong Kong comes alive in this unforgettable novel of a city in torment.

0 552 10437 X   £1.25p

CAPE OF STORMS BY JOHN GORDON DAVIS

This epic novel of whales and whalermen in the Antarctic seas centres round James McQuade, a young marine biologist from South Africa. Every summer he went south with the whalers to the Ice, and this season the crew was a particularly flamboyant mixture of personalities. On board was a beautiful nurse, Victoria Rhodes, who rapidly became the target for frustrated male lust ... Despite the mystery about her origins, McQuade fell violently in love with Victoria, and when the whalers returned to port, he could not bring their affair to an end ...

0 552 10447 7   85p

EXODUS BY LEON URIS

The courageous story of the rebirth of a nation ...

For Ari, the Israeli freedom fighter, his life's goal ...

For Kitty, the beautiful American nurse, a chance to find herself again ...

For Mark, the famous international reporter, another exciting story ... A miracle few could resist, the most dramatic event of the 20th century.

EXODUS tells the story of the Jews coming back after centuries of abuse, indignities, torture and murder to carve an oasis in the sand with guts and with blood.

0 552 08384 4   95p

THE DOGS OF WAR BY FREDERICK FORSYTH

Sir James Manson – smooth, ruthless City tycoon – discovered the existence of a ten-billion-dollar mountain of platinum in the remote African republic of Zangaro. With a hired army of trained mercenaries, Manson planned to topple the government of Zangaro and replace its dictator with a puppet president. But news of the platinum had leaked to Russia – and suddenly Manson found he no longer made the rules in a power-game where the stakes had become terrifyingly high ...

0 552 10050 1   95p

THE HONEY BADGER BY ROBERT RUARK

'There is a bloody brave little animal in Africa called the Honey Badger. It may be the meanest animal in the world. It kills for malice and for sport, and it does not go for the jugular – it goes straight for the groin. It has a lot in common with the modern American woman' – Alec Barr, hero of THE HONEY BADGER.

At the height of his fame, Alec Barr walked out on his wife and into a frenetic life of wine, women and war. This is a story of a man desperately in trouble with himself. As Alec Barr searches for a purpose to his existence, you follow him and his women through the feverish glamour of wartime Washington, into blitzed and battered London, among Manhattan's jet-set jungles – and into the real jungles of Africa . . .

0 552 08945 1   £1.25

VIVA RAMIREZ! BY JAMES S. RAND

This is the contrasting story of two professional hunters of entirely different schools and origins, each one critical and suspicious of the other's professionalism to the point of emnity. Their desperately dangerous forays and ultimate mortal clash with El Jefe Politico, the bitter, scheming enemy of Ramirez, who covets the hunter's fortune – and his daughter – make 'Viva Ramirez!' a compelling reading experience.

'Sheer encyclopaedic gusto of the writing in his straight tale of the beasts and beauties hunted by his hero in the cities, rain forests and savannahs of Central America.' Daily Telegraph.

0 552 08887 0   95p

A SELECTED LIST OF FINE
NOVELS PUBLISHED BY CORGI

WHILE EVERY EFFORT IS MADE TO KEEP PRICES LOW, IT IS SOME-
TIMES NECESSARY TO INCREASE PRICES AT SHORT NOTICE.
CORGI BOOKS RESERVE THE RIGHT TO SHOW AND CHARGE NEW
RETAIL PRICES ON COVERS WHICH MAY DIFFER FROM THOSE
ADVERTISED IN THE TEXT OR ELSEWHERE.

THE PRICES SHOWN BELOW WERE CORRECT AT THE TIME OF
GOING TO PRESS (MARCH '78)

☐	09769 7	**Operation Kuwait**	*Harry Arvay* 40p
☐	09789 6	**Eleven Bullets for Mohammed**	*Harry Arvay* 40p
☐	09895 7	**The Meirovitz Plan**	*Harry Arvay* 40p
☐	09475 7	**A Raging Calm**	*Stan Barstow* 60p
☐	10445 0	**A Kind of Loving**	*Stan Barstow* 85p
☐	09544 3	**The Terminal Man**	*Michael Crichton* 40p
☐	10437 X	**The Years of the Hungry Tiger**	*John Gordon Davis* £1.25
☐	10447 7	**Cape of Storms**	*John Gordon Davis* 85p
☐	08108 6	**Hold My Hand I'm Dying**	*John Gordon Davis* £1.25
☐	10244 X	**The Shepherd**	*Frederick Forsyth* 65p
☐	10050 1	**The Dogs of War**	*Frederick Forsyth* 95p
☐	09436 6	**The Odessa File**	*Frederick Forsyth* 95p
☐	09121 9	**The Day of the Jackal**	*Frederick Forsyth* 95p
☐	10269 5	**The Sons and the Daughters**	*Patricia Gallagher* 85p
☐	10149 4	**Dragonard**	*Rupert Gilchrist* 75p
☐	09898 1	**Trial at Monomoy**	*John Masters* 85p
☐	10345 4	**Touch the Lion's Paw**	*Derek Lambert* 75p
☐	09866 3	**The Yermakov Transfer**	*Derek Lambert* 60p
☐	07954 5	**Run for the Trees**	*James S. Rand* 85p
☐	08887 0	**Viva Ramirez!**	*James S. Rand* 95p
☐	10565 1	**Trinity**	*Leon Uris* £.160
☐	08866 8	**QB VII**	*Leon Uris* 95p
☐	08091 8	**Topaz**	*Leon Uris* 85p
☐	08384 4	**Exodus**	*Leon Uris* 95p
☐	08385 2	**Mila 18**	*Leon Uris* 95p
☐	08389 5	**Armageddon**	*Leon Uris* £1.25
☐	08521 9	**The Angry Hills**	*Leon Uris* 75p
☐	10495 7	**The R Document**	*Irving Wallace* 85p

*All these books are available at your bookshop or newsagent, or can be ordered direct
from the publisher. Just tick the titles you want and fill in the form below.*

CORGI BOOKS, Cash Sales Department, P.O. Box 11, Falmouth, Cornwall.

Please send cheque or postal order, no currency.

U.K. send 19p for first book plus 9p per copy for each additional book ordered to a
maximum charge of 73p to cover the cost of postage and packing.

B.F.P.O. and Eire allow 19p for first book plus 9p per copy for the next 6 books
thereafter 3p per book.

Overseas Customers. Please allow 20p for the first book and 10p per copy for each
additional book.

NAME (Block letters)..

ADDRESS ....

....